GERFALCON

GERFALCON

Young Raoul, heir to the barony of Marckmont, slipped away from the fortress of Ger, where he lived beneath the harsh guardianship of his uncle, the Count Armand, and set out across wild and dangerous country. For the moors had an evil reputation. They were haunted by witch and warlock, and gave sanctuary to renegades and outlaws.

So Raoul's adventures began: and grim and bloody they were to be. He soon learned the bitter lesson that sometimes one must kill in order to survive. He learned about love and anger and vengeance, the tricks of battle and the wiles of women.

He served—and finally slew—the mad Count of Campscapel, whose witch mistress, Red Anne, practised strange magic. And eventually the time came when he must return to claim his heritage—a greater heritage than he had expected, if he were strong enough to win it. With hardened fighting men at his back, the new Viscount of Ger rode to war . . .

Gerfalcon is an extraordinary, unforgettable novel. Set against a timeless mediaeval landscape of towering crags and dark forests, sinister marshland and foaming sea, it catches the true spirit of the old tales, of epic adventure and romance. Filled with the flash of swords and the gleam of heraldry, here indeed, if ever there was one, is a story to keep old men from the chimney corner and children from play.

GERFALCON

by

Leslie Barringer

The sunlit streets of Hautarroy
  Are filled with ladies, fair and free;
By garth and pleasance of Honoy
  The roses riot on tower and tree.
  The wine's deep red in Beltany,
And many a lance is splintered there;
  But give to me the northern sea
And the iron crags of windy Ger.

Raoul's *Ballade of Ger*

TOM STACEY

First published in 1927 by
William Heinemann Ltd

This edition published 1973 by
Tom Stacey Reprints Ltd
28–29 Maiden Lane, London WC2E 7JP
England

ISBN 0 85468 347 X

Printed in Great Britain by
C. Tinling & Co. Ltd, Prescot and London

TO

DOROTHY VAUDREY BARRINGER

CONTENTS

PARTS OF HONOY AND NORDANAY

I

SHADOWS AT SANCTALBASTRE

"The Countess Adela of Ger has a face like a horse!"

Black-haired Rogier spoke reflectively, with no intent to wound. Red-haired Thorismund took no notice; he was leaning over the low wall of the fish-pond, spitting with precision at the water-lily leaves below. But Raoul, propped against the trunk of the nearest tall sycamore behind them, gasped and sat upright, hardly believing his ears. Then he waited for Thorismund to turn on Rogier; and Thorismund continued to collect saliva with all the gravity of eleven summers. The Countess Adela was Thorismund's great-aunt and Raoul's grandmother; she it was who gave Raoul the knife with which he carved toy ships from odds and ends of wood collected in the monastery workshop.

A moment more, and Raoul got to his feet, sliding the cherished blade into its sheath at his belt, and hiding a tiny half-shaped boat amid the spreading roots beside him. His queer little face had flushed and greyed beneath its ivory-brown skin; fists clenched, eyes glaring at the tense hindquarters of the unconscious Rogier, he stepped softly forward. . . .

At Sanctalbastre time was bounded by the monastery bells, space by the blue mountains of Baraine and by the roofs and spires of Hautarroy. The minster, with its precious relic—a shard of that vessel broken by Saint Mary Magdalen above the head of the Sieur Jesus—towered between moat and river, on a wedge of fertile silt beneath the royal fortress of Ingard; and on a night soon after his twelfth birthday Raoul dreamed that the river-banks were widened, and that island, castle, monastery and all were sailing merrily southward against the stream . . . and then awoke to hear the ivy hissing in the breeze outside the dormitory window, to see the moonlight eerie on the steep roof of the minster nave, and to remember that his uncle Armand, Count of Ger, was coming to the capital at the bidding of René the King. . . .

At Marckmont were the marshes, and the four towers crowning the low mound above the causeway ; there grey skies lowered, and at dusk the poplars swayed against yellow streaks to westward. There, too, the land ran strangely in long wooded flats and shoals amid the water ; in misty autumn weather all the light was doubled by reflection, and at a breath of wind everything trembled upside down. It was a silent, happy place, for in the castle above the sleepy hamlet were only Countess Adela and a handful of old servants, with grizzled men-at-arms who remembered the battle at Harksburg, when the king was captured and the army ran away. That king was grandmother's brother ; King René was her nephew. Marckmont, once of the king's demesne, was granted to the Countess Adela and to the heirs of the body of her younger son ; one day it would be Raoul's own. . . .

At Ger, where the grey hold stood out upon terrifying crags, was never any silence ; there the waves came shouldering slantwise into the eastern cove, thumping ceaselessly amid the caves, or hurling tall shapes of spray against the dark cliff-walls and across the breakwater that masked the little harbour on the western side. There sea-gulls wheeled and screamed, and mists marched over the inland heather, and men cursed as they watched, from battlemented wall or dizzy window-slit, the dim shape of an Easterling pirate scudding far out along the lonely coast. . . .

But Ger and Marckmont were year-old memories ; Raoul was one of a score of noble ragamuffins whom the monks of Sanctalbastre strove to rear in ways acceptable to God and to the Neustrian king. Half the boys were nothing less than hostages for good behaviour ; King René was old and fat, but he knew his Counts of Barberghe, Montcarneau, and Ger. The brief and ghastly Jacquerie of Nordanay had somewhat sobered these restive lords ; the Constable, who marched to their assistance, found no difficulty in returning with the heir of each house suspect of flirtation with archducal powers beyond the frontier. So Sanctalbastre had become a school ; the king had placed therein his nephew Thorismund, Duke of Hastain and heir-presumptive to the throne, and sons and

wards of this and that great officer of state had followed
Thorismund. So arrived Rogier de Olencourt, brother of
Fulk the Castellan of Montenair. Presently from the south
came Conrad, son of the Countess of Burias—Conrad, whose
birth had so enraged the Count that the latter promised his
lady a dozen lashes for each month of the year he had spent
away from her when the event occurred. But King René
intervened, taking mother and child under his own protection ;
and then the Count of Burias died of a fever in foreign parts.
As for the little Conrad, the older he grew the more the King
regarded him and loved him ; but he and his mother were
ignored by the Prince René and hated by the queen. . . .

Last of all, Raoul, called of Marckmont, was brought to
Sanctalbastre by his grandmother, who welcomed an alternative to placing him in the household of her elder son,
Armand, the ruling Count of Ger. Failing Raoul and his
sons, Marckmont would revert to the crown, and Armand of
Ger was in no way his nephew's heir—a fact which angered
him, but also, in feudal law, gave him a claim to wardship as
the boy's non-inheriting next-of-kin. This claim, however,
Armand did not press whilst his own son Charles was beneath
the eye of the king at Sanctalbastre ; moreover, whilst the
Countess Adela lived he had no right to administer the
barony. Being hasty as well as avaricious, he had once
audibly wished his nephew in hell ; thereafter the old
Countess had kept Raoul out of her son's way. Nevertheless,
the time came when Armand of Ger, having obeyed the
summons to Hautarroy, rode down from Ingard to the
monastery gate and sent for son and nephew.

They came, an ill-assorted pair. Charles was ruddy and
round and dull, taller by half a head than his companion.
Raoul was pale and slim ; at Sanctalbastre he was sometimes
called Gipsy, because of his faintly Eastern cast of features,
and because he was born in Egypt, during the siege of Ajetta ;
but his parents, before they died, saw in their son a strange
resemblance to that great stone devil which sat, hands on
knees, staring out across the ruined temple-court where Raoul
first drew breath—the great stone devil with the weird half-
smile, who took no heed of woman's travail in the shadow, or
of knights and emirs at death-grips in blazing sunlight by the

water-gate two hundred yards beyond. For Raoul, as he grew, showed the same forward slant of a narrowing chin, the same big delicately-chiselled mouth with its hint of a smile at the corners, the same broad forehead and high cheek-bones, the same deftly-tilted eyelids ; but there was nothing of the devil of Ajetta in his eyes. The latter were wide and strange, being grey-green with little amber flecks in them. Thorismund of Hastain called them cat's eyes, and already most women looked twice at them ; but at this time they were disproportionately large, making of the heir of Marckmont a blend of elf and owl and boy. . . .

And into those same timid eyes Count Armand looked with less than his former disfavour, for that morning had healed the breach between himself and the King's Majesty ; the Count of Ger would return to his eyrie as Warden of the Coast March.

" Less muscle than I hoped to find in either of you," was his comment. " You, Charles, are flabby ; and you, Raoul, are puny. Dough may be turned to account, but thin air may not. Do you run and wrestle when you should ? "

The question was aimed at Raoul, who stood tongue-tied with downcast face. The plump Viscount sniggered and spoke.

" Half his time he spends in fashioning toys or *reading books*. But it is true that only Conrad beats him at archery."

" So ? But the book is for clerks, and the bow for churls. What of the quintain ? "

Charles laughed aloud, and went on :

" A week ago he was knocked clean out of his saddle, and lay down all the afternoon ! "

Raoul's head came up ; a spot of colour showed on each cheek-bone, and his big mouth twitched.

" I ride as well as *you*," he muttered.

" Better than I," amended his good-natured cousin. " But I can take a fall more featly."

" More fatly also," was the Count's gruff rejoinder. " Boy, when I come again *you* ride with me to Ger. As for Raoul, he seems headed for the cloister. But maybe I shall yet make men of both of you."

Then he gave them his hand to kiss, and mounted and

rode away, a masterful figure in the sunlight; and more
than once in the fortnight that followed Raoul had marvelled
that this grim Count, with his crimson face and blue-black
jowl and six tough feet of body, should be the father of the
placid Charles, and should himself have once been a boy
who sat on grandmother's knee.

The Countess Adela was the only person alive whom
Raoul both loved and trusted, unless it were Brother Ambrose
(who had been to Rome, Jerusalem, and Constantinople,
and was full of strange lore); and a sense of appalling out-
rage informed the kick which shattered the peace of afternoon
beside the monastery fish-pond. . . .

Rogier yelped and spun round, staring. No one at
Sanctalbastre took much notice of Raoul; Rogier was
thirteen, waspish if attacked, and the rival of Conrad of
Burias for leadership among the boys. But no one had
before seen Raoul's face grey with fury; and curiosity held
Rogier rooted for a moment to the ground.

" You—you said—— " snarled the diminutive attacker.

Rogier's surprise vanished. Rogier was a youth of few
words.

" Yes, little pig, I did," came his crisp affirmation.

And battle was joined before another word escaped them.

" Hi ! Hi ! Conrad — Alain — everybody ! " squealed
Thorismund, capering joyfully round the combatants.
" Rogier and Raoul are having a fight ! Come on ! Ahoo,
smack in the eye ! "

A dozen other boys appeared amid the monastery barns
or among the beechwoods above the pond; laughing and
whooping they plunged down the slope to ring the fighters
round, some cheering one and some the other. Rogier was
not having it all his own way; his bleeding lip matched
Raoul's half-closed eye before height and weight began to
tell.

Conrad of Burias stood in doubt, contemptuous of Raoul
yet bearing no good-will towards Rogier. Conrad's faction,
however, was of one mind, yelling shame on Rogier for his
advantages and the time it took for him to show them.
Sly Robin Barberghe and beautiful Alain de Montcarneau

ranged themselves as Raoul's backers ; and presently Robin
was fingering a skipping-rope and whispering in Conrad's
ear. Rogier had Raoul's head beneath his arm, and the
smaller boy was crying and choking with rage and pain,
when Conrad gave the word for action.

" Stop it, you coward, you hulking bully ! " he shouted.
" Stop it . . . very well, we'll see how you enjoy a thump
or two yourself ! "

The conflict underwent a sudden transformation. Conrad
gave Rogier a dexterous shove, Robin tripped him, two others
sat on him ; Alain twitched Raoul from his conqueror's
grasp and thrust an arm in front of the advancing Thorismund. Deftly the phalanx closed on its struggling victim ;
the skipping-rope flew free and tightened. . . .

" Ramon—Enguerrand ! " screeched the little Duke,
battering with ineffectual fists at the laughing Alain.
" Rescue—rescue ! They're going to torture Rogier ! "

But Rogier's friends needed no such summons ; a noisy
mellay locked round the beech-trunk to which the captors
strove to tie their prisoner. Raoul, crouching by the wall,
paused in his angry sobbing, and saw his cousin Charles
come lumbering up amid the straggling reserves. Charles
was of Conrad's party, but in this fray he served it ill ; someone immediately winded him with a shrewd thrust amidships,
and he collapsed, to sit up later and watch the fight with
laughter and applause. . . .

Rogier's followers were losing ground, and Rogier was
bound and helpless, when Raoul got to his feet again. What
made him do it he never knew. . . .

Rogier, finding his late opponent's tear-stained face
twelve inches from his own, gave a grunt of wrathful scorn.

" Go on, sneak ! Hit me now I can't hit back ! "

But Raoul's knife was out, and he was hacking at
the rope when Robin Barberghe leaped upon him from
behind and tore the weapon away, flinging it into the reeds
and kneeling fiercely on the ingrate's spine . . . whence
Rogier, breaking free with a yell, plucked him to bowl
him bodily at Alain. The two of them went down in a
heap, and Rogier turned raging on the rest of his would-be
tormentors. He knocked Conrad flat on his back, butted

another assailant in the stomach and sent him reeling and hiccoughing to the water's edge, and lifted his head for a whoop of victory which was never uttered.

For above him on the grassy slope was a blaze of scarlet and a glitter of steel ; three men had come unnoticed through the beechwood and out upon the scene of conflict. Raoul, still whimpering as he rubbed his bruises, became aware of Rogier's urgent voice.

" Pax, pax, you fools ! Get up, Alain—Ramon, leave him alone ! The Cardinal Count is here — the Cardinal Count ! "

As though by magic came silence and an end of strife. Up the summer wind rolled a soft tide of sound—the tolling of the great cathedral bells of Hautarroy. A battered, sheepish rank of boys took shape beneath the calm stare of the Cardinal Count of Estragon ; neither the disdainful smile of the tall Duke of Camors on one side, nor the scandalised frown of the mild Sub-Prior of Sanctalbastre on the other, had power to draw the awed gaze of a single boy from the parchment face of the little Prince of the Church.

The red robes stirred ; gems flashed on a thin raised hand. Down bobbed a score of tousled heads before the sign of the Cross. By twos and threes they were raised again ; the prominent grey eyes of the Cardinal Count searched once along the line, and came to rest on the brightest head of all. A moment more,· and his quiet melancholy voice went fluting up against the distant bourdon of the bells.

" Peace be with you, children. And among you. Let the Prince Thorismund stand forward."

A green-clad figure moved. Beneath the flaming hair was tilted a puzzled and obedient face. Those furthest away craned their necks to see. *Prince* Thorismund ? He was prince, of course, but his style was always *Duke*. . . .

" My lord Prince, I and my lord Constable are sent to acquaint you with grievous news, and to bring you before the King's Majesty that now has need of you. To-day it has pleased God to smite with a great affliction this kingdom and this people. An hour before noon, as he hunted in the Forest of Ecquerel, the Prince René was thrown from his horse and fell with violence, so that in a few moments he was dead.

I charge you, my lord Prince—and you, my lord's companions—pray for his soul, who was the flower of this great realm. Pray too, each one of you, that if death come thus suddenly upon yourself, your name may be as fair as his among men and with the Blessed Saints."

Thorismund gulped audibly, and blinked to check his tears. He was proud and selfish, but he had loved his jolly, noisy cousin.

"Bid your friends farewell, my lord, and come."

The little Duke wheeled, displaying wet blue eyes in a tragical pink face.

"I do not *want* to go away!" he announced, angrily.

Into the momentary pause that followed came the excited whisper of Conrad of Burias.

"*But now you will be King.*"

The Cardinal Count gave the whisperer a blank sidelong glance. The Duke of Camors smiled in his grey beard. But Thorismund, squaring his shoulders, took no notice.

"Farewell, all," he said. And then, less bravely: "*Farewell, Rogier.*"

"Farewell, Thorismund," came the ragged twentyfold reply.

More like a prisoner than an heir-apparent, the dejected prince trudged away between the scarlet and the steel. Behind him erstwhile friend and foe stood at gaze or gathered in chattering groups; but Raoul sneaked off to find his precious knife, and presently was gravely whittling at his boat again. . . .

It was not long before a shadow fell across his hands. He looked up savagely; Rogier de Olencourt stood near, thumbs hooked in his belt, grey eyes quizzical but not unfriendly.

"Why did you cut me loose?" he demanded curiously.

Raoul coloured up and looked uncomfortably aside.

"It was not fair," he mumbled. "Four to one, to begin with at least. And they pretended they were rescuing me, but they were not really. And then Alain is a brute, and Robin a sneak. Besides . . . I liked you till this afternoon."

It was Rogier's turn to colour up. He moved a step nearer.

" I am sorry, Raoul. I take back what I said . . . both times."

The sulky elfin face, with its discoloured eye and stains of earth and tears, came up ; Raoul smiled. That sudden bewitching grin was too much for Rogier ; he stooped and hugged the smaller boy round the shoulders. Clumsily they kissed each other on the mouth ; then Rogier straightened himself.

" Now we shall always be friends," he said.

Then he went gravely away ; and behind him Raoul drew a deep shuddering breath and went on with his task. The solemn bells, the strange news, Thorismund's going, the gentleness of Rogier's bruised lips, whirled together in his head ; bright blade and grubby fingers curved about the work, and Raoul was happy.

Happy, but not for long. His thoughts ranged backward . . . till suddenly his hands were still, and he looked up again. Throughout his life he was doomed to suffer from acute perception of uncomfortable truth ; and this, the first occasion of those subtle woundings, struck him rigid with bewilderment and pain.

He had done right. He had done the brave and honourable thing. He had forced Rogier — since Rogier was amenable to generosity—to unsay his words. But the more he thought of the occasion of the quarrel, the clearer the fact became that however kind and dear and splendid she might be, the Countess Adela of Ger had, had, *had* a face like a horse !

II

TOURNEY AT BELSAUNT

" My lord Count, if Charles may go to the tourney at Belsaunt, why may not I ? "

Raoul spoke beseechingly. He was just seventeen, and had lived three months in wardship to his uncle. To the grief of his grandmother's death had succeeded the pain of leaving Marckmont and the shock of his reception at Ger ; a dreamer whose frequent desire was to be alone found little comfort in the castle of the Warden of the Coast March. Outside, the spring gales howled along the coast ; on hearth and at board the gentle face and manners of Raoul provoked derision. Count and Countess let their contempt of him be seen, and forthwith men-at-arms growled in his hearing that women's care had made a wench of him ; pages grew insolent, servants moved slowly to do his bidding, and only the Viscount Charles displayed goodwill—Charles, who was far too indolent to bestir himself on behalf of another. Charles it was who told his cousin of the Count's decision ; Raoul had never doubted that he, too, would see the tilting at Belsaunt, and genuine astonishment projected him into his uncle's presence.

Count Armand, closeted in the winter parlour with his brother-in-law, the Count of Barberghe, looked up ; in the space of a silent half-minute his hard blue eye reduced his nephew's surprise to discomfiture.

" Since my lord Baron thus breaks in upon us, Barberghe," he said at length, laying down his pen, " we can only postpone our poor duties to attend upon his pleasure."

Crimsoning at his kinsman's tone, Raoul flung up his head.

" It is not my fault that I am a Baron," he protested.

The beginnings of a vulpine Barberghe grin attested this revelation of youthful insight ; the Count of Ger leaned forward and brought a great fist slowly down upon the table.

" Nor mine, by the blood of the Pope ! " he growled.

" To my own house, and in this hold, and up and down these
coasts, I give no reason for the asking. Yet since you are
my brother's son—I had his word for it, or, seeing the whelp
you are, it were a matter of sore doubt—I tell you this. Your
Marckmont is a barony of sand and water ; under my mother
its steward was thriftless or a thief. I will not spend its yield
of half a year in mounting and equipping one who seems so
little likely to benefit by sight of tourney. Do you think to
ride in the squire's mellay—you, whom the wind of a back-
handed blow from my son Charles, or from my lord's son
Robin, would unhorse ? "

" It is true Charles is too heavy for me, but Robin I will
any day——"

" Begone ! "

The sudden bellow of wrath blew Raoul like a leaf from
the room. He climbed to the battlements, and cursed and
cried a little in the gusty rain.

" If father were alive he would not dare—they would
none of them treat me as they do," he told himself. " Must
I stick a dagger in some one before they will leave me alone ?
Why did grandmother teach me courtesy, knowing what sort
of churls I must live among until I am of age ? Another year
of *this* . . . and first, I must learn to kill animals as though
I liked it."

A memory came to him of the cloisters at Sanctalbastre,
with the kind eyes of Brother Ambrose peering across the
garth as he repeated Raoul's question.

" Why do men like killing, boy ? Because it is an
usurpation of the power of God. What God began, they have
ended ; red with the mortal sin of murder, they feel a godlike
power, and fall into the mortal sin of pride."

" But wicked men, Brother . . . they must sometimes be
slain. . . ."

" Yes, or the good would perish from the earth. Yet the
slaying of men is forever ignoble. When *you* ride against the
wicked, Raoul, let your work be swift and sorrowful. Guard
against glee in torment or in killing ; for cruelty is of all
things most abominable."

" But animals . . . the mysteries of woods and rivers . . .
are *they* cruel ? "

" Only as life is cruel. Call off your hounds, and the boar
will one day meet his rival and go down. The crippled wolf
is torn by the pack with which he hunted. Children must
play unafraid in the village streets. Roads and crops must
be guarded. And as for flesh and fish to eat . . . I know a
boy who is inordinately fond of salmon. . . ."

Raoul had laughed, but the old monk's words stayed with
him. He had remembered them when, rocking with the
hunt through the forest towards Guarenal, he came upon a
kill, and saw his cousin Charles dismounted and transfigured
—bright-eyed, exultant, with a great splash of boar's blood
on his cheek, a reeking spear in his uplifted hand, and a
disembowelled dog between his feet. And now, with the
breakers surging and spurting far below him, Raoul
remembered the words again, and shrugged impatient
shoulders.

" I am a fool, I suppose. But I could never enjoy the
chase at Marckmont ; falconry is better, but here you must
be smothered in blood before they think you are a man."

With which reflection he turned from the damp embrasure
and dived morosely down a turret-stair. Gaining his own
small chamber, he bolted the door against intrusion, and
dragged from behind the ancient hangings a bundle wrapped
in a cloak. This bundle he had hidden when, after his arrival,
the thin-lipped disapproving Countess (a Barberghe of the
Barberghes) bade him lay out his clothing for her scrutiny ;
when sick for Marckmont he had several times unrolled it,
finding comfort in these things that came from thence and
were his very own. A short-sleeved shirt of fine link-mail
two sizes too large for him, a plain sword and sheath that
had been his father's, with a sword-belt of coloured leather
and a silver-hilted dagger murderously sharp—these were his
principal treasures. There was also a wallet containing a
purse and a small ballad-book which the Countess Adela
brought with her to Ger when, fifty years before, she fled with
the great Count Bors from Hautarroy. And now the ballad-
book was come again to Ger ; each word in it was copied by
the Countess Adela herself, and a faint perfume clung about
its mouldering cover of undressed hide. . . .

Raoul sniffed at it, squatting limply on the great press at

the foot of his bed. Immediately he was at Marckmont, gaily picking his way on stilts amid the half-drowned sedges where the marsh-fowl nested . . . going home to bathe in a noble tub where no daft page would snigger at his scraggy ribs, and no fat serving-girl would blunder in upon him as though by accident, backing out with a squeal of mock alarm, yet finding time to feast her little pig's-eyes on his shrinking body . . . going home to sup with the Countess Adela, and afterwards to sit on a cushion by her chair, plucking at his lute-strings or reading the ballads aloud, pausing to look up into the fierce old face—a face like bronze in candlelight and firelight. . . .

The embroidered purse clinked as he opened it ; its contents, emptied on the dark oak of the press, gleamed and glittered in the dull light of the dreary room. There were two gold rings—a signet bearing the swan of Marckmont, and a thinner loop giving rise to a falcon's claw that gripped and partly covered a cut sapphire. There were a dozen gold nobles and a few silver florins, an amulet or two, a string of amber beads with a little pectoral crucifix—a golden figure on a cross of jet—and a tiny image of Our Lady, carven in ivory, that Raoul's mother had worn around her neck through the heat and dust and agony of Ajetta. Raoul fingered it lovingly, staring down at the smiling ivory face. Its beauty was the same as ever, but life was very different. . . .

" This Ger is a beastly and barbarian hold," he thought. " If ever the chance came I would startle them . . . but that is folly, for I am not strong, except a little in my hands and arms, because I was born under the Sign of Gemini the Twins. . . . *Sancta Maria, gratia plena*, make me strong and brave. *Amen*.

" Perhaps my boorish lord intends not spite, but thrift, for I know nothing of these costs and charges. Still it is hard not to go to Belsaunt, and to live here, where no one will even play chess with me . . . and my lute will be spoiled at Marckmont, fool that I was to forget it . . . and now I must go down and hear these Barberghes yelping, and see the pages wiping their noses on their sleeves in open hall."

He sighed, and put his gear away, high on the dusty sill of a bricked-in window where bed-curtain and hangings hid it. Then, slowly, he prepared himself to descend and carve at the board of the Count of Ger.

On the morning of departure for Belsaunt Raoul stood by the steps of the great hall, watching the last bustle of preparation. Forty feet above him a biting sea-wind drove across the battlements, but sunlight slanted warmly into the inner bailey, meeting everywhere the sable gerfalcon of Ger—on the drooping banner of cloth of gold, on the yellow surcoats of the men-at-arms, on the gaily-painted horse-litters which would carry the countesses and their women, and on the device of tinted stone which capped the arch of the hall doorway. Steel glittered, silk and velvet shone, coat of charger and pack-horse glistened black and bay and chestnut; even the stable-dunghill gave hues of straw and brown and amber, as though for a background to the russet sheen of Robin Barberghe's marvellous new riding-boots, that came up to the thigh and were embroidered with crimson thread and clipped by silver spurs. . . .

Since Robin learned that Raoul was to stay at Ger his sallow face had lit with malice when the younger boy came near. Raoul knew perfectly that Robin watched from his saddle for signs of disappointment; so he, Raoul, turned a bright and interested face this way and that, admiring the mustering cavalcade. Presently he caught, amid the din, the words which Robin flung over his shoulder to the Viscount Charles.

" 'Ware gosling by the steps as you ride out," called Robin. " Someone left the gate of the poultry-run unlatched this morning."

Charles grinned, suspecting a jest. Raoul had actually peered among the horsehoofs before he took the allusion to himself and his heraldic swan. His lips tightened; threading his way sedately to Robin's stirrup, he paused and bent with simulated awe above the russet-covered foot. Then, straightening himself, he turned an anxious face to Charles.

" It is wise and seemly to draw attention from the other end of this chevalier," he cried, " but that tidy glory will never come off, unless it be by family enchantment. And what will the Jew say who lent it to him ? "

Charles grinned again, for a female Barberghe of another

branch had fled abroad to escape a charge of sorcery, and
part of the Count's plate had been given as Jew's security for
moneys to finance this present expedition ; but Robin's face
darkened, and he drew the tail of his riding-switch across the
back of Raoul's neck.

" Get hence, little stay-at-home," he advised. " Get to
your carving, poor little knave."

For answer, and before Robin could even raise the switch
to strike, Raoul caught at the boot beside him, twitched the
stirrup-iron from beneath the polished sole, and swung the
spurred heel high in air, spilling the startled Viscount of
Barberghe from his saddle into the drying edges of the
dunghill.

" Fiend rip you up, you little viper ! " screeched Robin,
scrambling to his feet and tearing out his new dagger as
though to make superfluous the invocation. But dismay at
his plight halted him in his second stride ; two pages of his
father's household flung themselves with shocked faces and
flapping hands upon their young lord's soiled magnificence.

Raoul, white-faced and breathing hard, had backed to the
steps. Charles rocked in his saddle, his fat face creased in
helpless glee. A Barberghe man-at-arms took a threatening
pace forward, but a tall archer of Ger lounged purposefully
athwart his path. Across an eddy of laden pack-horses Raoul
caught the eye of gaunt De Castlon, his uncle's chamberlain.
De Castlon's long lip twitched ; he made an imperative sideways gesture of the head. Raoul took the hint, and was half-
way down the great hall before the Counts of Ger and Barberghe came out upon the steps ; for those lords had lingered
in converse with the old Vice-Warden of the March—to whom,
as the most-trusted man in Nordanay, and a former comrade
of his father, Count Armand relegated at such times as these
the care of his official duties and the keeping of the hold of Ger.

From above the main gateway Raoul watched the head of
the long column cross the isthmus, pass the barbican, and
take the inland road towards the moors. The falcon of Ger,
the chevrons of Barberghe, woke to the cold north-easter and
danced above the slanting spears ; in less than half an hour
the last sparkle of steel had disappeared over the brow of the
rise above Gramberge.

"They go by Hastain for the better road," thought Raoul.

He eyed the heathery wastes, the dip and spread of scurrying cloud-shadows, the tranquil little town across the harbour, the surges smoking in the eastern cove ; and presently a great idea shook him. He gasped, caught at the cold iron of a cresset-foot, and glanced along the battlements to where two sentinel men-at-arms leaned on their spears.

"I am afraid to do it," he said darkly to himself. "I *must* do it, because I am afraid. Besides, grandmother used to say that I must always welcome a journey, because my birth-sign Gemini is ruled by Mercury, the planet kind to travellers . . . and if Saturn was high at my birth, yet Mercury will bear me up against too much sadness."

"But, lad, *I* cannot give you leave," said the Baron de Guarenal, smiling and pulling at his white goat's beard. "Your uncle told me nothing of his orders to you—indeed, he did not mention you—but there he is, on the Hastain road, and here are you ; the inference is plain."

"But, my lord, he did not *forbid* me to go to Belsaunt. He only said he would not be at the cost of taking me, because —because my lands are poor, he *said*. . . ."

The wrinkles deepened round the eyes of the old Vice-Warden. His thin red face was kindly ; and he was Raoul's nearest kinsman on the distaff side, though the actual relationship was distant.

"Ger *said* that, did he ? Well, he is careful of his own affairs, and no doubt extends a similar care to the affairs of his ward . . . but clearly, my adventurous lording, I cannot sit in your uncle's chair and bid you flatly disobey a command inherent, if not expressed. . . ."

"Then, my lord, I will not ask for your leave. I will ask you to let me go hunting in the forest."

"What, alone ? No huntsmen and no dogs ? "

"Well . . . if *you* should happen to ride out, my lord, with a falconer or two, and I were to——"

"God save me from conspiracy when you are of the covenant, lad. You mean you could disappear, and leave me to explain to your uncle's folk that a baron gone astray was no matter for search and outcry ? "

" My lord, I may seem foolish, but I . . . I beg you . . . "

" Grandfather, let him go ! It is a shame he should be
left behind ! A mean man's chair is not the place for *you*
. . . stand up and tell him he can go ! "

" Hey, now am I in trouble," sighed the old man, rounding
stiffly on the newcomer.

Raoul, too, had turned at the interruption. A brown girl
stood by the door. Beneath a round brown velvet cap her
thick dark hair was square-cut like a boy's ; her eyes were
brown and friendly, her face sunburned and vivid—wide-
browed, snub-nosed, with a full-lipped mouth and round
advancing chin. Her velvet riding-frock was umber-coloured,
and shortened to six inches below the knee ; beneath it both
high boots were spurred, for the new side-saddle was little
used in Nordanay.

" This, lawless one, is Raoul, Baron of Marckmont," said
the Vice-Warden, grimly ; " and this, my lord, is my—my
grandson Reine."

Raoul bowed ; the girl inclined her head impatiently.

" You are cousins in the third degree," added the old man,
twitching the lower half of his nose sideways in a fashion
twice observed by Raoul before he could believe it.

Reine sauntered across the room and perched on the table
by De Guarenal's chair, looking down on its occupant with
a smile that dealt Raoul a pleasurable wound. He was shy
of girls, but this one interested him because she was affianced
to his cousin Charles.

" Now why should I forward this lording's fell design ? "
inquired the Vice-Warden, eyeing his grandchild with mock
severity.

" Because *you* would have wanted to go at his age, dear
lord and grandpa ! "

" Umph . . . yes, that should I." Then, turning to the
expectant Raoul : " You know the roads are not of the
healthiest for solitary travellers ? "

" Till Guarenal the way is safe, my lord ; and from
Montenair to Belsaunt there are always pilgrims, and the
Castellan's archers ride a league this side each day. Only
from Guarenal to Montenair is there any risk ; and even
there, Saint-Aunay divides the journey. If I leave by noon

I can make Saint-Aunay by sundown. And to-morrow the Count's people will be on the road."

" H'm. It could be done. Have you a horse ? "

" Yes. Of my own." (This was Babee, a bay from Marckmont.)

" Arms and money ? "

" Sufficient."

" And you are not afraid of Joris of the Rock or of Lorin de Campscapel ? "

" Not until I see them, my lord."

But the names of the infamous outlaw and the mad Count of Alanol struck chilly amid Raoul's self-conceit.

" Would you like to examine the view from Château Guarenal ? " demanded the Vice-Warden gruffly.

Raoul hesitated, not yet sure of this red-faced old war-captain ; and Reine sniffed.

" Go on, stupid ; say *yes*," she urged.

" Yes . . . why, *yes*, my lord."

" Then go and look at it," came the command. " Three of my men ride thither in half an hour's time. You will accompany them ; and my steward will have orders to entertain you fittingly, to let you come or go as you desire. To-day is Monday ; you must be here again by Saturday noon . . . No, no, do not thank me ; thank this imp here. . . . "

Raoul seized the girl's hand between his own and wrung it joyously. Reine grimaced and dragged her fingers away.

" What a grip ! " she exclaimed half-ruefully. " Farewell Joris of the Rock, if he tries a fall with *you*. But truly I had rather have my knuckles ground together thus than kissed by Robin Barberghe."

" Why, what has Robin done ? " asked Raoul.

" Robin ? I do not like him. He asked for my colours to wear at the tourney . . . after kicking Charlemagne out of the room. Charlemagne is my little dog. He bit Robin, it is true. But I offended Robin by refusing twice. He was very angry, and very polite, and it was like a hot pudding on the back of my hand."

" But Charles should bear your favour," Raoul pointed out.

" Oh, Charles ! He forgot to ask me for it."

"Robin is persevering in anything he undertakes," said
the old Baron mildly. "And not easily discouraged, I think.
The Barberghe motto is *Sursum Corda.*"

"*Sursum Corda* — up, heart. Why, then" — Reine
grinned like a boy—"then Robin's heart was in his boots
this morning, just before he rode away."

Raoul was not displeased to know that she had seen
proud Robin on the dunghill; but he began to be aware
that his desire to reach the tourney was evaporating. Here
at last was some one who seemed to approve of him.

"You must be moving, lad," said the Baron, glancing at
the hour-glass on the table beside him. "As for you, Reine,
do you not wish you had accepted the invitation of my lady
of Ger?"

Raoul, half-way to the door, turned to hear the reply.

"No, my lord, not I. To see a great crowd of poor
sweaty wretches smelling so that it is near death to cross
the street; to see that sulky Castellan knock half-a-dozen
boys out of their saddles, one after another, like pots off a
shelf; to see Yolande de Volsberghe and Ermengarde de
Saulte look murder up and down the barriers, each knowing
that the other may be Queen of Beauty . . . no, not while
there are woods and streams in Nordanay."

De Guarenal chuckled, and again his nose twitched sideways at the tip. And Raoul went to his chamber, marvelling
that any one should not want to see the prowess of the Castellan
or the faces of the rival beauties of the North.

The drawbridge fell with a rattle of chains; horsehoofs
thudded a moment on the planks and clattered on the stone
beyond. The Baron of Marckmont, with three men-at-arms,
was on his way to Château Guarenal.

"I shall wave from the gateway turret," Reine had said;
and on the brow of the low ridge above Gramberge, a bowshot beyond the Count's great gallows, Raoul checked his
bay gelding and turned in the saddle. Across the curving
line of the cliff-edge, midway between two headlands, the
grey hold towered against a mass of landward-driving cloud;
and in the gulfs of air on either hand gulls flashed and fell,
bright-winged against the blue-green tumbling sea. Some-

thing fluttered from a crenel above the gateway; Raoul,
staring past the brown faces of his followers, pulled off his
bonnet of black velvet and stood in his stirrups to wave it.
Then, turning again, he shook the bay's bridle and led the
way down the league-long declivity to where the hamlet of
Gramberge lay dwarfed beneath the first dark steep of the
moors of Nordanay.

No track climbed that enormous rampart; beyond its
ragged crest the hills lay piled in deepening confusion till the
heather failed and the naked rock of Dondunor stood up to
crown the wilderness. So at Gramberge the road divided,
to hug the base of the massif for miles to left and right,
meeting again only at Belsaunt, twenty-five leagues due south
of Ger. In the tract of upland country thus surrounded—
a tract in shape like the outline of a nibbled pear, with
Belsaunt at its stem—Raoul was doomed to pass strange
nights and stormy days; but nothing of promise or warning
informed the sunlit afternoon as he turned his mount along
the eastern way. He was chiefly conscious of impatience to
pass Guarenal and find himself alone; also he feared that
his tunic of stout grey cloth sat badly over the too-large shirt
of mail. . . .

But when De Guarenal's bald and blinking steward handed
him a stirrup-cup he gulped the wine with relish, for his throat
was suddenly dry; the brown sandstone towers of Reine's
home were mightily alluring. Why not pass a night in
comfort, enjoying the respect which no one showed to him
at Ger?

No. The sun was still high above the forest. His horse
was baited, his sword sharp. He would go on.

" Terror will make of me a very butcher if the need arise,"
he reflected drearily. " If I had real courage I . . . why,
I should turn Babee's head and ride for Ger. Or if Rogier
were here it would be joy . . . but it is years since I saw
him, and now . . .

He shrugged his shoulders, and for the first time on that
journey touched spur to the horse's flank. For a mile or
two the sides of the rough road were cleared of underbrush
for perhaps a hundred paces; then, slowly, the forest closed
in upon the path, and Raoul commended himself to Our

Lady of Montenair and Marckmont, to Saint Michael the Warrior, to Saint Christopher the patron of travellers, to Saint Barruc of Nordanay upon whose day he was born, and to Saint Austreberte, patron of Belsaunt, whose eve was on the morrow, and whose shrine would no doubt benefit by many candles on the first day of the tourney.

" But on the second and third days not so many," thought Raoul. Then he prayed again, and made a promise :

" Sweet Saint Austreberte, bring me to Belsaunt, and safely home again to Ger within the appointed time, and I will offer a wax candle of my own height to be paid when chance permits it ; and because I am not tall, dear Saint, it shall be a very fat candle."

Then he loosened his sword in its scabbard, and whistled to show Babee that he was not afraid. There in the valley, beside the brawling stream, the dusk fell rapidly ; but far on the left, towards the frontier, the higher woods still caught the reddening sunbeams, and once, up a steep ravine to his right, Raoul had a distant glimpse of the sun-gilded peak of Dondunor. Pine-cones crackled beneath Babee's hoofs ; the darkening woods were full of the wet smells of spring.

Two charcoal-burners with a horse and sledge, and a mounted man-at-arms bearing the red owl of Guarenal upon his white surcoat, were the only living souls whom Raoul met in five leagues of his journey ; but when limestone cliffs beside the road told him that he neared Saint-Aunay he began to overtake pedlars and peasant folk who eyed him askance in the gloom. At length the muddy track was barred with banners of orange light from tavern doors and windows ; Raoul dismounted in a cobbled yard and followed the ostler to the stable to see that Babee had his due. The sight of a gold noble restrained the portly innkeeper from curiosity concerning this late arrival ; and from a dormer window Raoul craned his neck to see the glow of the castle courtyard high above the village.

Later, having dined on a capon, he sat glumly fingering a beaker in the corner of a crowded room, listening to the noisy talk and to the rap of empty drinking-vessels on the boards. And presently the quieter voices of a group of merchants claimed his attention.

" I am told this Count is very quick of temper," said one, who seemed to be a foreigner.

" Who, Saint-Aunay ? " responded another. " Ay, that he is. He thwarts and overbears this one and that ; and now for two years he has fallen foul and fouler of Lorin de Campscapel."

" Is that he whom men call the Butcher ? "

" You have it. Butcher Lorin, Count of Alanol. He has lain sick this winter, or Saint-Aunay might have rued that burning of three farmsteads under Dondonoy."

" But the Butcher has a brother ? "

" Oh, ay, Red Jehan. Both are mad, as their father was mad before them, and every cursed Campscapel in memory of man. But Lorin's blood-lust wakes on occasion only ; they say he is a very civil lord between times. As for Jehan, he is always mad—chiefly for women, so that virginity was once scarce in all the parts about Alanol. And Jehan has no head for war—his is the bull's way, charge and gore and utterly destroy ; and so, a month ago, he was outnumbered on the moors—Saint-Aunay being a cunning captain—and got a gash across the face which some say blinded him. At least, no man outside Alanol has seen him since ; and what that hold may be, with two such lords laid by in it, bears little thinking of."

" Then, I have heard there is a woman—— "

" Red Anne, the Butcher's mistress ? Yes, they say he is tame in her hands, maybe by witchcraft. Master Belyn here has it that she is a witch. Hey, Belyn ? "

To this appeal a third man made reply.

" Red Anne ? Well, who could conquer the Butcher and resist Red Jehan, were she not a witch ? It is said she flies from the turret-tops at night, and in the morning, when every gate is barred, raps for admittance with her broomstick. I saw her once ; four years ago, at Hastain Midsummer Fair ; her booth was covered with trashy ribbons and poor silks, but all the men were there, flies round the honey-pot. Indeed she was very fair—roses and cream, and hair that glowed for every woman's hatred. Tall, too, and powerful as a man ; I saw an archer make to steal a kiss, and she buffeted him on the jaw, ay, and gave him another when he swore at her.

Whereat I confess I applauded, and my good wife was angry, so that I saw no more. But the archer broke his neck that night; and when some complaint of the girl was lodged with the provost, he sent to apprehend her, and fell down in an apoplexy before she came. What spells she weaves at Alanol I know not; yet it is said—and Saints forgive me if I now utter falsehood—that the villagers of Capel Conan nigh worship her, for that one day she rode into the street, hawk on wrist, as Joris of the Rock and a mort of his murdering thieves broke in at the other end; and that at a word from Anne the outlaws avoided, leaving Capel Conan at peace."

Speaker and listeners crossed themselves, knowing that powers of evil are never so deadly as when they bear a shape of good; and Raoul went to his bed, and dreamed that laughing crowds made sport of him in Belsaunt streets, because he rode a broomstick and came a week too late to see the tourney.

An hour before noon on the following day he had traversed the northern limits of the Forest of Honoy, and come to Montenair, where the great castle crowned a limestone rock which overhung the road. For miles the roadside had been cleared again; trees and bushes were levelled, bracken, gorse and heather burnt. Merchants ceased to watch their pack-mules, pedlars began to quarrel, friars let fall their beads, peasant girls thrust out their tongues at Raoul because he did not smile at them. The track rose, the forest fell behind, the heather yielded to high pasture-land, and away to the left the last dense woods sloped down to gleaming fens, which Raoul eyed with a pang. For the only road across those marshes was at Marckmont, six leagues away, far out of sight beyond the curving edge of hills.

At the sunset-hour he doffed his cap to the image of Saint Austreberte that filled a niche above the northern gateway of the city of Belsaunt; and early in the morning, whilst the contestants knelt at Mass and every tavern yard rang like a smithy, he found a place among the gathering commonalty by the barriers of the great tilting-ground beside the river.

All day the dust and clang and thunder of the courses
rose in the long oval of the lists, between the painted palisades
and many-coloured awnings, beneath the cream-white galleons
of cloud that sailed the May-time sky. All day the jousters
rode *à plaisance*, singly and in groups, whilst lances of ash
and hornbeam cracked and splintered and flew wide, and
squires ran nimbly between the outer and inner barriers.
Beaten and brayed by kettledrums and trumpets, the rolling
cheers died down to murmurings, and the high voices of the
heralds gave the names and rank of the opposing chevaliers.
Aloft in a tapestried balcony, on a chair hung with crimson
silk, sat the Duke of Saulte, the Master of the Tourney,
bearing his white wand in a white-gloved hand ; to left and
right of him were the old Duke of Volsberghe and the portly
Bishop of Belsaunt, and about them nodded the horned head-
dresses of many comely ladies.

Beyond the wind-stirred banners and pavilions rose the
tiled roofs of Belsaunt, city of grey and ruddy stone ; pear-
blossom whitened the gardens, and gilded vanes swung flashing in the sunlight. Raoul was wedged in a press of burghers
of the better sort, who, no doubt, took him for a clerk ; he
had given his sword into the hands of the fat hostess of the
inn where he lodged, and his plain clothing passed unnoticed
amid the fur and velvet of the merchants.

Watching, he saw the newly-knighted Alain de Montcarneau break his maiden lance with credit on the helm of the
Bishop's champion. Rogier de Olencourt, also, first used his
golden spurs that day, with others whom Raoul had known
at Sanctalbastre. Alain, indeed, suffered the fate foretold by
Reine, for he flew backwards over his horse's crupper beneath
the Castellan's spear. As for tall Rogier, he rode against the
Count of Ger, and Raoul would have given much to see his
uncle thrown by his own one-time friend ; but Rogier, swept
from his saddle and hurled along the red-draped tilting-
barrier that separated the opposing chargers, clashed sideways into the sand and made no effort to rise. . . .

In the balcony nearest to Raoul a woman cried out ; Raoul
looked up, and saw—above green hangings sewn with the
silver fleur-de-lys of Olencourt—the wife of the Castellan,
and by her a still-faced girl whom after a moment he knew

for Fulk's and Rogier's sister Yseult. A page leaped from
the balcony into the outer lists, and scurried after the stagger-
ing squires who bore their fallen lord away. Trumpets
shrilled for the next onset; at the third shock a storm of
booing and hissing arose, for by mischance or clumsiness the
doughty Bertrand de Chevine had struck his opponent's
saddle; but Raoul threw no more than a glance at the
humiliated chevalier, for the little page had darted back
again and, standing beneath the balcony, piped words of
reassurance inaudible a score of yards away. . . .

Then Rogier was not sorely hurt . . . that was good.
Raoul saw the girl Yseult settle herself in her chair; and
presently he found himself unable to keep his eyes away
from her.

" Holy Mary," he said to himself, " that is the sweetest
face I ever saw."

About him was the thrust and press of heedless bodies;
the loose end of a scarlet liripipe fretted him with its blaze
each time the burgher on his right turned to a man beyond
him, and a goodwife's headdress exactly hid the distant figure
of the Duke of Saulte. Vaguely amid subsiding tumult he
heard an apple-cheeked boy ask his father a question.

" Nay, nay, nay," came the impatient answer. " Ten
years old, and knowing no more than that ? They aim *not*
chiefly to unhorse each other, but to break lance fairly—that
is to say, between a half-foot from the spear's point and a foot
above the grip—and when I was young, nigh as young as
you, I saw . . ."

" Poor soul ! " a woman was saying, her glance on De
Chevine's receding gonfalon. " I'll warrant he's glad of that
great helm, though it fry him in his own blushes. An inch
up or down, left or right, eh, it makes a difference, and so I
told my sister's daughter Maud that wedded the third son
of the Provost, when Griff cast the chopper at the Jew a
twelvemonth since come the octave of Saint Austreberte.
Chopper flew in at window like a thunderbolt; a finger's
breadth one way would have brained our prentice Luke, he
polishing the scales with his back turned, as I bade him stand
when I saw him watch the girls' ankles that go past that
window ; and less than a finger's breadth the other would

B

have shattered my great bowl of cream that stood on the
shelf out of reach of the cat, though indeed the wall is grievously clawed where the poor gomeril has leapt up at it. . . ."

" Wait until Ger and the Castellan meet. Then sparks
will fly."

" I wager an equal florin they do not meet this day. The
Bishop's champion will outface one of them."

" Your wager taken. I say they will meet. Look
now. . . ."

On and on went the voices ; in the sunlight at the far end
of the lists the creamy spikes of chestnut-trees stirred beyond
the red and gold of the Montcarneau pavilion ; Alain was out
again, wheeling his dappled charger in caracole and pontlevis
to the plaudits of the crowd . . . but still the alluring face of
Yseult held Raoul's mystified attention.

Once, with the Countess Adela, he had spent a night at
Montenair, and had played battledore and shuttlecock with
a maiden small and fat and even-tempered ; and now they
were both grown five years older, and Yseult was slim and
lovely, with olive skin, blue eyes, and an edge of raven hair
beneath the white and gold of a horned headdress. On
Yseult the thick black eyebrows of the Olencourts were arched
and fiendish ; she was yet not fashionable to the point of
narrowing them by artifice, and only her strong pointed chin
redeemed them from disharmony with placid brow above and
gentle girlish mouth between. To Raoul, heart-strung by adventure and the blaze and colour of the jousting, came a curious
consciousness of havoc and dissolution, a taste of silliness
that yet was graver than anything that he had ever known. . . .

" This is a very sudden magic," he told himself, aware of
his own willingness to fall beneath the spell of this sweet face,
yet frightened by some undertow that menaced more of him
than he was ready to yield to it. " Yseult de Olencourt . . .
in truth her name is different from any other name. Is this of
what the romancers talk so woundily ? Love at first sight ?
It may be called first sight. Yseult. Yseult. I am no
Tristram ; I am only Raoul—and you are the Castellan's
sister ! Yet I think *I* have no need of the philtre of Brang-
wain . . . and I think I would gladly serve you to the death."

A confused impulse to pray for some great worthiness, a

shame that he should watch like the meanest tavern-boy of
Belsaunt when his real place was with the waiting squires,
and a queer joy that deepened with the deepening sunlight
of the day, warred in him ; and when by chance the girl
glanced over his head towards the near end of the lists, a pang
of awe and fear assailed him—awe of her loveliness, fear lest
her gaze sought any individual crest among the colours of the
younger chevaliers.

" Still, I am Baron of Marckmont," he told himself.
" And a pitiful little churl she would think me . . . but this
journey is my own achievement, mine alone."

He had forgotten Reine's part in it.

That evening, when blue dusk ran in the Belsaunt streets,
he slipped from his lodging in the high town and bore down
narrow ways, beneath dim lanthorns, creaking shutters,
clanging signs, to where the banner of the Olencourts stirred
heavily beside the door of the Inn of the Four Swords.
Hooded against the east wind, he waited an hour for some
chance sight of Yseult ; but all he saw was golden-haired
Alain de Montcarneau bowing to the Castellan when the
latter met him at the tavern door.

"He goes to ask about Rogier," said Raoul to himself. "At
least, I hope so. No matter, *I* shall see her to-morrow. God,
and Our Lady, and all Saints and angels guard you, Yseult."

At which extravagant petition something stirred in him,
protesting mildly that God and Our Lady could manage it
between Them if They would ; but Raoul crushed the dis-
sentient murmur, and picked his way up garbage-littered
alleys whose odours mingled ill with half-awakened spring-
tide longings or with memories of the Countess Adela's tales
of the Sangreal and of the Courts of Love.

But in the morning, at a corner of the Street of Bells,
Raoul ran full tilt into Robin Barberghe, and destroyed his
own small hope of passing unrecognised by an astonished
spluttering of Robin's name.

" So ho, the gosling has grown wings ! " said Robin softly,
red mouth agrin, dark eyes aglow. " How gladly will my
lord our uncle hear of this emprise ! "

"Promise not to tell," advised Raoul simply, "or I will promise *you* full measure for your meanness—some time."

This calm assurance woke a curiosity in Robin.

"I promise," he rejoined, "if you will tell me how you did it."

"My lord of Guarenal gave me leave to ride to his hold with men of his; the rest was easy."

"Easy, was it? You little fool, I'll stretch your fond endurance till a dungheap will seem heaven to you."

"You go back on your word?"

"Pooh, that was all to draw your tale. Do you think——"

"Judas! Cur! Canaille! Take that!"

The blade of Raoul's dagger flashed between the boys, but Robin squeaked and dodged and ran, knowing from Raoul's face that it was for his life. And Raoul, shaken by rage—the blind rage of the house of Ger, that in the past had cost a king his crown—stood glaring after him, with one foot in the running gutter.

"Now all is done," he thought dully. "I had best flee before they search the taverns or set a watch for me at the North Gate. Robin, you shall rue this meeting. And so shall I. But I think . . . I *know* . . . I am not sorry I came."

Ten minutes later, as Babee carried him down a side-street, he felt a tug at his cloak and reached for his hastily-donned sword. This time, however, a friendly face looked up at him; Enguerrand du Véranger, a plump and modest squire of the Duke of Saulte, bade him good-day.

"A black and ruinous and bedevilled day," snapped Raoul. Then, seeing the other's storm-cloak and half-armour: "What, you ride also?"

"Ay, towards Volsberghe. A guest of my lord Duke has not yet come. A Franconian count. I go for tidings of him. You come my way?"

"As far as Saint-Aunay, yes. I go from frying pan to fire . . . oh, I will tell you all. . . ."

They rode ahead of Enguerrand's six men-at-arms, and Enguerrand's round face lengthened in sympathy as Raoul told his tale. And Raoul, omitting mention of Yseult and

her effect on him, realised that his companion was at a loss
to understand his sudden access of bloodthirstiness.

" Now, rot me if I thought it of you, Raoul," was Enguerrand's first comment. " To draw steel on him was great
folly, all the same. More dangerous in the end than disobedience to your famous skinflint of a kinsman."

" It showed me I could scare him," Raoul muttered, half
to himself.

" Yes, but your scared bully is the worst kind of enemy.
And his is a foxy breed. Now if I were only knighted we
might stir my lord Duke to speak for you to be my squire
when I set up at Le Véranger—if indeed a baron may stand
as squire to a simple vavasour."

" I may remind you later of that fair offer, Enguerrand."

" Well, it shall hold. Do you remember that day at
Sanctalbastre when Prince René died, and you fought Rogier,
and Conrad and the rest joined in ? "

" Yes, I remember."

" So do I."

Good comradeship—thought Raoul—and hatred, and
something stranger than either, which must be love. A
comely harvest to gather in twenty-four short hours.

At Guarenal he learned that Reine had returned from Ger,
but she was hawking in the forest, and he missed sight of her.
And when the trees thinned out towards Gramberge he halted
Babee by a clump of silver birches, and dismounted to divest
himself of sword and belt and shirt of mail. These, with
wallet and purse, he wrapped in his cloak and hid in a coney's
burrow high on a sandy bank ; he set a stone over the hole
and with his dagger, which he kept, he marked the nearest
birch-trunk. And with an invocation to Saint Barruc (Saint
Austreberte he thought it well to trouble no further in his
business) he left his treasures, rather than risk the laying of
other hands on them at Ger.

" Some day before you are rusted, sword, I will come and
fetch you," he said aloud.

And so he rode again to the grey hold and stood in
presence of the old Vice-Warden. . . .

" Here is a coil, my bold adventurer," was that dignitary's

comment when the story was done. " And now, I take it, you look to me further to compound your villainies ? "

The boy lifted a tired head and smiled a sickly smile.

" No, my lord. You had better lodge complaint that I abused your generous hospitality."

" Death and wounds, lad, do not talk to me like that ! I will speak to your uncle ; but remember, no man may skilfully command till he has learned expressly to obey. If I have helped you to indiscipline I have done ill. Ger is a wise and cautious captain ; had I a boy to rear, instead of madcap Reine, he would have paged it here, if not with the Castellan."

" Would *I* were a page with the Castellan," was Raoul's irrelevant reflection. But aloud he said : " My lord, I am indeed grateful that you stand my friend, and that you see my dagger drawn at Belsaunt to be no more heinous than Robin's in the bailey here below. And especially, my lord, that you have helped me to—to feel that I may win to my own life——"

" Hey ? What do you mean by that, now ? "

" *You* have dealt with me as a kinsman, not as a churl whose title is a jest, whose distaste of killing is a reproach. . . ."

" I see. By slitting Robin Barberghe's gizzard you would have proved nobility and manhood ? "

" I meant not that exactly, my lord. But surely that is the sort of proof that chivalry demands ? "

The Baron of Guarenal drew the tip of his nose aside and shook in the Warden's chair.

" In faith, Raoul, you are not far wrong. But do not take your vanity for pride."

" My lord ? Is not pride just vanity with a thick skin ? "

" Out, heretic ! But I think, lad, *you* would do well to grow a thicker skin."

And four days later, amid sick terror and despair, Raoul remembered that jesting advice, drawing even a moment's pleasure from his own appreciation of the grim aptness which events had given it. . . .

He stood in the courtyard, with the insides of his wrists against the smooth-worn wood of the whipping-post. The sun was warm on his naked back ; his fury at Robin's tale-

bearing, at this indignity, had dropped from him, and
nothing mattered but the torment to come. . . .

A thicker skin ! They had waited till the old Baron's
banner was beyond Gramberge, so that for a brief hour Raoul
wondered if a stern reprimand, delivered in the Vice-Warden's
presence, was to be the only sequel of his escapade. But the
Count of Ger had spoken only of disobedience ; no word of
the threat to Robin Barberghe had escaped him. And the
Barberghes stayed, instead of riding on to their own castle
beyond Basse Honoy. And Armand sent for his nephew
again. . . .

"Ha, Ger, what is this I hear ? " the Count of Saint-
Aunay had cried at the farewell banquet given by the Bishop
of Belsaunt. "Your brother's son defies you in patched hose?
I thought the Coast March had been better guarded."

The triple gibe had wrung a grim smile from Count
Armand and raised a laugh from noblemen in their cups ;
but possibly its rankling moved to Raoul's undoing more
than even the clamour of the Countesses or Barberghe's own
thin voice. . . .

"Now, little murderous whelp, attend ! " came the brief
afterword. "The Baron of Guarenal has interceded for
you in the matter of the tourney—though, having only a
maid to manage, he seems but half-aware that youth is not so
easily controlled as in my father's day. But for drawing
blade on the Viscount of Barberghe you shall have ten lashes
of the whip, in sight of all my household. If you would
have blood let, it shall be your own. *Lead him forth.*"

So the men-at-arms pulled off Raoul's doublet and shirt,
and clamped the wrist-bars down ; and the hushed crowd of
retainers gathered in the bailey, whilst the two Counts and
their families came out upon the steps of the great hall.

"Boy, where are you going ? "

The courtyard swung round Raoul in a blackening mist,
but at his uncle's shout he still had enough command of himself to turn his head and focus vision. Charles had tried to
sneak away into the hall, and now came shambling back
with an uneasy grin. The glad, dark gaze of Robin Barberghe was fastened on Raoul's face, and between Robin's
red lips his pink tongue came and went.

Swart Griffon, the Count's executioner, rolled high his sleeve upon his muscular arm. The whip hung from his fingers—a short-handled thing, with a pellet of lead at the end of each of its three lashes of plaited hide. A fearful clarity of sight swept off the cloud from Raoul's eyes, and showed him the coarse black hairs in Griffon's expanding nostrils, and the queer glaze of pleasure on Griffon's dull brown irises. Then the executioner was behind him, and he flashed a hunted glance round the tense watching faces— a glance from which more than one of the onlookers recoiled or turned—and sank his head low, shutting his eyes and bracing himself against the shock.

" I will not cry out," he promised himself. " I will kill every one of them some day. Except Charles. Oh, Blessed Virgin, help me not to cry out . . . *ah* ! "

The sound did not escape his lips, though his body leaped and writhed at the blow, and the red-brown dark behind his eyelids was seared with dazzling flame. A sigh went up from the watching servants—a sigh of pity and of satisfaction. Robin Barberghe laughed. . . .

Not till the fourth stroke tore the skin did Raoul shriek. His eyes flew open with his mouth, and as his legs were only chained he began to shuffle like a little dancing bear. Once he raised his head and caught back a yell ; when he looked down there was a crimson splash on the cobble-stones between his feet. Then there were no feet or stones, no whistlings or criss-crossed shapes of fire ; there was only the rolling red-brown darkness, with black night spreading from its core, and agony tearing the vitals of some soft thing that mooed and slobbered into swift oblivion.

He came-to lying prone on his own bed, with his head twisted sideways to enable him to breathe. There were cool tricklings on the fiery torment of his back ; gaunt De Castlon knelt by the bed, and an awed page held a basin of water.

" There, boy, there, there," mumbled the scowling chamberlain. ".I go for oil and bandages. Lie still. And you, sirrah page, empty that bowl and call the cellarer to me."

Raoul lay still, for he could do nothing else. Exhaustion weighted his eyelids, but a footfall roused him. A fat face

peered compassionately round the door, and he recognised
the wench who had come on him in his bath. Her round
cheeks ran with tears, and she slumped forward to bend
over him.

" Ah, poor lamb ! " she blubbered. " Ah, poor little
lording ! The vile cruel shame, the dainty back all torn ! "

An odour of onions assailed the prostrate Raoul. He felt
the girl's lips on his naked shoulder, and shut his eyes ; as
self-appointed servitor of the Lady Yseult de Olencourt he
found no immediate words for this occasion.

" Go away," he whispered at length.

The girl stood up as another step neared the door. She
drew aside, and Charles appeared—a shamefaced Charles,
who screwed up his eyes at sight of Griffon's work, and
thrust a handful of sugared comfits beneath his cousin's nose.

" Here, Raoul," he mumbled. " Yon Robin is a white-
livered marplot, and I told him so. Is this wench tending
you ? "

" No," said Raoul faintly. " De Castlon will be here
anon," he added, seeing the Viscount's dull eye lighten as
the fat girl blushed and giggled. Charles was already a
wencher of some experience, but Raoul found room for
surprise amid his pain when, hearing a word and a chuckle
two or three minutes later, he craned his neck and saw the
servant struggling not too hard in the arms of the heir of Ger.

" A good thing Charles is fond of onions," Raoul reflected
dizzily. " I am lucky that they do not turn me off my bed.
Yet De Castlon and they are all the friends I have in this
accursed place. But I have left my sword and mail and
money in the woods, and when my back is healed I shall
watch my chance and run for it. If Enguerrand would help
me with the Duke of Saulte . . . *Sancta Maria, gratia plena*,
make me strong and brave. How my head whirls again . . .
oh, friend De Castlon, hasten, hasten. . . ."

He groaned, but neither of the others heard him.

B*

III

THE MOORS OF NORDANAY

" GOD be good to all herrings," said Raoul softly to the silver birches, " but I wish I had my hunting-boots."

He sat on a sandy bank, four miles from Ger and within the fringes of the Forest of Nordanay. The precious shirt of mail already bulked beneath his woollen tunic ; sword and wallet, and the cloak in which he had wrapped them, lay beside him. For something over three hours he had run and walked and crawled towards this place ; and now, with his gear recovered, he paused to pull gorse-prickles from his hose and to consider his next move. . . .

At Ger, that morning, waggons laden with herring-barrels had rumbled in file across the rocky isthmus and into the outer bailey. Raoul, observing the Count's chief forester leave his lord's presence and make for the main gate, had mounted the curtain-wall that overlooked the harbour, and watched the official stride as on business bent into the untidy outskirts of the little town. Then, deviously attaining the great gateway on his own account, Raoul asked with simulated haste and flurry if the forester were already gone. The sentinel pikemen never doubted that a message from the Count lay behind this outgoing ; and, bonnet in hand, the docile-seeming Raoul trotted across the causeway and through the barbican. With pounding heart he swung down the curving road, past the uproar of the toiling waggons, and reached the first poor mud-and-wattle hovels of the fisher-folk ; diving away from the street, he took the seaward side of the earthen rampart raised near the cliff-edge to shelter the sheep from the sea-winds. Here, for three hundred yards, he was in sight from the turrets of Ger ; but all the bustle of the harbour lay between, and he risked a careless saunter till the curve of the piled sods afforded stooping cover. Then he bent and scampered, and at length the low swell of the cliff-top gave him dead ground. Climbing the wall, he struck inland, and made for the Ger-Gramberge road. Dodging across the latter from gorse-thicket to gorse-thicket, he hugged the southern slope of the ridge, and looked no more for Count Armand's battlements until the first clump of storm-bent pines brought surcease of the dread of open country. Then he paused, and shook his fist at the distant falcon banner, and turned away, shrugging the shoulders whose stripes were a fortnight healed.

" No use to threaten till I can perform," he told himself. " I have shown a duly-broken spirit these three weeks . . . now to test my own fair promises to myself."

So he came to the sandy slope where the marked birch-bole glistened silvery against the hues of fir and pine.

" If any noticed me by the sheep-wall," he reflected, " they will look for me towards Hardonek. Somewhere hereabouts is the wishing-stone through which the peasant maidens crawl before the new year, so that they may meet their husbands under the next moon. But I . . . by sundown I should be a bodkin in the haystack of those moors."

" Those moors " lay in front of him, between himself and Château Saulte, where he hoped to find Enguerrand du Véranger. They were moors of evil reputation, haunted by witch and warlock, giving sanctuary for renegade and outlaw, and forming—with the uplands of Honoy to southward of them—a vast rampart at whose core crouched the hill town of Alanol and the great hold of the Campscapels.

" But if I bear due westward it may be I shall meet not a soul till I come out above Hastain. Then, on the plain, it may be difficult. And now for food."

He stood up, cloaked himself, girded on his sword, and turned south-eastward through the scented, sunlight-shafted gloom of the pine-forest. As he went, the intermittent pipings of the birds and the soft crackling of his footfall were whelmed in each long surge of wind that stirred the tufted tree-tops.

" That sound is like the sea far off," thought Raoul. " Only there is no snarl in it. It says the same things in a friendlier way. Which is older, which knows better, the sea or the wind ? "

His question suddenly amused him, and he laughed aloud. He should be lonely and afraid, yet he was only hungry. He wondered, also, why he should feel happiest in just those moments when such unanswerable questions came to him. And presently the cleansing peace of his surroundings tore aside the cloak of shame that for long days had veiled his inward image of Yseult.

Thereafter the wind sang gravely of her and of lovers of old time ; the degradation of the whipping-post seemed at one moment a bar for ever between himself and a maid's honourable service, and at the next a mere awakening of the dreamer in him that must be disciplined for great achievement.

" Now which of these two certainties will move me when next I encounter man or beast ? " he pondered.

Immediately he became nervous and looked behind and about him.

" There may be wolves. I must take to heather before nightfall, crossing the brook beyond the road there, in case they scent me on this side. I wish I had bow and arrows. One wolf, yes ; but a pack . . . there would be little left for crows or worms. But their winter valour is past. . . .

" I wonder if they have missed me yet at Ger. Why do I feel a man out here, when there I knew I was a helpless fool ? Shall I always only feel a man when I am alone ? I wish a wolf *would* come along . . . just one. . . .

" What would Yseult say if . . . if she knew what she has done to me ? If some time I can tell her . . . some time I *will* tell her, Castellan or no Castellan. Perhaps I am too young to be in love . . . but if I can do some brave thing, if I can find Enguerrand, and if the Duke of Saulte . . .

" Bah ! There are too many ' ifs ' in it ! Next, my dinner ! "

He found prudence to avoid the first hamlet on the road, and courage to approach a woodman's solitary hovel by passing it, coming out into the road, and marching back as though he journeyed northward. To the sharp-eyed crone who sold him black bread and onions he talked of making for the coast ; and with some pride in his power of invention strode seaward out of her sight. Then he sought the thickets on the western side of the way, splashed through the stream, and in half-an-hour set foot on a sheep-track that wound across the open moors.

By sunset he was weary of skirting bogs and forging through deep heather. The ranges, sombre at high noon, donned menace like a shroud at the first failing of the light. The crying of curlews waned and died, the faintly-drumming wind grew cold, and Raoul, suddenly scared, looked round him for some rough shelter. At first he sought a ravine, and crouched amid damp dead bracken above a brawling stream ; but the sound of the water played strange havoc with him, for in it he seemed to hear words and laughter and the beat of horsehoofs, so that he started up and strained his ears, chilled along the spine and clutching at his weapon. Then he tried low crags to leeward of a heathery crest, and found dry sand beneath an overhanging rock ; and there—wrapped in his cloak, with his bonnet on piled bracken for a pillow—he watched slow-mounting cloud put out the southward stars, and prayed for Yseult and for his own courage and safety, and fell at length into uneasy sleep.

" Ha ! Stand ! Who are you ? "

The scream of challenge halted Raoul on the narrow bank of a cascading stream. He tore out his sword and stared ; dagger in hand against a moss-grown boulder a shock-haired lanky youth stared back at him.

" Why, he is mortally afraid as I am," Raoul told himself ; and aloud he said thickly : " No enemy. Only a wanderer— like yourself."

The other's pasty face relaxed ; his pale eyes flickered, and he showed yellow horse-teeth in a nervous grin.

" Put up your steel, then," he advised. " There are those would have it into me at sight. Perhaps you too—— ? "

" No," declared Raoul, driving home his hilt and stepping forward. " But I am fugitive."

" And outlawed ? " demanded the stranger. " I am out- lawed these three days," he added, with a boastful snicker ; and as he sheathed his dagger his gaze went curiously over Raoul's face and person. His own grey clothing was soiled and torn.

" You are no prentice boy, with those pretty hands," he broke out rudely. " What mischief turned *you* out of my lady's chamber ? "

Raoul was ready for the sense of the question, if not for the manner of it. Distaste lent curtness to his reply.

" I was lay-brother—no matter where. As for my hands . . . I wrote the prior's chronicle at his dictation. And you ? "

" A clerk, hey ? I was apprenticed to a saddler in—no matter where," the other mimicked. " But I taught the saddler's daughter more than the saddler taught me—he ! he !—and when he took his crutch to me I out steel and laid him dead as mutton. And here I am, asking no company, yet not refusing it, so be it shares out equal in fight or plunder. Two blades are better than one in these accursed moors. What say you ? "

" Which way were you going ? " asked Raoul soberly.

" Nay, nay," came the rejoinder—triumphantly spoken as though a point were scored. " I was seated when you came by—it is your place to make your destination known."

Raoul's heart sank.

" Hastain—perhaps beyond," he proclaimed, hoping that in Hastain the apprentice might have earned his outlawry.

" That suits me well," was the disappointing comment. And then : " I wish I had a sword like yours. How did you get it ? "

" Stole it."

" I'll warrant someone will have your ears off if you are taken, then."

" No," said Raoul indiscreetly. " My ears are worth a sword or two to the man from whom I run."

Again the pale eyes flickered.

" You fool," said Raoul inwardly and to himself, " have you set the thought of reward in his head ? Still, being outlawed he could not claim the price of betrayal. And he is none too valorous. But can I part from him without offence ? "

" Which way is your Hastain ? " inquired the apprentice, with elaborate indifference. " How do we go ? "

" Due westward," Raoul replied, with his mind on the Warden's map of Nordanay. " And we will keep off the tops when possible. A man seems twice his size against the sky."

The townsman held his peace, perhaps because he had nothing with which to cap this information ; and together they moved away along the narrowing ravine.

The wind dropped, and clouds banked sullenly to southward, hiding to its flanks the dark and dominant bulk of Dondunor ; but in the north the sky cleared, and where the hollows of the moors were waterless their slopes began to quiver in the heat. Glare of sunlight, scent of blossoming heather, low laughter of streams, and boom of passing bees seemed drawn through the substance of Raoul's dazed and tiring body, to fall in coiling coloured skeins to some dark cavern of the mind where—freed from consciousness of sweat and chafing and monotony of movement—a care-free Raoul wove a shimmering web of dreams. . . .

For warp were memories of swarded Sanctalbastre, misty Marckmont, fierce Ger, together with the fragrance of music and old stories that possessed Raoul's heart whenever he encountered them ; and for woof were desire of achievement and the grandeur of the moors. Only the features of Yseult he could not spin ; and then, when colour and sound and formless longing were a blur in his mind, the pale absorbed face with its dark hair and heavy eyebrows would stand out complete—to endure a moment in perfection, and then to fade into darkness where the spinning began again. . . .

No web of fancy, however, could long be woven in the company of the runaway apprentice. Like the flight of a sewer-fed horse-fly his converse tore and shredded the gossamer fabric. Street brawls and drinking-bouts, brothels and gaming-dens, had made this long-limbed youth a hero to himself ; and through the note of braggart invention, pitched to impress a listener clerkly-bred, rang a ground-bass of dreary truthfulness. Awhile Raoul marvelled, until disgust wore down his patience ; his brief mechanical comments ceased, and when the other turned a puzzled horse-face on his unappreciative audience, Raoul avoided the pale eyes and spoke to the skyline ahead.

" And if instead of seven moles she had seven hundred, it was to you she sold them, not to me."

" Hey ? What's amiss ? Do you not . . oh, pardon,

gentle tadpole of a cardinal, I only sought to ease the hour with honest mirth. But if you will we shall discuss the properties of herbs or the procession of the stars. Or would Your Eminence put up a prayer for our souls' salvation ? I fear this world is a wicked place, inhabited by lechers and blasphemers—— "

" And murderers," thought Raoul, but aloud he said : " I meant no offence. But for me one vow broken need not entail the breaking of the rest. And for you—you cannot be happy in your wenching, or you would not want to tell me of it."

" Happy ? " repeated the astonished townsman. " What think you . . . nay, you drone like a greybeard, but it means naught. Your head must be dank as the crypt of Saint Hiltrude—— "

At Montenair, thought Roaul.

" —— but one night a pretty wench will rid you of these humours. Take what comes, and turn it to account, say I ; these doubts and ponderings are well enough in the cloister garth, but I'm for a man's life."

" And a man's death," put in Raoul quietly, " if you are caught with me, for I shall not be taken alive."

" Eh ? Oh, ay, and a man's death," went on the other. " But plague on it, do not cross *that* bridge before you come to it. I knew a watchman who . . . "

This time the worldly manner lacked conviction, and presently its weaver fell silent, acquiescing moodily when Raoul suggested a halt where a hill-stream trickled into a little tarn that overflowed down a rocky slope beyond. There the pair ate the last of Raoul's food, and drank of the clear water ; and then Raoul stretched himself in shadow between two boulders.

" There may be adders here," he said, " but I shall risk a wink of sleep."

" Adders ? " repeated the other vaguely. Then with a sidelong glance at Raoul, he inquired : " Whose land are we now upon, say you ? "

" Saints alone know," affirmed Raoul, who was sure that somewhere near that spot the Duchy of Hastain met the Counties of Saint-Aunay and of Ger. " To whomsoever it belongs, his writ runs faintly hereabouts ; we might dwell here a year, and die, and none would ever know."

" And none would ever know," came the whispered echo.

Raoul raised heavy eyelids to observe the effect of a suggestion.

" Perhaps," he murmured, " it is royal land.   The County of Montenair runs far into these wild hills."

The horse-face twitched.   The pale eyes swept the south-ward ranges.   Raoul turned his head, gazed sleepily at the other's shadow hunched on the rock above him, and let his eyelids droop.

" Why does the fool sit brooding there ? " was his last conscious thought.   " He will find comfort in the shade.   Saint Barruc be praised, I have stopped his flow of sooty memories."

Raoul slept . . . and dreamed that an adder watched him.   He shrank away from its black blunt head, and, shrinking, woke.   His eyes flew open ; the shadow of the apprentice still darkened the hot rock above them, but now the shadow was crouching, with a hand that rose and paused and rose again, holding a dagger. . . .

With a cough, a splutter, and a hand raised to his own throat Raoul sat up ; above and beside him his companion struck out of sight into the heather, thereafter turning over his shoulder a staring face, with lips that crackled disjointed words.

" An adder !   It was an adder . . . close to your head . . . I dared not cry out . . . it turned away, and I *missed* ! "

Raoul's mouth was dry, and he kept his hand at his throat as he spoke.

" An adder . . . I dreamed it . . . I felt danger . . . I think I owe my life to you.   If you had not been there . . . but what colour was it ? "

" Colour ?   G-grey.   Silvery grey."

" Ay.   Very poisonous.   By Our Lady, I am weak and sweating from head to foot . . . you should have carved at it, not stabbed.   Doubtless your wrist shook, as would mine have done.   Oh, I am stupid and light-headed . . . your hand, friend.   I shall not forget."

The apprentice forced a grin as he dropped his weapon.

His palm was damp, and moisture glistened on his narrow brow.

" And now," said Raoul, " I must into the tarn to wash this fright away. Come you also ? "

" Ay . . . ay," muttered the other. " It will be good . . . what, you wear mail ? "

Raoul's belt and tunic were off, and he was plucking at the laces of the linked shirt.

" Yes, stolen with the sword," he grunted, peeling himself with puffings of relief.

He felt the other's eyes upon him, and rage and secret laughter quickened his pulse afresh.

" Either I have a touch of the sun," he told himself, " or this rogue waits for courage to do what he botched a moment ago. When I am naked, if he could get at my sword . . . but he shall not, and I must bring this matter to some end before I am afraid."

" Come," he urged aloud, " I shall be in the water before you."

With clumsy fingers the apprentice began to loosen his footgear ; Raoul, now unclothed, stepped into his own shoes again and stooped to draw his sword—aware, as he did so, that the grey-clad seated figure had stiffened to immobility.

" I trust the next adder may fare worse ! " he laughed, flourishing the blade as he stepped forward to the tarn. Skirting the peaty margin till the water rippled amber and steel-blue between himself and his companion, he kicked off his shoes and dropped the sword beside them, grinning across at the pale watching face before he leaped.

The splash, and his own joyful gasp as the tarn received him, roused the onlooker to swift action. Raoul had half-expected it ; his feet were on the bottom, and at sight of the grey darting figure he flung himself backwards in the water, and reached for the waiting hilt. . . .

Then he was out of his depth and swimming, head back and steel between his teeth. The apprentice had cried out in wrath and fear, and was already running back ; but this time he made for Raoul's clothes, snatched up the mail shirt from beneath them, twisted it round his left hand and forearm and whipped out his dagger.

Raoul trod water, turned for the far bank, and stood in his shoes before the other started to run round again. And now the servant of Yseult de Olencourt discovered himself to be cool and unafraid.

" Saint Barruc be *my* shield, for I have been a great fool," he murmured. " But a sword and shoes . . . h'm, this time again I must not attract the attention of Sainte Austre-berte."

Then he shouted across the water.

" Grey adders in these hills are rare, brave prentice. I dreamed of a black one, but woke to find him grey indeed . . . nay, bold Pendragon, cross the mere if you would gain Excalibur ! "

" You cursed little whelp ! I'll rip your pretty carcase into shreds ! "

And in a flash Raoul was tearing round the tarn, the bright drops flying from his limbs, the bright sword gleaming in his hand ; and behind him pounded and sweated the furious outlaw.

" Alehouse and brothel are on my side," thought Raoul, " but can *I* run *him* down if he bolts with my gear ? I had not thought of that. . . ."

Neither, it seemed, had his pursuer, until they had three times encircled the gently-stirring water. Then the latter darted up to the rocks, and halted to indulge in a blown grin.

" Run on, my jolly water-sprite ! " he cried. " I leave you to it. If the night be cold you will find the motion warming. As for me, I am the better by a shirt of mail, a cloak, a—what, you give battle ? Come, then—*ah* ! "

Raoul, halting a score of paces away, stood to recover full breath, and suddenly ran forward with upraised sword. To him the pale horse-face seemed swimming in a crimson mist ; for the third time in his life the murderous rage of Ger had raised its head in him. A sweeping downstroke bit his own good mail, jarring the bones that hewed and the bones that parried ; the whirling dagger-point went past his chin as he gave ground, and with a crouch and a wide outward fling of his sword-hand he sent a shearing horizontal blow beneath the other's guard. . .

The mail-wrapped fist beat him on the mouth as the

apprentice shrieked and toppled forward; the sword was fearfully home, and Raoul lost hold of the hilt as he stumbled aside. Then he clutched it again as it drove into the heather, and wrenched the broad blade reeking out, and backed, and stared, and gasped . . . and then in pity and horror smote once and twice and thrice at this wailing, writhing thing which he had split asunder. . . .

Then he reeled away and was deathly sick by the margin of the tarn. And when he raised his head a hooded crow sat watching him.

" So that is how it feels to kill a man," said Raoul to the black expectant shape. " Poor wretch, God assoil him; it was he or I, for he would have murdered me asleep this night."

He climbed into shirt and hose, and crossed himself before bending to unwrap the mail from an arm still limp and warm. By that time three crows waited for his going; and when, five minutes later, he gave the place a last unhappy glance, the ghoulish company was grown to eight.

The rage of Ger was spent. Raoul cried out, and flung the dead youth's cap at them, and fled.

IV

THE SINGING STONES OF HASTAIN

NEAR sunset on that same day Raoul passed from the dark grit crags of Nordanay to the limestone of Honoy, where the hot rocks glittered grey-white and took on shadows sharply blue, and where the streams were hushed below-ground, so that rowans stood pale-green and lonely in dry watercourses. Now Dondunor was sunk and lost behind, and the south was fretted by the steeps of the twin upland monarch, Dondonoy. And suddenly, a league away to his right front, Raoul saw what might have been the bricks of a child of Anak, once built in a ring of uprights to support a continuous architrave, and then two-thirds swept down and scattered by an idle hand.

" The Singing Stones above Hastain," he said aloud.

Again he crossed himself, for the Stones were accounted the haunt of witches ; then he thanked Saint Barruc in his heart, for beyond the dark crest just above those strange grey shapes the moors sank in a swift slope to the bank of the Nordenne and the plain of Basse Honoy. And presently threads of smoke climbed listlessly out of a ravine ahead of him, whilst at his feet a stream leaped into daylight and flung its rippling tribute down towards the river. There Raoul drank, and then strode forward into climbing shadow, wondering with some trepidation whether news of his disappearance could possibly have reached this corner of the hills.

A bend of the ravine discovered grey-white huts, standing amid the débris of which they were builded ; below them stood a row of rough hill-sledges, some with shaggy ponies harnessed to them. Men shaggy as the ponies and grey-white as the stone moved to and fro and paused to stare at the approaching wanderer. These were the lead-miners of Prince Thorismund, Duke of Hastain ; among them appeared a muscular rascal with a great whip thonged to his wrist, and

an eye so trained in menace that Raoul capped his hilt with
one hand before fumbling in his wallet with the other.

" Account for yourself, youngling," growled the overseer.
" No good thing comes the way you came."

" One good thing comes all ways," cried Raoul, holding
up a silver florin. " My last coin for a wallet full of food ;
I have pined four years on monastery fare, and now would
test the flesh-pots."

" What monastery ? "

" Saint Gudule in Belsaunt," Raoul replied—adding
inwardly : " A candle the length of my sword to Saint Gudule
if I come out of this." For there was nothing to prevent his
questioner from setting the mining serfs to bait a wayfarer to
death for their amusement.

" Where do you go ? "

" To Hastain, to seek service with the Prince."

" The Prince, as you call him—here he is our Duke—is
not at Hastain. He is not yet seventeen, and still eats pap,
for aught I know, at Hautarroy."

" His seneschal is there, however ; he assembles a household against the Duke's coming into full possession of his
lands."

" Oh, ay . . . well, come your ways and let me feel your
bonny silver."

" Yes, when I get my fingers in your provender."

The overseer spoke aside in a dialect so broad that Raoul
could not follow his words ; and ten minutes later the wallet
was full and its owner munching, with a sense of danger
lately overpast, as he crossed the stream below the mines.
There the waters, so limpid a quarter of a mile behind, ran
thick and milky-grey ; and to the sound of their brawling
Raoul breasted the first stir of the evening wind and caught
a glimpse of the level fields beside the shining river.

" Somewhere here, then, is the end of this murderous
day," he told himself. " I shall sleep soundly if I can cross
the water."

Fatigue had blotted out all emotion relating to that noon-
tide killing by the tarn, and his anxiety to be beyond Nordenne was only on account of quicker travelling on the
morrow ; but for him the end of the day was not yet. When

he was half a mile below the mines he came on a single serf—
a miner by his grey-white garments—who shuffled in the path
and beat with a cudgel at something humped in the heather.

Raoul stared and quickened his pace ; the humped thing
was a woman—a woman whose head was bowed upon her
knees, whose hands lay limply beside her bare feet.

" None of my business," reflected Raoul uncomfortably,
feeling that he was going to interfere.

At his sharp challenge the miner turned a stupid hairy
face and stayed his cudgel in mid-air.

" Who are you ? " he growled.   " This foul hag is a witch.
Last New Year's Day she stole a burning peat from my
hearth ; my child is sick because of it, and my she-goat gives
no milk.   Stand away now, whilst I score her with iron above
the breath."

He had lowered the stick to his shoulder, and now began
fumbling in the breast of his tunic.   When the other grey
paw was withdrawn it clutched a rusty knife ; the sight put
an end to Raoul's irresolution, and his sword came out with a
vicious scrape.

" Touch her again and I split your skull for you," he
snapped.   " Begone ! "

To his surprise—for the serf overtopped him by a head—
his threat was seriously received.   The fellow backed away,
crossing his cudgel and knife-blade in front of him ; then,
with an unintelligible growl of abuse, he edged round the
newcomer, took to his heels, and fled up the winding path.

Raoul watched him for a moment before turning to the
woman ; she had not moved, and gingerly he laid a hand on
the matted spread of her coarse black hair.

" He is gone," he said gently, aware of an odour of rags
and garlic.   " Are you very sorely hurt ? "

The dark head was lifted so suddenly that he started back.
The woman was middle-aged, and life had roughened and
wrinkled her sharp brown face, but shoulders and breasts
were round and smooth where her torn bodice parted, and
there was vigour and even laughter in her harsh voice and in
the eyes that peered through her tangled elf-locks.

" I thank you, stranger," she said, in a manner something
above her apparent station.   " I had already lost my pleasure

in that cudgelling—indeed, I wondered how best to startle the poor lout away ! "

" You wondered—your *pleasure*— " stammered Raoul. " But woman, your arms, your back—you are bruised from head to knee ! "

" Ay, but with naught that oil of Saint Jehan's wort will not ease. My bed was never of swansdown, stranger. I teased yon oaf into beating me for a purpose of my own . . . but see, we must not linger here. At sundown the miners come this way to their huts at the valley's end ; if you are seen by the stream they will run along the height where the gorge narrows, and stone you before you can get away."

" Stone me ? Why—because I drove that knave —— "

" Ay. None but a witch would save a witch from honest men, unless it were that witch's own familiar—a comely boy, springing from fiend knows where in the lonely hills."

" Then you *are* a witch ? "

Backing another pace, Raoul rubbed on the skirt of his tunic the fingers that had touched the woman's head, and crossed himself with his drawn sword. The creature showed white teeth in a grin, hugging her elbows, and watching the bright point as it moved against flushed cloud and shadowed heather. As it sank to earth she leaned forward and caught the steel betwixt thumb and finger ; before Raoul understood what she was doing she had scratched herself on the back of her other hand and let the blade swing free. . . .

The blood welled out, and Raoul gasped ; but the woman laughed and held the hand aloft.

" Yes, I am a witch, but by this token you are safe from me, fair Christian youth. No need to cry ' a rowan-tree ' or call upon your gods ; you have done me kindness, and that will afford you better protection."

" That is blasphemy," said Raoul sulkily, digging his sword-point in the peat to cleanse it. " There is one God, and you know it."

" There are two at least," came the grave rejoinder, " or you would need no sign to ward the Other off. Come, let me set you on your way."

Baffled and shaken, Raoul stared about him and down at the witch-woman's face. Only the topmost edge of the ravine

still glowed in sunset-light ; and here was company stranger
than any loneliness. There had been little noise of witchcraft
at martial Ger, quiet Marckmont, or hallowed Sanctalbastre ;
traffic with witches might be called damnable, but beneath
Raoul's dreams and vanities lay that stony honesty which
sometimes disconcerted him, and he found himself curious
and unafraid. This woman might be Satan's paramour and
agent, but there was neither fear nor malice in her face. There
was even a hint of contempt in that extravagant gesture of
good faith . . . and suddenly the smeared hand rose again.

" Hark ! They are moving ! "

Raoul stiffened and strained his ears ; but he heard nothing
save the restless murmur of the wind-stirred heather.

" Come, then. I know a way. Your sword is one, and the
pickaxes are many."

The woman shrugged her beaten body, rose in one movement, snapped her fingers, and plunged up the steep immediate
slope. . . .

" I follow," called Raoul, sheathing his sword.

Thereafter he slipped and climbed and scrambled as best
he might, until a darkling reach of bog lay between him and
the lip of the ravine ; once a faint tumult swelled in that
direction, but Raoul barely raised his eyes from the horny
heels and strong brown calves of his guide until she halted a
mile or more from the path where they had spoken together.
Puffing, he sank down in dead bracken and watched the
witch-woman as she scanned the southward quarter of sunset-
reddened and deep-shadowed desolation.

" Have you lost the way ? " he hazarded.

She turned to him with a smile.

" No, Christian. I watch for my companions. Now,
whither would you go ? "

" To Château Saulte, avoiding Hastain, Santloy, and the
abbeys," was Raoul's frank reply.

" So ? It will be easy enough, if you but trust yourself
to friends of her you have befriended."

" Why should you take such trouble ? " he demanded.

" Had you not torn your hand, I should believe you mocked
me. You could have saved yourself—or so you claimed in
your first words to me."

"You heard the accusation, gentle youth; yet you intervened. Besides . . . I think most women would do as much for you."

"Why?"

"By your bearing you have lived where there are mirrors. If not, when daylight comes look into the nearest pool."

"But . . . tell me, who *are* you?"

"My name is Cordula, once wife of Bleis the miller at Dor, now cattle-doctor to three hamlets on the plain. But among the witches I am called Sabelle; in the first or last house in any village of the moors you must say these three words: *Nos tol venko*; adding thereto: *Sabelle sent me*."

"'Nos tol venko, Sabelle sent me'—and then?"

"They will give you food and shelter, and pass you on your way. And now, if you hasten, I can point out to you the ford which . . . ah, hearken again! You hear?"

This time no human outcry stole across the hills. A faint and eerie double note, a harmony of groan and whistle, swelled and died and swelled along the rustling wind. And now the sun was going down amid slate-purple cloud; Raoul sat listening, and felt the cropped hair stir at the base of his skull.

"What is it?" he whispered.

"The Singing Stones."

"Are they near?"

"Half a mile away or less, beneath the crest yonder."

"You go to an assembly?"

"No, to a council of the coven. There will be little to see to-night, but if you care to watch in hiding ——"

"God forbid! I pray you, set me on my path."

"As you will. But I must come with you to the last hill-brow, for all these ridges are treacherous with bogs. See, how the country darkens; you will need to hasten."

Raoul stood up and gazed across the plain, now visible through several heathery gaps beneath them.

"Is that the Rambard road, then?" he demanded, pointing to a distant line of poplars.

"Yes . . . I was in Rambard yesterday, and saw the Duke ride through. . . ."

"What? The Duke of Saulte? Which way rode he—
and who rode with him?"

Sabelle wheeled at the sudden questions, and watched his
face as she answered.

"Ay. The Duke of Saulte. He rode for Hautarroy . . .
they say the Constable is sick to death, and Saulte, belike,
would be at hand when the king looks about for a successor
. . . and with the Duke rode his two brothers, and the Sieurs
de Chevine, de Belfrancourt, du Véranger——"

"Enguerrand also! What a curst mischance! Are you
sure?"

"I am sure . . . lording," said the witch-woman slyly.

The title roused Raoul to his self-betrayal. Sullenly he
looked Sabelle in the eyes and groped for his purse.

"Here," he muttered, proffering a coin. "Will this buy
your silence? You know who I am?"

"I know nothing, lording . . . oh, I will pouch the good
gold noble, but . . . it was my familiar saved me in the
gorge."

Raoul flung himself down again, and stared into the
twilight. Here was a brutal end to his fond plan . . . and
suddenly he realised his desperate weariness.

"It is no use my going on," he growled.

Then, with a sudden smile at the dark watching face, he
added: "Gentle witch-wife, I must trust you further. Is
there a night's shelter anywhere within my reach?"

"There are caves beyond the Singing Stones . . . come,
before darkness falls."

Again Raoul set eyes upon her swiftly-moving heels;
and, save for the occasional whiff of garlic that reminded him
his guide was of earth, the strangeness of hour and place and
circumstance would have borne heavily upon his mind. As
it was, perplexities irrelevant to his own welfare filled what
thought he could spare from his stumbling feet; and at
length impatient curiosity had its way with him.

"Tell me truly, good Sabelle—how dare you face man's
fury and reproach in this life, and the good God's damnation
in the next, for any gift or promise from a fiend? What
happiness is there in trudging ragged over weary moors to
prove a foul allegiance or to whirl in a hell-taught dance?

I have heard of witches dying in torment with their Master's name on their lips, steadfast as any martyr of the True Faith. What power sustains this damnable delusion? Why did *you* seek to be thus miserably beaten?"

Sabelle had slackened speed and turned her head to listen. Was he deceived by a trick of afterglow, or did her eyes go bright and blank as a cat's and then take on humanity again?

"I must show bruises that I may have comfort of my Master . . . lording, what do *you* know of the great miseries endured among the poor? The lords and chevaliers have right over their bodies, the priests claim what is left—bidding them suffer patiently, in that Christ who died to save them suffered worse than they. Christ rose again, it may be; I have never seen Him on these moors. *My* Master I have seen a score of times in a year . . . seen and touched him, ay, given myself into his strong cold arms. . . I have had potent charms of him, and gold when my husband was hanged for killing the deer of the Prior of Dor . . . but of the dancing and the night-riding ointment it is useless to tell you, for only one who knows them can ever understand. . . ."

Magical, sombre, unutterably sad, the last light brooded over the uplands of Honoy. For Raoul the harsh voice of the witch-woman filled darkening hollows, lessened in the wind, and rang to leeward of piled rocks as she swung her head towards him and away again. Each time a further question rose to his lips, some phrase, some half-caught fragment, of that weird monologue headed his thought into new channels—disclosing to him deeps of unconsidered life that stirred and agonised to prop the schemes of governance and chivalry. And ever, behind and beneath her utterance, breathed the soft clamour of the Singing Stones.

"My daughter would be little younger than yourself if she had lived . . . at least, I know not if she lives or no. When she was fourteen the warrior Abbot of Saint-Maur-by-Dunsberghe took her to pour his wine, and since that day I have not heard of her. . . .

"My husband did not slay the deer at all, but some one had to pay for that great wickedness. . . .

"My grandam was in Rambard when the Butcher's

father sacked it. She was foully slain by the ravening Riders of Campscapel. My mother was then six, and she remembered it. . . .

"You think the witches but exchange one bondage for another and a viler? Have I not told you of the help that waits for them, the garnering of knowledge—ay, of life and death if the lessons be well learned? Deal not too harshly with the witches, lording, if you come to power over a countryside. I tell you our assemblies and our ritual, being forbidden, give outlet for that wild spirit of revenge which stirs at times amid the serfs—finding little easement in the pale ceremonies of your Church. . . .

"You are too young to remember the Jacquerie of Nordanay. It was madness . . . but how the dull hinds rose! I saw the Fox of Barberghe fleeing for his life . . . and saw him grinning, three months later, when he rode along his row of seventy-two gibbets. The Count of Montcarneau fired his own granaries and flooded half his fields, and famine had nigh done his work for him before the Constable came north to finish it. As for the Count of Ger, they say he laughed and lived on fish. . . .

"At La Roselle there were orphan children eaten before the winter ended. And always wolves ran up and down the village streets. . . .

"Even Joris of the Rock found few pickings in that turmoil; he stole the Butcher's cattle and hid far in the forest. . . .

"And in those days, lording, I had bread of Yaan."

"*Who is Yaan?*" cried Raoul, reeling with fatigue.

"My Master . . . he whom you call Satan. See, lording, here are caves in plenty. Some of them we are wont to use when the weather is stormy; but in a dozen of the smaller holes you may sleep undisturbed till the clang of the Doom Trumpet."

Raoul set his hand against the limestone lintel of a cave and peered within.

"Adders," he thought. "Wild-cats. But once I get my shoes off not a cockatrice itself shall drive me out."

He turned, and found that now he could see the Singing Stones—a medley of dim squared shapes, some with a side still faintly grey, some dark in silhouette against the eastern dusk, three hundred yards away from him. Drawing his sword for the last time that day, he knelt, and was poking cautiously amid the gloom of the little cave when Sabelle cried out and pointed to the last yellow rents and gashes in the western sky. Two mounted figures, jet-black against the lowest light, drove hard across a neighbouring ridge and vanished. . . .

" Who are they ? " asked Raoul.

" The Mistress of the Coven and her little friend . . . lording, I must leave you. Make no noise and none will interfere with you. Remember, *nos tol venko*, and my name, will stand you in good stead among poor folk for twenty miles around. . . . Farewell."

" Farewell," said Raoul stupidly ; but the witch did not move.

" Lording," she whispered suddenly. " A kiss for Sabelle ? "

Raoul, still squatting on his haunches, looked up and smiled and put out his empty hand. The darkness of Sabelle enveloped him as she stooped ; fingers gripped him above the elbows, rank hair fell all about his face, a fierce kiss came flatly on his mouth . . . he blinked and endured.

" Garlic this time," he told himself. " Last time it was onions. Holy Mary, she has sinews of steel ; she could break me between her two hands. . . ."

Then he was freed, and in a moment Sabelle was a vanishing blur in the gloom. He bent to cut and gather heather, for the cave-floor seemed naked rock ; and as he worked he became aware of a little piping tune that threaded in and out of the wind's wuther and rose against the ghostly blowing of the Stones.

" What now ? " murmured Raoul, turning once more to peer about him. " Fiends of the Pit and angels out of Paradise shall not delay my sleep much longer . . . ah, there, a lordly stag at gaze. Can he see the piper, I wonder ? "

Magnificently antlered, the dark head rose in profile a score of yards away. For a moment Raoul knelt still, but when the antlers stirred he started and bit back an exclamation.

The stag had something in its mouth, a straight and slender stick . . . or . . .

The stag moved higher . . . the stag had a man's body, a man's arms and hands, and fingers playing on a shrill-voiced little pipe.

But now the levity of extreme fatigue was upon Raoul ; he eyed the apparition as it moved away towards the Stones, and did not even raise his sword-hilt for a cross.   Instead, he thrust his bundle of heather into the dark aperture before him, rolled after it, and wrapped his cloak around his body.

" Sieur Yaan," he whispered sleepily, " you may have all your moors to-night, save this one little hole. . . . Oh, Holy Saints, have they begun ? "

A dreadful screech rang out, and distant laughter followed it.   Faint voices hailed and answered, and the piping was no longer audible.   Horsehoofs drummed near Raoul's hiding-place, and he craned his neck to see two riders come careering by—their cloaks blown out, their horses plunging recklessly in the dense heather.   As they passed him in the darkness one of them cried out, in a deep laughing woman's voice that rang like a festal bell : " *Hola—hola !   Avoy—avoy—avoy !* "

A mingled din of welcome rose around the Singing Stones, whilst Raoul clutched his sword and let his thoughts go wandering where they would.

" That must have been the Mistress of the Coven," he mused.   " *Hola—avoy !   Nos tol venko !*   I am half a witch myself by now.   Well, Saturn my birth-star is the liege of witches.   But I meant to ask a score of things of yon queer woman.   In truth the serfs fare badly . . . at Marckmont there was never any famine.   Nor will be, if I have my way . . . but shall I ever win out of this devilish domain ? To-day I must have covered twenty miles of roadless country . . . and to-morrow I must strike back into it again, for Guarenal is now my only hope.   That girl there, Reine, she may be able to help me.   She helped me before—to my own undoing, it is true.   Ah, no, that is false ; had I not gone to Belsaunt I should not have seen Yseult. . . ."

Again that ghastly screech ; but this time nothing external had power to stir his weary senses.

" I shall never forget Reine ; she helped me to find my dear lady. . . .

" I am *not* too young . . . it *is* love . . . nothing else could fret and flame as this thing does. . . .

" A day may come when I see how that taste of garlic, and those three words of gibberish . . . ay, even the torn guts of that pitiful knave by the tarn yonder . . . have led me to my chalice of the Sangreal."

His chalice of the Sangreal was then to serve Yseult, asking nothing in return.

In the morning he ventured down to the Singing Stones, but found no strange or startling trace of the night's meeting. Round orange mosses clustered on the weathered slabs, and gorse bloomed between the uprights that remained ; only the flat altar-stone bore stains and ashes as of some recent sacrifice. The wind-song flew in booming organ-notes and piercing whistles from crevices above his head ; and as he stared about him a thin rain began to fall.

Till about noon he sat in his cave, dry but worried. A new alternative had suggested itself to him. Why not make for Montenair and seek out Rogier de Olencourt ? Rogier served as a chevalier with his brother Fulk the Castellan ; Rogier was silent as Fulk was grim. Moreover, the Baron de Guarenal held office under Armand of Ger ; the Castellan was Armand's equal in military rank, and touchy concerning his own rights. Perhaps an appeal to the Castellan . . . besides, the sister of Fulk and Rogier was Yseult.

" At any rate I may see her again," Raoul reflected. " I have food for about two days. I must aim for the road between Guarenal and Saint-Aunay, and then find out if Sabelle's password carries weight thus far."

A gleam of sunshine sped him on his way, but by mid-afternoon he was caught in drizzle ; the June dusk found him wandering, forlorn and soaked and utterly lost, beneath the mists that surged along a terrifying mountainside.

" I am too far south," he told himself. " This is still limestone. . . . God help me, it is Dondonoy. Whilst I have strength I will climb . . . where there are screes there are

no bogs . . . maybe I shall reach some sort of shelter before
the light fails utterly."

And not too hurriedly, lest he should weary himself beyond
measure, he began to march up hill. Night fell, and still he
clambered, for only whilst he moved could he hold off the
horror of the black towering steeps and endless gulfs disclosed
and hidden and disclosed again as the gusty mountain wind
parted or rolled together the armies of the clouds. . . .

Far up the slopes a raven croaked at him, turning him
sick with fear, so that he shrieked aloud. A gruesome echo
gave sharp answer, blasting him dumb ; and there amid
dripping mist he flung himself prone in the heather, sobbing
with fright and exhaustion, whispering prayers and curses
into the evil darkness, drowning at last in deep and heedless
slumber.

The wind freshened with the first grey light, and as the
clouds dispersed a leaden-eyed Raoul found himself gazing
at the dawn from an eastern flank of Dondonoy, a mile or
more from the grisly-looking ridge, six leagues in length,
which linked the monster to its rival Dondunor. Presently.
over the lowest point of that same ridge, the sun got up in
splendour ; bread and beef and apples restored the wanderer
to some confidence in himself, so that he laughed when the
watching raven rose and flapped disconsolately away.

" Not this time, carrion-thief ! " he shouted ; and now the
noisy echo failed to startle him.

His sodden clothes dried in morning sunshine as he
neared the crest of the ridge ; blue sky dispelled the terrors
of the night, and his stiffened limbs gained a new elasticity.
Presently he was crossing up-ended limestone strata where the
moisture was already fading ; a slanting two-mile ascent, and
the bulk of Dondonoy seemed shaken off behind him. Then,
amid the wet freshness of the topmost heather, he ceased to
climb ; the tumbled hills to southward of the ridge burst on
his view. Far to the right appeared slopes giving signs of
cultivation ; between were pinewoods and sheets of water,
whereby the Butcher's savage rangers guarded the Butcher's
deer. And ahead the remotest uplands were darkened by
the fringes of the Forest of Honoy.

Raoul began to stride downhill.

c

Hot noon had settled upon Capel Conan when the wife of
Piers the hay-ward carried her leathern bucket to the rushing
stream.   To her appeared a slender youth, with a tired face
austerely carven, and shining, smiling grey-green eyes.   This
youth was girt with a fair sword-belt, and had a heavy cloak
folded across his body.   His woollen tunic sat ill, as though
some thicker garment lay beneath ;   and his hose showed
wonderful rents from thigh to ankle.   As for his shoes, they
were half cut to pieces ;   but the hay-ward's wife forgot them
when the black velvet bonnet came off the thick brown hair.

" Give you good-day, mother . . . *nos tol venko !* "

" Give you good day, pretty stranger, and who sent you ? "

" Sabelle sent me."

" Sabelle of the Coven of the Singing Stones ?   You come
a strange way—but no matter.   What is your need ? "

" Food and rest, and word of a by-path to Montenair."

" You shall have all these things."

All these things Raoul had ;   in a roomy barn he sank on
straw beside a plough and watched the motes dance in the
narrow sunbeams that fell from great cracks in the dried mud
of the wall.

" Another twenty miles, I'll warrant," he told himself
contentedly ;   and then :   " Yon Sabelle was no liar in this
matter, come what may."

Then he was asleep.

In a dream he heard hideous uproar, a rhythmic crashing
which seemed to shake the earth.   He turned to Sabelle, who
stood near, and borrowed her own words that had remained
with him.

" Is this the clang of the Doom Trumpet ? "

Her features blanched and lengthened into those of the
outlawed apprentice.   Raoul flung a hand to his hip, and
twitched himself awake. . . .

He started up on one arm, bruising his elbow on the
handle of the plough.   The tumult was real enough ;   there
was shouting and screaming, a slamming of doors, a stamp
and shuffle of feet, a gabbling of poultry, the smash and tinkle
of a roof-tile—the whole sawed through and through by the
demented braying of a donkey.   Raoul leaped to his feet and

snatched up his weapon; where the motes had danced in the sunbeams was now a wavering crimson glare, and through the smells of straw and cattle and rotting wood came a sudden whiff of smoke. Hoofs clattered on the cobbles; from outside something struck the wall of the barn with a crash, and dried mud flew this way and that within. The donkey's voice rose deafeningly to an incredible screech, and was suddenly cut off, so that the lesser mingled din broke out as though from silence. . . .

Raoul stole to the door, unlatched it, and peeped out. Ducks flapped and waddled distractedly in the dusk-laden street; at the far end men with steel caps and corselets moved obscurely in a growing spark-shot smother. A score of yards from the barn, and almost at the threshold of Piers the hay-ward's cottage, a villager lay motionless on his back.

" By the beard of Beelzebub ! " boomed a great voice close at hand. " At last I have seen a dead donkey ! "

Raoul leaped back along the wall and flattened himself against it. A thunderous kick beat the unlatched door wide open; but the peering man-at-arms had looked at fire, and the barn was pitch-black to his eyes. He made a pass with his pike, grunted, and backed away; Raoul heard him turn with a stamp, and slid again to the door. . . .

A ragged child, a girl of five or six, had dodged out of an alley between two crazy hovels, and now stood dumb with terror, her back against a wall, her little paws outspread as though she were already crucified.

" Hey, mistress ! " roared the laughing man-at-arms. " Where have you hidden the Red Witch ? "

There came a clang and a clatter, and he reeled sideways with his steel cap beaten over one ear; the hay-ward's door had burst open, and a slim gowned figure had darted forth and launched a cobble-stone at the armoured head. The child was snatched aside and bundled towards the cottage before the pike was raised; Raoul yelled and shot like a slung stone from the barn as the pike-head flashed and disappeared. Nailed by her clothing to the wall, the little rescuer screamed and struggled; growling with fury, the bull-necked man-at-arms spun round to confront his new attacker. Before his sword was out Raoul had cloven the mail on his forearm ; then blade and voice went up together, and Raoul, crouching, felt his end was come.

" Gilles ! Hamo ! This way ! " thundered the man-at-arms as Raoul parried his slamming downstroke and dodged aside. " To me—to me—here is the hell-cat's earth ! "

" This is my life, then," was Raoul's fleeting thought ; but the swinging sword flew free from the hand above him at a sound—*twang-whiz*—from the hay-ward's door. The man-at-arms straightened up : the bright point of a cross-bow quarrel, driven through the bull-neck, broke out beneath the angle of his jaw. With a choking sound he gave at the knees and pitched forward ; and little hands seized Raoul and dragged him backwards as shouting men raced down the street towards them.

" Quick—quick—in here ! " gasped the girl.

Together they plunged for the doorway. A leap, a stumble into odorous gloom, and the door crashed to behind them. Bolts were shot, and the gleam of a candle dazzled Raoul's eyes.

" O mercy ! " clucked the voice of the hay-ward's wife. " It is the boy I let sleep in the barn ! I had forgotten him ! "

Hard on her words came the deep twang of the cross-bow and a swelling roar without. Raoul blinked and stared about him ; there seemed a dozen people, young and old, humped on the earthen floor or crouching by the walls of the cottage room. One candle in a corner threw enormous shadows ; indeed the room was chiefly shadow, for an old woman held a brass bowl half over the flickering flame.

" Are you wounded, stranger ? " said the girl's voice in his ear.

" No . . . and you ? "

" No, only my new cloak is torn. Who are you ? "

For this emergency Raoul was ready.

" My name is Herluin," he muttered. " But tell me, what in God's name is it all about ? "

" Saint-Aunay's men came on us in the hills and chased us here."

" Chased *you*—why, who *are* you ? "

" Red Anne and I . . . they will fight to the death for us in this place. *She* is there, with her long-bow "—the girl

pointed, and Raoul saw a narrow doorway leading to some
tiny inner room—" and now you have come there are seven
of us to reckon with."

She glanced up at the roof, where dried herbs swung
in bundles from the beams ; her profile came against the
candle-flame, and Raoul saw that she had a long nose and a
delicate mouth and chin.

" Piers with his cross-bow, the two other men with axes,
the good-wife and I with spears . . . I am Lys . . . see,
the baby has gone to sleep again, poor mite . . . it is quieter
outside, but I think they are mustering . . . if the roof were
thatched a torch would finish us."

Raoul thought of the bright yellow clay in which his day's
march ended, and blessed the tile-bakers of Capel Conan.
The walls, he noticed, were all of stone ; Piers had builded
well.

" If we can hold out for an hour," said Lys between her
teeth, " these hell-dogs of Saint-Aunay may regret their
foray. As it is, half-a-dozen are done for."

Raoul and she were seated now—he nursing his naked
sword, she digging with the broad blade of her boar-spear
in the hard earth of the floor. Piers crouched on a stool, his
cross-bow ready at a loop-hole. The girl-child whom Lys
had rescued was huddled against the old dame who guarded
the candle-flame. And suddenly the humped shapes that
were men and women started at a deep female voice that
belled from the blackness of the inner room.

" Piers, set your great hutch fast against the door. I
think they have a beam with them. Let the women come in
here, or you will have no room for axe-play. Stay you,
granny, by the inner door here . . . then stand ready, all."

The shadows slipped and sprawled whilst the heavy oaken
chest was dragged into position and the unarmed women
crept into the sleeping-hole. Raoul, tugging with the rest,
could scarcely credit the reality of this strange siege until
the reawakened infant set up a determined yelling. . . .

Outside someone laughed. Then came a shout, an
ordered tramping, and a mighty crash upon the door. . . .

Long-bow and cross-bow hummed and twanged, and the
stout door-planks held fast till the sixth swing of the ram.

A seventh and eighth, and they gaped, showing sky and steel caps, swords and axes. Someone began beating in a shutter ; Raoul posted himself behind it with a caught-up palliasse, whilst at his left elbow Lys waited with her spear . . . wild threats and filthy promises came hailing from without.

"The roof!" screamed the good-wife behind them. "They are on the roof!"

"I will see to the roof!" called Red Anne easily. Then, to one of those by her : "Soak this blanket and keep it stuffed in yon slit with your stool."

A stamping above them, a thudding of blows, the crack and ring of tiles that flew ; then a rattle on the cottage floor, a laugh from above, a single deep oath from Red Anne, and the fierce note of her bow. Something dropped like a sack and slithered down the roof to fall heavily among the snarling besiegers. . . .

"Stand by with water, goodwife!" said the rare voice. "We shall have a torch through this hole anon."

So it proved ; a red glow and a resinous reek, a quenching splash and a long hissing, proclaimed the failure of the first attempt. And now Raoul was hacking off the pike-points as they pierced the shutter beside him ; from near the door the hay-ward fired and fired again into the bucklered press, whilst his two comrades swung their axes murderously behind the smashed planks and the waist-high hutch.

Then, with a crashing impact, a stone the size of a quartern loaf tore half the shutter from its hinges and gave Raoul a glimpse of jagged sky as it crushed him, palliasse and mail and all, beneath it to the floor. Gold and black and grey the interior scene spun round him ; Lys stepped across his body and stabbed furiously at something already darkening the window-space. Raoul tried to drag himself aside, and found his left arm would not move, whilst grisly pain ran through the shoulder-joint above.

He cried out, twisting his head, and so for a moment saw the centre of the room. There furtive candle-light had half-revealed the tall and glorious figure of a woman—a figure sturdily bent for a deadly upward shot. Past massive milk-white throat and forearm swung twin ropes of flame-red hair ;

and from a full-lipped scarlet mouth broke most unwomanly
a mighty war-shout.

" Face Campscapel, face death ! "

For Raoul the vision swayed into rushing night, and the
besieging uproar dwindled to a thread of sound that died in
utter silence ; but that one clarion call sent a quick certainty
with him into darkness.

" Red Anne," he thought, " is Mistress of the Coven of
the Singing Stones."

" Who is this lad ? "

The impatient growl broke out of spinning gloom over
Raoul's head. From near at hand Red Anne's rare voice
responded.

" The goodwife has it he fled from some abbey in Basse
Honoy, wandering here out of the mountain. Lys would
have died on a pike in the street but that he charged from
nowhere, fighting like a wild-cat. Give him to me for a
page, Lorin, and you will reap a likely squire when he is
grown."

" As you wish. We have room for another boy."

" We have room for half a score, but it needs another
Jacquerie to give us them."

Only Red Anne would have dared to use the Butcher's
given name, or, laughing, to remind him of his isolation, as
one who said : " Banish your wild beast of a brother, and
your peers will deal with you again." And Raoul, who in
the past few days had opened eyes on so much that was new
to him, felt his heart leap at first sight of the Butcher's sombre
steel-girt face, with its long yellow nose and ravaged cheeks
amid the thick black hair and beard. . . .

" His arm is broken," whispered the girl Lys.

" Strap it to his side," commanded Anne.

" We have a cart," said a new voice. " There are two
wounded who must travel in it. The boy can go with them."

Cool night air. A woeful rocking, a creaking and grinding, as the springless wicker-sided cart plunged forward
along the rutted track. Torment that made him screech
when the writhing man-at-arms beside him rolled on his

mangled arm and blew spittle and fetid breath into his face.
Then sudden easement and the strange sound of a death-
rattle.   Black shapes of horsemen, humped against the stars,
with visors lifted and lances leaning backward.   Curt words
and laughter, vague sounds of hoof and steel and leather.
Tunnels of over-arching trees, and rushing water falling
away and away from beside the road.   Sleep that was half
delirium, and an awakening sprinkle of heather-scented rain.
Lastly, the clash and rumble of stone under wheel and horse-
shoe, and the black uprising of towers and curtain-walls
beneath a misted moon.

"I am no longer Raoul," he remembered. "I am
Herluin the runaway novice—Herluin, befriended of witches
and saved by the Riders of Campscapel."

V

THE HOLD ABOVE ALANOL

FROM the corridor by the entrance to the pages' turret bed-chamber a window gave out upon the steep ravine dividing the chalk rock of Campscapel from the walled town of Alanol. This window was double, consisting of two round-arched lights with a dog-toothed pillar between them; being on the second floor, in the utterly inaccessible north face of the keep, it was builded with no eye for defence, and any one slim-bodied, kneeling on the stone seat in the deep splay behind it, could get his head and shoulders through and stare down at the rushing stream and the grass-covered slope beyond it, or sideways along the wall to where the grey bridge spanned the gorge between the crenellated towers of gateway and barbican. Below and beyond the barbican rose the topmost roofs of the little town; a few houses of a larger kind clustered behind the wall immediately opposite the overlooking castle ramparts, but the bulk of them lay out of sight on the receding slope to northward of the lip of the ravine.

"Campscapel has Alanol by the neck," said Ivo. And indeed the grey fortress crouched like a beast of prey above the unhappy town, laying bridge and outworks like a paw against its backbone of a steep main street.

"Time was," said Ivo, "when Red Jehan broke out every week or two and lifted a burgher's wife or daughter from her bed to his own; but in the Jacquerie the townsfolk stood by the Butcher, and he gave them a charter of rights, renouncing seigneury over such of them as were his serfs. So that now they have market and fair and watch of their own, and Jehan has no excuse for filling the gutters with red-headed bastards. Which mightily grieved him at first. But, mad as he is, he yet obeys the Butcher in everything touching the two of them. Hence he rides abroad for ease

C*

of his lusts—or did so ride, till Saint-Aunay broke his nose for him."

" Herluin would not believe *me*," said Gervase, " when I told him Jehan is ruled by the specks on his finger-nails."

" It is so," agreed Ivo. " And if he sees a ram in the pastures, he kills it or has it killed, because of a prophecy that the slayers of the last Campscapel shall come behind a ram."

Herluin—who had been Raoul—sat with his arm in a silken sling and looked from one face to another. Ivo was dark, with bright blue eyes, and a white skin, freckled, and reddened on cheeks and nose ; Gervase was sallow and girlish, with curly ash-blonde hair. Both were orphans of the Jacquerie, and neither was as old as Herluin ; but both were taller than he, and both seemed older in knowledge of the world—as, indeed, befitted the pages of Lorin de Campscapel and his resplendent mistress. But Gervase and Ivo had not yet borne arms in earnest, much less killed a fellow-creature ; they had hung upon Herluin's words when he described the swift fight by the tarn, and his invented tale of flight from a monastery found full belief with them.

"God help me, I am a grievous liar," was Herluin's constant thought in those first strange days, whilst he fell as though without a ripple into the dark pool of life on the rock of Campscapel. " But what else can I be ? I ran from Ger, and maybe when my arm is whole I can run from here. Meanwhile—lies, and my window."

To the Butcher himself, to Red Anne when she set his arm in splints for him, to the girl Lys who bathed his face and shoulder on that first night and brought a scarf for his sling, and to these boys, his room-fellows, who helped him to dress and gave him kindness and respect, he lied most valiantly ; and since his injury prevented him from carrying out any but the lightest duties, his first weeks were devoted to a wide opening of ears and eyes and to a careful guard upon his tongue. . . .

" Behind a ram," repeated Gervase thoughtfully. " No house in Honoy or Nordanay bears a ram, or even a ram's head, for crest or blazon, to my knowledge. Do *you* know of any, Herluin ? "

" There was a Franconian baron at Belsaunt, at the tourney," was Herluin's unuttered thought.

Then he smiled; he had taught himself to be slow of speech, as he had taught himself to answer to his adopted name. Gervase saw and misinterpreted the smile.

" I suppose, in the monastery—— " he began.

" We were not told much of blazonry," finished Herluin. " That is so; but I picked up a little, just as I learned to play the lute."

Ivo grinned, showing wonderful white teeth.

" I found it hard to imagine Herluin a novice," he interjected, " until I learned his wonderful innocence concerning women. By the beard of Saint Anthony, Gervase, I saw Mathilde bend down in front of him when they fed the popinjays yesterday, and rather than look at her breasts he turned his head away ! "

Herluin blushed, and Gervase laughed at him, but not unkindly; it was plain that both Gervase and Ivo thought virginity comical, if in Herluin's circumstances comprehensible.

But Herluin was the grandson of Adela of Ger, who married for love in defiance of the custom of the age; and if the old Lady of Marckmont made of her heir a youth too delicately-minded for any easy happiness, she had at least enabled him to grasp at contentment of spirit and senses beyond the reach of many about him. So that he liked to sit alone by the high window, watching the drift of far cloud-shadows, the still shapes of pines against the northward shreds of afterglow, and, in the heat-haze of the long June afternoons, the faint glare of limestone crags on the summit of his late enemy Dondonoy. There many strange thoughts of Yseult were born in him, and there he first began to weave rhymed verses out of his own head.

" What am I doing here ? " he would ask himself, coming out of a boy's long reverie, turning to gaze along the stony passages, eyeing askance the red and green embroidered curtain that hid the entrance to the Count's Tower, or, in the other direction, the massive ironwork on the door of the dungeon stair. This was the keep of Campscapel, where the dreaded Butcher held his state, where Red Anne filled with gorgeous furnishings the rooms of the Lady's Tower, where stores and arms lay piled against a siege that no one—not the king himself—had even attempted for half a century ; and at first it seemed to Herluin that one northern hold was very like another. But that was before he saw Red Jehan—who had a tower to himself at the south-western angle of the inner ward—and before he heard the Butcher dispensing what passed with him for justice beneath the blackened beams of the great hall. . . .

Sturdy vassals cloaking their nervousness as they called on their lord for settlement of their disputes, shivering peasants brought to book by bailiffs scarcely steadier at the knees than they, farmers with tales of stacks destroyed and cattle lifted by retainers of Saint-Aunay or by Joris of the Rock, and along the walls the evil hairy faces of the Riders of Campscapel . . . blows and laughter and fearful screams, the slamming of great doors, the dull glow of branding-irons, the shuffling feet of mocked and ruined men who dared not raise their eyes for the fury and hate that was in them . . . and above all, in the red-draped oaken chair, the dark unsmiling gaze of the Butcher, and his long yellow hand clamped in the blackness of his flowing beard. . . .

Yet when Herluin stood dizzily before him on the morrow of the fight at Capel Conan there was no hint of blood-lust in the Count's ravaged face ; and Herluin came to understand that this Butcher Count was one man, and Lorin de Campscapel, the lover of Red Anne, another. . . .

" This is the boy, lord," said the red-haired beauty.

" Look up, sirrah," commanded the Count. " Who are you, and whence come you ? "

" Herluin . . . never knew my surname . . . the Abbot of Saint-Maur-by-Dunsberghe found me in the fields by Santloy during the Jacquerie, and gave me into the keeping of the Prior of Saint Remigius at Hardonek . . . and there I became a novice, but . . ."

" But what ? "

" I—I grew very weary of the life, my lord, and ran away because the infirmarian beat me."

" His back bears witness to it," interjected Red Anne.

" And then ? "

" I came to Château Saulte to seek service with the Duke,
but he was going away and none would speak with me."

" What service can you render ? "

" I write well, my lord, and I know Latin.   Also I can
sing a little, and play the lute, and hold my own at chess. . . ."

" H'm.   Is Saint Remigius on the eastern or western cliff
at Hardonek ? "

" On the western, my lord.   Saint Eloy is the other."

A boy called Raoul had once stayed for a week at
Hardonek, and had gone with his grandmother to see the
relics in the church of Saint Remigius.   But the youth called
Herluin began to sweat profusely beneath this catechism.
He had expressly pitched on country beyond the Duchy of
Saulte, knowing the Count to be on bad terms with all the
neighbouring tenants-in-chief, and he felt as though sawdust
were trickling out of his heels before the next query reassured
him.   He even lost his sense of the nearness and heartening
friendliness of the tall woman sitting at the Count's left hand ;
and he had no time to promise a candle to Saint Remigius.

" How came you by sword and mail ? "

Herluin began a long and somewhat involved explanation,
in which he made the apprentice lure him into the hills with a
promise of employment at Saint-Aunay ; but after the fight
by the tarn the Butcher yawned, and bade him hold his
peace and serve the Lady Anne with care and discretion.

" And except in my own presence," he finished drily, " go
not near the person or the dwelling of my brother, the Sieur
Jehan."

This curious afterword interested Herluin until he learned
the reason for it.

" There was a page called Brunel," said Gervase when
pressed to explain.   " Jehan, in his cups, mistook him for a
girl, and when he found he was not a girl he wrung his neck."

So Herluin, in common with all the castle folk save a few
choice gentlemen-at-arms and Jehan's own body-servant Ord,
gave the Sieur's Tower a wide berth, and was marvellously
circumspect in his behaviour on those evenings when the
Butcher had his brother in his own rooms to play chess with
him. . . .

" *But what am I doing here ?* " would Herluin ask, in

those strange moments when, before his arm was set, he had the pages' quarters to himself and felt the wild disharmony between his own desires and those which seemed to fill the bosoms of Butcher Lorin and Butcher Lorin's garrison. " No one *asked* me if I wanted to stay.   H'm !   Imagine the Butcher : ' Young sir, if it please you, make free of our hospitality till you wish to move on.'   No.   I am lucky he did not send me to the kitchen. . . .

" When my arm is whole again, perhaps. . . .

" Strange.   This is the one castle in the north where news of my flight may not have penetrated.   Yet surely if Sabelle knew, then Red Anne herself or Lys must have heard of it. And if the Count discovered I was Raoul . . . like as not he would fire me back at Ger out of a mangonel, for I do not remember my uncle speaking of Campscapel without an oath.   Crack !   Whiz !   And a bundle of bones . . . flying, I judge, straight between Dondunor and Dondonoy.   But I should scarcely reach the top of the opposite slope . . . these are not pleasant thoughts. . . .

" Yet it is true I am in great danger. . . . God speed the feuds of Campscapel, so that no one who knows me may set foot in this place. . . .

" No, that is miserably said.   Enough of beastliness goes on hereabouts without new quarrels. . . .

" Since leaving Ger I have shamefully neglected my regular devotions, yet never have I so required them. . . .

" I wonder what Yseult would think if she knew that which she has come to mean to me. . . . Sieur God, bless and guard Yseult.

" I think I will say my morning prayer to the Blessed Virgin, and then an Ave, a Paternoster, and a Credo ; and after that it will be time to feed the popinjays again. . . .

" *Sub tuum praesidium confugimus, Sancta Dea Genetrix ; nostras deprecationes ne despicias in necessitatibus nostris, sed a periculis cunctis libera nos semper, Virgo gloriosa et bene-dicta.   Amen. . . .*

" *Ave, Maria, gratia plena : Dominus tecum : Benedicta tu in mulieribus, et benedictus fructus ventris tui Jesus. Sancta Maria, Mater Dei, ora pro nobis peccatoribus nunc et in hora mortis nostrae.   Amen. . . .*

"*Pater noster, qui es in coelis, sanctificetur nomen tuum. . . .*"

The feeding of the popinjays or parrots entailed a certain embarrassment even before Herluin realised the laxity of life within the great keep.

" Saints save us, here is a solemnity ! " said plump fair-haired Mathilde when first she had watched Herluin for five minutes. Loud banter and allusions recondite to the new-comer flew free when Red Anne was not present ; but beneath her eye Mathilde and Agnes were soberness itself, and only Lys gave rein to her sharp tongue. Lys, like the pages, had been orphaned in the Jacquerie ; the other two girls seemed by their slighting references to the town to have come out of it, in what way Herluin did not at first appreciate. It irritated and depressed him to find that once again his demeanour awakened ridicule ; and after a few days Lys noticed his added glumness.

" Clouds upon Dondonoy," she intoned, as though to herself, whilst Roland, the grey popinjay, ate out of her hand, and Olivier, his evil-tempered green companion, clashed his formidable beak upon the tray held gingerly by Herluin.

" You said, demoiselle ? " inquired Herluin politely over his shoulder.

" I ? Naught. The feeding of popinjays must be conducted in bleak silence."

Mathilde giggled, twirling in her fingers a new string for Red Anne's great lute of painted wood and ivory.

" Your pardon," said Herluin, with grim deliberation.

Behind his back he heard Lys make a movement. Mathilde burst into a shriek of laughter, and the green popinjay clawed thoughtfully at his own green poll and delivered himself of staccato speech.

" *Quiscut sonitus spinarum . . . fssssss !* " he croaked and hissed. " *Quiscut—quiscut—quiscut sonitussssss !* "

" *What* does he say ? " demanded Agnes, shakily. " I have heard him make that noise before . . . why, our solemnity is all to pieces ! "

For Herluin's gape had changed to a grin, and Herluin's

body rocked as he held the tray towards the gilded perch of
Olivier.

" God help us, what has taken him ? " demanded Lys,
stepping away in mock alarm. " I thought when feeding
Olivier he always recited the Seven Penitential Psalms. What
ails you now, poor soul, flashing from dumps to mirth like
that ? "

" *Quia sicut !* " hiccoughed Herluin. Then, to Agnes :
" You say he has spoken so before ? Tell—tell me truly, was
it when Demoiselle Mathilde had laughed ? "

" Why, yes, now you ask ; but what——"

" Whence came this—this miracle of wisdom ? "

" I know not. The priest had him once, the priest that
fled. But tell us, Herluin, what did he say ? Is it some
Latin filthiness ? "

" No, no," cried Herluin, his amusement dwindling at
sight not only of Mathilde's contracted brows, but of dark
pretty Agnes all agape for dirt. " No . . . it . . . it was
Holy Writ. . . ."

" But not a Penitential Psalm," he added with a touch of
malice. " It was the beginning of a verse from Ecclesiastes
. . . *Quia sicut sonitus spinarum* . . . and it goes on *arden-
tium sub olla, sic risus stulti.* And it means, ' As the
crackling of thorns under a pot, so is the laughter of a fool.' "

Agnes and Lys gave vent to mirth restrained by sight
of Olivier's fluffed neck-feathers, but plump Mathilde got
flaming to her feet.

" You beastly little bent blade ! " she screamed. " Take
your poor empty hose away before I pull them off and
baste you across my knee ! Go to, with your airs and your
Latin——"

" Mathilde ! "

The blonde girl's cheeks lost colour, and she backed
against the blue and yellow arras. Red Anne stood tall and
watchful in the doorway ; there was anger in the musical
deep voice.

" Mathilde, remind me once again of that lair where I
found you and back you go thereto—or elsewhere as it pleases
you, so be it you stay not here."

The girl sank stricken to her knees, and Herluin, having

bowed when Red Anne first spoke, now bent a knee of his
own to the rush mat on the floor.

" Pardon, lady, it was my folly angered her."

Grey Roland emitted a sudden piercing whistle and rattled
his silver chain.

" Olivier has no knees," said Lys calmly, " or his place
were on them also.   This was how it happened. . . ."

" Red Anne believes she is a great lady," thought Herluin,
whilst the fluting voice of Lys prepared a reconciliation.
" And here they all dance shrewdly to her piping," he added
to himself, seeing Mathilde's bright tears on Anne's strong
hand. . . .

But before many weeks were out he too was a convert to
Red Anne's belief.   For this round-faced, blue-eyed witch—
this flame-haired and deep-bosomed huntress who, drawing
all men's eyes to her, cared no whit for any save the morose
and afflicted Butcher—spread where she dwelt some curious
good-nature that baffled explanation.

In that walled den of darkness, where men held rank
according to brutality, and where any comely woman (excepting only the girls about Red Anne herself) could gain no
peace save as the accepted property of this or that tall warrior
—in that walled den the Butcher's mistress ruled more surely
than if she had been the Butcher's wife.   At the Count's
court she seldom appeared, but when with hawk on wrist and
quiver at hip she rode among the grey hill-hamlets, the sound
of her silver bridle-bells brought ragged wretches by the dozen
to her stirrup ; and Herluin, on the first occasion when he
rode behind her with her falconers, suddenly realised the
power she wielded.   The Butcher's black depression never
irked her, and the sound of her rich low singing above the
soft notes of the lute drew little groups of silent men-at-arms
to listen beneath the windows of the Lady's Tower.   When
she left the keep and moved abroad in the castle no Rider of
Campscapel looked at her with the glance he used for other
women ; a leer, a whispered insult, or even a well-meant
pleasantry—and anything might follow, from a blinding lash
in the face delivered by Red Anne's own powerfully-wielded
riding-whip, to a dance on air at the Butcher's gallows-tree.
Indeed, there was no religion in the great hold above Alanol

save the worship of Red Anne. Even in Alanol, where
burgher and apprentice spat aside when the black surcoats
passed along the street, Red Anne commanded the civility
due to one who spent good money in the shops and booths,
and was well known to exercise restraint upon the black
moods of her lord.

Only Red Jehan held aloof from Anne's influence ; and
that, it seemed, was because he feared her witchcraft—a
power accepted as deadly, though no one spoke of her making
any evil use of it. And Herluin, scared at first when she
changed the bandages on his arm and dressed the ugly graze
above it, came shyly to enjoy the moments when her perfumes
rose about him and her strong hands touched his body. . . .

She, humming and absorbed, made nothing of that task ;
one day Herluin discovered that she had a brown mole like
a ladybird, just where the down-shot whiteness of her sturdy
shoulder rolled to the hollow between the shoulder-blades
and fled beneath her embroidered gown. Tales of dim vileness wrought by witches stirred in his memory, and he began
to blush. He shut his eyes and set his teeth and willed the
rising blood to stop, but it spread along his scarred back and
half-bared side, and round about his bruises, reaching his
breast and neck and flooding at last into his face.

" Have I hurt you, Herluin ? "

" No, my lady. But when you took the bandage from
my arm the blood seemed to stir. . . ."

" In fact, you blush most prettily. One would have said
you were ashamed. Tell me, are you in love ? "

" I .   . I think so, my lady."

How strange, how violent, how disturbing was this sudden
raid upon his secrecy, and his own pleasure in surrender !

" And the lady has looked kindly upon you ? "

" She—she knows nothing of it at all."

" So ho ! A silent lover. And is she the fairest lady in
the world ? "

" Yes . . . no . . . yes."

" A most ungallant hesitation, Herluin. Are you not
sure ? "

" I was sure till I came here, my lady."

" O fie, this is turn-coat talk."

" By your leave, my lady, it is not. I love that lady, and I think I shall always love her, though I have seen her only twice ; but that does not mean I think she must be the *fairest* lady in the world."

" She would not thank you for saying so. And many would cry out on you for that great heresy, but there is something brave in it. And you have found in this poor hold a face to match your lady's ? "

" Yes, my lady. Or very nearly."

" Tell me in secret now : is it Agnes ? She looked kindly on you when you strove to shield that barnyard-voiced Mathilde."

" No, my lady."

Now for it, he told himself—aware in one breath of some resentment of this forcing of a declaration to Yseult as it were by proxy ; of curious certainty that this magnificent red-haired creature, with her dark power and wisdom, her mannish valour, and her great love of the Butcher Count, could still be flattered by a page ; and of a stir of admiration for himself, who carried his flame-winged memory of a girl above all present fear and favour—and yet aimed skilfully to please his questioner.

" I . . . I crave your pardon, my lady ; you may be mocking me, or you may be angry when I have spoken ; but only one lady has ever seemed so fair to me as the lady I love . . . and that one lady is yourself."

Red Anne chuckled deep in her throat.

" Now am I honoured, Herluin. No, I do not mock you ; you speak a subtler flattery than you know."

" I have scored," thought Herluin, half-sad at the success of his confession.

" But give some day a word to Lady Best from Lady Second-Best : Tell her, before she refuse your honourable love, to see you half out of your shirt. If she find you not irresistible, her heart is of stone, and the humours of her body are gone to mud together . . . what, have I raised the blush again ? "

Could not even generous Red Anne realise that there was another, rarer way of loving than that she knew and jested at ? The knights who went to death with a word, a look, at

most a kiss or a scarf for sleeve or helm—*they* would have
understood the feeling of Raoul for Yseult de Olencourt. . . .

"Your shoulder is a rainbow at the back, but this scar
needs no more bandaging. I think, for the rest, I can hand
you over to Lys. . . ."

"My lady . . ."

"Well ? "

"I fear to presume . . . but Lys is . . ."

"Too edged of speech ? "

"No, my lady. Too *young*."

Red Anne laughed abruptly, and twirled him round before
her, so that her broad face with its clear pink and white, its
wide red mouth and tilted nose and laughing pansy eyes,
was on a level with his carefully diffident gaze.

"Very well. But, little Chevalier Sobersides, you must
not be too grim. Kiss me ! No, not my hand, my mouth ! "

Neither garlic nor onion this time, but a most disturbing
perfume. No rose had petals so soft and warm. But—and
what folly !—his eyes smarted with sudden tears. . . .

Concerning Lys he was grateful, for Lys was becoming a
problem to him. When he lay dazed and bleeding it was
nothing that she should have helped to tend his body ; but
recovery found him shy of this girl-witch—this slim foil to
Red Anne, with her long nose and light blue eyes, her smooth
brown-ivory face and humorous pale mouth and thick mouse-
coloured hair. And she, who had at first been frank with
him, was repelled by his shyness, and did not hesitate to
mock at him with her companions.

Lys it was who told him how the Butcher, long sick of
low fever, with a great imposthume on the inside of his
sword-arm, leaped from his bed when the hind from Capel
Conan brought news of Red Anne's danger. The imposthume
broke beneath armour, the fever disappeared as if blown
out of him in that wild moonlit ride. . . .

"But how was it that she and you went unprotected in
the hills ? " demanded Herluin curiously, remembering that
he was not supposed to know the meaning of their journey.

"We went to buy a salve and a febrifuge from—from one
who understands such things. But as you see, my lord
recovered without them."

" But is not my lady herself very skilful in the preparation of remedies ? "

" Oh, ay.   Yet she learns from another.   Some day I may tell you more of that."

And on the day of the quarrel in Jehan's tower it was Lys who ran down to the tilting-ground in the outer bailey—where Gervase and Ivo were steering the Count's destriers up and down in the windy afternoon—and bade all there take heed, since the Count and his lady had not returned from hunting, the chamberlain and comptroller were with them, Bruin the war-captain was in Alanol, and Red Jehan and five of his cronies were slashing at each other's throats up and down the steps of the hall and over the grass of the inner ward.

" Herluin, come you with me along the ramparts," she commanded.

So Herluin, following her, first saw Red Jehan. . . .

Sergeants tugged at their beards and growled in each others' ears ; archers and pikemen, and even the tall Riders of Campscapel themselves, stood grinning and uneasy by their guard-rooms ; servants and grooms ran madly for shelter, and from a window of the Dungeon Tower some wretched prisoner raised a wild cackle of laughter to see the bloody antics of his captors among themselves.

Jehan, his servant, and another seemed to be fighting four ; as Lys and Herluin slipped out upon the rampart wall one luckless gamester—for the quarrel was over the dice—tripped near the wooden opening of the wall and sprawled upon his face.   Like a great ape Red Jehan was upon him, stabbing, trampling, roaring with gleeful rage ; the red-veined face, with its prominent wild eyes, crushed nose, and wolfish mouth agape in a ruddy tangle of beard, gave Herluin a shock at the midriff.   Wherever lay the blame of this en-counter, he felt, no man could more deserve extinction than the owner of that beast-face and those long arms, on one of which a gashed sleeve showed red hair thick almost as fur . . .

" Why do they not fill him full of arrows ? " he muttered, staring down in fascination.

" Hush ! " whispered Lys.   " The Count's brother !

You must not say such things aloud! There is hump-backed Dirck . . . a good thing he is deaf, indeed ! "

Hump-backed Dirck was the Butcher's personal attendant. Being old, lame, deaf and deformed, he seldom stirred from the keep ; half his time he spent in the Count's own armoury, where everything glittered from his ministrations. And he grinned as he watched his master's brother lay dead a second of his master's troop-captains. . . .

" Come away ! " urged Herluin, after a sickened glimpse of blood-lust in the watching faces near him.

" Not I," answered the girl blithely. " There is always something to watch when Jehan's sword is out."

" Then watch it alone," snapped Herluin, and bolted past Dirck into the keep.

" I am a fool," he told himself. " That is just the kind of fray I must train myself to witness unmoved. As for Lys . . . Our Lady help her in this den of beastliness . . . and yet, she risked herself for the child at Capel Conan."

He reached the ramparts again in time to see the Butcher's return. A shout and a gesture from the saddle, and Red Jehan was ringed by advancing pike-points ; slowly the rage in his face abated, and by the time he had backed to the doorway of his own quarters he looked like a monstrous sulky boy, caught stealing apples or trapping pigeons, and sheepishly defiant in his knavery.

The Count rode up and dismounted ; the men-at-arms made way, and the dark beard towered over the red as the elder brother pushed his brute cadet out of sight. . . .

" Why do they call the Count mad ? " whispered Herluin to Gervase. " No man in Neustria seems more sane than he . . . and no man but he would have dared touch that . . . that eccentric gentleman, his brother."

" It is only in the spring that something very evil comes to him," muttered Gervase. " This year his sickness seemed to ward it off. Last year it . . . he trapped wolves in the forest, and buried men and women to the breast in the bear-pit, and turned the wolves loose on them."

Gervase seemed to shiver in the gathering twilight.

" It was very ghastly," he went on quietly. " I do not think God will forgive those who stayed to watch it. I got

a grievous clout over the head, for as I ran away I was sick
on the comptroller's new furred gown. . . .

" Every one went in fear of death.   The little priest fled—
that is why there is only drunken old Father Benedict to say
the Mass here now.   Two archers were racked and hung for
withholding plunder of one of Saint-Aunay's farms.   I knew
the madness was coming, for I saw his face twitch dreadfully
for a week before.   Even my lady could do nothing, until
after Easter she . . . she disappeared, as she is wont to do
at certain times, and came again (no man having seen her
depart) with some strange medicine that eased him. . . ."

" You mean she flew . . ."

" Ssh !   I know not.   But for the medicine, it is as I
have said."

Herluin went and stood by his favourite window, drawing
no cheer for once from its glimpse of soft pine-masses and
star-shot evening sky.

" Before the snow comes I must flee from here," he said.

His arm was still in the sling on the first afternoon when
Red Anne and Lys did not appear at dinner in the hall.

" Where is my lady ? " he asked of Ivo.

Deliberately Ivo winked.

" To-morrow," he murmured in Herluin's ear, " is the
Eve of Saint Jehan, but my lady has another name for it."

Herluin understood.   Midsummer, known to Christians
as the Feast of the Nativity of Saint Jehan Baptist, was the
witches' Beltane, the time of the gathering of herbs.   So
again Red Anne and her slim companion were on their way
to the Singing Stones. . . .

At midnight Herluin awoke and found himself alone.   A
great wind boomed in the corridors, and all the outer darkness was alive with flying music of the stream and crashing
of storm-smitten trees.   Rain beat against the shutters of
the pages' room, and from the ramparts rang the faint calls
of the watchmen. . . .

Somewhere far off across the heathery wastes Yseult was
sleeping ; or, if the wind had wakened her, what thoughts
went flitting in her mind ?   Perhaps she pictured a gift from
Fulk or Rogier, or recalled the memory of an old tale, of a

falcon's stoop by Olencourt along the river-banks . . . but nothing, nothing at all of a boy who stood in a crowd at Belsaunt, who now drowsed in the keep above Alanol— feeling something sorry and scornful because his new friends had crept through draughty blackness to the beds of Agnes and Mathilde. . . .

None of the culprits shared his morning's shame for them ; and Herluin experienced a certain broadening of the mind. On the second day`following, the wanderers returned, each carrying a bundle ; and thereafter the Lady's Tower reeked with strange vapours for a while. Lys seemed withdrawn into herself, and Herluin avoided her when possible ; a witch was, after all, a witch.

But when his arm was fully set and healed the routine of the castle gripped him, and he began to acquire those dexterities which his position at Ger had rendered difficult of mastery. Here on the rock of Campscapel no one expected a stripling supposedly monastery-bred to vault without long practice into the saddle of a destrier standing sixteen hands high ; and in the rough sports he was soon on equal terms with Gervase and Ivo. At wrestling his disproportionately strong arms threw them both, and even the sturdiest of the younger grooms could scarcely break his hold. The use and care of weapons and armour, the exact knowledge of horses and horsemanship, the tricks of quintain, quarter-staff, and archery, filled his days and toughened his muscles, until the greater part of the garrison of Ger would have passed him without recognition. And in the evenings he read aloud out of his ballad-book (from which with grief and pain he had torn the emblazoned title-page, hiding it with the rest of his treasures in the straw of his thick palliasse) or took turns with the others at the lute. At table his deft service pleased the Count ; with hawk and hound he followed Red Anne far into the hills, singing in glen and pinewood for her delectation ; and presently he found himself on good terms with all who had the freedom of the keep, excepting only Dirck the hunchback, and the unfathomable Lys. . . .

The dog-days came and went, and August mellowed into September, and Herluin had been three months on the rock

of Campscapel. He flinched no longer at the seamy side
of feudal state, and watched the daily coarseness and brutality
with no more than a sense of his good fortune in being lifted
above it to the more tranquil existence of the keep. And
even among the Riders of Campscapel the iron hand of the
Butcher kept alive a code of conduct comparable with that
of the retainers of Saulte and Ger and Olencourt ; some of
them growled in their beards that the summer with its one
poor bicker at Capel Conan was a summer wasted, but for
the main part they hawked and hunted, feasted and jousted,
gamed and drank and whored without complaint of their
inaction.

"Wait till the spring," they said among themselves.
"Saint-Aunay has gone too far. The Butcher bides his
time ; his flesher is none so rusty yet."

A week before Holy Rood Day Lys fell ill, and Herluin
found that he missed the very strangeness of her ; he was not
sorry when, on the fourth day of her sickness, he and the
others were summoned to Red Anne's tapestried chamber to
make music for their lady and for the convalescent, who sat
silent amid cushions in a corner chair. Her oval face was very
pale between the thick mouse-coloured braids of her uncovered hair, and her long-fingered hands seemed helpless
against the carven blackness of the heavy oak. In response
to greetings she smiled faintly, but when Ivo crouched by
the great harp and struck up a little hunting-song she stirred
and laughed. Then Herluin took the lute, and found his
fingers trembling as he tuned it ; for hours of brooding by
the dog-tooth pillar had borne fruit, and he was bent upon
experiment.

" This, my lady, is called *Ballade of Karmeriet*."
Then he struck a chord, and to his own light fingering sang:

> *A score of spears he led that day,*
> *For strength can woo if prayer be vain,*
> *And smiled when o'er the mailed array*
> *His banner took the wind again :*
> *Remembering, as he tightened rein,*
> *A song she sang of old Provence,*
> *A ballad with an odd refrain :*
> *" Plus faict douceur que violenz."*

When sank the sun on flame and death
He held her on the saddle's bow,
She cried Our Lady 'neath her breath,
And snatched at steel ; he foiled the blow
And kissed her pallid face aglow.
But silent scorn was her response ;
The winds of twilight whispered low :
" Plus faict douceur que violenz."

In carven chair before the fire
Alone and grim he sate all night,
But tore his soul from out the mire
And free'd her in the growing light.
Yet ere her troop had spurred from sight
He saw the maid look backward once,
And heard the gale cry down the height :
" Plus faict douceur que violenz."

Herluin turned on his stool, and softly addressed the
Envoi to Red Anne :

Lady, yourself the tale shall end :
Lied that old singer of Provence
Down the long years this word to send ?
Plus faict douceur que violenz.

" Prettily sung, Herluin," belled the mistress of the
Butcher Count. " The tale I have heard, but the song never.
You learned not that in your cloister-garth."

" No . . . no, my lady."

" Where then ? " asked Ivo softly, with a grin that flashed
in the gathering dusk.

" I made it myself a week ago."

Then there was outcry, and he sat blushing, fingering
the silken ribbons of the lute. In Hautarroy and the South
the nobles might employ their leisure with such trifles, but
in the gloomier northern airs a poet, however minor, was a
rarity. One voice only Herluin missed in the chorus ; the
sick girl in the corner said nothing.

" Agnes, a beaker of wine of Estragon for our troubadour,"
commanded Red Anne, " and one for each of us to drink to
his contriving."

Amidst the clink of horn-and-silver standing-cups a giggle
rose from behind Mathilde's embroidery-frame.

" He-he ! Poor Lys ! Herluin has made her cry ! "

Up bounced a contrite Herluin, and bowed to Red Anne before crossing the room to the sick-chair.

" A thousand pardons, Demoiselle Lys . . . I did not so intend to afflict. . . ."

" Oh, granted every one of them ! " said Lys wearily. " But sing of a murder, and I shall be more grateful."

Herluin laughed and caught her limp hand to his lips. What fortune that she should so have led him to a second of his songs !   With a little grimace, a half-derisive flash of her wet eyes, and a light pressure of her fingers on his hand, she motioned him back to his seat.

The formal salutations were not in great demand on the rock of Campscapel ; it was hardly polite to invoke the Trinity or the Mother of God on behalf of one devoted to a cult opposed to Theirs.   Thus, when Agnes handed Herluin his beaker he merely raised it and said :

" To the great glory and happiness of our good lord the Count, and of our dear Lady Anne," and so drank deep of the dark red wine.

Then with a " By your leave, my lady," he sang his *Lay of the Portcullis.*

> *Demoiselle, are you dreaming yet*
> > *Of his raven curls in the breeze astir :*
> > *Of his laughing eyes, when he said to her :*
> *" Amour qui rougit, fleurette, fleurette,*
> > *Amour qui pâlit, drame du cœur " ?*
>
> *You saw her beautiful face rose-red :*
> > *Did you know your own was blanchèd and drawn,*
> > *Your eyes the eyes of a wounded fawn ?*
> *Hers were aflame as she tossed her head,*
> > *There in the light of the windy dawn !*
>
> *Now he has ridden away and away ;*
> > *His banners have faded beyond the hill.*
> > *Demoiselle, you are strangely still !*
> *Why do you stay, and why do you stay,*
> > *Fronting the dawn-wind damp and shrill ?*
>
> *She, that other, so sweet and tall,*
> > *Stands where the last farewell was said*
> > *Beneath the arch ; and her mirth is sped,*
> *And she leans her hand against the wall*
> > *When the iron teeth hang overhead.*

Gleams a chain in the niche deep-set,
  Demoiselle, where your fingers were ?
  A touch, and a creak, and a clashing stir :
" Amour qui rougit, fleurette, fleurette ;
  Amour qui pâlit, drame du cœur ! "

" Oh, bloody-minded Herluin ! " laughed Red Anne, motioning Agnes forward to refill the singer's cup.

" Ah, the poor maid beneath the cruel spikes ! " lamented the impressionable Mathilde.

" That," said Lys quietly, but with none of her customary decision, " was splendid."

" Matter or manner ? " came Ivo's chuckled question.

" Both," said Lys.

" Now you have learned to sit still, my pretty one, you shall wear a varvel.   Come you along to my lady."

Herluin was training a ' hagard '—a young wild falcon caught when its plumage had already changed—and Red Anne had promised him a ring and bell of silver for its leg when he should sufficiently have tamed it.   So, quenching the fierce orange eyes beneath a small embroidered hood, he let the grey-white feathers fluff and subside, and watched the murderous claws shift grip upon his heavy gauntlet.   Then, with his left elbow held away from his side, and the forearm stiffly right-angled as became a good falconer, he bore his cherished hagard out of the hawk-sheds and across the sun-browned grass of the inner ward.

Noon-heat of mild September lay upon the keep of Camps-capel.   Behind him he left his fellow-pages in earnest consultation over a ' falcon-gentil ' that would not follow the food drawn past it on the lure ; in the guard-room above the steps a seated pikeman roused himself, scraping the iron-shod staff of his weapon on the flags to show that he was awake.   At the foot of the stairway leading to the Lady's Tower Herluin made way for some one who descended ; it was the crone who doused and swept the living-rooms and infuriated Dirck by shuffling up behind him to touch his hump for luck. . . .

From a slit in the wall beside the spiral stairway Herluin saw, on the shadowed stone seat above Red Anne's bright flower-beds, Mathilde and Agnes playing at cats'-cradle, with painted battledores and shuttlecock on the ground where they had flung them.

The Count was riding in the forest; Dirck, no doubt, dozed in the armoury, his mean grey face reflected and distorted in a score of polished steel convexities. There came no breath of wind to stir the faded silver lion of Campscapel on the curtain of sable velvet that hid the antechamber door. . . .

Herluin knocked, listened, waited, knocked again, softly raised the latch, and entered. A looseness of the hinges swung the door to behind him when he let go of it ; and he blinked a moment at the glitter of a grisaille window which overlooked the inner ward.

Then he frowned and blinked again and stepped backward in astonishment ; Lys rested on the broad damask-covered bench by the other window. Among the red and green and blue of gold-embroidered cushions she lay and watched him, hands behind her head, with nothing but a half-transparent shift of azure silk to hide her ivory-tinted body and its slim, sprawling limbs.

" I—I—most humbly I crave your pardon," stammered the intruder. " I fear I wakened you . . . or I did not hear your answer. . . ."

He swung groping round to the door, and the hagard lurched and tightened its grip on his gloved wrist. Then the girl's voice struck coldly into his confusion.

" No need to frighten the little falcon. . . . *Herluin !* "

The mingled notes of command, appeal, and exasperation turned his unwilling head upon its shoulders. Lys lifted her hands from her neck and deftly caught a pair of cushions to her body.

" Herluin, why are you such a fool ? " she demanded crisply. " Fiend rot it, child that you are, what harm have you done ? At the worst we are only quits . . . throw me that cloak from the chair-back there, and tell me why you have brought the hagard."

Some sense of scornful rightness in her bearing cut Herluin's mind adrift from its top-hamper of romance, its cloudy awareness of the swoons and tears and protestations

which some old ballad-mongers would have found inseparable
from this situation ; and as he walked across the room and
lifted the cloak he nerved himself to look straight at the girl
when he should turn again. . . .

Try as he might he could not keep his eyes on hers ; the
cushions fell apart as Lys reached out a slender hand for the
proffered garment, and from lifted shoulder to extended foot
the strangeness and beauty of her body assailed him. His
face, that had been crimson, went white as her perfume rose
to his nostrils ; through the vague aroma of herbs (such as
were used in the baths of those days) came like a subtle
blessing from Mother Earth herself the faint scent of the
half-naked girlish flesh.

" Gramercy, Herluin," and the crimson cloak fell like a
pall across that disturbing vision. " And now that we have
saved your soul from danger of immediate damnation, sit
down and tell me why you came . . . and by the bones of
Huon the Foolhardy I swear there are no eggs here."

Then Herluin laughed, for he had indeed taken a seat
with marvellous circumspection. He set himself more at
ease, and spoke his errand, whilst the girl bunched crimson
velvet beneath her shapely chin and bestowed a mock-
magisterial frown upon her uncovered toes.

" My lady is gone away," she said shortly. " This hand-
some spark must wait for his varvel," and she put a caressing
finger to the falcon's breast.

" Yet I have not seen her leave the keep," objected
Herluin. " I have been in the hawk-sheds since we broke
fast, and I swear she has not passed through the inner ward
or along the curtain walks. . . ."

He broke off, conscious of a half-smile at the corners of
the girl's pale mouth ; and curiosity overcame the convention
of the place, which was to mention witchcraft as seldom as
possible.

" Demoiselle Lys," he began again.

" Well ? "

" Has my lady flown over the battlements in broad daylight ? Or has she made herself invisible ? Tell me—it will
do no harm, for indeed I believe we are all in her hands here.
You have great knowledge of her craft ; it may be you your-

self could grievously afflict me were you not gentle-hearted. It may be also that I blunder on powerful and forbidden things, but . . ."

" Things forbidden by whom ? "

" By . . . by my lady. I mean that you may be bound to secrecy. . . ."

" ' Maybe—maybe—maybe,' " mocked the girl, her pale eyes starred with malice. " Listen, Herluin, it is Holy Rood Eve. Last time my lady went I went with her ; had I had full health I should have gone with her to-day. The second time before that, we found you at Capel Conan ; do you think Saint-Aunay's men had trapped us there could we have flown on broomsticks up the hay-ward's chimney ? "

" No . . . no, I had thought of that."

" You have heard of the Miracle of Dunsberghe ? "

" Yes."

Lys spoke of the great scandal, ten years past, at Dunsberghe on the feast-day of Saint Hilgarde, when the wooden image of the martyred virgin was accustomed to bleed at the breast between compline and vespers, what time the saint was tortured for her Faith. There came a feast-day when the image did not bleed ; instead it screamed in a manner horrible to hear, especially from one whose face remained entirely impassive ; but this circumstance was explained when the image broke open behind, and a little sub-deacon of the church flung himself out, crashing to the tiled pavement, dying of his fall and of a dozen wasp-stings in the face and neck, whilst the sewn cow's bladder in his hand tore on the plinth of a Crusader's tomb and made one ghastly splash of the devoted drops within it. . . .

" If the Church use such artifice to hold the ignorant and childish of her flock, think you the witches lag behind in deception ? I, for one, shall never launch myself in air upon a broomstick ; nor have I met a witch who could. But there are potent brews, as no doubt you have heard. . . ."

" And the waxen mammets thrust through with pins ? "

" I have only known them take effect in conjunction with subtly-administered philtres, or when the bewitched man *knew* he was thus bewitched."

" And the . . . the taking of the shapes of brutes ? "

" Ah, now you touch a mystery . . . of that you will learn nothing from me. Nor of the witching of crops and cattle, In any case I have told too much already . . . but stay a moment. Lest you think the power of the witches nothing but fraud, I will show you a thing. . . ."

She sat up, circling her knees with her bare arms, and whistled three short notes, up and down and up again ; and into the chamber stalked the jet-black cat which kept down rats and mice in Red Anne's tower. At sight of the hooded hawk perched against Herluin's breast the beast's eyes flamed and narrowed ; then, with uplifted paw, it looked at Lys.

" Ha, Bloton," she demanded, " what do you see that is strange ? "

" *A silly boy and a silly bird.*"

Herluin recoiled where he sat, for the harsh whisper came from the black cat, although its mouth seemed not to have moved. He crossed himself, and the brute's pink tongue flicked round its lips.

" *Cross the hawk also,*" said the malignant voice.

" Not at your bidding, you accursed beast ! " cried Herluin, starting up and laying his free hand on his dagger-hilt. " Avaunt . . . I carry cold iron here . . . what damnable sorcery is this ? "

" *You are safe enough, you fool. To each his own magic.*"

That time the black-furred jaw had moved ; and the bewildered Herluin caught at the whispered words.

" Magic ? " he muttered. " *I ?* I have no magic and you know it . . . but . . . but . . ."

He rounded on the watching girl beside him.

" *Nos tol venko !* " he faltered, and saw amusement fade to a hard question in her brooding eyes.

" Yes ? " she parried. " And what next ? "

Herluin looked from her to the cat and back again.

" *Someone* sent me," he hazarded. " By your art I doubt not you can find out who it was. But from this convocation I beg leave to retire. . . ."

" Bloton, go away ; you have frightened our clerkly visitor enough. *Out !* "

She waved a hand, and the black cat mewed and turned obediently, stepping haughtily towards the half-open door of

Red Anne's bedchamber. When the raised black tail had vanished Lys leaned forward and caught at Herluin's hand.

" Are you convinced ? " she demanded whimsically. " It seems you have helped a witch in some distress, since she trusted you with those words. Herluin, I think you know more of the witches than your questions served to show."

Herluin looked down at the slim clutching fingers, and a great pity and sadness stooped upon him. He thought of the stag-headed thing by the Singing Stones, whose influence seemed to have filled the room where humanity was mocked and affronted by a talking cat. . . .

" God forgive me, I think I know too much," he muttered, pressing against him the gauntleted hand whose wrist sustained the hagard. Beneath his shirt the little ivory image of the Virgin fretted the skin, as he had intended. " But . . . if that beast indeed spoke . . . what did he mean by *my* magic ? "

Lys let go of his hand and leaned back on her cushions.

" If that beast indeed spoke," she said mockingly, " I take it he meant that a poet's magic may be as compelling as a witch's."

" How so ?   *I* cannot make a cat speak ! "

" No doubt ; but you achieved a deadlier thing."

" You talk in riddles, demoiselle."

" You made a witch regret her witch-hood for a while."

" But from what I have seen both my lady and you are white witches."

Lys shook her head, and now her mocking was gone.

" Grey at the best, with a twilight greyness, dusking into dark. We are not to be stopped by your cold steel, unless it rive our bodies, or running water, unless it be too wide to swim. Horseshoes and branches of rowan have never oppressed us ; half the remedies against our art are as much a tale of the chimney-corner as half the powers claimed by witches for their own. But for the other half . . ."

Her voice tailed off into silence, and Herluin moved uneasily.

" All the same I do not believe you are very wicked," he muttered. " You are brave and loyal. . . ."

" Poor Herluin, are you still so young that you believe

courage and loyalty are good of themselves ? You have seen
Ord, the Sieur Jehan's servant ? He is brave, and loyal—
to his master. Jehan is brave, and loyal—to his brother.
The Count and my lady are brave, and loyal to each other.
The Riders of Campscapel are brave . . . and so on. But
what fame have all of them outside these walls ? "

" Very evil fame, it is true. But except Red Jehan, and
perhaps Ord, they are none of them so bad as folk believe
who have not sat at meat with them."

" All bad enough to be damned, I'll warrant. And all
sufficiently hated to be torn in pieces if Saint-Aunay's men
could manage it. Besides, you have not seen the Count with
his madness upon him . . . no, Herluin, all your charity
will not cover the multitude of our sins. Nor can I understand why those same sins should trouble you. . . ."

" I cannot understand it myself," admitted Herluin, after
a moment's thought. " I am not devout as I should be, and
I love beautiful things to excess . . . or so my confessor once
told me. . . ."

That was Brother Ambrose at Sanctalbastre ; but it
sounded well enough.

" What beautiful things ? " asked Lys.

" Sunsets. The hovering of a hawk. The violet shadows
of clouds on the pale green sea at—at Hardonek. The
flowering gorse, and the wind in pines, and the thick silence
of a church. And carvings in ivory, and bright colours of
shields and banners and jewels. And helpless things like
puppies. And shapes of trees, particularly cedar, yew, and
poplar. . . ."

Careful ! Poplars were scarce in Nordanay. . . .

" And faces of people," he added quickly.

" Only faces ? "

The question came so gently that it might have risen in
his own mind.

" No," he whispered gravely, staring up at the silvery
blaze of grisaille in the opposite wall, and feeling a slow flush
rise to his forehead.

" You mean that because my lady is very beautiful you
cannot condemn her, even though she lives in sin and is a
witch ? "

" I mean . . . her voice especially. How can one be
anything but good with a voice like hers ?   And as for living
in sin, that is folly . . . she and my lord are more nobly man
and wife than many who have benefit of clergy. And for
her witchcraft, I am altogether puzzled.   Yet in those matters
the Church must be right, and she wrong."

" Of course," said Lys with a hint of her usual sharpness.
" It is as I said ; we are all damned . . . particularly my
lady and I, unless your God is as powerless in the next world
as He shows Himself in this."

Automatically, Herluin crossed himself, but the only shock
he felt was that the blasphemy aroused no horror in him.

" I wonder you endure our company," went on the girl,
almost as though to herself. " You might have fled a dozen
times already. Do you not fear corruption of your own
sanctity ? "

" My ' sanctity ' is nothing but hatred of ugliness."

" Is Agnes ugly, or Mathilde ? "

" No, but their . . ."

He was confused. Why had he not fled ? He did not
know. Perhaps he had felt that Alanol would do as well as
any other place until he was eighteen and able to claim his
barony. The plan of reaching Rogier at Montenair had
somehow faded of late ; and by now the Duke of Saulte was
home once more (the office of Constable having gone to his
rival, the Duke of Volsberghe), so that Enguerrand was
again available if Herluin rode hard. Yet he did not move
to adventure it. . . .

" Every one is good to me here," he confessed aloud, more
in answer to his own rapid thought than in explanation of
his pause ; but Lys read another meaning into his words.

" Master Weak-at-the-knees," she observed, " temptation
is visibly upon you. This soft response to kindliness will be
your undoing. One day you will be so sorry for poor Agnes,
who has lost her soul, that you will risk your own by comforting her in the only way she can understand."

" I am in no temptation of that sort," muttered Herluin,
sullenly.

" Why not ? "

" I . . . there is a maid . . . I cannot tell you. .   ."

" Ah, there is a maid, is there ?　I thought the catalogue
of things beloved rang somewhat hollow.　A maid to fight
and die for, eh ?　A maid you cannot even discuss with the
cracked pots of Campscapel ? "

This was the old Lys, wide-eyed and something shrewish ;
but never before had Herluin seen pink colour on her cheek-
bones.

" I think there is nothing I could not discuss with *you*,"
he said simply.　" But now you are angry, with life and with
yourself, I think, as much as with me.　And everything I
say you will distort and make a mock of.　If any one here
could bewitch and ruin me, it is yourself, because my Ballade
made you cry."

He rose to his feet, but again the girl leaned forward
and gripped his unencumbered wrist, smiling into his
eyes.

" Brave Herluin ! " she gibed.　" Do you dare me to
enchant you ?　See . . ."

She flung the cloak aside, and rose to her knees with a
lithe movement.　The swirl of her perfume surrounded him,
her quick fingers tore the flimsy shift from breast to hem, so
that she faced him with the last shreds of her garment
floating and subsiding down her arms and away from her
ivory nudity.

" Let me go, I beg you ! " he cried, backing and dragging
her with him, but she laughed and clung with both hands
to his arm, and her words came in a half-chuckled stream
most curious to hear.

" Oh, I will loose you in a moment . . . I am not the wife
of the Sieur Potiphar . . . but, Herluin, do you know how
wicked we are ?　Can you guess how my lady bought the
medicine from the Devil ?　*You* do not know how terribly
he comes . . ."

" Yes, I *do* know, I *can* guess—I have seen your Yaan by
the Singing Stones—of all things most abominable—let me
go."

" Ha, you have seen him ?　But you have not felt his
strength . . . some of the witches will tell you his body is
cold as ice, and his seed as icy water . . . but they are not
so to me, Herluin, not to me !　If you come to possess that

maid of yours look well for moles on her body, Herluin . . .
see, I have three. . ."

" I will not see !   I will not listen !   You are distraught,
and bent on driving me from this hold, but I will not go for
all your devilry. . . ."

Why had he said that, he wondered ?   He had not meant
to challenge her, but now he was more angry than ashamed.
Hampered by the bird on his wrist, he could not struggle
violently ; to set the hagard on the floor meant picking it up
again, and against his will he heard the vileness of her words.
But suddenly an idea smote him ; bending rapidly forward
so that the girl's head came against his shoulder, he kissed
her thrice, on hair and cheek and neck, before she knew what
he was about.   Her voice was cut off as though by death
itself : her fingers loosed their hold, and with a gasp she fell
away from him, white-faced and cowering amid the colours
of her disordered couch.

" *In Nomine Patris, Filii et Spiritus Sancti !* " growled
Herluin, as he turned and fled from the room. . . .

At the stair-foot he met Mathilde ; and on that same
evening he was discomfited by Ivo's jesting voice.

" Now, by the beard of Saint Anthony, we have no longer
in the keep a cure against the king's evil ! "

For in those days the remedy for scrofula was a touch of
the king's own hand—or, failing that, a touch of the hand
of a fasting naked virgin of either sex, who should also spit
three times upon the sore and say : " The Holy Trinity deny
that the heat of the plague increase where a naked virgin
quencheth it."

Herluin shrugged his shoulders.   If Lys had chosen to
let Mathilde misunderstand that which passed in the antechamber, he would not trouble to combat what Mathilde
had told the others.

When next he met Lys, in a corridor, she shook her finger
at him without a trace of anger or embarrassment.

" You never brought the hagard for his varvel after all,"
she said.

VI

FACE CAMPSCAPEL, FACE DEATH

THEREAFTER Herluin began seriously to ponder his escape from the hold above Alanol and the domain of Lorin de Campscapel. It seemed sufficiently easy; he had only to fall behind or somehow lose himself in the chase, to set spurs to his mount in country already half-familiar to him, and he would be his own man again—Raoul or Herluin as occasion served. The Butcher had strewn his marches with watch-towers, but these might be avoided; and a certain urgency began to possess Herluin's mind. Already the wind was whirling bronzed leaves in the woods, fluting eerily in the creviced stone of Campscapel, drumming like iron across the autumn hills. . . .

Rogier at Montenair should be his mark again. There he might see Yseult; at least he would hear of her. The shameful memory of Count Armand's whipping-post, the sinister undertones of life in the Butcher's hold, and lastly a half-scared perplexity aroused in him by Lys, combined to send him questing in strange realms of fancy, where all roads led at length to one bright shrine, and all adventure stilled to worship before one sweet unheeding face.

Discomfort smote him lest Lys should betray his confidence and fall to open mockery of that guarded side of him; but the witch-girl gave no sign that she remembered his embarrassed avowal. Red Anne, indeed, had at times a mischief in her face, and once or twice she confused Herluin with a whisper that reached no ears but his own.

" What do you see beyond the hill ? " she sometimes asked; or, nipping the lobe of his ear, she would say : " Fie, here is molten stuff; did you lie when you said she knew naught of your dreams ? "

Then, on a wild October evening when the Count's chase had ended in pouring rain, Herluin found himself lugging two great cans of scalding water up the winding stair to his lord's

bedchamber. When he set foot on the top step he was staring
straight ahead of him as though the stones of Campscapel
were dissolved in air ; within him hardened the resolve to
dash for freedom if the Butcher hunted on the morrow. But
Red Anne, turning silently in the corridor near by, thought
her page tranced with love-longing, and smiled, and spoke
sharply to him.

" *Come back, Herluin !* "

The boy jumped ; one of the cans tilted, and Herluin
drowned its falling clash with a yell of agony. Then he reeled
against the wall, whilst the spilt water dripped and steamed
far down the stony stair. Red Anne half-carried him to
the pages' room, and at her call came running Agnes with
bandages and oil and wine. . . .

" Oh, clumsy Herluin ! " crooned Red Anne as she knelt
by his bed. " May that lady of yours be skilled in leech-
craft ! Bid her line your harness with swansdown and send
you very seldom to the wars ! "

Ivo, entering before the bandaging was done, stood staring
for a moment, and then backed out with more than sympathy
in his face. Later, when he and Gervase came with Herluin's
supper, he turned at the door, and scowled, and launched a
sudden snarl across the room.

" Why in the fiend's name do *you* have all the luck ? " he
demanded—and stumped off down the passage with his head
in air.

" What the devil ! " gasped Herluin. " What ails him,
Gervase ? "

Gervase chuckled, and whispered in his ear.

" No ! " exclaimed the listener, incredulous. " He would
never presume . . . no one in his senses would dare. . . ."

" Watch him and see," sniggered Gervase.

And it was true that when next the Butcher in his great
furred bedgown had shot the bolts of Red Anne's scented
chamber, Ivo stood staring out of a window, gnawing his
finger-nails with a face unpleasant to behold.

Ivo had fallen in love with Red Anne.

" Well," sighed Herluin, considering him askance, " after
all, it is not much greater folly than mine, to have dreamed of
the sister of Fulk the Castellan."

Then he caught himself sharply up for comparing the jealous desire of Ivo with the exalted flame of his own tender and chivalrous passion for Yseult. . . .

Of Yseult he mused on the still morning a week later, when Dirck's great wooden shoes clop-clopped out of the armoury and the door was locked before Herluin was aware. He shouted, but the deaf hunchback either did not hear or heard and would not trouble to retrace his steps. However, Dirck was never absent from his charge for long at a time, and Herluin shrugged his shoulders and sat himself down behind the stand of war-shields—glad, indeed, of a respite from his tyrannical company, for he had spent the best part of his time of enforced inaction in polishing armour. His skin, though healed, was still tender, and now that flight seemed at hand his mind was often busy with the reception he might hope to receive at Montenair . . . where he might see Yseult. But at Montenair there must be dozens of men who watched her when they could—chevaliers who linked their two hands to give her a step into her saddle, war-captains who would tear the heart out of any who offended her, and so on, down to the very pages who ran to fetch her a footstool or scrambled when she dropped a glove. And amongst all these what place had Herluin, the skulker in the hills, the slayer of apprentices, the servant of the Butcher and of Red Anne?

His glowering and distorted reflection watched him from a cuirass of the Butcher's; on his knees he held a naked sword in case the door should open suddenly and Dirck should peer round the war-shields to see if his assistant idled over the work.

"Perhaps when the mirror is flat I am good to look at," he decided. "But also I look queer . . . I suppose because the great stone devil watched my mother before I was born. Yseult might think me ugly. . . .

"At any rate I am no fool with a lute."

Then he laughed at himself, and checked his laugh because it split the reflected face in a ghastly manner.

"It is good to be alone," he felt. "Why am I happiest when alone? Because then I can think of Yseult, and of

Marckmont, and of my little songs.   But they hold only the
splinters of beauty and dread left over from the home I have
built for her in my heart.   If I were to save Rogier's life
in battle, now, or cut my way to the Castellan with some
important news, she might look kindly at me . . . more
kindly I mean, than at another.   She might even, perhaps
. . . if it was a bad wound . . . come and see me, bringing,
it may be, some flowers.   Roses.   No, lilies.   Lilies of
Olencourt.   Lilies of the valley. . . ."

There sprang into his mind a picture of a battered Herluin
—no, a battered *Raoul*—wounded in the more picturesque
places, and lying motionless in a half-shuttered room.   Beside
his bed, in a yellow vase admired in his childhood, a bunch of
delicate lilies of the valley, brought by Rogier, sent by Yseult.
Some time she had smiled at him with clear grey eyes ; that
was like swords of blessed martyrdom, for she would smile
in kindness only.   But when Rogier had gone the wind would
sing about her, and the lilies would nod assent to . . . to
what ?

It was beginning to be a poem.   Some promise in the
onset of the wind.   Onset, sunset.   It *would* be sunset.   Hills
dark against it.   Yseult looking up from the lilies in her
garden.   Thinking about him, just for a little while, as the
boy . . . the man, the Baron of Marckmont . . . who had
saved Rogier.   *When my home hills were dark against her
sunset* . . . damnation, Marckmont was east of Olencourt,
and she would be looking the other way.

Very well, into the third person with it . . . a disguise.
Just a man and a girl, west and east.   *When his home hills
were dark against her sunset. . . .*

Footsteps, and a key that clicked in the lock of the armoury
door, interrupted the dreamer and shattered his high postula-
tions.   Deftly he snatched up an oiled clout, and silently he
fell to work on the sword-hilt, wondering what Dirck had done
with his clattering wooden shoes. . . .

The door grated open ; snowy lilies of fancy were torn
and scattered by a dusky lily of flesh and blood, green-cloaked
and booted and spurred, with hood thrown back and a tight
green cap on her thick braided hair.   In one gloved hand
she bore a key ; and without looking aside she sped to the

far corner of the armoury, where a narrow flight of three steps dipped to the tiny chamber in the thickness of the wall where Dirck slept. This narrow stairway had faded hangings on both sides of it ; Lys twitched aside the right-hand arras, sneezed as the dust flew out, and rammed her key into some hole hidden from Herluin by her body. Again the grating of a lock ; a push of the girl's hand, and a door swung open before her. Then she glanced over her shoulder at the entrance to the armoury, and saw the staring Herluin.

" Oh ! " she said, and then again, but in a different and thoughtful key : " Oh ! "

" It is Michaelmas Eve," thought Herluin. " *This* is how Red Anne flies over the battlements."

But aloud he said : " Your pardon, Demoiselle Lys ; I fear I startled you. Dirck locked me in by accident . . ."

He stopped. The girl's face had gone white and tense.

" Be still ! " she hissed. " Get into the corner there, and stand fast as you love your life ! "

Her urgency admitted of no question. Herluin, still gripping the sword, stood up and crowded himself behind a suit of plate-armour, so that he was almost completely hidden from her view. And there he stood, with loins weakened by excitement and suspense.

" Lys . . . oh, the key is here," said Red Anne's voice a moment later. Her heavier tread came on the armoury floor ; she changed to the inner side of the door the key that Lys had left on the outside, and turned it in the lock before withdrawing it. Then she too padded down the chamber to where Lys stood beside the arras, and there came to Herluin's nostrils a scent of burning tallow.

" Child, you look sickly," she said to Lys. " Would you rather stay behind ? "

" I . . . I . . . dear my lady, I had so hoped to be with you this time, but my head is like to split," muttered Lys.

" If it is like that you must stay. Here is the other key. Be off with you, and bear a happier face on my return, or I shall dose you rarely against the migraine. Pouf ! how my lantern smells to-day. Bid me success in this task I am now set upon. . . . Farewell."

The sound of a kiss, the slam and locking of the hidden door, and silence. . . .

Then a gasp of relief from Lys, and her rapid returning footfall. She was unlocking the outer door again before Herluin glared round the elbow-plate of the great suit of armour. Lys held the door wide, and glanced along the passage ; then her quick speech whipped the air.

" Go quickly to your own room—anywhere ! When Dirck asks, tell him I let you out—I alone, saying I came to see him. Do not mention my lady, or you are sped. Later I will explain. Now *go !* "

Herluin went.

" What follows is best said on a turret-top," observed Lys grimly, when Herluin had followed her up the spiral stair and out into pale autumn sunlight. " And if Agnes or Mathilde appear, do you try to put your arm round me, and I will box your ears for you."

Herluin, accustomed to unusual instructions from this strange creature, merely nodded ; and elbow to elbow they leaned in a crenel of the battlements and stared down at the woods or across at the western hills.

" Well," began Lys, " you have seen how one pair of witches flies, and in the act of seeing you nearly looked your last on this world. Had my lady come upon you there would have been an end . . . no, owlet-eyes, I am not jesting now. Because she has been ' good ' to you, do you think she would hesitate a moment to crush you like a fly, if she knew you shared that secret ? My lord Count is her life ; she and he, and Dirck and I—and now you—are all who know of it in the hold ; and there is one outside. And even though you never know the other end of the passage, your knowledge of the bare fact of a hidden way into her lord's keep would have sealed your fate . . . as it sealed the fate of the poor wretches who made it for the Butcher's father."

" What ? "

" Five serfs dug the passage, Dirck feeding them—for they never left the keep again. Near the far end he had them widen the way and dig a pit ; and when it was done he called them one by one to receive payment, which payment took the shape of a dagger in the throat. He dragged them down to their pit and buried them ; so that was the end of *them*. And before the old Count died he told Lorin. And now Dirck has one key, and my lady another."

" But the Sieur Jehan does not know ? "

" No. He might talk of it in his cups."

" And who is the one outside ? "

" I shall not tell you that. As it is, I have broken faith with my lady for the first time since she carried me into the castle."

" Lys . . . *why* ? "

Lys frowned.

" I do not know. At least I am not sure. Maybe my sins do not include child-murder."

Herluin was silent for a moment ; his thought included a wonder as to the nature of the task Red Anne had mentioned in the armoury.

" Well," he whispered at length, " I do not know enough of your passage to work harm to you or any here, even if I wished it. But I owe you my life a second time, and if I can ever repay . . ."

Again he fell silent. Lys shrugged her shoulders.

" As for child-murder," went on Herluin thoughtfully, " what childishness I brought here is clean dead, I think."

Lys laughed abruptly.

" Clean dead, not cleanly dead," she murmured.

" But life is strange," mused Herluin aloud.

" A great and original thought, my Herluin."

" I wish . . ."

" Wish on."

" I wish I could do something, Lys, to show I am not the silly oaf you take me for, to be dragged from death at one moment and chidden as though I had stolen sugar at the next. Set me a task, as the ladies of Pendragon's court set tasks to the chevaliers."

" Better not press that fond comparison too far."

Herluin affected to misunderstand her.

" No, I am no chevalier, it is true. But . . ."

" Curse you, Herluin, do not plague *me* with your fantastical chivalry. Keep that for your little maid elsewhere."

" If it *is* chivalry," said Herluin sententiously, " it should be at your bidding no less than at hers."

The pale face of Lys went a dark and dangerous red, and Herluin's exalted sentiments were lowered by a curious qualm.

" Life *is* strange, as you say," and now the girl's voice was thick and unsteady. " Herluin, I will give you your task, and see what your chivalry makes of it."

" Now, what have I done ? " cried an unhappy Herluin silently, within himself.

But he felt he had played with the girl's strange service to him, and his knees trembled. He knew he lacked the fortitude of that Sieur Gareth who became a server in Pendragon's kitchen.

Lys turned and faced him, hands behind her back, eyes wide and fierce.

" Beloved little fool," she whispered stonily. " This is your own fault, for I believe you are only half-blind. You owe me a life ; if you win your maid *she* will owe me her joy. If she be worth a lifetime of you she should not grudge me a night or two of the love of your dear body."

" I see," said Herluin.

It all seemed sensible enough ; and certainly he had himself to blame for it.

" Not *love*," he began, hopeless of an ending ; but Lys cut short his words.

" No. Chivalry, kindness, gratitude, or any other mischievous abstraction, so that life that has fooled me in part does not fool me altogether."

Herluin floundered in the recesses of his mind. He had not even coloured up until a hunger woke behind defiance in the steady eyes two inches below the level of his own.

" Give me a week," he said.

Incalculably, a dimple appeared beside the girl's pale mouth.

" To nerve yourself ? " she demanded. " Poor Herluin— it will not be so terrible."

" No. To decide which way lies my greater knavery."

" Your greater . . . yes. So be it. But, Herluin, do not make me hate you."

" Perhaps it were better for both of us if you did," he replied gravely.

" I promise not to hate you for a week," said Lys.

Then she left him alone with the revolving aspects of his problem.

To begin with, he was wholly in her power. A word to Red Anne, and a word from her to the Butcher, a sign from the Butcher to Dirck, and no more Herluin. Nor would the end be necessarily swift . . . sweat started at the thought. Dirck's lined, grey face, and a cell in the dungeon tower, and things that made the misted steeps of Dondonoy a very hearth of comfort to imagine. . . .

But would Lys let it come to that ? Was she, in spite of her own word, a Potiphar's wife whose lust, if repelled for long, would turn to ruinous spite and destroy him ? And was her strange fierce tenderness a cloak for lust, or evidence of a nobility that strove against the darker passion ?

Lys, no doubt, set his scruples down to monastic training ; but what was it that really restrained him ? Had Lys been no witch but an ordinary wanton, nine boys out of ten in his position would already have sought and enjoyed her favours, thinking no more of them than Ivo thought, or Gervase. But Lys was a witch, and many a hardy wencher would have shrunk from sharing his little mistress with the devil ; yet Herluin could not easily summon the religious horror which that circumstance demanded. Issues such as this rose straightly in the legends ; but in life, it seemed, they came aslant and end-long, bearing strange discomfitures and complications. . . .

Now had it not been for Yseult . . . yet his shrinking from Lys had very little to do with his thought of Yseult. His image of Yseult shone so aloof from contacts of the day that it was hard to bring even this question to her shrine. To keep himself unspotted for Yseult . . . yes, that was a sustaining thought, holding at certain moments a rainbow splendour spilt from Paradise. Yseult, wide-browed, still-eyed, who moved to the music of faëry horns and, all unknowing, filched from him that wondering devotion which at

Marckmont he had offered to the kind-faced image of the
Mother of God. . . .

Paid to Yseult, that devotion seemed thankless enough ;
or so the baseness in him whispered. Supposing she was
already betrothed . . . supposing he fell in some scuffle on
his way to Montenair . . . supposing . . .

I promise not to hate you for a week. Take that at its
worst, as a definite threat. If he could not fly from Campscapel before the week was up, was he not setting a lunatic
value on his poor virginity ? Was the whole coil a judgment of God upon him for abiding in the tents of wickedness ?
Or for his most abandoned lying ? Did God demand truth,
even to the Butcher ? *That* would be easily set right : *My
lady, I know of your secret stair.* . . .

Herluin bent and caressed his tender leg.

" If I cannot run for it in a week, I must go to Lys," he
said.

A shiver passed down his body. He remembered much
more than he had yet admitted to himself of that comely
vision in Red Anne's antechamber. A dimpled knee, a
blue vein in a slender arm, the flawless swell of little eager
breasts . . . and all these Yaan. . . .

" I am a coward and a liar and a fool," thought Herluin,
covering his face with his hands. " And now I am going to
be a lecher. And as she said, it will not be so terrible. But
what else can I do ? I am not made for martyrdom. Once
I get away from this accursed place, Great God and Holy
Mother of God, I will atone so far as may be . . . and you,
dear Saints, to whom I owe the candles—you would not have
had me pay them in the little dirty chapel here ? Help me
and give me time, and strength and courage."

He fumbled in his memory for King David's prayer
against a lying tongue.

" *Domine, libera animam meam a labiis iniquis, et a
lingua dolosa . . . Heu mihi, quia incolatus meus pro-
longatus est ; habitavi cum habitantibus Kedar. Cum his,
qui oderunt pacem, eram pacificus.*"

That was the hundred and twentieth Psalm. Herluin
stared across the Butcher's ranges, and there rose in his
memory the clang of the hundred and twenty-first.

"*Levavi oculos meos in montes, unde veniet auxilium mihi ; auxilium meum a Domino, qui fecit coelum et terram . . . Dominus custodiat introitum tuum, et exitum tuum; ex hoc nunc, et usque in saeculum.*"

"All the same," said Herluin gloomily, "the help that hitherto has come to me out of the hills was that of Sabelle of the Coven of the Singing Stones."

Two days later, when Herluin stood with the Butcher's hunting-cloak in his hand, Dirck brought news to his master of Red Anne's return.

"Is she alone ? " asked the Count, drily.

"No, lord. A fat rogue comes with her, sweating and uneasy."

"Good. Send the Captain Bruin here to me. Go ! "

The short hairs prickled on Herluin's neck, for the Butcher's face was suddenly distorted by a twitch that shot his eyebrows high and dragged his mouth an inch aside.

"Boy, take that cloak away. Here, pull my boots off first. . . . How old are you ? "

"S—sixteen, my lord," came Herluin's flustered reply.

"H'm. Too young," growled the Butcher, waving him aside.

"Who is that swithering knave with my lady ? "

Herluin shot the low-voiced question at Ivo when the two of them were setting up the trestles for the Count's board in the great hall.

"Fiend knows," responded Ivo grumpily.

But later, when he had spoken to Mathilde, he passed behind Herluin whilst the latter shook out a great table-cloth, and whispered in his ear.

"There is something afoot," he said. "It is Saint-Aunay's steward."

Herluin stiffened and stared ; then, with unsteady pulse and awkward fingers, he fell to work again, spurred by the critical eye of the Butcher's chamberlain.

That night Gervase came and sat on Herluin's low bed before they went to sleep.

"Herluin," he whispered shakily, "did you see ? "

" My lord's face ? Yes. Is that *it* ? "

" Yes. I . . . I am afraid. It is not spring yet . . . if his madness is on him again it is strangely delayed or forwarded."

Ivo came in, with an ill-fitting air of unconcern.

" You two had better sleep, instead of catching fleas," he announced. " Soon after midnight we must rise again."

" What ?—why ? "

" Some little jaunt of my lord's. Oh, *we* must stay here, worse luck. . . ."

" By way of garrison," he added, thoughtfully making the best of it.

Then he opened a shutter and poked his pink nose out into the night.

" New moon, and like to freeze," he observed. " Brr ! I wish I was seven foot tall and fifty inches round the chest."

" Then you would have to ride two horses at once," gibed Gervase, restored to his usual self by Ivo's normal bearing.

" And we should have a new Count of Alanol," said Herluin.

Ivo laughed, and banged the shutter to ; then he caught up a pillow and turned starry eyes on Herluin.

" Not of necessity," he cried, and slam went the pillow across the stony floor.

" What ails him this time ? " wondered Herluin, as he flung the missile back.

" Never mind, Ivo," chuckled Gervase, who by now was sitting up beneath his blankets. " Beef is not everything. The cockatrice slew the lion, but the weasel slew the cockatrice."

Ivo slid half into bed, and blew out the candle. Herluin lay for a restless hour listening to the faint rush of the stream far below the windows. Once Gervase laughed in his sleep, and Herluin grappled with the thought that not only gentle Gervase and blithe Ivo, but every human being in the castle, had almost certainly some deep absorbing problem of his own. Meanwhile, he hugged his body-belt that he had made to wear under his shirt. It was pouched, and in it he had sewn his money and his rings.

At midnight a leaden-eyed Herluin lurched from bed and dressed as rapidly as might be. Five minutes later Dirck caught him by the neck in the corridor and thrust him into the armoury. Gervase presently suffered the same usage, and together they buckled the Count of Alanol into his great panoply of plate. Only the casque they left on the table; and whilst they worked the lightning of the disfiguring twitch ran in the blackness of the Butcher's hair. When the long beard was tucked behind the projecting beaver Gervase brought the heavy sword-belt with its great slung sword; Herluin knelt and buckled on the vicious spurs, and the Count turned himself about, a glimmering tower of steel, with the rampant lion of his house agrin in silver on his sable surcoat.

" Dirck, in my absence my lady is Captain of Campscapel."

" Speed you well, my lord," piped Dirck, bowing and rubbing his hands together. " A merry day and a trim homecoming, and death and damnation to the enemies of your house."

" Amen to that, you old fool," growled the Butcher, laughing a direful laugh as he pulled on his gauntlets.

Then Herluin bore the grim lion-crested casque, and Gervase the black lion-dight shield, down to the inner bailey, where Ivo and lean Ord held the bridles of the great barbed destriers of the Campscapels. Presently, through the cheerful hum of the outer wards, a nearer sound of singing came flatly to Herluin; and the Sieur Jehan—helmed, though with his visor up, so that his gingery curls were all but quenched in steel—came lumbering down his stair and out into the torchlight.

One stalwart rider of Campscapel had a horse roped to his own; this, it seemed, was for the bulky steward whom gold had prompted to betray his master. Herluin watched him mount, and saw that he was pot-valiant—saw, too, that Bruin, the grey war-captain, spat aside when the steward hailed him. . . .

Then, without sound of trumpet, the portcullis grated aloft and the drawbridge-head crashed down. First moved the Count and his brother, then the banner-bearer and grey Bruin, then the steward and his bodyguard, and after them, two by two, the savage Riders of Campscapel. Morning, that yet was night, swallowed them up to the number of two hundred ; and the subdued clangour of their going rounded the southern end of the castle rock and died along the east-ward road.

On that still autumn day the townward gate was opened for an hour about noon, but the other stood fast as it had shut behind the outgoing array. When he had fed the hawks Herluin climbed to the pages' room and tried on his mail shirt.

"I am growing into this thing," he told himself with satisfaction. "Next time I ride out with my lady I will wear it . . . and with any fortune I shall not come back."

Then he took the mail off again, and lay on his bed in shirt and hose with a blanket over him, and went on with the poem about the lilies until sleep claimed him.

At sunset he awoke, and dressed and moved abroad in the castle. A waiting hush had fallen on the rock of Campscapel ; only about the kitchens was there light and sound and move-ment. After one tour of the ramparts Red Anne had kept her own tower ; Herluin looked in at the antechamber door and found Mathilde and Gervase whispering together.

"Where are the others ? " he inquired.

"Lys and Agnes are sewing upstairs," replied Mathilde.

"And Ivo ? I have not seen him since noon."

Mathilde giggled. Gervase looked comically at Herluin and jerked a thumb at the door of Red Anne's bedchamber.

"So-ho ! " said Herluin. "What—— "

"Ivo was playing the harp for nearly an hour," muttered Gervase. "But that has long since ceased, and the door is bolted."

Herluin nodded and wandered away. He had noticed that Red Anne drank more wine than usual with her supper, and wondered if Ivo owed his joy to it.

"Now is that a great wickedness ? " he mused. "Or is it the noblest thing in Ivo's life, and gentleness and good-nature in Red Anne ? By all the Saints, these things are difficult. But certainly a little wine might help *me* when the time comes. *Et vinum laetificet cor hominis.*"

An hour or two later, when the first dismay of that grisly night was on him, he remembered King David's cheerful words again. The chill October twilight had yielded to cloudy darkness, and by twos and threes and dozens the blood-mad Riders of Campscapel came yelling home. The Butcher's iron-grey charger trampled into the torch-light; the Butcher sat like a man drugged, with his raised visor beaten flat against his casque, and his teeth gleaming through his beard in a fixed grin of triumph. Red Jehan sang loudly and obscenely, waving his gauntleted hand when the pikemen and archers cheered him; his helmet swung at the saddle-bow, and his beast-face glowed above a riven breast-plate. Behind the noble brothers came the day's prisoners, humped and wretched, bound on the saddles of led horses; and at sight of them Gervase exclaimed in Herluin's ear:

" Christ ! See the tall one, hook-nosed, on the grey . . . it is Saint-Aunay himself ! Caught hunting, by his dress . . . ay, ay, and that woman in green is the Countess . . ."

Herluin stared at the reeling figure; by the gateway the outer bailey was as bright as day, and a face still lovely in pallor and distress was turned continually towards the helpless Count.

" Why, there is half their household," muttered Herluin. " I suppose they will hold them to ransom ? "

" God knows."

" But surely, the women . . ."

" You fool, nothing is sure."

" But my lady will never permit . . ."

" My lady is very wisely getting drunk to-night. *She* can do nothing. Moreover, when we have disarmed and served my lord *I* am going to get drunk also. And I advise you to do the same. . . ."

There was nothing reassuring about the manner in which captives, men and women alike, were hauled from their saddles and thrust or kicked into a guard-room. Herluin looked for the Count and Countess of Saint-Aunay, but they had already been haled away. The Butcher sat watching until Bruin the war-captain, who brought up the rear of the cavalcade, rode forward and saluted him. Ivo, bright-eyed but sleepy, had appeared from nowhere to take his lord's bridle, and presently Herluin was carrying the battered casque into the armoury. The Butcher said no word whilst the boys stripped him of armour and clothing in his bedroom ; not till the water of his steaming bath lipped the black mat of hair on his great chest did a growl of content escape him.

" Arrrrh ! It is good ! Dirck, old dog, where are you ? "

" Here, my lord," and the grinning hunchback shuffled forward.

" Make ready my stool of penitence for my lord of Saint-Aunay. I fear he is not yet penitent ; but the end will show."

The Butcher's stool of penitence was a low wooden block set against the wall in the room adjoining the armoury ; nailed to the panelling above it was an iron collar, hinged to shut on the neck of any one seated on the block.

Dirck chuckled and withdrew, whilst the Butcher lathered his own war-scarred arms ; and the dreadful twitch ran up and across his yellow face between the darknesses of hair and beard.

" I grow heavier in the saddle," he grumbled suddenly, and then, to Ivo : " Hey, rat, what weight are you ? "

" Barely eight stone, my lord."

" I was once as light myself. More hot water, one of you ; and the other go lay out my black velvet on the bed. If the comptroller come, or Captain Bruin, admit him instantly. . . ."

Here and there they scurried at his bidding ; once the Butcher called Ivo a foul name, and Ivo, pausing for an instant behind his master, lifted his forefingers like horns by his own forehead.

" Mad fool," thought Herluin. " What would happen if . . . but Red Anne knows that none of us would do that."

The drunkenness began at supper. Even the Butcher drank more than usual, so that his step was ponderous as he left the hall. Herluin, falling to at the high table, saw that half the Riders and many of the lower sort were already in their cups. Red Jehan had lurched away, with face inflamed and muttering mouth ; Bruin, the chamberlain, and the comptroller disappeared, and the troop-captains ruled the roost. Pursuant to his plan, Herluin had hastily swallowed

a cup of mead and three small beakers of wine of Estragon ;
torches and candles wavered and tended to multiply as he
looked down the hall ; and when a side door opened and a
score of men and women were thrust through, even the roar
of brutal glee that went up did not at first enlighten him.

He poured out a fourth beaker, but never lifted it to drink,
for a scuffling arose in the hall, and he saw that the clothing
of the newcomers was being torn from their bodies.

"They are heating irons," croaked Gervase. "Come
away. Ivo, you too. For Christ's sake, come away."

Ivo shook his head, and dipped his little red nose into his
beaker.

"I am hungry," he said, after a long draught.

So the other two slipped out, and found themselves in the
chill air of the inner bailey. Here and there, by doorways
in the stone, torches were burning low ; the windows of the
great hall cast a dim glow on grass and gravel, and beyond
the blackness of the higher ramparts the unheeding stars
winked in a clear sky.

"It goes on and on, and then you suddenly find it is
devilish," muttered Gervase.

"What ? " demanded Herluin vaguely

"Life in this hell-hole. Last year . . . I told you . . .
and since then I have thought I must have dreamed it, all
that horror. But now it is on us again."

"We . . . we cannot help it," mumbled Herluin.

Then, as they turned towards the keep, both boys were
rooted to the ground by an appalling scream. It came from
high above them ; and as they stared the orange of a horn-
filled slit in the Sieur's Tower went black and blank. A
second fainter scream was suddenly cut off ; and now, behind
them, a mingled tumult swelled and died in the hall.

"*That* is the little Countess," whispered Gervase. "That
foul beast Jehan. . . ."

He shivered and caught at Herluin's arm ; and together
they blundered into the keep. The winding stairs seemed
unfamiliar and treacherous ; and when he reached the first
landing Herluin halted by a black curtain and addressed the
silver lion that ramped across it.

"What are *you* doing here, beast ? "

" Say, rather, what *you* are doing here," said the clear voice of Lys in the corridor behind them.

" In truth, I had it we were in our corner tower," said Gervase apologetically. " Now I come to think of it, we never crossed the lesser hall when we came in. You see, Lys, Herluin has drunk too much, and I . . ."

" You were taking him to bed. I see."

The girl stood watching them, and a faint squeal came from behind the curtained door. Herluin, aware of weakened limbs and a slowly-spinning head, leaned against the wall and gestured vaguely.

" What is the matter *there* ? " he inquired.

" My lady is beating Agnes. Agnes is a fool; she was jealous because of Ivo this afternoon. I tried to interfere, but my lady marched me out."

" And Mathilde ? "

" Mathilde went to the chamberlain's room to dress his wounded hand. We shall see *her* no more to-night."

Lys laughed unpleasantly.

" *I* went to the minstrel's gallery over the hall," she added, " and now I am going to bed."

She shot one glance at Herluin, and stepped past him to the foot of the upward stairs. Then Gervase clucked his tongue and fumbled with his belt.

" By all the fiends in hell," he swore, " I have dropped my little dagger. It was loose in the sheath, and too heavy for it. I had it at supper ; it must be on the steps or in the bailey."

" One moment," said Lys, " and I will bring you a light."

She dived upward into the gloom, and Herluin stood working his fingers and trying to think. A waxen taper burned by the curtained door ; along the stony vaulted passage a rat's eyes shone and disappeared to the accompaniment of a faint scuffle. Obscure sounds drifted from the blackness of the other corridor, beyond which lay the rooms of the Count's Tower. A little wind woke in the slit at Herluin's elbow, breathed weirdly, and died down again. Then the footfall of Lys came cautiously above him on the stair. . . .

Lys carried a rush-light and a wooden cup in one hand,

and a tiny crystal flask in the other. She handed the rush to Gervase, who lit it at the taper ; and then she pulled the stopper from the flask and poured a little of its contents into the cup.

"Here, Gervase," she snapped. "This is a cordial which will pluck up your heart and at the same time sober you."

Gervase drank, and Lys refilled the cup for Herluin. He took it, and the still amber liquid burnt his tongue delightfully.

"It is like the stuff the monks distilled at—at Hardonek," he said faintly, feeling a queer reviving fire in all his veins.

"Yes," said Lys firmly. "Like it, and yet not altogether the same. And now, poor scared Herluin, go and help Gervase find his dagger . . . and good-night to you."

"Lys," began Herluin mistily ; and she turned on the stair to look at him.

"Said I not we are all damned ? " she inquired mockingly.

Then she was gone again, and Gervase bore his rush-light valorously down the steps.

"Come on, Herluin ! " he called when he had passed from view.

And presently Herluin followed, finding himself compelled to a strange mincing gait by reason of the stuff he had swallowed.

"God help me, I am more drunk than ever," he reflected. "But at any rate I can walk straight. It is like walking upon air. Lys is a mischievous little cat . . . when that dagger is found I have half a mind to try her door. No use holding aloof any longer . . . I perceive half my virtue was nothing but timidity . . . *et vinum laetificet cor hominis*."

Hither and thither shone the rush-light ; and presently Gervase called out and stooped.

"I have it," he said.

Then he looked at his companion, and Herluin saw that his face was flushed.

"And now I have it," he went on, "I am minded to stick it into the paunch of that damned chamberlain."

"That is because of Mathilde," thought Herluin. Then : "Jesu, are we both bewitched ? That draught Lys gave us must have . . . oh, there are potent brews, sleek demoiselle, and this is one of them, to turn a page into a stallion . . . well, let us all be damned together."

Gervase threw down his rush-light, stamped out the smouldering end of it, and stared over Herluin's shoulder. Herluin turned, and saw the Sieur Jehan's body-servant Ord approaching them on his way from the gate of the inner bailey to the door of his master's tower. The boys drew together as they saw what he carried; torch-light faintly showed the stricken face and staring eyes of a little serving-girl who, maybe, had happily polished the brass bowls and platters at Saint-Aunay twelve short hours before. Now she was moaning and distraught; from shoulder to foot her clothing was in rags, as though her captor had torn her from another's grasp; and from the uproar in the hall it seemed that many were fighting there. But Herluin and Gervase saw the droop of a thin bare arm, the parted lips of a terrified child, and their lusts sank and shrivelled in a fire of shame and wrath.

" Ord, Ord ! " cried Gervase. " Let her go ! For God's sake let her go ! "

Red Jehan's servitor stared as he stalked on his way. He had a lean hound's face, with one dark eyebrow half-burnt off, and a red scar in place of it. In the gloom of the inner bailey they saw him grin and shake his head; and both of them started forward, trotting by him as he strode.

" Not likely," he said. " And have you younglings take her on the grass ? No, no ; get you to the hall and win your own ! "

" But, Ord," yammered Herluin, clutching the servant's woollen sleeve, " she is too young ! Christ in heaven, you swine, she is only a little maid ! "

" And fiends in hell, you rat, I like them young—and for your other objection, it is a matter of moments only. Stand aside."

Ord swung contemptuously by; and now he was on the steps, so that Herluin let go, rasping his knuckles on the stone. Like many such approaches, the low stair ran side-ways up the wall to the doorway, being designed to prevent a frontal attack on the latter ; and the long-limbed Ord was up it in two strides. Herluin, following, was thrust aside by his furious fellow-page.

" Ord, you bloody beast ! " screeched the once-gentle Gervase. " Drop her, or I cut your liver out ! "

And in a flash he was at the other's back in the darkness of the Sieur's Tower. . . .

Ord must have turned on the inner stair and set his foot on the boy's chest ; for Gervase grunted and shot backwards through the doorway, crashing in a limp heap against the low parapet at Herluin's feet. Herluin, aghast, bent over him ; there was enough light from the nearest wall-torch to see that his skull had struck the stone. When Herluin touched the soft warm hair the head rolled sideways in a way that turned his stomach ; it was clear that no matter what else had happened to Gervase, his neck was broken.

As Herluin stepped back there came the clang of an iron-bound door within the tower ; and a great sob of fury tore its way out of him. Then he was down the steps and half way across the bailey ; but he hardly knew what he did, for presently he found himself at the hawk-sheds, and then beside the well. Lastly he screamed aloud, and made for the door of the keep ; and this time he bore past the stairway of enchantment and plunged across the dim-lit lesser hall. Then stairs again—for all that gruesome night he seemed condemned to pass up and down stairs—and the cold corridors and the armoury door, iron-studded against his beating fists. Then a creak, and a slit of light, and Dirck's inquiring face. . . .

" Dirck—Dirck—Gervase is dead ! Ord has killed him ! What shall I do ? "

Dirck scratched his long nose with a crooked finger, and considered, holding the door half open.

" Well," he grated, " if I did not already know you for a parlous little fool, I might send you speedily to join him. Do ? What do you want to do ? Why do you come to me ? It is true you will have more work in the armoury now, if that little slave is indeed dead ; but if you want masses said for him . . . look you, silly varlet, come here and see what happens to the enemies of Campscapel, and *then* tell me if you think a page's death a thing to worry for."

And in a trice he had the sobbing Herluin by the neck and in the armoury.

" No sound, or your bones are like to be cracked," he growled, thrusting his captive powerfully towards the door of the Count's own room. " Now look your fill, and page me no more pages."

Herluin looked. The low-backed chair of the Butcher Count was turned away from the door, and towards the stool of penitence. A table stood at the Butcher's elbow, with wine and comfits on it ; and the black velvet arm of the Butcher lay along the polished wood as he admonished with uplifted finger the bound and ghastly thing before him. Saint-Aunay's nose was gone and his tongue also, so that when he opened his mouth it was like a second hideous wound in his grey-white bleeding face. He made a gobbling sound, and stirred from time to time ; tears ran from his staring eyes, but the latter were not visibly cowed. Wide movement was denied him, for his wrists were chained to the block, and his knees had been broken with a cunning instrument of springs and bars that stood in the dungeon torture-chamber. . . .

" They took no chances," Herluin thought—for now his mind was numb with horror, and had it not been for the medicated draught that Lys had given him he might have vomited or swooned. As it was, he sobbed no more, but watched and listened, with fists tight-shut and cold sweat stealing down his spine ; and beneath the numbness in him stirred a cold and deadly rage.

" Man after man has raised his hand against Campscapel," said the Butcher sombrely, " and no one of them all has died in his bed, save that crippled Saulte who fought against my father. And *his* son's turn, it may be, is now on the way. Face Campscapel, face death ; but you, Saint-Aunay, crossed me in the matter of my promised wife. . . ."

" I never knew that," thought Herluin.

" And burned my farms and slew my hinds and wounded my brother, and would have taken my mistress Anne and burned her at the stake. Thus and thus has it befallen you. . . ."

Dirck's grip tightened, and Herluin was hauled away.

" Since you are here, boy, fetch me a jug of water,"

growled the hunchback. " And swiftly," he added ; and
for the first time Herluin noticed that his hands were
red.

That meant the kitchens ; and Herluin tottered into the
dark passage with a great brass ewer in his hand. But he
took the wrong turning, and presently brought up at the
entry of the corner tower, where his favourite window showed
a double blue-grey shape in the jet blackness.

" Perhaps there is water in our room," he thought, and
blundered forward. . . .

" Who is there ? " said Ivo's voice from Ivo's bed.

" Herluin. Is there water here ? "

" No, I used it all. Who wants it ? "

" Dirck. But Ivo . . ."

" Well ? "

" Gervase is dead. Ord killed him. . . ."

" You were fools to interfere," said Ivo, when the other
had finished. " But that is very beastly news."

" It is the least beastly thing afoot in this damned hold
of hell to-night," came brokenly from Herluin's lips. " But
you—you do not care. Was it so wonderful ? "

" It was," replied Ivo simply.

" I saw in the hall you were like one drugged . . . what
were they doing when you came away ? "

" Oh, *that*. Making them dance and jump over red-hot
rods."

" Oh, single-minded Ivo," said Herluin tragically in the
darkness.

Then he stole out, and in a minute or two was peering
down from the minstrels' gallery into the fume and uproar of
the great hall. Once or twice he retched, and then stood
motionless save for a chattering of the teeth. More and more
of his mind was slipping beneath the mounting wave of icy
madness that he knew for the famous anger of his house ;
yet still he could watch himself watching, and wonder at what
point the wave would break in action.

" I think this is the end," he told himself. " God cannot
show me this without intending me to do a thing. . . . God
keep my head for me until I find a thing to do . . . but God
has gone away and forgotten, and I will keep my own head

until I see how best to lose it. Holy Mary, there is a girl
like . . . something like little Reine de Guarenal."

All that was dear in the past rose up in him, and his
wrath broke free. Seizing the great brass vessel, he held it
poised, as if to hurl it down into the hall ; then he checked
himself and lowered it, and turned unsteadily away into the
blackness of the passage.

The armoury door again, this time ajar. Dirck was not
in sight . . . ah, he was in the Butcher's room.

" My hands are cold," thought Herluin as he set down
the empty ewer near the steps that led to Dirck's dark sleeping
place. " But not too cold," he added, taking a broad short
sword from its place in a rack. " Fie, Dirck, you have given
it an edge like a razor."

The Butcher's voice boomed loudly as the door opened,
and Herluin skipped down the three steps into the hunchback's evil-smelling lair. There he waited, but this time
with no trembling of the loins. He had his plan.

" Tell the Sieur Jehan that it is discourteous to keep man
and wife apart all night," commanded the Butcher. " Let
them see each other again ; I'll warrant both will find an
alteration . . . hey, my lord ? "

Dirck shuffled into the armoury, his grey face wreathed
in a grin. His wooden shoes clop-clopped in haste ; near
the door of his den he saw the ewer, and stooped to
lift it.

" Hasten, Dirck ! " bellowed the mad Count.

But that consummation of beastliness was never achieved ;
for as the hunchback stooped, a sword, and a boy behind
the sword, crept out of darkness up the shallow steps. And
as the hunchback straightened himself and piped an answer
to his master the sword was swung in a frantic sweep. Not
for nothing had Herluin hewn diligently at wooden blocks
shaped like men in armour ; the hiss of steel was silenced in
a strange thudding slap, and Dirck the hunchback raised
his arms a little and sank down like a sack with his head all
but severed from his body.

" Christ and Our Lady, Saint Barruc and Yseult," said
Herluin beneath his breath. " Who would have thought
that dry old monster had so much blood in him ? "

Then he stepped across the crimson tide towards the door of the inner room.

"*The cockatrice slew the lion*," he thought, "*but the weasel slew the cockatrice. . . .*"

Then again, as he peered in : "*Face Campscapel, face death* . . . keep your back turned, my lord ; if ever I face Campscapel it shall be with good swords all about me. Keep your back turned, my lord ; drink again. Set down your glass and bow your head to ease a hiccough. My lord, you are nearly altogether drunk . . . my lord, you have a red and swollen neck this night . . . my lord, my lord, *have at you* ! "

Perhaps some alteration in the tortured eyes of his victim made the Butcher slowly turn his head ; and perhaps he saw the white blur of the mad young face and the flash of the whirling down-stroke. At all events he made to rise in the instant that the steel shore deep into his neck. Indeed, his half-turn exposed the jugular vein ; with a grunt and a frenzied roll of eyeballs he made to rise in his chair, clawing with one great hairy hand at the air between him and his slayer. Then he swayed sideways over the chair-arm ; lower and lower sank the huge black head, the great beard heavy and running with blood. Again the big paw rose ; and Herluin, who had torn his blade away with an unforgettable jar of steel on bone, slashed downwards in snarling terror, and severed two fingers from the hand as it fell back. Then he stood staring, whilst a last convulsion shook the bowed giant, toppling chair and body over across the floor. . . .

Herluin sprang back ; but now the bearded face was twisted upwards, and its clay-coloured dreadfulness admitted of no question. Lorin de Campscapel, the Butcher Count of Alanol, was dead in the hour of his triumph. . . .

His murderer bent a glassy stare on the wretched captive against the wall. The maimed face wagged, the maimed mouth gaped and gobbled, and Herluin shifted his sword from one hand to the other and made the sign of the Cross.

" God help you, my lord Count," he said. " I must lock the outer door . . . one moment, and I shall be with you again."

Then he was out of one death-chamber and in the other ;

and as he barred the armoury door he wondered what his duty was to this poor wreck that had been lord of Saint-Aunay.

But when he stood again by the dead Butcher he saw that the prisoner's eyes were fixed on his own wet sword ; and an eager gobbling shook the suffering frame.

" My lord, do you wish me to make an end ? "

Emphatically the ghastly head was nodded ; and the eyes, half-human with pain, grew wholly human for an instant as Etienne de Saint-Aunay straightened himself for the blow. Herluin read gratitude in their glance ; and desperately he raised his sword again.

" God and sweet Jesu and the Holy Ghost have mercy on our souls ! " he groaned, and sent a swift thrust into the chained body.

One shudder, and the prisoner was freed ; his eyes shut and opened again, and his body hung limply, held to its seat by chin and wrist. And so Herluin left it, staring as though at the lifeless bulk of its late tormentor.

Treading delicately over the dead, he saw a sparkle amid the dark blood on the floor. Stooping, he grimaced and fumbled ; it was the signet of Campscapel—a gold loop bearing a beautiful intaglio, the rampant lion in topaz—and, being on one of the severed fingers, it was easily detached and wiped on the dead Butcher's sleeve.

" Now I will keep this as long as I live," said Herluin with drunken gravity, " be that ten minutes or forty years. For no man will ever believe the tale of this night's work, and if I have not evidence I shall cease to believe it myself."

Then he blew out the candles, and passed into the armoury.

" Ho, baseborn Dirck," he muttered as he cleansed his wet blade on a cloth, " you have mingled your blood at the last with the blood of two great houses, and died at noble hands. God rest *your* soul at the least ; for your master's I will say nothing. And now that the door is fast and the hold far gone in heedless arts of hell, I will borrow such arms as I need, and win out if I may."

Like one in a dream, he took the keys from Dirck's girdle, searched patiently until he found the right one, and turned it in the lock behind the faded arras. Presently he had a

new mail shirt beneath his tunic, and a plain cloak of the
Butcher's own; sword-belt and dagger, and sheath for the
sword he had used; boots of Dirck's, each with a rag stuffed
into the toe; a candle, a flint and steel and box of tinder;
and, at the last, a round buckler and a small steel cap that
his hood would hide if need be. His money-belt was safe
about his middle, and only his own sword and mail, with the
ballad-book that had been Countess Adela's of Ger, would
remain of his belongings.

" Some day I may come to fetch you," he promised them
in his heart. " But if I do, I shall not come alone."

Then he lit his candle, quenched all other light, and
cautiously unlocked the door by which he had first entered
the armoury that night. And at last, with half the keys of
the keep at his belt, he was descending endless secret stairs
that turned ever to the right in flights of seven. The ceiling
of this staircase was barrel-vaulted; presently moisture
dripped through the bricks, and the great spiders ceased to
run and drop on him as he tore their countless webs. Ten
sevens of steps he counted, and then he stood in the close
air of a passage hewn through the chalk rock.

The passage sloped slightly downwards, and soon Herluin
had to stoop to move along it. Forthwith a dread of the
weight of earth above him gripped him by the throat, so that
he sweated and began to run as well as he could. His sense
of distance suffered eclipse, and he could not tell whether he
had gone a hundred yards or the eighth part of a mile when
the passage rose and widened and showed him an arched
alcove to one side.

" The serfs' grave," said Herluin. " God keep their
souls also. And here is a door. Lys said *key*, not *keys*.
Ah, it fits again. Now, sword and buckler and Saints in
heaven defend me . . . so, a second door. . . ."

Again the key fitted; and this time the door was very
narrow, opening on a little stone-paved cell. Fresh air blew
in at an unglazed window opposite, and water rippled near.
And in one corner of the cell sat up a white-haired old woman,
smiling shyly from a heap of blankets and shading her eyes
from the light in Herluin's hand.

" Are you Saint Michael himself ? " she asked.

" No, mother.   Who are you ? "

" I am Clotilde the Anchoress.   Where is the red-haired lady who is so kind ?   Is she not coming this time ? "

" Not this time, mother . . . tell me, how do I get out ? "

For the cell was sealed, and the old woman evidently lived on the charity of those who thrust food and drink through the shuttered hole, a foot square, in the wall opposite the bed. A narrow curtained doorway gave out an evil stink, but the cell itself was clean and dry.

" The ladies stand in the empty niche there, and push open the trap in the roof," said the old woman.

" I see," and Herluin stared round him.   " And how long have you been here, mother ? "

" Oh, a many years.   Since Jehan builded the cell for me."

" Jehan de Campscapel ? "

" Ay, father to the great Count that is now—my lady's lord, I mean."

" Oh.   And now, mother, will you hold the candle for me whilst I climb out ?   Stay, is there a path away from here ? And whither does it lead ? "

" There are two paths ; one I can see, that leads along the stream to the ford and into the sunset.   The other my lady goes along with her little friend.   That I have not seen since I came here, but I think it goes to Capel Conan."

" I thank you, mother.   God be with you ; and I pray you blow the candle out and give it to me through your little hole . . . and forget you ever saw me.   Remember in the morning that I was a dream."

So saying, he slung his buckler on his shoulder, sheathed his sword and drew his key from the lock.   The door swung to behind him ; and he saw that it was cleverly contrived to look like a carved wooden screen set against the brick wall of the cell—a screen standing behind a canopied wooden bracket that supported a gilded image of the Virgin and her Child.   Bracket, image, and canopy, fastened to the door, swung forward on it ; and the keyhole was set in a whorl of the rude carving on the screen.

All this Herluin saw and admired.   Then he locked the door, and mounted to the niche, whilst the anchoress held the light for him.   Boards and thatch rose cunningly together ;

E

and Herluin was out in the night air.   Ten feet he dropped, and the trap fell to behind him.   Then he took the blown-out candle from Clotilde, bade her good-night, and turned to consider his whereabouts.

" Yes," he said.   " I am at the north-western corner of the rock, in the pine-woods above the stream.   Here I must wait till the first light . . . no, I will not, I will risk the ford by starlight.   And now, by God and all His Saints, I hold a secret worth the telling to my lord Castellan at Montenair."

And by dint of sounding with his sword, he got across with no more than a soaking to the waist.   Many a time he turned to look at the few lights in the black bulk of the castle; by them and by the Pointers he steered a course into the thick woods to the north of Alanol.   There, with the town between him and his late home, he dozed till the first daylight ; and then he aimed for the dawn and the hold of the grim Castellan.

In this way Herluin, who had been Raoul, added a post-script to the great feud of Saint-Aunay and Campscapel, and broke from the hold above Alanol into the Forest of Honoy.

VII

THE FOREST OF HONOY

WITH the grey dawn-light came reaction from enchantment Herluin stumbled amid rocks and bushes, trotting to keep at bay the chill that invaded a body ravaged by the witch-cup of Lys ; and as he steered and plunged through the wet woods his fortitude began to fail him. He knew that food and sleep would tune his jangled nerves again, but now there was time for neither ; before he paused he meant to pass a watch-tower by the stream, where the road curved north-easterly towards Capel Conan, and thus leave nothing but deep forest between himself and Montenair.

" How the mist thickens in the hollows . . . *what was that ?* Only a pheasant, God be praised. Now, there should lie the stream and above it, round the shoulder of the hill . . . yes, Lorin's watch-tower. Now am I thankful for this mild October season, that has yet left a screen of leaves. . . ."

He was hard put to it, as the daylight grew, to keep above the mist and yet find cover that felt sufficient. Dark against the sunrise stood the tower ; to skirt it Herluin must move along a ridge into the sun's eye, and now he halted to hide steel cap under hood and buckler under cloak, that no glitter of bright steel betray him.

" Outpost of hell," he called the tower in his mind ; and his thought flew back to the dismal awakenings which this sun-up must bring on the Rock of Campscapel. He marvelled at his two murders and at that other, stranger killing ; and desperately he strove to block the entries of thought against his memory of the doings in the great hall and in the Sieur's Tower.

" I might have stayed and fought till I was killed," he thought. " I might have nailed Ord to his bed, or waited for him when he came out. I might have slain half-a-dozen in their cups when I had the chance . . . but what use was

there ? It would not heal the evil they had done . . .
though it is true it would prevent them doing any
more."

And now the fear of Campscapel sat like a weight between
his shoulder-blades ; the stress of hunger began to complicate
the urgency of flight. Dirck's boots, being large, were none
too comfortable for a twenty-five mile tramp ; hose drenched
in the ford beneath Alanol and dried by running in the
dawn-lit pinewoods were soaked again in undergrowth heavy
with October dew. Pinewoods yielded to beechwoods, beechwoods to glades of oak and chestnut ; leaves fluttered down,
pale brown and gold, showing translucencies of amber against
the morning sunlight. A fitful twittering of birds was
audible ; great brown squirrels leaped and ran, spilling
acorns in their flight. Once a solitary grey wolf stood at
gaze by an alder thicket, flitting noiselessly from sight when
Herluin halted and tore out his sword. . . .

Then a smell of smoke, and a clearing where huts stood
and charcoal-burners worked. Again Herluin employed the
device of rounding the habitation and coming upon it from
the other side. Awkwardly, with his dagger, he had slit the
money-belt beneath his shirt and loosened a florin ; with this
he purchased food from the astonished serfs, and circled the
clearing before hurrying on his way.

"Queer souls, who never leave the forest," he reflected.
"Do they know the king's name, or the Pope's, or their own
over-lord's ? How long before they learn the Butcher is
dead ? Is my passing the sort of topic that will serve them
for a year ? Do *their* thoughts glow and gleam and fade as
mine do ? Are they coward and valorous in the same five
minutes, as am I ? And is not God almost confused when
He sets about reward and punishment of His so great diversity
of creature ?

"Now if I said that to Ivo he would grin and tell me I
needed a purge. That is because Ivo never thinks of aught
except with himself in the middle of it. Yes, even Red Anne
whom he adores must minister to his delight . . . whereas
I . . ."

Herluin laughed for the first time that day.

"I minister to my own comfort by claiming deeper

thoughtfulness than Ivo. And now, among these thickets, let me find a place to sleep. . . ."

When he awoke it was mid-afternoon. A breeze was rustling and rushing in the trees, and leaves came slanting thickly against disorderly wisps of cloud. As he pressed forward the ground rose again ; undergrowth gave way to fading bracken and pink-brown earth amid another belt of pines. These heights must be half-way on his journey, and it seemed to him that the woods wore a more peaceful aspect, since they stood within the jurisdiction of the Castellan of Montenair. . . .

The thought was scarcely formed when he heard a shouting in the distance—a shouting, and the faint clang of smitten steel. Herluin paused and listened ; then he rolled his cloak and unslung his buckler, and with bared sword and scowling watchfulness of mien bore slant-wise, hoping to pass unseen whatever fray might be toward at the foot of the slope he now descended.

" I must keep out of forest brawls," he told himself. " No more blood for me awhile, kind Saints ! Still, it may be well to see what . . . ah, there goes some one running. Now does the distance baffle me, or is it only a child ? "

A little fleeting figure bobbed amid the pine-trunks on his left front. At sight of him it stopped, leaned against a bole, and sunk dejectedly to earth. Angrily Herluin broke into a trot, aware as he neared the tree that the fugitive was small and slim, with ill-fitting black garments and a brown childish face beneath disordered golden hair.

" What is the matter, boy ? " he called.

The little face was strangely smeared, and anguish stared from bright blue eyes.

" They are fighting down there . . . Ferrand is fighting evil men . . . oh, look . . . *oh !* "

Hard on the gasping words came a pounding of feet ; a thin-faced, ragged-looking rascal swung up the slope towards them, carrying a war-club and a battered targe of hide. At sight of Herluin's bright steel he slackened speed to a walk, then, confident of height and weight, came on again at an easy stride.

" Give up the boy and go your way, whoever you are," he

barked. " If not, I have comrades behind, and it will be the worse for you."

" Oh no, no ! " sobbed the crouching child. " Do not let him take me——"

" I will not," said Herluin simply.

Then, since there seemed nothing else for it, he ran at the newcomer as once he ran at the apprentice. This time he was frightened, but his opponent's reference to comrades behind had not bespoken too great a confidence ; and the club crashed on his buckler as his sword-point seared the ragged thigh. Then the targe swung out and blocked his rising blow ; the club rose high again, and Herluin stooped to his left, whisking his blade beneath the disc of hide and flinging his buckler up to shield his head. Then he dived forward, and the club flew free from the descending hand as he drove his thrust home in the other's belly. A dreadful screech smote into Herluin's ear, and then he was rolling on the ground beneath his stricken enemy. The buckler saved his face and throat ; his sword-hilt, driven up against the other's body, bruised his own ribs as he loosed it and groped for his dagger. Two quick jabs, and it was finished ; a breathless Herluin thrust the weight from him and stumbled to his feet in time to see a second assailant making up the slope towards him.

" One more and I am done," thought Herluin grimly. Then he dropped his dagger, dragged out his sword and tossed it into his left hand behind the buckler-grip, and stooped to lift the war-club, that had fallen against a tree and rolled back almost to his feet. . . .

" Something to throw," he told himself.

But when the second attacker saw above him a ready and unwounded foe he halted, swinging a long sword and frowning dubiously. And Herluin, realising that this rogue might dog him and the child for leagues, shouted he knew not what and launched himself down the hill. For shield this second man had a cloak wrapped round his left arm ; when he realised that the club was about to be hurled at him he gave ground with a yell and darted behind a pine-trunk of girth sufficient to hinder Herluin's aim.

" We shall be dodging here all night," thought Herluin ;

and a ruse came to him.   Lifting the club high, and gazing
past the sidling figure in front of him, he shouted aloud :
" This way !   This way !   We have him ! "
Like a flash the man wheeled and ran, but the flung club
fared faster ; it thudded on his shoulder-blade and spun him
half round in his tracks, shouting with pain.   He made to
lift his sword and could not ; his face went grey as Herluin
scuttled forward to finish him. . . .
" Where is your Ferrand, youngster ? " Herluin cried
when that untidy work was done.
Shakily the child pointed.
" Come along, then," Herluin called ; and obediently the
queer little shape, wide-eyed and something knock-kneed,
stole down the slope to him.
" You are quite safe now," said Herluin gently, wondering
if such a lie would tempt some demon of mischief to unmask
it.   " How many were there of them ? "
" Three.   But one F-Ferrand overthrew at first."
So it proved.   Ferrand the man-at-arms sat bowed against
a tree, with his third assailant dead beyond him ; and
Ferrand's eyes and wounds said clearly that Ferrand's race
was run.   Also Ferrand was mumbling at a clod of earth, in
token of unworthiness of the Last Sacrament and desire to
receive it.
" No, leave me alone," he croaked, when Herluin knelt
by him.   " Do not touch me ; listen.   You, my lady, step
aside ; I must speak to this stranger apart."
" My lady ? " repeated Herluin, as the little figure drew
sorrowfully back.
" Ay, daughter of Saint-Aunay.   Thirteen, but she does
not look it.   Yesterday the damned Butcher of Alanol took
my lord and lady as they hunted ; Bertrand the steward's
work it was.   And they won into the hold in open daylight
by putting my lady the Countess on a horse in front of them.
. . . I leaped into the moat when the slaughter began, and
the old nurse lowered the child to me by twisting sheets
together . . . bidding me take her to her aunt . . . ah !
I am nearly done ! "
" What aunt ?   Where ? "
" Abbess of Our Lady's Abbey at Montenair.   But I . . ."

" You are far out of your way, then."

The horror in the man's sunken eyes gripped Herluin's heart ; he bent closer and began to whisper comfort.

" Now, surely you have made a very gallant defence of this little maid ; and for the rest, I will deliver her safely to her aunt at Montenair, not forgetting your name and honour. . . ."

" Ah, ah, God pity me ! " broke out the dying man. " I die unshriven of a most abominable wickedness . . . God will not pity me. He cannot ; I have not confessed, I am not absolved, I die in black and miserable sin ; I shall suffer all torments of the damned for ever. You . . . you are not a priest . . . no matter, let me tell you aloud . . . so may God know I die repentant . . . but do not tell the little maid, for she thinks me faithful . . . and I . . . was taking her, not to Montenair, but through the forest to Belsaunt, to sell her to a hag that keeps a brothel . . . but God is just, and sent these villainous outlaw thieves to kill me before I could accomplish it . . ."

" I do not think God moved yonder wretches," whispered Herluin grimly. " Yet it may be He sent me to save the maid. But do you consider this ; your sin is not committed. Your intent was wicked, but the maid has come to no harm, nor shall if I can prevent it. God would not suffer you to work this wickedness ; you have at least saved the maid from present peril at cost of . . . but now let me look to your wounds. Maybe . . . ."

" No *maybe* in it ; I am sped . . . here, in my belt pouch is a ring, the maid's ring that I took from her, telling her it was for safe keeping . . . and, stranger, I charge you keep faith with me . . . can you—do you know a prayer ? something in Latin ? Latin is God's language, and He may attend more to it. . . ."

" Yes, I will say the Paternoster for you . . . and the verse against the noon-day devil . . . I was once in a convent —the great monastery of Sanctalbastre. Shall the little maid come also ? "

The man-at-arms nodded feebly ; his face was very pale now, and his eyes bore a strange film. Herluin, sick at heart for the terror and loneliness of this passing, beckoned to the queer little figure a dozen paces away, and motioned her to her knees. With curiosity and dread she watched the dying face, and at the first Amen she caught the nearer blue-white hand between her own brown paws, holding it to the end.

"Now this is the piece against the noon-day devil," said Herluin gently.

"*Scapulis suis obumbrabit tibi : et sub pennis ejus sperabis. Scuto circumdabit te veritas ejus : non timebis a timore nocturno. A sagitta volante in die, a negotio perambulante in tenebris : ab incursu et daemonio meridiano.*"

"Go on," muttered Ferrand. "Go on with the good Latin. Hold up my sword for a crucifix."

Herluin lifted the weapon, and plunged haltingly into the Miserere. Once or twice he stuck, and the girl's voice helped him out.

"*Miserere mei, Deus, secundum magnam misericordiam tuam. . . .*

"*Amplius lava me ab iniquitate mea : et a peccato meo munda me. Quoniam iniquitatem meam ego cognosco : et peccatum meum contra me est semper. . . .*

"*Asperges me hyssopo, et mundabor : lavabis me, et super nivem dealbabor. . . .*

"*Averte faciem tuam a peccatis meis : et omnes iniquitates meas dele. . . .*"

In the midst of the Miserere Ferrand's mouth fell open. The watchers crossed themselves, and Herluin stood up.

"God assoil him," he said. "I think he may not fare so badly, despite the noon-day devil. But now the shadows lengthen . . . come, little lady, do not cry any more. Pray for him when you reach the abbey . . . see, we must press on. You will not be afraid to come with me ? "

The child watched him as he donned his steel cap and wiped his sword on a handful of fallen leaves. Then, solemnly she rose and held out her hand to him.

"No," she said. "You are kind and very brave. I will tell my father, and when he comes back from the war he will make you a chevalìer."

"When . . . yes," said Herluin unsteadily. "But now we must start quickly . . . what is your name ? "

E*

" Dionysia de Saint-Aunay. But my father and mother call me Denise for short. And who are you ? "

" I am . . . my name is Herluin."

" Herluin de Marckmont ? "

Herluin stopped and stared.

" Why Marckmont ? " he asked.

" Because when you ran to kill the evil man—the second one—you shouted *Nôtre Dame de Marckmont* ! "

" Did I ? Well, She was once my patron. But I am called Herluin—Herluin Forester. And now, Lady Denise, how long is it since you had anything to eat ? "

" Oh, hours and hours . . . and I am very tired. Shall we reach my aunt Catherine before it is dark ? "

" No ; we must sleep in the woods to-night."

" Again ? It was cold and dreadful last night, and F-Ferrand walked about and talked and cried."

" I will find you somewhere warm and quiet and safe . . . see, here is a piece of bread and meat ; let us eat as we walk, and we will drink at the stream down there. You must be very hungry."

" Yes, I am. I only had a little piece of bacon this morning, and some of the dried figs nurse tucked into my hood. Nurse cried . . . but will it be a very long war ? Ferrand said so. Whilst I was eating he cut off my hair with his sword, and gathered berries to crush and rub on my face to make me brown. Poor Ferrand . . . my father will be sorry he was killed. Where do you come from ? Have you ever seen my father ? "

" Yes. At a tourney in Belsaunt."

" Close to, I mean. He is the finest, bravest man in all the world. He will like you ; but you will only come up to the spiked plates in front of his shoulder-armour . . . it was so strange yesterday. The fighting began so quickly that father had no time to say good-bye, and mother sent word that she would stay in the castle till he had beaten all his enemies and I could go home to them again. Do you think our castle will be taken ? It is a very strong castle. Have you ever been in a castle ? Oh, Herluin, it is better with you than with Ferrand ; he was afraid all the time that we were being chased, or that we should meet someone. And yesterday evening we got lost in the forest. . . ."

On their right as they went the sunset flamed, to die in rose and coral afterglow above the darkening forest of Honoy. The rounding moon got up, and Herluin watched it from the shelter of a hollowed oak. Beside him in the darkness slept Denise, her head upon his shoulder, his cloak about her body, and through the soft rhythm of her breathing came the unending saga of wind-harped oaks and beeches.

" Herluin," whispered Denise before she was still, " your clothes smell more nicely than Ferrand's did. Will you kiss me good-night for my father ? I hardly remember a night when he did not come to kiss me. . . ."

Once a wolf howled, and Herluin's feet grew tense against the buckler that nearly filled the hole by which they had entered. He had arranged it so that he had play for a shrewd thrust at any wild beast making to disturb them ; and there he dozed, roused now by the hooting of owls, now by the distant belling of a stag. One gruesome sound he failed for long to recognise, only to smile at last, knowing it for the rubbing together of two branches high above him in the darkness. . . .

" Now if beside me," he mused, " were Yseult, instead of this little Denise . . . why, I am a fool ; I should be in agony at her peril in these sombre forests. . . .

" Denise must be heiress of Saint-Aunay. Was there not a boy who died ? But the Count and his lady were young enough still to have a quiverful. . . . Ai, me, poor lady, who gave life to this little creature in my arm, not knowing that the hand which slew her lord should guard her child. . . .

" Lord God, I pray you, bring this maid and me in safety to Montenair."

He crouched and peered into the night, where the black branches of the oaks sprawled and swayed against ragged cloud and grey-blue midnight sky. And as he watched, a meteor slid silvery to vanish just above the horizon ahead of him.

" I thank you, God," he said. " That sign fell full on Montenair. . . .

" But I dislike the thought of this Castellan, Yseult's

brother though he may be. Now why? He is a great captain, but I would be free of all great captains, and especially of those whom captains gather round them. Yet there is never any peace from them, except in the cloister— where dwell their cowled and mitred counterparts. I want to be free and alone at Marckmont, and yet I want to gain great honour in the eyes of Yseult and of the world . . . but chiefly of Yseult. Why do I want these things that must destroy each other ? Honour must come first, and then peace at Marckmont, and then, perhaps . . ."

A sudden passion of gentleness assailed him : the weight of the body of the trustful child set his thoughts straying in paths strange to them. Denise might grow beautiful as her mother, and bear tall sons to some brave husband ; or she might die in the robes of an Abbess or the sackcloth of a witch ; yet never, he told himself, would she spend a stranger night than this, wherein she lay in the arm of her father's slayer. . . .

Beneath Herluin's fingers, under the girl's coarse woollen tunic and linen shirt, stood warm the first curve of a little breast. Once he had moved his hand away, and then his cheek burned in the darkness, for the movement told him that none could come unspotted from the rock of Camp-scapel. And then again a queer ferocity of tenderness swept clean his mind.

" In so far as I can," he told himself, " I will never harm human creature except to prevent him from harming another. For the thing which sets men naturally at each other's throats, and the other thing which bids them blush or grin or frown at touch of a woman's body, there must be somewhere a reason, but it is beyond me. . . .

" Fine words, from one who may be a corpse at daybreak. . . . How drily sweeps the wind through the dying leaves— a song so different from the rushing sound of spring. It is getting up, too ; by morning it will be a gale. To-morrow— what is it about to-morrow ? Why, dolt, to-morrow you may see Yseult . . . when the gusts die down the beeches say *Yseult*. . . ."

A crust of bread and a drink of water for Denise, and a

tightening of the belt for Herluin, started the pair on their
way at dawn. And now the wind came shouting through
the forest : high up the trees were bared, and suddenly a
grey embattled shape stood out upon the eastward skyline.

" Look, Denise, there is Montenair."

" Oh ! Still so far away ! "

" Only five miles. Here, let me see your shoe."

Hand on a tree-bole, Denise flexed a knee and cast a
doubtful glance backwards.

" There *is* a hole," she said. " And at home I have seven
pairs, three of them with gloves to match. Herluin, you do
look cross ! "

He cut and tore a long strip of cloth from his cloak, and
wound it round the broken shoe, knotting it on the instep.
Then, as they slunk on their way, swift storms of rain swept
out of the south-east, blotting from view the ranges towards
Belsaunt and the towers of Montenair. Herluin was drenched,
for he had given the torn cloak of the Butcher to the daughter
of the Butcher's enemy ; and now, so near to safety, he was
more than ever scared lest some mischance befall her.

Above a slope waist-high in sopping bracken the child
called out and pointed, and Herluin's heart seemed risen to
his throat ; then he stared, for far ahead, beneath a ragged
edge of dark low-driven cloud, a glow of tawny sunlight fell
as though into another world. There water gleamed, and
poplar-studded flats gave tints of green and gold beyond the
sombre fringes of the forest.

" What is it, Herluin ? " squealed Denise through wind
and rain.

He turned to look at her—at her fair face with its childish
curves, with its ill-smeared mask of brown that had not
touched pink ear or little cream-white throat—at the slender
figure whelmed to its ankles in his flapping cloak ; and
again he wished she were Yseult, that, trusting her utterly,
he might say " That is my barony."

Instead, he smiled and stepped to where Denise stood
beside a grey and wrinkled beech-trunk.

" The Marshes of Marckmont," he cried. " And just
beneath us is the road. Come . . . and, Lady Denise, will
you remember that my name is Herluin Forester ? "

" Will I remember—— ? "

The blue eyes were puzzled, the full lips parted.

" But of course.   Why should I have forgotten ? "

" Oh, it is no matter," he replied, giving her his hand
across a rain-filled hollow.   She seemed to have no memory
of his unguarded war-shout ; nor, indeed, would it greatly
have mattered had she known who he was, but the instinct
of secrecy was now so strong in him that he felt a danger had
passed him by.

Noon.   A twelve-foot ivied wall, a niche holding a blue-
gowned Mother of God, a massive oaken door half-covered
with plates and studs and scrolls of iron, a chain that woke
a muffled clangour in the grey-white gate-house.   Then a
wait in the relentless rain, a sharp sound as the panel moved
behind the little grille, a steady scrutiny from beady eyes
beneath a huge starched coif. . . .

" I pray you take this ring to the Lady Abbess," said
Herluin wearily.   " And if it please you to return before
we are drowned, I verily believe Our Lady will be glad."

At last the great door opened noiselessly, and haggard
youth and limping child passed into cleanliness and gloom
and silence, along corridors that bore faint odours of sweet
herbs and new-scoured stone. . . .

The Abbess was young and stout and grim ; her capable
fingers crisped on the arms of her great chair, and the gold
cross heaved on the broad bosom of her grey habit.

" This is she who they say goes corseted with iron,"
thought Herluin, who was again falling into a recklessness
of hunger and fatigue.   " In which case I behold a miracle."

But aloud he said, with an unsteady bow :   " Reverend
Mother in God, I, Herluin Forester, have the honour to
render to you your niece, the Lady Dionysia de Saint-
Aunay."

Denise had already scuttled forward and fallen on her
knees, clasping and kissing the plump white hand that came
out to her ; and over the wet gold of the bowed curls the
Abbess looked fixedly at Herluin.   Her other hand moved
to a tiny silver bell that stood on a table at her elbow ; at
its melodious tinkle a door burst silently open behind her.

Into the room stalked a gaunt nun, her face creasing in anxious tenderness at the child's plight.

" Sister, my niece. A bath and clothes for her as soon as may be—— " and a gesture seemed to sweep nun and child away.

" And now, young stranger, who are you, and how came you into this guardianship ? "

" More lies," thought Herluin, embarking on a tale of flight from the town of Alanol. Of his meeting with Denise he told all save Ferrand's confession ; and at the finish he pled urgency of news to be communicated to the Castellan.

" One moment," said the Abbess shortly. " Tell me, what do *you* know of this great wickedness of yester-eve ? "

" Naught, Lady Abbess. That is to say, I heard the din in the Castle ; that is all. And in the town there were rumours that . . . that my lord your brother and his lady were slain out of hand . . . but how the rumours got about I know not."

The Abbess compressed her lips and crossed herself twice ; otherwise she betrayed no emotion.

" Why were you fleeing ? " she demanded.

" I—I quarrelled with one of the Riders of Campscapel, and in Alanol it is not safe to do that."

" You look for a reward ? "

" No ; unless some day, since the little maid is safe, I might ask shelter for another fugitive knowing it would not be refused."

" It would not be refused," said the Abbess roundly. " But tell me, were you apprenticed in Alanol ? "

" No . . . no." Then, urgently : " Reverend Mother, I pray you will give me leave to seek my lord the Castellan."

" I give you leave ; but if you are wise, Master Herluin, you will answer his questioning more straightly than you have answered mine."

Again the bell tinkled, and presently Herluin found himself once more out on the road, plodding wearily through the puddles towards the walled village that nestled beside the castled rock of Montenair. Rain had ceased, and shapes of blue sky widened behind the limestone crag ; neither the

steep which his fasting body must encounter, nor prospect
of fronting the grim Castellan, could rob the wanderer of a
stir of heart's delight in that the face of Yseult might shortly
be revealed to him.   As if to seal some promise of felicity, a
shaft of sunlight broke and brightened athwart the bulk of
the castle ;   and Herluin doffed his steel cap and crossed
himself.

" Sweet Jesu send me sight of her," he whispered.   " Holy
Mary guard me from fear and folly and despair."

Then he capped himself again—too tired to resent the grin
with which the elderly sergeant of the gate had watched his
movement, yet not too tired to achieve a grin himself when he
brandished the signet of Campscapel beneath the sergeant's
goggling eyes.

" Death and damnation ! " wheezed the ancient.   " Who
are you ? "

" No matter.   Bid someone lead me to my lord Castellan."

So Herluin dragged one foot after another up the cobbled
way above the village, keeping his eyes for the most part
fixed upon the steel of an archer's scabbard-tip that winked
ahead of him.

" You come from Alanol ? " asked the guide presently.

" Yes."

" Saw you aught of the raid on Saint-Aunay ? "

" Yes."

" What, then ? "

" Yes."

The archer wheeled, observed a grey face, and caught his
charge by the arm.

" Come, we are nearly there," he grumbled kindly.   " By
the Mass, your gear is soaked.   Had I known you so far
spent I could have found a stoup at the guard-house . . . well
do I know the torment of long marches . . . I'll warrant
your shirt is round your neck and the tail-end of you on
fire. . . .

" Nevertheless you did well not to tarry.   My lord
Castellan is hard, but he rewards stout service.   Yesterday
he rode to the ruins of Saint-Aunay, he and the Sieur Rogier ;
and bleak of face they were when they came again, for the
little Countess was of their kindred.   And the Sieur Rogier

halted only to change horses, and then was off like the wind
along the Belsaunt road. But I believe him bound for the
Duke at Saulte ; for the damned Butcher is so guarded by
his hills and bogs that even my lord cannot engage him
without assistance. And there is need to hurry if aught is
to be done before the weather breaks. I do not remember so
fine and dry an autumn in twenty years. As for the other
lords, Guarenal is old, and Ger sends word the Easterlings
are out along the coast ; the Prince's seneschal has fallen
foul of Barberghe, and only Montcarneau is with my lord
as yet."

"Montcarneau ? " mumbled Herluin, roused by the name.

"Ay. The new Count, this tall young Sieur Alain. We
were surprised to see him, for his father hated my lord
Castellan."

"Alain is here . . . and Rogier is away ? "

Herluin lifted his eyes to the castle, only half-aware of the
archer's startled face and more respectful grip.

"I am no longer Herluin," he reminded himself. "Now
I am once more Raoul."

Curious stares of men-at-arms and grooms. Words
between his guide and another—words ringing hollow
beneath a gloomy arch, yet seeming far away. Glistening
cobbles, flagged and vaulted passage-ways, a trim reach of
grass, dark splendour of yews against a limestone wall ; and
all the time a crooning of wind through the enchanted wards
of Montenair. . . .

A curtain of green velvet, thickly sown with lilies of new
cloth of silver ; to tired eyes the brightness of the stiff heraldic
flowers advanced them strangely from their sombre field.
Then another passage, plastered white and leading to an open
door, beyond whose flanking columns the leaves of a creeper
shivered, blood-red in sunshine of the autumn afternoon.

And beyond again . . .

Raoul checked his shambling stride and leaned against
the plastered wall ; he endured thick heart-beats and a spasm
of the midriff, and then lost every sense save that of sight.

Out in the garth Yseult de Olencourt stood gowned in
colours of amber and silver amid a whirl of feasting pigeons.

Pink-brown and blue-grey, with rainbow-feathered necks and breasts, the plump marauders mobbed their benefactress ; to the soft tumult of their cooing they alighted on her shoulders and extended arms, pecked at the corn in her open palms, and brushed her bright côte-hardi with their wings as they fluttered down to fight around her feet.

" No, no, you must not quarrel," fluted Yseult, staying one combat with a flip of her slim fingers. " Knave Joscelin, I know you by your ring ; shame on you for a bully. And you, whoever you may be, avaunt your muddy claws from my new headdress ! "

The turn of a cream-white throat as Yseult shook the intruder off—the little grimace, sun-dazzled, comical, which brought her fierce brows down and pouted her gentle mouth —held the onlooker bewitched. One ruffled blue-grey head came thrusting beneath the girlish chin ; one questing beak assayed the little pearls set in embroidery about the square-cut neck of the amber gown, and, thwarted of food, nudged boldly at the miracle that was the shoulder of Yseult. . . .

" Oh God, the silly, happy pigeons," whispered Raoul . . . and started as the archer's voice resounded from the gloom ahead of him.

" Not that way, stranger. Along here."

" I follow," Raoul called unwillingly.

Yseult heard their voices, and glanced between shifting bodies and whirling wings towards the creeper-clad doorway. For an instant her steady grey eyes met the worshipping glare of the halted wanderer ; then, unperturbed, she looked away, and Raoul knew himself for nothing and less than nothing— a wraith, a scarecrow planted in the mud far down the slopes that led the valorous and the true to Paradise.

Dropping his mired hand from the wall—the proud wall that her cloak had maybe brushed in passing—he stumbled forward, drunken with joy and riven with humility. And presently, seeing a snub-nosed page hold wide a curtain and look straight through him, he came to the end of his flight from Red Jehan and Red Anne and the red night on the rock of Campscapel.

VIII

PARLEY AT MONTENAIR

FULK DE OLENCOURT, Count of Olencourt and Castellan of
the royal hold and county of Montenair, was deemed formidable even among the harsh lords of Honoy and Nordanay ;
his lands were so trimmed of disorder that Joris of the Rock
himself would harry the farms of the dreaded Butcher before
he thrust his outlawed nose into Fulk's marches. Thus it
was not without trepidation that Raoul faced the eyebrows
conjoined in one black furious bush upon the bronzed face
of the Castellan.

" Stand fast, fool," was his inward exhortation to himself.
" You are a man now ; you have seen your love and slain
your foe."

But it was utter weariness that steadied his dogged answers
when the floor-boards thrilled to the great war-captain's voice.
Fulk the Castellan was saving of speech, and not until the
Butcher's signet shone on his horny palm did a surly comment
pass his lips.

" I doubt not the Count of Alanol lay very dead before you
came by this ring."

" My lord Castellan, you do not believe I slew him ? "

" I do not. He is dead, it may be ; and you have his ring
. . . that is, you had his ring. Much of your tale I can test ;
but by your mien you could barely lift the sword of such an
one as Butcher Lorin, and this talk of a witch-brew rings
idly on the ear. If you be that runaway Baron of Marckmont
what thought you to gain by coming here ? "

" My lord," said Raoul, forlornly but with black anger in
his heart, " I hoped you would allow me to remain until I
am of age, and then would aid me in the obtaining of my
barony. If you wage war on Jehan de Campscapel I ask no
more than to follow Rogier into battle ; indeed I can be of
service. . . ."

" How ? "

Raoul swayed on his feet, and a veil of changing green
and purple seemed to float between his own eyes and the
hard grey eyes of the Castellan ; but the hint of derision in
that curt challenge sealed his lips upon the secret of the stair.
Heedless of any complication that might ensue thereafter, he
let spite rule him, and broke into a faltering reply.

" I . . . I know the town of Alanol, my lord, and the
marches of the Campscapels. But if you think me a liar
I would beg to be allowed to go my way."

" Whither ? "

" To my lord Duke at Saulte."

" H'm. Page ! "

The snub-nosed boy bounced into the room and stood
attentively before his lord.

" Bid my lady the Countess attend me forthwith, and tell
my lord of Montcarneau that I ask immediate speech with
him."

The page bowed and disappeared ; Raoul fixed a blurred
gaze on the gleam of the Butcher's signet, which the Castellan
had slipped upon his own ring-finger. And whilst they
waited the Castellan spoke again.

" How fled you from the hold above Alanol ? "

Raoul summoned the lie direct.

" I—I am not large, my lord. I crawled through a
window, dropped into the moat, and swam across ; then I
ran through the woods, helped first by darkness, and then
by morning mist. But . . ."

" But what ? "

" M-may I have my ring again, my lord ? "

" No."

" Then let my curse abide with you for ever, you hulking
hog of the forest," thought Raoul dully. " Yseult's brother
or no, you gain no help from me against Red Jehan, unless
Rogier move you to more courtesy on his return."

" Now, hearken," began the Castellan, reaching out for
paper and a quill. " How many men has the Count of
Alanol in garrison ? "

And Raoul was floundering in reply to searching military
inquisition when the curtains parted to admit a buxom woman
with the fair aquiline features of the house of Saulte.

" My lady, do you know this lad ? "

For all her fairness the Countess had brown eyes—eyes kindly if commanding as they searched the wanderer's face.

" Not I," came her blithe avowal. " But whosoever he be, my lord, in God's name let him seat himself ere he fall to pieces. Page, ho ! A goblet of wine of Estragon from the cupboard in my chamber . . . here is the key . . . be swift, and bring the flask as well. And now, my lord, who is it ? "

" Perhaps my lord Count here can tell you," said the Castellan.

Pink-faced and golden-haired, with the radiance and stature of the Sieur Achilles before Troy, the Count of Montcarneau lounged into the room.

" This ? " he drawled, in a voice well-nigh as deep as the Castellan's own. " I do not know . . . that is . . . one moment ! "

Recognition dawned in his blue good-natured eyes, and he smiled.

" Sanctalbastre ! " he exclaimed, so that the name held the sound of an oath. " It is Raoul of Marckmont, nephew of Armand of Ger ! Raoul, what are you doing here ? I heard tell you were dead."

The Castellan grunted, and the vigorous voice of the Countess checked and overwhelmed the beginning of Raoul's answer to Alain.

" Sweet Mary save us, Alain, you are right. Page, serve my lord of Marckmont."

" Gramercy, gentle Countess," croaked Raoul. " I pledge you, and you my lords, in this fair goblet."

" Poor lad, you look nigh done," cried the compassionate lady. " I mind you now—you came here on a time with the old Countess Adela . . . page, fill up again . . . it may be Yseult will remember you, for you played together in this room."

" It may be so, my lady," responded Raoul darkly, in a voice he scarcely knew for his own.

There came a flush on his cheek, a pleasant swirling in his head, and a great ease through all his body ; he set about

rising from his chair, and when he spoke again his words
were thickened and portentous.

"I hope it may be so, my lady; and I pray the Sieur God
we may all meet in Paradise. But as things are . . ."

As things were, Raoul was too drunk to stand upright.
Vaguely he heard a boomed command from the Castellan;
then a tall squire lifted him and carried him away, to strip
and tub him as though he were a child.

He slept in the bath-tub, and slept at table before a half-
consumed dish of venison and eels; and at length he slept
like a log in the bed of the absent Rogier.

On the night of the following day, when Raoul entered
the Castellan's winter parlour, it was plain that Yseult had
quite forgotten him. She gave him a polite considering
stare that racked him with its half-amused indifference;
then she shook her comely head, and there came again the
whir of her spinning-wheel and the deft movements of her
strong slim hands.

"I never remember further back than my last going to
confession," she complained, with a mischievous glance at
the Countess.

"I myself," ventured Raoul hardily, "am otherwise
blest . . . or curst. Shall I tell you, Lady Yseult, the
colours of your arrayment at the Belsaunt tourney six months
past?"

Ruefully his divinity smiled at him.

"Of your pity, forbear," she exclaimed. "Only to-day
I looked at that dreadful antiquity, wondering what mischief
I could work that I might not wear it again."

Raoul forbore, growing hot and cold by turns; this time
the shuttlecock between them was of conversation, and
woefully it fell and lay when she had struck her blow at it.
Thereafter he pretended to watch the fire, stealing as many
glances as he dared at the pure untroubled profile above the
spinning-wheel. . .

Yseult had smiled at him . . . as though he were a figure
in the arras. He thanked his Saints that he had spoken
apart to the Countess and Alain concerning his adventures,
without care for his suppression and evasion of the truth;

for to lie to Yseult would have been a kind of blasphemy, and
he was well content that she displayed no curiosity to hear his
story.   Nor, since the chief personages in the room made no
reference thereto, could any of the household gentlefolk well
entice him into speech ;   and for the greater part of the
evening the ardours of Raoul burned smokily behind a pale
impassive face.

From beneath the mesh of a gauzy sleeve the faint gleam
of Yseult's round forearm mazed him ;   it was as though he
had never seen a maid's arm before.   Yet barely a fortnight
had gone by since he struggled in the embrace of naked
Lys . . . a year of growth and hazard seemed compressed
between that strange hour and this—between black art on
the rock of Campscapel and white enchantment on the rock
of Montenair.

Meanwhile, Alain was telling an interminable hunting-
tale to the Countess ;   and Raoul listened idly to the hum of
conversation as it reached his corner of the room.

" . . . but in sooth the Countess of Burias has one ear of
the King, and the Cardinal Count the other.   The Queen is
naught, poor lady, especially now that she is fallen sick.   So
that Saulte and my lord are without support in Hautarroy ;
for Thorismund of Hastain is, to speak the truth, an idle
little rip ;   and the Archbishop is very old.   No, ladies, I fear
there are those will condone the Butcher's raid for the hatred
they bore to Saint-Aunay, and for spite of my lord and the
Duke of Saulte. . . ."

" Yet if the Butcher be dead indeed . . ."

" Sst !   The little Baron there will hear you."

" Let him withal.   I would say, if the Butcher be dead,
there is naught to prevent my lords from luring Jehan out
into the hills . . . it is only a matter of provocation."

That was the comptroller of the Castellan's household,
himself an Olencourt and a proud chevalier.   Humped
against the wall in his shadowy corner, Raoul marked the
speaker down for hatred.   If only Rogier were come !

And then . . . how, if you were a maid, look on the fairness and bigness of Alain without a fascination ?   Alain was
modest, courteous, something dull, but in the lists a very
lion. . . .

"He could take me by the ankles, whirl me round his head, and throw me twenty yards," reflected Raoul drearily. "Saint Barruc aid us, how he drones on!"

"By that time," Alain was saying reminiscently, "we had two boars of pride, but my best hound was dead as I have told you. And coming to a stream we found two stags at battle royal, and Robin winding his horn. . . ."

"That will be caitiff Robin Barberghe," mused Raoul. "No matter where I listen I meet with some reminder of despite and woe. Yet Alain is only here to help the damned Castellan against the thrice-damned Jehan de Campscapel . . . and I am a jealous half-wit, lacking grace to grasp what happiness is offered me by the Sieur God."

Three pages, smooth-faced boys in liveries of green and silver, sat or stood in his range of vision. He suspected them of adoring Yesult; any who did not must be clod and churl, yet one presumptuous little hound—he of the fair hair and snub nose—seemed too attentively to watch her. . . .

"Mary Mother," was Raoul's silent exclamation, "am I fallen to wrath against her servitors because they serve her? Next I shall hate herself because I love her, because she sits ten feet away from me and feels no faintest ripple of this my desperation. . . ."

His roving and splenetic gaze came next to rest on the tapestried figure of Saint Sebastian, who meekly endured the inconvenience of a dozen arrows in his limbs and body.

"Ay, sweet Saint," thought Raoul, "but were you ever in love?" And then: "Now, who is this who comes in jingling spurs? Ah, it is the squire who tended me."

The tall half-armoured squire strode straight across the chamber and bowed to the Castellan's lady before whispering in the ear of the Count of Montcarneau. A spinning-wheel was checked and moved again; Alain stood up.

"My lady," he said, "my lord Castellan would have speech with me. I crave permission to continue my tale another time."

"God aid you, poor Countess," rose in Raoul's mind. Then he shrank in his chair, lest he be called upon to take the place of the departing paladin; but the Castellan's wife had had her fill of manly egotism for the while.

" Boy, give us a song ! " she called over her shoulder ;
and the snub-nosed page sat down by the great harp and
raised a youthful chirp.

" What song will please you, my lady ? "

" Oh, *Huon's Hunting* or *Now Raveth Alured* . . .
something with a lilt in it."

The harp spoke quietly, and the page sang :

> *Full fiercely Dom Cupid*
> *Doth plague and annoy.*
> *Alured is mournful,*
> *For Meldreth is scornful ;*
> *Alured is dupéd,*
> *For Meldreth is stupid,*
> *He deemeth her a creature*
> *Of gold sans alloy,*
> *Outmatching in feature*
> *Dame Helen of Troy.*
> *In dolour and distress*
> *For lack of his mistress*
> *Now raveth Alured*
> *Bereft of all joy.*
> *In folly immuréd*
> *He deemeth her above him,*
> *But if she should love him*
> *Then hapless Alured*
> *Perchance would be curéd.*
> *For Meldreth is stupid,*
> *Alured is dupéd,*
> *So fiercely Dom Cupid*
> *Doth plague and annoy !*

" A silly idle round," thought Raoul when the page began ;
and " Well sung, Jorian ! " cried the Countess when he
finished.

" A good song," mumbled the Castellan's aged chamberlain, who had entered meanwhile. " Ay, a good song. Did
ever I tell you, my lady, how on the eve of Harksburg we——"

The alarmed brown eyes of the Castellan's lady sought
swiftly round the room and came to rest on Raoul's face.

" It may be the Sieur Baron will sing to us," she interrupted hurriedly.

" My lady, I sing but ill," lied Raoul with gloom.

Then he too had the harp against his shoulder, and the

room fell still. For a moment he strummed thoughtfully, and then went white, and overrode his fear, and spoke.

"This, gentle Countess, is a *Song of Lilies from a Lady's Garden.*"

And huskily he began:

> *When his home hills were dark against your sunset*
> *Stood she ever beside you for a space,*
> *Or ever saw you, in that shadowed place,*
> *Bowing your frail heads at the wind's shrill onset,*
> *And touch'd you gently ere she rais'd her face?*
>
> *Came there never a mist of doubt or wonder*
> *In those clear eyes, far-set upon the west?*
> *Did no fleet-winging prayer or behest,*
> *A golden echo in the wind's low thunder,*
> *Assail her, eloquent of love distrest?*
>
> *Softly they answer, nodding all together:*
> *"We saw her, listening when twilight fell*
> *To clamorous wind and chiming vesper-bell;*
> *We heard her laugh in the wild summer weather;*
> *Now hope thou on; thy love hath wish'd thee well."*

Yseult glanced up when he had done, but he dared not meet her eyes. The snub-nosed page chuckled, and turned the chuckle to a cough. Amidst feeble applause a lady giggled openly, and somewhere a man snorted.

"Gramercy for your song, my lord," cried the Countess with a too-emphatic cheerfulness.

"Plague me if I understood a word of it," quavered the old chamberlain. "But now, my lady, on the eve of Harksburg, when we sang in our tents . . ."

"Much better to have run away at Harksburg," thought Raoul with bitterness, "than to play the fanciful clown at Montenair. What under Heaven made me sing that folly? Raving Alured himself could have done no worse."

No one asked him where he got the song. His misery became so exquisite that it pleased him. He even ceased to want the vitals of the snub-nosed page dispersed about the rush-strewn floor. . . .

That night he slept ill, and in the morning rose with a feeling of wan splendour. He fancied that winks and grins were exchanged behind his back; and after he had broken fast (Yseult, alas, a table's-length away from him) it occurred

to him to sally forth and inquire after the health of Denise
at the abbey gate.

But before he set foot on the drawbridge the steel of a
pike-head descended before his face, and to his astonished
query came a stolid answer :

" My lord Castellan's orders : you, my lord, are not to
leave the castle."

The Castellan had ridden out with Alain and a dozen
gentlemen. To plead or argue with the Countess would
further shock a battered self-esteem ; and furiously Raoul
retraced his steps through the ominous wards of Montenair.

When he had flung his bascinet and belt and sword upon
Rogier's bed he stared awhile from Rogier's window, which
gave out on the curtain-wall and on a dead end of rampart-
walk above a small yew-bordered garth which Raoul had
noticed when he first traversed the hold. Walls almost blank
stood over the garth, which was plainly meant for ladies' air
and privacy ; and from the walk above it was visible a lordly
westward sweep of forest, moor, and mountain. But beneath
the rampart-wall . . .

" A drop of a hundred feet and more, plump on to the
main road," thought Raoul miserably. " And now I still
might gain my liberty if I revealed to the Castellan the secret
way into the hold of Campscapel. But I will not, yet.
Rogier, old friend, come soon."

" Lady Yseult, can you tell me when Rogier is expected
to return ? "

" Oh, it is you, my lord. . . . I do not know, but it
should be to-morrow at the latest."

November sunlight laid pale banners across the floor of
the winter parlour. Faint music of the harp had drawn him
to the door ; Yseult was practising, alone.

" Where have you been, my lord ? "

" This morning I have found I am your brother's prisoner ;
and I have since been praying in the chapel."

" God grant your prayers," said the girl absently.

Raoul grew still as a stone.

" But I am sorry Fulk should hold you against your will.
He is too stern sometimes. . . ."

" It cannot be helped till Rogier return," muttered Raoul ;
and then, more clearly : " But I beg you let me not interrupt
you ; and I will listen if I may."

" Listen if you will.   It is not much to hear."

She reached for a silken kerchief, and a weird gust of
thinnest ghost-music woke beneath its brushing touch along
the strings.

" The war-horns of the host of faëry," murmured Raoul.

" Too much beeswax," amended Yseult.

And presently her fingers roused a plaintive melody that
wrung the listener's heart.   Seated upon a cushioned stool,
Raoul leaned against painted panelling and watched the
player. . . .

Faint sunbeams had their will of her ; beneath the gauze
frontlet of her steepled headdress her wide, childish forehead
moved in a pearly dusk, and little ghostly shadows played on
her round neck and in the folds of the long veil that hung
behind her shoulders.   And again it seemed impossible that
she should sit there, calm and intent, as though unconscious
of his presence ; something *must* reach her of this stress that
mounted to his throat. . . .

The little melody ran sombrely towards fulfilment ;
Yseult's grey eyes looked far away, but once her red mouth
twitched at a slur of notes.   Why did she not sit still ?   She
did not do herself great credit on the harp. . . .

Ashamed to stare too hard, Raoul tore his gaze away from
her and fixed it fiercely on the gilded gryphon's claw at the
harp's foot.   The glitter of the claw began to maze him ;
three final chords dispersed what sense was left to him. . . .

" Gramercy for your fair playing, Lady Yseult."   (Was
this hoarse voice his own ?)

" It is not so fair as yours."

" Ah, that . . . tell me, what thought you of my song
last night ? "

" It was . . ."

" In brief, you did not approve it.   It shall not be sung
again."

The oddness of his tone arrested her attention ; for the
last time she had looked at him as at a figure in the
arras.

" Why should it not be sung again ? It was a pretty little song, if difficult to understand."

" It was a memory of a thing that never happened . . . and you did not like it. You have silenced it for ever."

Yseult looked away, with a faint line between proud black brows, and the slightest shrug of cream-white shoulders. And Raoul sympathised with her impatience.

" What difference does it make whether I liked it or not ? " she asked incuriously.

Raoul rose from his stool, and stood, with hands behind him, looking down at her half-averted face.

" All difference in this world," he said unsteadily. " And for aught I know, the difference also between heaven and hell."

Yseult's head turned ; Yseult's long lashes rose. A frankly curious stare, as old as Eve, as young as seventeen, took tribute in innocent triumph before the grey eyes clouded with amused distress.

" My lord," she murmured, " this seems to me a very sudden folly."

" Folly it may be ; sudden it is not. It has been six months in the weaving—since May, when I saw you at the Bishop's tourney in Belsaunt city. Graciously you said, ' God grant your prayers ' ; my chiefest prayer was, as it has been since that day beside the lists, that one day I may hope to . . . to ask you to be Lady of Marckmont. . . ."

" *Lady of Marckmont*," exclaimed Yseult, and laughed.

Embarrassment, and not disdain, might well have prompted that quick stifled laughter ; but it checked the flow of Raoul's eloquence and sent him down upon one knee. Four towers above a causeway, and a waste of sand and marsh and forest . . . all seemed blown to shreds by the light breath of a maid. . . .

" Hear me, Lady Yseult. All that forbids my hope I know. . . ."

Yseult had risen in her turn, and her eyes darkened as she interrupted him.

" You do *not* know ; your words betray the depth of your unwisdom. Say no more to me . . . you do me honour of a . . . you do me honour, and I can only wound you. Besides, in a little while the Countess comes. . . ."

"And, if she find me thus, will deem me madder than ever? My barony, then, is one with my song and my slaying of the Butcher—matter for mirth at Montenair. So be it. Yet you have long borne my love between your hands—oh, well I know you had no least thought of it " (for Yseult had made a little loosing gesture with her fingers) " —and what is comical to you is dear and desperate to me ; but I would serve you to the death if I knew how. As for honour, I can bring none yet ; all the honour is mine, that I have told my love to the loveliest maiden under heaven."

"I pray you have done."

"I will have done . . . I may have no hope at all ? "

"None."

"Why ?—ah, no, I have no right to ask. Forgive me."

In a strange exaltation of defeat Raoul stood upright, trembling as he had not trembled before the Castellan ; deep down in him an elfin stave seemed piping : *The arras comes to life*. Silence heavy with unresolved emotion was cleft by Yseult's cool voice.

"Forgive you ? There is nothing to forgive, except that . . ."

"That what ? "

"No matter."

"Tell me."

"No."

"Then . . ."

The life in Raoul went overstretched and limp, for all the world like a ruined bowstring. Words that had crowded to his lips fell away and were lost. Nothing mattered ; the sunlight was dim, the world preposterous and awry. Even the lovely breathing shape of the girl grew foreign to his eyes.

"Then I will even forgive you that you are Yseult," he said.

He bowed, and somehow reached the door. His fingers shook on the wood, and he looked back. Yseult stood watching him, her gaze half-pitying, half-askance ; but when he halted she turned aside to the harp.

"Back into the arras, fool ! " said Raoul to himself. "You would now look well indeed beside good Saint Sebastian."

As the door closed behind him there came one little

random sweep of music from the room.   It was a queer and
lonely sound, he thought—as though the Sieur God had set
a useless heart upon His thumb and flipped it idly into bound-
less night.

Dusk at Montenair.   Raoul, who again had slept as one
dead throughout the afternoon, slipped out of the window of
Rogier's room, and, standing on the rampart-walk, leaned
in a crenel and peered down the castle cliff.   It was as he had
expected ; the road ran greyly far below.   As ever, the height
played havoc with his body ; he braced himself against the
parapet and scowled across the darkening ravine.

"Now might I brand my love into her memory," he
mused, "by yielding to this deathly tug of the abyss.   But
mine is not the anatomy of a martyr.   Nevertheless I would
risk a broken leg to part with my lord Castellan . . . the
forest that was full of menace wears a homelier look to-night.
Now, who are these ? "

Voices and footsteps rang in the passage opening on the
little garth, and all Raoul's desire that evening was to shun
his kind.   The two thick yews nearest Rogier's window
overtopped the rampart-walk by three feet or more ; in a
trice Raoul was prone behind them, invisible to any standing
in the enclosure below.

"Saint Barruc send they do not mount the walk," went
through his mind.   "So Modred lay to spy on Guinevere,
until Lancelot plucked him from the wall."   Then, as a
double footfall checked and softened on the grass : "Holy
Mary, my thought was apter than I knew.   It is Yseult with
Alain de Montcarneau."

"No, no, Alain, not here ! " came the girl's fluting whisper.
"You must not . . . we may so easily be seen ! "

"The rooks flew high this sundown, Lady Yseult,"
responded Alain with a loud solemnity.   "It should be fine
to-morrow."

The deep drawl caught on a stifled laugh, and Yseult
gave a little gasp of pleasure and alarm.

"And to-morrow," went on Alain in a lower key, "I
must to Ger, to press for aid from the Count Warden.   I
could not refuse . . .   I will yet force your grumpy Fulk to

lay aside his enmity towards my house . . . and then, sweetheart. . . ."

Except that Raoul's spine seemed crawling of its own motion, he was stiller than the stiff yews beside him ; and whilst the ruin of his hopes was sown with salt he clenched his teeth and fought to keep his breath inaudible even to himself.

"But you will come again with speed," said Yseult happily. " You will not wait for that grim Count of Ger ? "

" No, even if the Easterlings be out I swear to run away. And Armand should be glad to see me, for I shall take and render to him, in token of Fulk's amity and hope of aid, this woeful chicken Raoul of Marckmont."

The woeful chicken shut his eyes ; worse even than dread of Ger and fury against the Castellan was the mention between these two of his own name.

" She has told Alain," he thought. " Or if not, she will tell him now."

But Yseult was silent for a moment, and when she spoke again her voice was grave.

" Poor Raoul," she murmured. " He is not so foolish as you think, Alain."

" ' For he loves *me* ! ' " rang the frantic secret gibe in Raoul's brain.

" He is foolish enough, God knows, if he thinks he slew the Butcher. I doubt not the drug of which he spoke worked wonders in his poet's noddle. I would I had heard his daft little song. Sunsets and promises and lilies, the comptroller said."

Then Yseult, too, laughed.

" He may be an oddity," she said, " but I call it shame to send him back to Ger. He should rather be put into the Church. I do not think he will be happy out of it."

" Maybe. I find small hope of cheer in his morrow's company."

" Nevertheless you must be courteous to him. He is gentle, and cousin to the king, and I would not have him altogether rue his memory of Montenair."

" Oh, I will bear with him . . . but now . . ."

" No, no, Alain ! "

" Yes, yes, Yseult ! "

" No . . . ah, but you are strong, and I am glad. You hurt me, and it is sweet. Let be, dear thief ! "

Alain's voice when he spoke again was sunk and blurred with passion.

" Yseult, my life's delight, there blossoms no such fruit as this in the orchards of Paradise ! "

Man's scorn and maiden's pity were nothing now ; Raoul, mindful of what fruit was yielded to Alain, felt his whole being tilt and swither on the verge of madness. One hand twitched backward towards his dagger-hilt ; but he checked it, and again grew rigid in his place. The blood sang curiously in his ears, and through his clothes the chill of stone invaded all his body.

" I pray you, Alain, have done," said Yseult, hoarsely.

A laugh that was half a sob, a kiss, and receding footsteps, the lighter first, the heavier following after. Then . . . nothing but the stir of autumn wind across the darkling reaches of the forest and the stark walls of Montenair.

Night fell. Raoul had dragged himself back into Rogier's room. Fallen face downward on the bed, he lay dry-eyed and motionless, in battle with the fiend of his adversity.

" I would she had mocked me for Alain's diversion," he told himself. " Then I might hate and despise her, and find some ease. Why did she spare me ? Was she ashamed of my devotion ? *Lady of Marckmont*, she said . . . and laughed.

" I made of her a divinity scarcely to be loved for reverence. I find she is flesh and blood. What quarrel have I with her that she is herself, and not the painted image of my dream ? *None*. . . .

" Even Alain I cannot hate as I would wish, or I might warn my lord Castellan that his orchard gates are down. Some would now name her wanton, hearing what I have heard . . . and more would call it folly for a maid to yield so much so soon. . . .

" But if Alain be true she has done no wrong. . . . Saints witness she has done no wrong, to herself or any other. Alain is worthy as any man can be of . . . go hang yourself,

F

Alain . . . yet even out of your carcase your love tore strange
and gentle words. Fell passion which could make a poet
of *you*. . . .

"But if you be false to her, Alain, by God and all His
angels I will somehow cut your heart out, ay, though you
wring my neck the while. . . .

"Yet she loves him, and he her, in a way she seems to
understand. Sunsets and promises and lilies are poor
watery stuff beside the plundering lips of a paladin. And
indeed she is only a maid like any other maid. Yseult, your
fool is madder than Alured in the song; since you are mortal,
and therefore in some measure to be pitied, he loves you
more than ever, and would comfort you because you are
neither so fair not yet so pure as the Holy Mother of God. . . .

"Perhaps Red Anne is even more glorious of face and
body than are you; and Lys, maybe, is braver, and Denise
more innocent. But it is you I love. Shall I tell Alain the
secret of the Butcher's stair, that he may use it to gain favour
with Fulk the Castellan? That would bring you to his arms
with none to overhear. . . .

"No, I will not. That were a slavish meekness to which
I am not yet descended. Let Alain buy that secret with my
liberty to-morrow. But there is yet one Olencourt to see,
and maybe I shall not 'altogether rue my memory of Montenair.' "

To Fulk he was a pawn, to Yseult a wisp of irrelevance;
now remained Rogier.

Upon the following morning, when Raoul got to horse,
the blaze of a score of Alain's surcoats lightened the mid-
November gloom of the bailey of Montenair. Yseult looked
curiously at him, as a child will watch a fly whose wings he
has torn off; and Raoul contorted his features into the
semblance of a smile before he looked away.

All in a creeping mist the banner of Montcarneau hung
slanted from its pole in the hand of a grim squire; its field
was quartered red and yellow, and in each quarter grinned
a wolf's-head of the other colour.

"I would gladly exchange you, beasts, for grey wolves
of the forest," thought Raoul.

Then Alain came to mount, drawing on shining gauntlets, and there was a great jingling of bits and stamping of horse-hoofs.

" You will accompany the Count Alain to Ger," the Castellan had said to Raoul on the previous night. Since then he had not deigned to notice him. Only the Countess had been kind, giving Raoul a new cloak and leathern gloves ; but no one thought of finding him any spurs, and the gelding assigned to him moved sorrily enough amid the trampling destriers.

Nevertheless he was not obviously a prisoner ; he wore his sword, and the Countess had sent the snub-nosed page to polish up his steel cap and clean the boots of humpbacked Dirck that one Herluin had stolen from the keep of Campscapel. . . .

Alain had clashed into his saddle when the watchman's horn wailed twice from a gateway turret. Raoul stiffened where he sat and fixed his eyes on the bailey entry. . . .

Mud-splashed riders and weary horses filed beneath the arch ; and under the foremost lifted visor a haughty Olencourt face lit with a tired smile at sight of the glittering Count of Montcarneau.

" Ha, Rogier ! " boomed Alain. " Well met ! I will in again to hear what the Duke has said."

As Alain swung to the cobbles Raoul edged his mount forward.

" Rogier ! " he cried joyfully. " Rogier ! You remember me ! " Tall Rogier treated him to a puzzled stare.

" Why, yes," he said vaguely. " You are Raoul of Marckmont. What in the name of the Pope are you doing here ? "

And with one quick hand-clasp from the saddle he swung past towards the steps of the keep, where the Castellan awaited him.

" What indeed ? " murmured Raoul, looking after him. " But . . . no, I will not dismount until he comes again. He must have ridden from Belsaunt before dawn. At least he knew me. And now to wait."

The gay group on the steps dispersed. Alain's red and yellow vanished in the wake of Rogier's green and white.

Rogier's half-dozen armoured riders got stiffly to earth, growling and jesting with the grooms and with the men-at-arms of Montcarneau. Odours of stable and kitchen mingled on the damp air. Raoul counted the bricks in a row on the wall in front of him, counted the merlons on a reach of crenellated rampart, counted the years since he last saw Rogier, the months since he went to confession, the weeks since he fled from Ger. . . .

The quarter of an hour went by. Coarse voices and muttering laughter died to the ring of sollerets upon the steps. Deliberately Raoul looked round.

It was Alain, and Alain only.

Alain got thoughtfully to horse, and nodded to the squire whose duty was to lead the way. Elbow to elbow, with no word spoken, the lovers of Yseult de Olencourt rode out of the great hold and down the limestone steep of Montenair.

IX

ASSAY TOWARD SAULTE

WHEN they were jogging along the level Raoul cleared a nervous throat and addressed himself to his towering companion.

"What said my lord Duke at Saulte ? " he asked.

"This and that," replied Alain, without so much as a sideways glance at him.

Raoul flushed and tried again.

"Pledge me your word as a chevalier that you will look the other way whilst I ride off," he said, "and I will do you a service such as you cannot dream of."

This time the polished casque was turned ; beneath the lifted visor the blue eyes of the Count of Montcarneau were solemnly aware of the youth beside him.

"Belike you carry a phial of that witches' potion," drawled Alain, "but I want none of it. I am pledged to render you to Ger."

"So be it," Raoul rejoined with savage meekness.

"So will it be. But now you pledge me *your* word as a . . . as a nobleman that you will attempt no escape throughout this journey."

"Not I," snapped Raoul. "If you have entered service of my lord Castellan as a catch-pole, look not to me to ease your task for you."

Alain's mouth twitched behind his shining beaver.

"So dark a threat demands a desperate remedy," he intoned ; and added in a milder key : "There are some would kick your hinder end for that same pleasantry ; but I own I would not willingly stand in your shoes myself, so let it pass."

"Gramercy, good my lord. But I warn you, let not my lord Count Warden abate the reward for my apprehension ; for it would please him to do so, on the score that you are only agent for the man who took me."

Alain looked steadily at Raoul, and this time Raoul could

not hold the stern blue eyes. Then Alain motioned to a squire behind him, growled an order, and gave Raoul the broad back of his wolf-bedizened surcoat to contemplate as he rode ahead. The squire drew level, and presently a cord hung slackly between his saddle-horn and the chain of the gelding's bit.

It was come to this, then. The promise of lordly sunsets, the elfin glamour and alarum of many a midnight wind, had led to nothing but a muddy captive ride through the November-darkened Forest of Honoy. . . .

Most of the trees were bare now, but below the greys and blue-greens of the conifers a wrack of dull brown leaves clung hardily among the ancient beeches ; gnarled lateral beech-boughs were hobgoblin arms that pointed along the road of shame and of frustration. Mist thinned and thickened in the hollows, paling the glitter of plate-armour, spangling with tiny drops the braided manes of the horses, closing at bowshot-length the dim perspective of every autumn glade. . . .

Resentment against Alain gave place in Raoul's mind to anger at the slight accorded him by Rogier. But presently this latest quirk of Olencourt behaviour fell likewise into a rearward place in his dark convoy of imaginings ; after all, what right had he to expect more than had happened to him ? Rogier and he had not met for a matter of five years. Rogier had grown up and away from him, become a chevalier, maybe fallen in love ; at all events he had forgotten a sunlit afternoon when news of a prince's death came with steel and scarlet and the sound of bells to the slope above the fish-pond at grey Sanctalbastre. . . .

" But Enguerrand had not forgotten that," mused Raoul. " In Enguerrand is my last hope. I was a fool to anger Alain. How can I yet escape and make my way across the forest ?

" But even were I free, the Castellan's men must now be strung along Red Jehan's marches. I should need to go far south, maybe across the river—or far north, and again into the moors—to avoid encountering them. And what if in the end the Duke proved obdurate as the Castellan ? Well, at the least, I should have shortened my days of bondage, for in April I come of age according to law, and then my barony is mine . . . however poor it be."

At a turn of the mired way he looked behind him ; the
wolf-heads on the banner of Montcarneau seemed to send a
fierce unanimous grin along the road to Ger. . . .

Not only to Ger.   First must be passed the ruins of Saint-
Aunay   . . then the sandstone towers of Guarenal, where the
kindred of Raoul's mother—the old goat-bearded Baron and
the blithe brown maid—must see him and know that he had
failed in whatever thing he had set himself to accomplish. . . .

Raoul clenched his teeth and swore in silent rage and
shame.

Towards noon began a thin drizzle of rain.   Raoul drew
the pointed hood of his new cloak over his steel cap, and
inwardly praised the Castellan's lady, especially in that her
gift included gloves ;   for he hated getting his hands wet
without reason.   And immediately he realised that his spirits
had touched rock-bottom of dejection and begun to rise again ;
Mercury rounded on Saturn in him, and the forest ceased to
pass in a blur of heedless woe.   Presently he noticed that the
masses of the trees were thinning out on his left and crowding
closer and more thickly on his right ;   that meant the end of the
Forest of Honoy and the beginning of the Forest of Nordanay.
And when at length Alain halted the troop by the crazy inn
of a wayside hamlet, Raoul noted how thickets of gorse
and briar rose gently for a hundred yards from behind the
clustered hovels to the edge of the dense woods above.

A squeak at his near stirrup startled him ;   looking down,
he saw a tiny ragged child who cowered against a mud wall
in terror of the trampling horsehoofs.   Whether the elf were
boy or girl it was impossible to tell ;   but its smudged brown
face was barred by eyebrows which hinted that not every
Olencourt was continent as Fulk and Rogier.

" Some by-blow of that damned comptroller's, like as
not," reflected Raoul ;   and, moved by the resemblance as
much as by the child's distress, he reined in sharply and swung
out of his saddle.

" Hey ! " roared the squire in charge of him.   " Stand
fast, there—what game is this ? "

But when Alain looked round it was to see his prisoner
gathering the mite into his arms and offering it to a scared-

looking serf whose shaggy head projected from above a half-door in the hut immediately opposite.

" Here, take this imp out of harm's way ! " commanded Raoul ; but the peasant backed and answered something unintelligible, pointing up the street with one hand, whilst with the other he sketched the sign of the Cross.

" What the devil ails you ? " grumbled Raoul, looking over his shoulder at the dwelling thus indicated.

Immediately a queer shock assailed him at the midriff ; for the child belonged to the last hovel in the village, and the serf was afraid to take it in. . . .

Alain was bawling at the innkeeper when Raoul passed him. Behind Alain the men-at-arms were dismounting, thrusting their horses towards the wayside drinking-trough, or loosening straps and reaching for their knives. Only the squire whose mount was roped to Raoul's, and the other who had ridden ahead, sat grimly in their saddles, watching this latest baronial antic ; their eyes seemed gimlets between Raoul's shoulder-blades as he tightened grasp on the whimpering and unsavoury morsel of humanity, and bowed his head to step into the gloom of the mud-and-timber hut.

" Ho, there," he said, as the odours of garlic and onion attacked him—this time together, with a ripe grounding of unwashed peasant to cement them. " Keep the little one indoors when . . ."

His utterance failed, for never had he seen the like of what confronted him. Stirring the stew in an iron pot that hung above a smoky fire stood an enormous woman, whose age might have been fifty, but whose eyes were shrewd and bright in her wide coppery slab of a face. She was not tall, but solidly fat—blackavised, moustached, with an iron-grey mop of hair and two great hairy moles, one on her cheek, the other on her chin—and as she gazed at the intruder she paused in her task and cocked aloft a mighty wooden spoon.

The shock of her, the mingled reek about him, and the brown-green of gorse beyond the half-shuttered window which broke the opposite wall of the hut, set Raoul's head spinning. Quickly he lowered his little burden to the earthen floor ; then, leaning against the door-post, he steadied himself and summoned soft and desperate speech.

If she were deaf, or stupid, or merely ill-disposed, this
bolt was shot in vain ; but garlic . . .

" *Nos tol venko, mother. Sabelle sent me—Sabelle of the
Coven of the Singing Stones.*"

His voice was hoarse ; but hoarser, and deeper than many
a fighting-man's, came the strange churning whisper of reply.

" *Oy, oy, oy !* Sabelle I know not, but the words I know.
I am Gunnore of the Coven of Culdesang. What would you,
friend ? "

" Escape—escape from these behind me in the street."

" Whither ? "

" Anywhither, and at once. I aim for Saulte."

" I take you. *Oy*, be still now. Be still for a moment."

The moment seemed an age ; Gunnore thrust her spoon
back in the pot, and stirred reflectively, once, twice, and again.
Then, suddenly, she grunted and spat noisily into the stew,
loosing the spoon amid the drifting steam. With startling
speed she turned and lifted an earthen bottle and a cow's
horn from the floor behind her, pouring out a measure of
mead as she surged round the iron tripod of her fire towards
the staring onlooker.

" Quaff your stoup in the street . . . here, a bite of barley
bread with it . . . let them see you breaking fast at ease."

Raoul seized horn and manchet and stepped forth into
view of any who cared to look. Out of the corner of his eye
he saw the leading squire, still mounted, wheel his horse
beneath the trees across the way to escape the all-pervading
drizzle. A man-at-arms was bringing food and drink—
perhaps Alain felt some compunction for his harshness—but
at sight of Raoul's tilted horn the fellow deflected his stride
towards the waiting squire. His footfall splashed at Raoul's
back, first up the street, then down ; meanwhile Gunnore had
pressed her bulk beside a slit that flanked her door ; and the
muted thunder of her whisper broke on Raoul's straining ear.

" *Quarterly or and gules*, and the wolf-heads, is Montcarneau. A pox devour him and all his iron breed . . .
stranger, let me fill up again. *Come inside.*"

Raoul held out the drinking-vessel and stepped into the
hut ; and immediately the beldame slammed the door, raising
a genial bellow audible half-way along the street.

F*

" Little vagrant pig, would you be out again ?   First let
the horses pass . . . name of a foul name, does granny want
you jellied for the pot ?   Wait till you wear more flesh upon
your bones ; and till that day sit still when you are bidden,
or I will tie you to the roof-beam and starve you of your
dinner ! "

The tiny child looked wonderingly up, in no wise terrified
by the sudden objurgation ; but Gunnore laid a red hand like
a ham upon Raoul's sleeve, and motioned towards the window
in the rear.

" Now hearken," she murmured huskily.   " Bear slant-
wise, *so* "—she gestured to the south-east—" until you have
two blasted larches between you and the hamlet.   Then half-
left, straight along the hill-top ; there is good going among
the pines for nearly a league. . . ."

Wide-eyed and trembling at the knees, Raoul listened to
the bass whisper of instruction.

" And if you are not afraid," came the chuckled ending,
" you will find shelter for the night amid the rocks of Culdesang.   Now pouch this bread, and cheese, and a piece of
horse-flesh. . . ."

" But *you*, when they find me gone . . ."

" Nay, I am old and wise.   Not for nothing, when I was
your age, did I travel the way I tell you of.   On the left, near
the top of the gorge, you will see a jutting crag ; thereon are
carven rings and ladders . . . *oy*, *oy*, but I have found
surcease from care up yonder, dancing to horn and bagpipes
under a goblin moon !   See now . . ."

The weight of Gunnore's hand was gone from Raoul's
arm.   Gunnore bent and scooped up a handful of wood ash
and peat from her fire, clapped the mixture to her forehead,
and sat down heavily against the wall, a monument of
battered and unvenerable eld.

" Behold me, stunned by the wretch who ate beneath my
roof ! " she muttered ; and then, ferociously :   " Get you
gone !   *Away !* "

Raoul gasped, broke free from a rigidity of fascination,
and darted to the window.   With one leg over the sill he
paused to clear his sword ; looking back, he saw the multiple
chins of Gunnore settling gravely down upon each other.

Her eyes slewed round, and she gave him an awesome wink, a wink of wicked and portentous glee. . . .

Like one in a dream he slipped out upon damp sandy soil and stood to get his direction. Thickets lipped the very walls of Gunnore's dwelling ; neither her immediate neighbour, nor the squire who munched in his saddle a score of yards away, could have seen him as he flitted from the drip of the thatched eaves into the mass of wet and scented gorse that climbed the slope towards the thunder-smitten larches.

" Mary Mother requite her if I cannot," prayed Raoul confusedly as he tripped and stooped and dived. " I spoke not a word of thanks. . . . Alain may not be deceived, but by all Saints she looked as though I had beaten her senseless . . . what a world of adroitness is that of the confederation of the witches !

" God help them . . . or, at least, be merciful to them as they have been to me."

Presently the last thatched roof was hidden ; after one pause to listen for sounds of pursuit, and to thank his patron saint that Alain had no dogs with him, the fugitive trotted until his wind went and his knees gave under him. And when at length he sank down on a fallen pine-trunk he was a mile or more from the hamlet and deep in the southward limits of the Forest of Nordanay.

Then, and then only, exultation mounted in him ; he hammered the red bark with a clenched fist, and cried aloud amid the quiet drizzle and the sighing stir of chill November wind.

" Fulk, and Alain, and my good uncle Armand — be damned to each and all of them. I am free again despite their lordliness and their devices. Gunnore, brave Gunnore, one fine day I will come again with gifts for you and for that grimy imp who drew me from my saddle."

The beldame's parting wink recurred to him ; it seemed to clang in his mind, a very portcullis of a wink slammed down between past servitude and present freedom.

" Servitude of the body, yes," he muttered, suddenly dashed again. " But servitude of the spirit . . . in truth though I be miles away I am still bound by chains to Monte-nair. Yseult's word has no more power over my love than my word over hers . . . and in a little, if she have her way, it will be a kind of sin to love her. She will wed Alain, and he will be good to her, and she will maze him with all her secret beauty, and bear him children lovely as the day. . . ."

The thought of Yseult love-possessed and travailing in child-birth goaded him to his feet and forth on his trackless journey.

" To find her woman's fate a desecration is a poet's whim and a fool's," he realised sullenly. " Poor Raoul, whose love brought nothing but confusion to him . . . poor Raoul, whose pleasure is self-pity, whose occupation is running away ! "

It was best to forget Yseult, and that was clean impossible. But if he could laugh at himself for loving her, could his love be of that heroic weft which something in him craved, and something in wind-song and autumn colouring demanded ? Would this despairing heaviness about the midriff be with him now for ever ?

Thus musing, tormented by self-mockery, and careless of all but the immediate future, Raoul fled deviously through two leagues of high forest and came to the foot of the gorge called Culdesang.

Four miles in length, smothered in blue-green spruces from each lip down to the hurrying stream whose ironstone bed had earned the place its name, dark Culdesang climbed southward into the naked moors that lay between Raoul and his barony of sand and water.

" In the morning, if it is clear, I shall see the marshes," he told himself. " Not Marckmont, perhaps, for that must be five leagues distant ; but at least the colours and the shimmer of the water. And I must turn my back on it and dive again into the Forest of Honoy. . . .

" But unto each day its sufficiency of woe. I do not like the name of this same Culdesang."

Indeed the word had a grimmer connotation than that of ironstone browns amid the leaping water. At the top end, where the spruce-jagged sky-line failed, there would be heather and dark tarns, and tumbled rocks ill-famed as the Singing Stones themselves.

" Has Gunnore drunk the blood of new-born babes up
yonder ? " wondered Raoul.   " And am I damned for thrice
availing me of pass-words of the brood of midnight ?   At
least I escaped this time without kissing my benefactress. . . .
Saints, what if she had offered me a bowl of stew ?   But I
will not stand shivering here.   The sky is clearing.   God be
good to Gunnore and her wooden spoon ! "

Then he set foot beside the brawling stream and began to
ascend the ravine.   The drizzle ceased, the wind freshened
to a steady roar amid the stirring spruces, and all the middle
distances grew clear and grey beneath a scud of broken
cloud.   Once he surprised a herd of drinking red deer ;   once
a wild-cat, crouching aloft in a tree, snarled angrily and
flogged the air with a black-ringed tail ;   and once the lonely
wanderer thought he heard the grunting and snuffling of a
boar where a score of oaks stood islanded amid the spruces.

But of mankind he found no trace ;   the shades of early
dusk discovered him still pressing southward between the
rush of water and the roar of wind.   By that time the
tree-masses were lessening ;   to westward, across the stream,
a gash of smouldering yellow fire ran secretly behind the
ranked boles of a side-ravine.   And at length a turret-like
crag stood out upon the eastern side of the now shallow gorge ;
there must be the carven rings and the playground of the
witches.   By the stream the spruces began to straggle, like
some forlorn-hope exposed to arrow-sleet and blast of
mangonel ;   presently they dwindled to groups and solitary
ill-grown spears, and then ceased altogether.   Save for a
twisted hawthorn here and there that clung amid the rocks,
only the heather remained to break the driving wind.   But
there on the bleak moor-crest Raoul's gloom-accustomed
eyes seemed granted a new lease of daylight ;   and with its
aid he found a hole in which to sleep.

His wallet still contained the flint and steel and tinder
taken—so long ago it felt—from the armoury of Campscapel ;
and when with difficulty he had lit his stump of candle and
explored the hiding-place he cursed because he had left the
buckler behind at Montenair.   There was nothing for it
but to blow the candle out, wait until he could see again in
the half-darkness, and then sally forth to cut down hawthorn-

branches with which to block the entry against any prowling beast.

This done, he drank of the iron-flavoured stream and barred himself in his den, to eat his black bread with the rank horse-meat and ranker cheese that Gunnore had given him. . . .

Presently rose the waning moon; when flying cloud permitted it she filled the head of Culdesang with wild disturbing shapes of rock and tree and heather.

"A Sabbath," said Raoul, "a Sabbath frozen in mid-frolic or humped in obeisance to a coming fiend. But for me, I am going to sleep, with my sword ready and a prayer said to the Virgin and my own good Saints."

When his prayer was concluded he spared a final chuckle for Alain's predicament in face of Warden and Castellan, and a last sigh for the harsh fortune that had sped him on his second assay toward Enguerrand du Véranger at Saulte.

Not until pale sunlight pierced his screen of hawthorn-boughs and glittered on the blade between his knees did the wanderer wake upon the following day.

"The Sieur God be praised for a fine morning," he said, and crawled stiffly out of cover, to stretch himself with a creaking of joints and a chattering of teeth. "And now to rinse my face in the stream and eat what is left of Gunnore's gift of food."

Before he embarked on his day's adventure he climbed to the turret of rock, crossed himself, and stood for a few moments staring at the emblems graven in the topmost surface of the crags.

"You are heathen and accursed things," he told them doubtfully, "yet I am loth to spit on you, for there are staunch and kindly folk among your friends."

His gaze slid down the slope to the forest margin, and a dark stir of fancy made of it a grove of Ashtaroth.

"I wonder, have *they* been here?" he muttered, half-pleased and half-ashamed. "No need to fend such visions off these days. I am quit of extravagant loyalties once and for all. Duty against evil-doers, and worship for beauty of the flesh, and guarded memory of old friendship . . . one

by one the Olencourts have flung them in my face. Lys
would not need to beckon if her body shone down yonder . . .
but I will go now, for I think this is an evil place."

He turned from ring-markings and spruce-shadows, and
made his way athwart open moor to the crest above the head
of Culdesang. And there again he halted, with Lys and her
allure forgotten ; for below and beyond the southward slope
of the watershed lay a flat tide of mist, with clumps and rows
of poplar-tops emergent, tiny in the distance—and now and
again, at a shifting and thinning of the grey-white veil, the
steely sheen and brown ripple of his own marsh-water.

Raoul stared fixedly and long into the vague, and belied
his own denial of extravagance in loyalty.

" You dear despiséd Marckmont," he said aloud, " twice
since I left you I have neared you ; the next time I approach
I vow I will not turn away. You are mine, and I love you
and will hold you though every maid in Neustria laugh, and
every Count in Christendom say nay."

And presently he was headed west-south-west towards the
point where the Conan Beck at last ran slowly and wound
to lose itself in the fen.

" This is the maddest venture of all," he told himself,
" for I must pass again within a league of Montenair, buy
food in the Castellan's villages, and dodge his men, and any
skulking rogue or outlaw—and maybe wolves as well—in the
deep forest south of Alanol. Still, better forest than moor
in mid-November. God grant the weather hold till I make
Basse Honoy."

For there on the plain were abbeys that refused food and
shelter to no wayfarer ; by now the rumour of a baron's
flight from Ger would have died on that side of the hills.
And as for the Duke, the Saultes were a genial breed—witness
the wife of the Castellan. Moreover, there would be Enguerrand to speak for him. . . .

Before noon he had forded the Conan Beck and climbed
into the heather ; and mid-afternoon of that mild day discovered him gazing across high pastures at the grey towers
of his late prison Montenair. By sunset he had found a
shepherd's hut where a tall serf and a ragged girl looked
curiously at his good gear, but did not deny him food at his

own price.   And in the late dusk he flitted across the roadside clearings and the muddy track between them, listening
fearfully lest a jog-trot of hoofs and a rattle of harness herald
a passing troop of the Castellan's mounted archers.

To the east of the road pine-cones had given him not too
wet a going, but on the western side he was speedily soaked
once more by bracken and long grasses.   Before full darkness
fell he crawled on to damp sand amid a gorse-thicket, and
there composed himself for a comfortless night.

Strange dreams came when he dozed, flinging him awake
to consciousness of clammy gear and utter wretchedness.
Once he toiled leaden-limbed up a turret'-stair, with the
Butcher clanging in pursuit ; and he knew that the Butcher's
head hung sideways and half-severed.   Once Denise cursed
and struck at him, because he had not taken her to the
Belsaunt brothel.   And at last he lay again on the rampart-
walk of Montenair, with Armand of Ger and Red Anne and
the Olencourts hunting along ward and corridor to kill
him. . . .

In that dream a stony chill struck through his limbs, and
terror reinforced its grip when the battlemented wall at his
left hand dwindled and disappeared, so that he hugged a
dizzy ridge of masonry and glared down at the vengeful face
of Lys—Lys, stirring a mighty cauldron with a bright
guisarme, and bidding him leap into the boiling brew.   Yet
as he shrank away from the outer steep his dominant horror
was not of cauldron or abyss, or even of the sharp swords in
the hold beside him ; it was that Lancelot of the Lake, with
more than the Castellan's stature and more than the beauty
of Alain, should rise behind the yews and pluck him from
the wall and hold him up to sempiternal shame. . . .

He flung himself sideways against the stiff yew-tops, that
yielded like air to the sickening swoop of his fall . . . and
awoke in a cold sweat, to find relief in the rustle and drip of
rain that scourged the midnight forest.

" My enemies hunt me hard," he thought, when the first
trembling of his fright had passed into shivers normal for
time and place and season.   " Brrr !   Lords and ladies,
there was no need to call the Sieur Lancelot to aid
you. . . .

" By all the Saints there is another side to that old story. Had I been Modred's self . . ."

Not all his bodily woe could quench the easing flame that suddenly possessed him. Then and there came leaping into life the first wild scenes of a romaunt of doom and hatred that should occupy the winter evenings when he came into his own at Marckmont. Then—so he told himself—these present perils and adventures should inspire fair-written pages, with only the friendly murmur of the fire and the mysterious plaint of wind in the wide chimney to break the brooding silence of the marsh. . . .

" I will call my story *Modred, Prince of Britain*," whispered Raoul, wrapping the skirt of his cloak more closely about his knees, that the loose boots of hump-backed Dirck should not admit the creeping wet. " And I will plaster it thick with misery and woe. No hey-day of the Table Round for *me*. Indeed, these *gestes* of frisking lambs and stainless dames and perfect chevaliers give me a kind of toothache. Mine the decay of power and loyalty, the sneer of Agravain, the brutish mirth of Kay. And Modred, biting his black hair while Nimüe tells him of his dreadful birth."

Towards dawn, before he fell into a slumber almost happy with exhaustion, he chuckled grimly and grew grave again.

" There will be no room for Tristram in this galley," he reflected. " It would cut too near the bone to expound the loves of two queens called Yseult."

An hour after dawn Raoul woke again, and ate, and staggered forth upon his journey. The night's rain had long ceased ; sunlight was with him, shafting amid the beech-trunks, stirring the embers of autumnal glory in the Forest of Honoy. Over the piled dead leaves, beneath bared branches, across hollows odorous of decaying bracken, down gorges where moss and lichen patterned the glistening rocks, he strode south-westward, aiming as he judged for Olencourt, beyond whose towers he meant to strike the road along the river.

Without setting eyes on man or beast he came soon after midday to a ridge that showed him Varne as a silver ribbon laced through the lower forest a league away.

" Now, God be praised," said Raoul thankfully, " that
I have come thus far without encountering visible danger.
Modred, too, shall have more sense than to joy in battle. . . ."

Then he halted and stiffened where he stood, for from
somewhere ahead came once again a sudden shouting and
the clang of smitten steel.

" Ah, now ! " groaned Raoul, laughing at his own discomfiture. " God send this is not Joris of the Rock. But
maybe it is best to see the fray in order to avoid it ! "

A little wind was stirring again in the forest ; a brook
swept noisily beneath a bank where its swirl had cut the
ground from beneath a network of sturdy beech-roots. Wind
and stream together blurred the din that rang along the glade,
so that Raoul all but stumbled over a dead man before the
conflict opened to his view.

Backed by deep gorse and flanked by thick-set holly-
bushes, two men stood at bay ; and before them in the
coppery-tinted bracken dodged and snarled some six or
seven others. There had been more ; the ragged wretch at
Raoul's feet was only one of three who lay in sight, and in
the first moment of his watching a fourth went down with
his hands flung wide. . . .

The odds were long, yet not too desperate, for the pair
had chosen their ground well ; moreover, Raoul could see
only one of them—a thick-set, fair-haired man who fought
with a two-handed sword—for his left side, and almost the
whole of his companion's body, were guarded by a small
" mantlet " or siege-shield of wicker and hide, set at a slant
with its prop deep-earthed behind it. From that broad cover
protruded a swiftly-moving spear, and against such deft
machinery of defence the swords and pikes of the attackers
made slow headway.

Yet the latter were determined, and numbers were telling ;
a poleaxe-blade was hooked over the top of the mantlet,
dragging it slowly upright, and there was blood on the fair
man's wide pink forehead as he backed and cleared his
formidable " estoc " to meet another rush. A deep short
oath went up in a foreign tongue ; and Raoul tore off his
cloak and wound it tightly round his shield-arm. Then
he was flitting forward through the bracken, tugging out his

sword ; for it seemed a foul thing to let two such stout
travellers fall to a pack of ruffianly forest-thieves. As he
moved he noticed a grey mule tethered amid the trees ; and
then he selected his man and made for him. . . .

" God knows I am a fool," he growled. " This, too, is
no affair of mine . . . a thought in my mind against war,
and there comes a battle round the next corner. . . . *Ai, ai !
Out on you, dogs ! Friends, stand fast !* "

With a great yell to hearten himself he plunged at the
attackers in the instant of the mantlet's toppling over ; and
with an answering yell a figure slight as Raoul's own bounced
up behind, trampling on the hide above the poleaxe-man on
whom it had fallen, swinging a sword in one opponent's face
as Raoul stabbed another in the side. Then the sturdiest
rogue of all, the only one among them to bear body-armour,
sent a shrewd back-handed blow at the newcomer ; Raoul
parried it, but the blade glanced heavily and shore into his
thigh. With a scream he backed and staggered, and an axe-
head crashed flatly down on his steel cap ; it was as though
his brain burst in a shower of sparks that whirled and died
in sudden night.

With the impact of light on his eyeballs came a jagged
pain in his temples and a surging of blood in his ears. He
moved, and a dreadful certainty assailed him ; he could not
feel his left leg any more.

" Lift his head, Nino. Let the blood run out of it."

" Ah, for Christ's sake let me die ! " he muttered.

" Not we, friend . . . here ! "—and his face was suddenly
soused with water.

The boy who held him in his arms had a round brown
face, a kindly, jolly face with honey-coloured eyes. A yard
or two away knelt the fair-haired man—sweating, enormous,
his blood-stained jowl distorted as with teeth and fingers he
fastened a rag round his own right wrist. Then the bandaged
limb came down, and Raoul saw that the man had a little
humorous slit of a mouth and a pink battering-ram of a jaw,
square beneath the ears, yet pointed at the chin.

" My leg—— "

" Ay. We bound it tightly to stop the bleeding. Drink."

And out of his own dented cap of steel Raoul gulped cold water. For a blessed second or two the aching torment of his head was stayed ; then back it rolled, so that he closed his eyes and groaned.

" I am sped," he whimpered miserably. " Oy, do that again ! "

For the other had crushed a handful of wet bracken on his forehead.

" Now what ? " said the deep voice, the voice with a strange burr in it, which he had first heard on coming to his senses.

" Belsaunt once more," responded the round-faced boy called Nino, in softer southern-sounding accents. " We can set him on the mule. Plegmund the armourer will take him in. One moment . . . stranger, does that hurt ? Or that ? Or that ? No. Then I think no bones are broken. Listen ; these rogues may well be Joris of the Rock's, by God's grace only a half-score of them together. But four are fled, and we must not delay, or the whole pack may be upon us. Can you sit up ? "

Raoul sat up, blinking with pain and faintness.

" I knew not," he whispered, " there were any Good Samaritans in this damned Forest of Honoy."

" Ten thousand little fleeting devils ! " said the other, pleasantly. " Do you think we should leave you here after that stout intervention ? But for you we were dead or mangled by now. Lift him up, John."

And presently Herluin was swaying dizzily on the back of the plodding mule. Beside him stood the fair-haired man, whose murderous estoc hung at his back, the hilt sticking up at the right shoulder. Over the other shoulder he bore the prop of the mantlet, so that from behind he must have looked like an enormous playing-card on sturdy feet ; and his free hand was ready should Raoul show signs of losing his balance. Ahead, with dark curls stirring above his back-thrown hood, went the soft-spoken Nino, carrying two of the mule's saddle-bags, and using as a staff his own broad-bladed spear.

Twice they halted and laid him down to rest ; and at the first halt Nino told him their names.

" This swordsman's name is Doust," he explained, with a

wave of the hand. " His given name, as I should say it, is Giovanni or Gian ; you would say Jehan ; but in his England, a land of fog and long-bows, it is short and swift, like a blow ; thus, *Jon*. His motto is : *Trust in God and mount your archers*. And his home is at a place with a most barbarous name, Yorvic I make it ; but John calls it—now, *per Bacco*, what is it ?—*Yorr-k !* Even so croaks a frog. . . .

" As for myself, I am Giovanni da Chiostra, a graver of gems. Being, as you observe, in stature no Goliath, I have been known as Giovannino, a diminutive longer than its ordinary ; but John tells me that his mother called him ' Johnny,' so that one habit holds in tongues most marvellously dissimilar. But John calls me Nino ; and you, I trust, will do the same. I am out of Tuscany. . . ."

" And Tuscany is well rid of you," grunted John Doust.

" Alas, yes, perhaps the old bear growls aright. I assure you the charge was false \. . . malice, sheer malice, born of soured virginity. . . ."

" Call me Herluin," said Raoul, feebly. " And say I fled from a monastery. It is not true, but I have said it often enough. I am . . . a wanderer, born under Gemini ; Saturn and Mercury dispute the fortune of my days, and Saturn has the best of it. And this *is* true—I have a belt beneath my shirt, with money in it. Take what you will in payment for your broken journey. . . ."

" Now, by the harrowing of hell, say naught of that ! " ground out John Doust. " We have silver of our own for once ; we were making for the coast and England . . . but come, we must push on. A rogue misled us with a tale of a short cut to Olencourt ; you know the rest."

In this way—dazed and stirrupless upon a mule, with little thought save how to keep his balance—Raoul-Herluin rode for the second time in seven months beneath the image of Saint Austreberte that crowned the arch of the north gate of Belsaunt.

X

STREET OF ANVILS

Tink-a-tink-a-tink-a-tink-a-tink-tink-tink !
Tink-tink. Ding, ding, dong, dock !

Street of Anvils was awake before the misty autumn
sunlight touched the triangular jut of the dormer window so
that the crippled wanderer could see it from his bed. It was
pleasant to be Herluin again, to lie there with nothing to do
until his bowl of broth and manchet of black bread were
carried up the ladder to him. Sometimes good Marthe
herself, the armourer Plegmund's wife, came puffing through
the trap-way, pink-faced and trim as one of the apples which
lay behind the partition of the loft and scented all the air.
Sometimes her pretty daughter Godelieve came, blushing a
little as she bent to set the bowl in place. And sometimes
came Florette, the swarthy, worried, and un-flowerlike serving
maid, who dumped the breakfast down with one scared glance
at Herluin—keeping an ear cocked lest the shrill voice of her
mistress ring out from below.

Then, before the last spoonful was drunk, a shock of dark
hair and a pair of bright and curious eyes would pop into
view.

" Hey, Berel," Herluin would call, " what news from
Camelot to-day ? "

The small boy would scramble up and approach the bed,
seating himself cautiously at Herluin's undamaged side.

" The Sieur Gawain was wounded yesterday, fighting the
Red Chevalier by the Windy Tower. The Red Chevalier
tied him backwards way on his horse, and sent him home to
the Court with a message to the king, and . . . *you* go on,
Herluin ! "

Then Herluin would go on—inwardly tickled by the
contrast between the tales he told to Berel and the dark
endings of the Table Round that swam at the back of his

mind—till terce rang from the convent church of Saint Mary
Magdalen in the high town.

" And now be off with you to school," he would say.

Again the noises of the street, the hammering and clinking
of the forges, would drift up to the silent chamber under the
tiles, until Marthe or Florette came to straighten the tumbled
bedclothes and hold the great brass bowl for Herluin to wash
in. Once or twice this office was performed by the apprentice
Berthelin, a sullen disregarder of all persons save his master
and his master's wife and daughter ; Herluin, perceiving that
his own receipt of kindness from them was an offence to the
silent youth, gave him his dagger, and thereafter gradually
thawed the stiffness out of him.

But at that same kindness he himself lay marvelling day
by day.

" Nay, a friend of John Doust and of Nino Chiostra is a
friend of mine," said burly Plegmund, the master-armourer,
when Herluin first spoke to him of it. " Two pack-mules
and a new suit of plate they saved for me by Pont-de-Foy ;
and two stouter, merrier blades never sat in to supper at my
board. I would they had stayed longer."

For the valorous pair had left the morning after they
brought Herluin to Street of Anvils ; and Herluin smiled
each time he remembered John Doust's injunction to the
little barber-surgeon who would have bled the remains of his
strength out of him.

" Dress the wound with warm wine only," said John
Doust, " and lift no lancet against this young swordsman, for
he was born under the Sign of Gemini, which is opposite in
all things to the Sign of Sagittarius. Therefore the sight of
pointed weapons induces in him a kind of madness ; and he
is very handy with a cutting edge himself."

So Herluin's blood stayed in his veins, and the gashed
quadriceps had a better chance of healing than was given to
many such wounds in those times ; and in warmth and cleanliness behind his horn-filled casement Herluin lay for the wild
end of that November season. By now the weather had
broken ; no matter what word Alain de Montcarneau had
borne to Ger, the winter gales were roaring through Honoy
and Nordanay, and Saulte and the Castellan must needs

draw off their men from valleys flooded and impassable, leaving Red Jehan in peace at least until the coming of the spring.

So much Herluin gathered from the news that came to Plegmund's ear in the high town of Belsaunt; and in the intervals of story-weaving he wondered what would be the end of that evil whereof he had seen and furthered the bloody beginning.

But on the rare mild days, when his casement stood open, he came to recognise certain voices drifting up from the street or across the few feet separating the overhanging house-fronts; and presently a world foreign to him—the world of the ordered townsmen—thrust its own problems and observances before his notice.

There were echoes of a great dispute set on foot at the Michaelmas assembly of the Armourers' Guild, when the Canons of Saint Augustine were sued in the Court of the Bishop of Belsaunt for toll of a passage-way in the armourers' ward. There was a stabbing in the liberty of the Duke of Baraine, where the burghers' provost had no jurisdiction, and the Bishop would not interfere, since the stabbed man was suspect of sacrilegious theft. There was the coming Christmas Mystery, of which a third part of the expenses was to be defrayed by the armourers. And there was the constant bickering between armourers and blacksmiths or makers of horse-harness as to the limits of their craft. . . .

" Ruan is amerced a half-florin for crying out a foul name in the Weavers' Hall. . . ."

" Three pence a ton a mile for the haulage of elm-timber ! It is robbery. I told the knave, I said . . ."

" That new priest is too fond of slipping in for a horn of ale when Odger is down at the wharf . . ."

" They say she has the Evil Eye these days. . . ."

" Give me the good old times when an honest woman might empty what she liked out of window, with no by-your-leave or if-it-please-you no straining downstairs with a great bucket, for fear of a rogue of a watchman who is paid by the town to keep down thieves, not to interfere with worthy folk. What is the street for, say I ? Because some one has splashed the gown of the justiciar's red-nosed clerk, are we all to . . ."

" Trimmed with marten, as mincing as you please, quite forgetting her father was only a foreigner from Montenair. But I passed her with never a wink, I swear. . . ."

" And she said . . ."

" And I said . . ."

" And she said . . ."

" I would not live always in a town," mused Herluin. " ' No. Not while there are woods and streams in Nordanay.' "

Who had said that ? Why, Reine de Guarenal, that sturdy little person with the dark brown eyes, whose interference on his behalf had set eight months' adventure going. . . .

" Was that a good turn or an ill one ? " he wondered. " At least it has brought me now to peace and comfort in the home of these good people. And I have seen much—maybe too much—that I should have missed had I stayed soberly and obediently at Ger. Ah, there is that harsh-tongued rogue again. By his voice I know him for a rogue ; that is the tenth time at least that I have heard him vaunt his service in the Jacquerie."

" Demoiselle Godelieve," he said, when next the pretty shy girl came with his food and drink, " who is the brawling knave in this street who was out in the Jacquerie and cannot forget it ? "

Godelieve smiled.

" That is Drogo," she replied. " He is the youngest master-armourer in Belsaunt. He is . . ."

" In fine, you do not like him."

" No. But father says he will be provost yet. But Berthelin says . . ."

" What ? I thought Berthelin never said anything."

" Master Herluin, Berthelin is my good friend ; I pray you do not laugh at him because he cannot talk like Master Nino Chiostra."

" Your pardon, demoiselle ; and Berthelin's. I grow peevish, mewed up here. Berthelin I salute ; he is fortunate in friendship . . . more fortunate than most. I wonder . . . could you lend me a sharp curved knife and a stick of black-lead, and find me any odds and ends of wood ? I used to carve little things ; carving would keep my temper more as it should be."

"Why, Master Herluin, you talk as though . . . but I will find you some wood . . . there is Drogo again. Alas, he beats his little sister Alys because she does not wish to marry old Hamund the horner."

"Is Drogo, then, a bully?"

"Well . . . I suppose he has the right. He is her guardian. Hamund is rich and gentle, but he is *old*. It is not good, is it, for sixteen to marry fifty-three?"

"No . . . no. But is there no one to take Drogo by the neck at times?"

"He is a bitter enemy, they say. Why, at the Lammas Fair he nearly slew a man-at-arms of the Bishop's; and after all, he *was* out in the Jacquerie. Why, he *has* killed a man! And he is big and tall."

"So? H'm. There is no getting away from these lovers of strife. But surely your father can influence this Drogo?"

"Yes . . . but father is not anxious to offend him. . . ."

"Nor he your father?"

Godelieve sighed.

"Nor he my father, it is true. Yet I must do as my father would have me do, when that time comes."

Herluin was silent; and in the days that followed he fell to carving stiff little wooden warriors with arm-pits pierced for lances and legs hoop-shaped, so that they sat on stiff little wooden horses.

The boy Berel squealed with delight when he saw the first three figures and learned they were for him to play with.

"Who are they, Herluin? This one with the crown?"

"Charlemagne."

"And this one with the mitre?"

"Archbishop Turpin. And the paladin is Roland."

"And whom are you doing now?"

"Olivier."

"And whom will you carve next?"

"Ogier and Aymon."

"And then?"

"Ivon and Berengar."

"And then?"

" Oh, Ganelon the black traitor. And some Paynims. We must have Paynims. . . ."

Thereafter, one by one, the family was dragged up to see the wooden warriors.

" This is fair carving," said portly Plegmund, with one hand holding Paladin Roland, and the other flattening Berel's shock of hair. " In good faith, Master Herluin, the Bishop might be glad to see it. There is work even now on the rood-screen here at Saint Mary Magdalen's, but the craft rules would not permit you to raise chisel to it. Nevertheless the Bishop can do as he wills in his palace ; and for the first time I should be content to see a stranger working in our city, if you desired to seek employment there. He has these new wooden mantel-carvings. . . ."

" I do not much enjoy the households of great lords," said Herluin thoughtfully. " But I thank you for the word ; if my little money runs out I must think of it. God knows I am content here for the present."

" Well, now," said Marthe the goodwife, " did you ever see the like ? Look at the beard and crown ! And this one with the great war-horn slung behind him ! Berel, I hope you thanked good Master Herluin civilly ; and Saints witness you need never whine again on a wet afternoon."

" Why ! " said Florette after a long stare. " They look like little men on horseback ! "

Herluin and Godelieve smiled at each other ; and when Florette had clambered down the ladder Godelieve laughed and clipped her little brother round the body.

" Oh, Herluin ! " she exclaimed. " They are lovely ! " And then, blushing : " Your pardon, Master Herluin."

" I pray you, no more *Master*," Herluin hastened to ask. " As for these, if Berel is as glad to use them as I am to carve them, all is well enough."

" But you are often sad," said Godelieve softly.

Herluin narrowed his eyes and cocked his head to survey stout Olivier.

" Yes," he said simply. " I am often sad."

" We have a friend—another friend, Hubriton, clerk to the notary in Street of Bells. And he is sad too. Mother says it is because he reads the notary's books. And he writes little songs. And he even keeps a chronicle of the town, but that he will not speak about, lest it reach the provost's ear. Yet sometimes he reads to us out of it ; it is so strange to hear what happened on a day two or three years ago. But I should not have told of it. . . ."

" That secret is safe with me," Herluin assured her. " And I think I should like to meet this Hubriton."

" He is grave and shy. And he says strange things."

" Such as ? "

" Oh, that the land were better without its nobles, and that . . . dreadful things. And he is kind and good. I cannot understand it. Berthelin says Hubriton is a poor thing, because he is not skilful with the quarter-staff. . . ."

" And Berthelin, I take it, *is*."

" Yes. He bore away the apprentices' purse last Midsummer Fair."

" But Berthelin makes no songs ? "

" Oh, no . . . but that is different. They do not like each other, and that displeases me ; I want all my friends to like my other friends."

" Perhaps those two have more than songs and quarter-staves between them," hazarded Herluin.

Godelieve blushed again.

Hubriton's black eyes flashed in his gaunt young face when at their first meeting Herluin sang to him the *Ballade of Karmeriet*.

" There speaks true chivalry," he said sardonically. " I see your sword in the corner here. Would you like to hear my *Song of the Sword* ? "

" Yes . . . but what do you mean ? "

" ' Flame and death,' hey ? Not all his gestures of nobility could restore that which was burned and spilled. Now hearken to a townsman's view of it."

Then he hummed a moment in a tuneful bass ; and suddenly the words came.

Safe lands have strong kings :
This is what the sword sings.
Dove-cote and corn-patch,
Stout beam and firm thatch,
Trim hearth and caught latch.

Cradle by the bed-stead ;
Grey head and dark head
Lifted at a homing tread.

Flies a word 'twixt strong kings,
And this is what the sword sings,
This is what the dawn brings.

Fouled hearth and burst latch.
Tumbled cote and trodden patch,
Flame leaping in the thatch.
Grey hair mired and red ;
Dark hair still and spread,
Reft life and maidenhead.
From the beam a corpse swings,
And faint the cradle-cry rings.
Gaily strive the strong kings :
This is what the sword sings !

" Yes," said Herluin thoughtfully when Hubriton had done. " That is a good song.   Better than mine."

He was amused to see that Hubriton had hoped to shock him—that Hubriton was in one way disappointed and in one way pleased.

" You are the first to like it, Master Herluin."

" Am I ? Well . . . listen, Master Hubriton. That poor sword of mine has not yet been raised except . . ."

And he found himself telling his tale with only elementary precaution as to name and place and circumstance.

" God send some more like you will break out of that monastery," was Hubriton's grim comment.   " But say, now —what is it to us in Belsaunt if this lord cut the throat of that lord, or if a bishop quarrel with a cardinal ? "

" Would you have Jehan de Campscapel for governor ? "

" No, not if . . . oh, our Bishop is well enough, but bishops die, and what is to prevent that lecher Thorismund from sending us a churchman like the Abbot of Saint-Maur-by-Dunsberghe ? "

" Naught, it is true.   Yet that is how things have been done and will be done. It seems to me, Master Hubriton, that we have oftener to choose between two wrongs than between a wrong and a right."

" Truly but most heretically spoken, Master Herluin.   It

is time for one of us to say ' But it is all in the hands of the good God.' "

" It is not for us to know all things."

" But all things bear upon us, Master Herluin, and it is for us to be damned eternally if we go altogether wrong. Yet I think God must be more merciful than many men suppose Him, for He plays with loaded dice."

" Hush, Master Hubriton. These are grave matters."

Herluin, in fact, was thoroughly uncomfortable. This notary's clerk who cut so shrewdly at the roots of ordered life had a gentle bitterness that at once attracted and repelled him.

" One moment, Master Hubriton. If a great lord, or indeed any lord, should offer you a not ill-paid post as his steward or secretary, would you close with him ? "

" That question is ridiculous . . . yet it is fair. I should say *no* at once ; but honestly . . . I do not know."

" That honesty would well serve any lord, I think."

" Maybe. Until it came to racking rents out of his wretched hinds. But I do not know . . . you have me there."

" Not I, I believe, but something far stronger."

Hubriton brooded with set face.

" Love is the devil," he broke out sharply.

" No. I have met Love, and I have seen the Devil. They are marvellously unlike."

" You have met—you have seen—— ? "

A sudden change came over the clerk's face, and Herluin read the quick suspicion of a tormented lover.

" Ay. Months before I came to Street of Anvils," he said, quietly.

Suspicion was replaced by curiosity.

" Then I trust you fared better than I am like to fare . . . unless your unwary lord appear in search of a clerk."

" Oh, I fared no way at all. It was madness."

" It generally is. If I am writing out a deed and, glancing up, see the pear-tree in my master's garden, leafless and fretty against blue sky, I find in it a sign from Heaven, since Plegmund has a pear-tree, and Godelieve once let fall a pear which I picked up and kept till foul things walked in it."

" Ah, *I* know. . . ."

For a space they were silent, peering each into his inward desolation. Then Hubriton remembered.

" But the Devil, Master Herluin ? You saw him ? "

" Ay, by the Singing Stones of Hastain. Why, now, you cross yourself ? "

" Oh, Saints, yes. When talk of the visible Fiend goes on, I know God watches somewhere ; else how could so much that is fair yet shine on earth ? "

" An argument invincible. Well, as to the Devil, I was journeying . . ."

" In good faith, you have lived adventurously," commented Hubriton when that was ended.

" I suppose I have. Yet the true adventures I believe are in one's heart. . . . I cannot say what I mean, but I feel it is so."

" That was graciously said, Master . . . may I call you Herluin ? "

" Yes, Hubriton. What, you must go ? "

" Ay. But I will come again, often."

When Hubriton had gone Herluin lay back and shut his eyes. He heard a half-derisive hail from Drogo, and Hubriton's flat-voiced reply. Then he fell to considering the procession of those who had crowded into his life since last he was at Belsaunt.

" Friends and foes and all the pattern of their motion," he thought wearily, " are less to me than the shadow of Yseult, the shadow of her arm which fell on me that second night at Montenair. Why is that ? I have been fortunate in everything save the one thing that most matters to me. If there be a jest in it, God grant I see it as levelly as poor Hubriton regards his plight. I hoped to have a love story of my own ; I see I am like to be no more than the confidant of other lovers. . . .

" Yseult, Yseult, Yseult ! It is all one to you if I am slain or go into the Church or mark my days by carving little wooden men."

Paladin Olivier was finished the morning of Herluin's uprising, when he walked stiffly to the window and first stared forth on the huddled roofs of the high town. By leaning out and looking sideways he could see the steep fall of the cobbled street, the medley of jutting eaves and gables where dark upper stories seemed to nod in conclave across the narrow way. Immediately beneath him was a corner ; just opposite him a flight of stone steps climbed the gloomy gulf between two house-flanks and led along an alley bounded by high garden walls. Red and grey and red again the tiles and walls and chimneys straggled away downhill, pitted and sown with windows blackly open between their shutters, or blank and closed with horn ; and beyond them, bland in intermittent sunlight, soared the steel-grey bulk of the cathedral of Saint Austreberte—course on round-arched course, with a pearl-grey central tower rebuilded by the ruling bishop, and a cluster of scaffolding hiding the great window at the western end.

Down in Street of Anvils stood Godelieve, chatting with a pale-faced girl who started and scurried away when Drogo's voice resounded amid the clangour of his forge. Harsh-smelling smoke blew gustily across the house-tops ; a distant yelling of schoolboys pierced the ceaseless dinging of a score of hammers. Herluin, watching a lean, grey-bearded citizen picking his way carefully across the garbage-littered cobbles, marked him for Hamund, the pale girl's would-be husband ; for he disappeared into a corner doorway, above which hung the bleached skull of a cow with long horns painted red.

A man-at-arms, wearing the bishop's blazon and carrying a pair of shining sollerets, elbowed an aproned apprentice into the gutter ; the youth scowled after him and spat. From the ale-house next to Drogo's forge some one began faintly roaring a bawdy song.

" No," said Herluin. " Not while there are marshes by Marckmont, and woods and streams in Nordanay."

Paladin Ogier last felt his creator's steel on that dull afternoon when the great bells of Saint Austreberte were tolling for the queen.

" Poor lady," said the goodwife Marthe, in tears. " I mind me Berel was born the day the Prince René came of age. And when Berel was three all but a week, the Feast of the Name of The Sieur Jesus falling that year on a Wednesday—or was it a Tuesday?—no, a Wednesday, for Wednesdays I went to Low Mass before marketing, and the chasuble was white—and when I got back Godelieve came running, for the young limb had fallen souse into a salting-tub, and no sooner had I stripped him and dried him and got him across my knee than—*boom!*—the bells were at it for the poor sweet Prince. I waited, hand in air I vow, for Master Hamund to come across; and when he told me what was amiss I looked down, and there was the lad's little hinder end, all pink from the towelling I had given him, and as I hope to wake in Paradise I could not smack it—I who was that day luckier than the queen!"

"You wept instead," said Hamund reminiscently. "Thereby salting Berel a second time," he added with a smile.

Herluin, halting on a crutch, looked across at Hamund, and wondered if the mild and elderly horner would not after all make a good husband—for more and more as strength came back to him was Herluin growing curious as to marriage and its endless complications. But now Plegmund was speaking. . . .

"They say the king is risen from his bed, swearing that he will follow her bier on horseback if not on foot."

"God save him, gentle soul!" cried Marthe, with fresh use for her kerchief.

"He had much better have kept to her bed while she lived," muttered Hubriton.

"And the Cardinal Count is gone to Avignon," continued Plegmund gravely.

"Oho!" commented Hamund, plucking at his beard.

"And the King of Franconia has sent his brother, the Archduke Welf, to Hautarroy—what for, God knows. But this afternoon go you, wife, to Saint Austreberte to pray for the soul of the good queen."

"All Franconians are devils," said the hitherto silent Berthelin, spitting aside.

"Berthelin," murmured Hubriton, "have you ever seen a Franconian?"

"I?—seen a Franconian?" growled Berthelin. "None

G

of your pleasantries with me, Hubriton, unless you want a fist laid to your loose-hinged jaw. Seen a Franconian ! "

" Well, *have* you, beyond the Envoy and his men (all horned and tailed—I saw them too !) when they passed through last year—and the cross-eyed friar who jumped into the Varne to save a drunken man—a very fiendish thing to do, no doubt ? Any more ? "

" Now hearken to me, you singer of little songs . . ."

" No more, I see," said Hubriton, poised for rapid retirement. " Well, let me tell you, most Neustrians are devils too."

" You chattering ape ! " ground out the apprentice, only restrained from dealing a blow by the fact that Plegmund could still see him from the forge.

" But obviously. All men whom Berthelin has not seen are devils. . . ."

" Go away, Hubriton ! " urged Herluin. " One Jacquerie in the street is enough," he added—indiscreetly, since black-browed Drogo had come to his door to see what the noise was about.

" Ha ! " exclaimed Drogo, acknowledging Herluin's existence for the first time. " Come here, you ! "

But Herluin took no notice ; instead, he began to plod quietly towards Plegmund's entry.

" Lame duck, turn round ! " rasped Drogo.

In four strides he was up with Herluin, catching him by the shoulder and spinning him about.

Herluin cried out with pain and would have fallen had the other not held him up. Then, meeting with diffidence the practised stare of the bully, he spoke.

" Your pardon. I thought you spoke to some underling."

" I did, hound. I spoke to *you*. Now you have crawled from shelter like a maggot out of cheese, keep a civil tongue in your head, or that will be broken also ! "

" Civility is due to one who gives so much of it," said Herluin, blanched with rage.

" I see your tongue is sharpened like the tongue of that poor flat-fish there," growled Drogo, with one contemptuous glance at Hubriton. " Well, think on *this* ! " and he suddenly gripped his captive's arm with all his strength, thereafter casting him loose so that he staggered against the wall.

" That I will do," snarled Herluin ; and he did, for his arm was black and blue for a fortnight.

" Small chance with Drogo for a swordless man," said Herluin to Hubriton that same evening.

Hubriton nodded, and pondered awhile.

" Drogo was somehow born astray," he remarked at length. " I feel he was intended for a nobleman."

On the morning when Herluin laid aside his crutch, Paladin Aymon rode the famous destrier Bayard insecurely over the blankets of Berel's bed. Berel awoke, saw his new warrior, and clutched him joyfully ; then, skipping naked from beneath the clothes, he stood up and flung his arms round Herluin's neck, sticking one of Bayard's legs with violence into his benefactor's ear.

That day they sallied forth together to a chandler's in the low town, and there Herluin and his sword were measured for the votive candles he had promised months before. Since Herluin might not wear his weapon belted in the city streets, he gave it to Berel, who cocked it under his arm and stalked most gloriously past the homes of schoolfellows, one of whom planted a piece of bacon-rind neatly beneath the swaggerer's ear. Then, as Berel had half-drawn the sword, and riot and butchery seemed imminent, Herluin carried it himself.

Paladin Ivon stood forth with his peers on the night when Herluin returned in sober mood from the cathedral, from confessional and Mass and from a round of the chapels. . . .

God the Father, the Sieur Jesus Christ, and the Holy Ghost, as Three and as One ; the Holy Mother of God, especially for her patronage of Marckmont and Montenair ; Saint Barruc his own patron ; Saint Austreberte of Belsaunt, Saint Michael the Warrior ; Saint Gudule, also of Belsaunt, and Saint Remigius of Hardonek, whose names he had used to embellish his lying ; Saint Peter because of the Keys, Saint Mary Magdalen of Sanctalbastre, Saint Christopher the traveller's friend, and even Saint Guthmund of Ger, about whom he had hardly ever thought : all these received his prayers and thanks and explanations.

It was easy enough to stick a candle on a pricket, and

kneel, and shut the world out and speak to a Holy Presence.
It was good to open eyes on the interlaced arches of the chapels
round the choir, where now and again a sunbeam pierced
the deep-tinted window-glass and wrought unearthly blending
and confusion of colour on precious metal and sparkling
jewel and gaily-painted wood and stone. But confession
was exhausting, with its tale of continual deception, of seven
killings, of lust for a witch's body, of momentary doubting
and despair. . . .

"Sometimes, Father, I am tempted to believe that Satan
whom I have seen is unconquerable, so manifest are his
workings in the wake of wicked men; and sometimes to
feel that there was some strange lack of . . ."

"Continue, my son."

"That the Good God could not have intended so much
evil to attend His creation of the Devil. . . ."

"My son, you have come perilously near the accursed
heresy of the Manichees, which in many guises lurks continually for the confounding of those of light and unstable
faith. Most earnestly do I admonish you to set all such
doubts under your heel, lest growing they consume you.
Has God vouchsafed you so much mercy, brought you
through such manifold dangers, for you to inquire as of
right into the mysteries of His will ? Is not the very presence
and work of Satan but a subtle evidence of the might and
goodness of God, Who having sent this enemy to try His
faithful, daily overcomes him in their lives ? "

"Yes, Father."

But somehow there were dissatisfactions, even after pro-
nouncement of absolution and strict injunction to prayer.
Perhaps that was only because Herluin had fasted since
the previous night, and that his head was swimming and his
back numbed with cathedral draughts, whilst his knees were
stiff and sore from depressions in the pavement worn by
countless other knees before the shrines of Belsaunt.

It was pleasant to sup in the room behind Plegmund's
shop, and comforting to feel again the curves of Paladin Ivon.

Paladin Berengar took his place with the rest no more
than an hour before a ragged figure reeled through screeching

wind and stinging rain to batter feebly on the bolted door of
the forge. The little hump-backed man who worked the
bellows ran to open it, and Nino Chiostra stumbled into the
red glow cast by the furnace.

" Ah, Holy Mother be good to us, what ails you, and where
is Master John ? " cried Marthe as she ran forward.

Nino sank upon a box and held his hands to the roaring
fire.

" Hunger and weariness and a festered foot," he said.
" But John Doust . . . a foul fiend fly off with that bull in
armour, the Arch-thief of the Coast-March, Armand, Count
of Ger !   To Ger we come, meaning to take ship for England ;
but this accurst Count Warden catches sight of John and bids
him stay, he being in need of just such swordsmen.   John
says no ; we fight a score of them.   No Herluin to succour
us this time . . . John carves a man-at-arms or two, is
overborne and pushed into the harbour, and half-drowned
before they haul him out.   Then, bound, he is given a choice
of gallows or the Count's service, and chooses the latter like
a sensible man.   But I—*I* am not large enough to meet the
Count's requirements.   *I* am whipped with bow-strings from
the quay, and all our gear is stolen by the master of the ship ;
for it was already on board. . . . *Per Bacco, Donzella Godliva*,
I kiss your hands and pledge you in this God-given cup . . .
and Christ and Our Lady requite you all for . . . for . . ."

Godelieve had brought him wine already warming for the
evening meal ; and Herluin, who at mention of his own
name had flung an arm round the soaked shoulders, was
not surprised when the cup clattered to the floor and Nino's
dirty face came blindly against his breast.   There Nino
cried and steamed till Plegmund lifted him and carried him
upstairs. . . .

" Friend Plegmund," said Herluin that night, " you had
better take down that rusty corselet from over the forge door,
and paint instead a legend : *Hospital for lame ducks.*"

XI

A VISCOUNT COMES HOME

THERE is here no space to tell of the winter which Herluin
and Nino spent together in Belsaunt—of the Mystery at
Christmastide, when one of the apprentices who was to have
played a devil fell from the Cathedral scaffolding and died,
so that Nino Chiostra took his place—of Nino, dancing so
merrily in his red suit before the mouth of hell that saints
and angels could not speak their parts on earth and in heaven
until a roaring crowd had had its fill of that diabolic capering ;
or of snow-fights between apprentices (Herluin and Nino being
soundly rolled in a drift because they were foreign to the city),
and of ice-games played along the frozen moat on skates of
whittled bone.

At length came the day when Godelieve found snowdrops
in the little garden behind the armourer's house, the day when
a thrush woke sudden music in the pear-tree, the day when
Berel was allowed to go to school without his wooden shoes.
The February floods abated along slow-rolling Varne, the
March winds ceased to rattle and bang the shop-signs and to
blow tiles into Street of Anvils, the April rains poured off the
eaves and lisped in the steep gutters. Nino Chiostra would no
longer accept free hospitality at Plegmund's hands ; he refused
to live on Herluin's diminishing store of gold pieces, and
January saw him painting queer frescoes on wood in the
Bishop's palace. At Florence, it seemed, he had spent a
year in the studio of Messer Baldassare della Chiava before
turning his hand to the cutting of gems ; and his anxiety to
bring Herluin's carving to the Bishop's notice drove the other
to casting up Plegmund's accounts as a form of honest
employment.

It became Herluin's habit to walk down to the Cathedral
precincts with bread and cheese and ale for his own and Nino's
midday meal. If the day was wet, they ate in the cloisters (for
Saint Austreberte's church was a minster before the bishops

came) ; if it was fine, they sat on their cloaks beside a buttress of the southern transept, watching the people in the market-place and listening to the singing of the monks and to the growl of the cathedral organ. And there, in an hour of fitful April sunshine, Nino chuckled, raising with discretion a paint-stained forefinger.

" Do you see ? " he whispered.

Herluin looked, and saw little Alys, Drogo's unhappy sister, with unaccustomed colour in her cheeks and blue eyes staring something mischievously ahead of her. Beside her, speaking low and rapidly, slouched a stocky, red-haired lad, her senior by three years or more ; and there was nothing of mischief in his earnest freckled face.

" Who is he ? " Herluin asked when the unseeing pair had passed them by.

" Ruan, son of a fat weaver by the South Gate. Drogo may look to his plans ; it is not easy to thwart hair of that colour."

" Is that Ruan who was fined for calling names in the Weavers' Hall ? "

" I know not, but it is likely ; he is something of a blade, I believe."

" Alys seemed mistress of herself," said Herluin, idly.

" Ay. Ruan is paying for Drogo's heavy hand. None so cruel as a slave come suddenly to power."

" A slave come suddenly to power," repeated Herluin, softly. Then : " What would *you* do, Nino, if you were such a slave ? "

" Hang the tall Warden of the Coast March on his own noble gallows, and set John Doust at liberty," came the prompt reply. " And then, perhaps, we would go to England . . . or lead a company of free-lances back to Tuscany and settle another score or two."

" And then ? "

" Oh, God knows. Find a tower by a marsh, and hawk and fish, and harry my peasantry for money to buy precious stones."

" You like marshes ? "

" Ay. Better than hills. In hills I always want to see the other side, and there is seldom anything there but a bloody nose—as the Emperors find when they go trampling down into the Lombard plain."

" Nino ! "

" Yes ? "

The Tuscan turned, but Herluin was gazing out across the square. . . .

It was spring-time, and Nino's fond desires seemed strangely incomplete.   Only a week before, when Herluin had glanced out of window, he had seen in Drogo's house across the way what Ruan might have given his soul to see —Alys, not quite as King David saw the wife of Uriah the Hittite, but as a dainty shape that stretched and yawned and innocently let fall the shift from round white arms and girlish body.   Herluin had drawn quickly back ; but three times in the week he had dreamed despairingly of Yseult, and once—and shamefully—of Lys. . . .

" Nino, what is it like to wake in the morning in arms you do not love ? "

It was Nino's turn to stare silently over the cobbles at the pigeons cooing and strutting after crumbs which often as not were swooped upon and stolen by the jackdaws that flocked and squeaked around the bishop's chimneys.

Then Nino laughed, and his brown face went red.

" Plague me if I know," he answered simply.   " I have never touched a woman's body in that way."

" But . . ."

" Oh, yes, I am a grievous liar.   But have you never found that most men demand a certain sootiness in you before they will admit you to their kindliness or counsel ? "

" Do you mean John Doust ? "

" No . . . no.   Only twice or thrice in the year I have known him has John gone wenching of a night.   Once I went with him . . . and when he was safe with his charmer I gave mine the slip . . . handed her money, told her to fetch another stoup of wine, and bolted like a frightened puppy.   And plague me again if I know why I have told *you* that.   But for mankind in general I find affection of a like beastliness with their own a passport to good fellowship. . . .

" In Messer Baldassare's studio, of course, I saw a mort of pretty models in their skins ; and the first time I used a memory of one to adorn a dirty tale I felt as though I had spat on all the Ten Commandments. For God in Heaven knows it was a blasphemy, though not one priest in fifty might so have understood it, and maybe you will not understand, it either."

" I think I do. But at least you need not pretend *that* any more to me. I am glad, for now I can tell you about . . ."

He paused and considered. No, it was too much to hold in any more. Nino's confidence in him ; Nino's realisation of sacred beauty ; dreams, and the spring, and the whips of Ger, and (spur somehow most urgent of all) the mention of dear marshland : all these drove him to clear his throat for confession.

" Nino, it is my birthday in a fortnight's time."

" You speak as grimly as though it were your last on earth."

" It is my first *and* last—as Herluin. You see . . ."

Out it all came ; or nearly all.

" Ten thousand little fleeting devils ! " said Nino once. And later : " So *that* is why you showed such stubborn objection to working for gain ! "

" Yes. To exchange my accounting for Plegmund's food and shelter is not *dérogeance*, but paid employment would be. And though the Holy Trinity be my witness I have had no friends, or only two, like those of Street of Anvils since my grandmother died, yet I am not of the town and never shall be. And in the end Raoul must stand by all that Herluin has done."

" Ay. But will Raoul . . . will the Baron of Marckmont want Herluin's friends about him ? "

" Nino, you devil ! In three weeks' time, if the king still lives—and they say he is like to now the winter is gone—the Bishop gives another tourney to the lords of Honoy and Nordanay. Hither will come, I trust, that Enguerrand du Véranger to see whom I have made two foiled attempts. He has the ear of the Duke of Saulte. I will possess my barony, and we will somehow haul John Doust away from my noble kinsman. But at Marckmont you shall hawk and fish to your heart's content. And although I shall not be rich, there may even be some little cutting of gems. . . "

G*

" It sounds too good to happen," sighed Nino. " And
do you know, in Tuscany the nobles have mostly left their
castles and come to squabble in the towns."

" More fools they," said Raoul-Herluin.

" And there are even merchants rising to be nobles."

" What ? " cried Raoul; and a moment later Herluin
added : " Well, why not ? "

The Bishop's tourney was come round again, but this time
it drew no muster of the greater lords. Saulte and the
Castellan sulked at home, for they had been restrained, by
machination of those opposed to them in Hautarroy, from
striking at Jehan de Campscapel. The Constable Volsberghe
dwelt in the capital ; Ger and Barberghe found excuse to keep
them on the coast. Sons and younger brothers led famous
blazons and diminished trains towards the lists, and of the
lesser nobility there was no lack ; but Herluin looked in vain
for Enguerrand among them. Alain de Montcarneau he saw,
and Robin Barberghe, and Rogier de Olencourt, all of whom
he eyed askance ; and his heart stood still when Street of
Anvils showed a half-score of yellow surcoats charged with
the sable gerfalcon of Ger. Ahead of them rode his cousin
the tall Viscount Charles, drawing rein at Drogo's door ;
and Drogo's surly face grew bright at a noble order for arms
and equipment.

Berel hung out of a window and cheered ; Herluin and
Nino backed and watched for John Doust, but he was not
there.

" Our noses were better indoors to-day," said Nino. " But
I must to the palace . . . by way of the garden wall, I fancy.
I dusted a yellow surcoat or two myself by the harbour of Ger."

So Herluin brooded alone by his attic casement, carving
half-heartedly at a fierce Paynim, restless to test the efficacy
of the prayers he had put up on his coming-of-age a week
before. Yet, failing Enguerrand, there seemed nothing to
be done ; and, watching, he smiled when Alys leaned
interestedly from an overhanging window that brought her
near to the quickly-lifted head of mounted Charles. Words
passed ; and later in the day pre-occupation clouded
Godelieve's pretty face.

" I know not what has come over Alys," she said sadly
when Herluin chaffed her. " That big Viscount of Ger . . .
Herluin, are these great lords really wicked ? "

" Some of them are. Charles of Ger, no ; but he is like a
baby for his pleasures . . . or so they say," he added hastily.
" You had best tell Alys to be careful what encouragement
she gives him."

" I have already told her that, and she only laughed."

" Is it true that Drogo has threatened to beat Ruan the
weaver if he hangs about the entry there ? "

" Yes."

" Poor Ruan. This morning I saw him down the street,
watching with a face like doom. But Drogo did not offer to
beat the Viscount ? "

" Oh, Herluin, Drogo dare not. In any case he *could* not.
Besides, he has to make a whole suit of plate-armour, and a
chamfron and bards, and six steel bascinets for men-at-arms,
and what-not else."

" I see."

Gusty May afternoon, three days later, and apple-blossom
bright above the walls of the alley. The northern end of
Street of Anvils was empty save for a few starveling dogs and
a watchful cat or two that nosed amid the garbage by the
gutters. Sparrows fluttered and fought on the gable almost
at Herluin's elbow, and barely any noise but theirs was
audible ; forge and shop were closed, for most of the people
of the high town were down by the lists amid the water-
meadows. It was the last day of the tourney, when the
townsmen had their own sports ; once or twice a long tumult
of cheers and counter-cheers came thinly up the wind,
marking some dire crisis of quarter-staff mellay or tug-of-
war. . . .

Two days of standing in packed crowds had wearied
Herluin of uproar and of indiscriminate enthusiasms, and
now he was man enough to seek what he wanted rather than
what he felt he ought to want. So he sat alone by his dormer
window, subtly pleased by the hundred planes and angles
of the red-tiled roofs, by the fretwork of golden sunlight and
blue-grey shadow in the narrow street ; and in the flotsam of

his idle mind came words spoken by Hubriton : *All things bear upon us, Master Herluin.* . . .

Hubriton had talked something blasphemously of God's loaded dice ; but that was not now Herluin's concern. Herluin was wondering how anything that befell in Street of Anvils could possibly affect himself. Here Drogo boasted, Hamund watched Alys with patient kindly eyes, Berthelin scowled at Hubriton behind the comely back of Godelieve . . . and Herluin waited, living an inner life that excluded all these active shapes of men and women about him. They were wraiths in his eyes, and he was a wraith in theirs. When he had gone there might be one or two in Belsaunt who would remember him for a while ; and then they would forget.

" There is precious little room for me in any one's life but my own," mused Herluin. " To-morrow I will buy more paper for *Modred, Prince of Britain.* I have neglected the poor wretch of late."

Then his eye fell on a red head that appeared by Hamund's shop ; Ruan the weaver, wearing a short cloak over his tunic, stood hesitating at the corner of the street, staring now down the slope, now sideways towards Drogo's door. Ruan was grey-faced and haggard ; when he lifted his head the watcher had a glimpse of bloodshot eyes and restlessly-moving lower jaw.

" Now, who goes there ? " he wondered—for the red head suddenly vanished, and a quick footfall came in hearing from the other direction. A tall man, hooded and with a fold of cloak across his mouth, swung into sight where Street of Bells ran up to Street of Anvils, and strode beneath Herluin's window, whistling . . . whistling the air of *Now Raveth Alured*, that silly little song.

On the first floor of Drogo's house a window-shutter moved ; the whistling ceased, the tall man turned, and in three paces he was across the street at Drogo's shop-door.

" Now, by the Rood ! " swore Herluin—for the door opened at the stranger's touch ; and a certain thrust of head and limpness of hanging hand confirmed his intuition that this was his cousin, Charles of Ger. . . .

It seemed a long time that he sat there, staring at the shuttered windows of the silent house across the way. That

morning, he remembered, Godelieve had said Alys was
sick.

" The silly puss . . . the little fool," said Herluin.
" What, red-head, you still there ? Ah, God ease you, poor
damned wretch ! "

For Ruan had dragged himself round the corner again,
only to start and fling a hand across his face as though a
whip-lash seared it ; but the lash was a girl's laugh, full and
joyous, trilling into Street of Anvils from a shuttered first-
floor room.

Then Ruan was gone again, and only the stray 'dogs
prowled between the gutters. The sunlight had a redder
hue, and the shadows climbed and deepened ; the wind took
a shriller note, and Plegmund's rusty corselet swung grating
on its nail. . . .

At length the shop-door stirred ; the bulky figure emerged,
again with a corner of cloak across the lower half of a hooded
face . . . three strides of the long legs, and Herluin jumped,
so suddenly the red-headed weaver shot from his lurking-
place and padded soundlessly in pursuit. . . .

" Charles ! *Charles !* "

Herluin began his warning cry with insufficient breath ;
the result was a strangled yelp that Charles could scarcely
have heard. If he heard it perhaps he ascribed its origin
to the wrong side of the street ; burgesses' sisters were not
always too discreet, and this one might not understand that
the affair was finished . . . the long stride quickened, but
not till a second too late did the hooded head begin to turn. . . .

Herluin sat staring. The stocky red-headed townsman
seemed weirdly dancing at the Viscount's back ; three times
his broad dagger-blade went furiously home. Charles
grunted audibly, swung body and flail-like arm, sent his
attacker reeling against the opposite house-wall, and caught
at his own right side. Then he coughed and sank to his
knees ; then he was flat on his chest, spewing blood into the
gutter.

Ruan had bunched himself together where he fell, and
sprang erect in one swift movement. A shutter crashed
wide in Drogo's house ; a fearful scream resounded, and the
clatter of feet on a wooden stair. Alys flung open Drogo's

door, recoiled at sight of the red-headed death upon her, and
screamed again as she turned and ran. . . .

A louder clatter of feet on stairs . . . from somewhere a
woman had scuttled out to Charles, and two men were lumbering up the street beyond her, but Herluin spared them no
more than a glance ; for at the unshuttered window appeared
Alys, agrin and grey with terror, propelled from behind till
her protruding eyes could see her lover's body. Ruan had
her by the nape of the neck ; his mad face lowered behind
her, and she squealed a squeal like that of a trapped rabbit
when the dagger ran up to the hilt in her side. . . .

Herluin heard himself gasp ; the murderer had twisted
his victim in his arms and kissed her even as her head
fell back in death. Then the grim group vanished ; three
minutes later a man in the gathering crowd yelled and pointed
to the roof-tops. Ruan had climbed through a trap where
Drogo's gable overtopped his neighbour's ; and there for a
moment he stood poised astride the ridge-tiles, laughing and
crying and waving his dagger. Then he looked at the wet
blade, and drove it deeply into his own body beneath the arch
of the ribs ; and silently he lurched down the steep slope of
roof to plunge with arms extended to the cobbles forty feet
below. . . .

The crash of Ruan's end brought Herluin to his feet.
There was uproar now in the street, and he took a step
towards the door. Then he halted, suddenly aware that it
would be better not to run a risk of meeting any man from
Ger or Barberghe who might know him and, knowing him,
wonder how he came so near when Charles lay dead. . . .

Charles must be dead by now. No use to thrust into
that noisy press below . . . poor Charles, who only followed
where his man's senses led him, and maybe had flouted a
half-score of desperate lovers, to meet at the last an eleventh
with red hair . . . poor Alys, whose drab life had maybe
filled with gladness when chance sent trampling horse-hoofs
and a black gerfalcon into Street of Anvils. . . .

" At least she laughed once," said Herluin sombrely.

Poor Ruan, too, whose mind had maybe run on two chairs
by a comfortable hearth, with red-haired babies chuckling on
the floor . . . three poor unshriven souls, let loose together

in the westering sunlight, leaving behind them dismay and confusion and clattering tongues. . . .

Hamund would now grow old alone. Drogo would curse most vilely, for dead noblemen had no use for armour ; he would marry sooner than he had intended, needing a wife to slave for him in place of his sister. Ruan's father was doomed to shame ; and in a great hold on the northern coast the Warden of the March and his proud lady would find themselves lacking an . . .

Herluin stared out again across the roofs of Belsaunt, and a strange tremor shook him.

" Holy Mary," he said aloud, " I thought that nothing in this street could touch me . . . and Ruan has made me Viscount of Ger ! "

The Warden of the Armourers' Guild, the watch, a surgeon, fat Brother Fugatius of the Friars Minor in Street of Bells, the Provost of Belsaunt, stricken Drogo sweating from the lists, and lastly Robin Barberghe with a score of his own and his dead cousin's men-at-arms, came into Street of Anvils before the bodies were removed. That night the mortal semblance of Charles lay in the Chapel of Saint Jehan Baptist by the north choir aisle of Saint Austreberte ; and by the bier, twin shapes of steel in flickering candle-light, watched Robin Barberghe and Alain de Montcarneau.

But in the hot gloom of Plegmund's kitchen Nino Chiostra spoke softly in Herluin's ear.

" Your Sieur du Véranger is gone to the Vice-Warden, this old Baron . . . I forget his name."

" De Guarenal. How do you know ? "

" I heard it said in the Inn of the Four Swords, by a chevalier who wore the Saulte colours. Sent by the Duke, he said. But *now* . . . what do you think to do ? "

" I know not yet."

And in the morning, when amid a silent crowd he stood outside the little chapel and stared through the gilded iron-work of the grille, Herluin was still undecided. To what-soever expiation Charles was doomed in Purgatory, his dead grey face was utterly contented ; hands that had plundered the sweets of many comely bodies lay austerely crossed on an

ivory sword-hilt, and Herluin's eyes were filled with sudden
smarting at a tumbling stir of memories. . . .

Charles imperilling his neck for gulls' eggs on the cliffs
at Ger—a risk which his small cousin dared never adventure
. . . Charles guzzling at his father's board, answering all
questions with a nod or shake and a mild gleam of eyes
above distended cheeks . . . Charles swimming powerfully in
dangerous seas, foremost and undismayed in face of bear
or boar or wolf, giving blow for thunderous blow in lists or
tilting-yard . . . Charles falling on his knees to mumble
prayers by rote, crossing himself mechanically with his eyes
on a girl's ankles . . . Charles sprawling on a settle in the
winter parlour, losing with entire good-humour game after
game of chess. . . .

Charles, too, must have had an inner life ; but Raoul had
never considered it, and now, when Charles was dead,
Herluin thought of it for the first time. Perhaps Charles
had never considered it either. Strange to be alive and
strong and lusty, and yet somehow never *aware* you were
alive . . . never conscious of something in you that could
side with other people against yourself. . . .

" The wages of sin is death," said Herluin to himself.
" But the wages of everything else is death too. That must
mean eternal death, damnation, torment that is no death . . .
but Charles was like a child . . . what will the Sieur God
have to say to him ? "

Charles, lonely on the jacinth floor of some aloof and
glittering Judgment Hall, seemed suddenly to have some
case against the Power that gave him strength and kindliness
and wandering desires. . . .

Herluin passed into the Lady Chapel in the apse and
prayed for the Virgin's intercession on behalf of his cousin. . . .

" Holy Mother of God, if *I* went whoring it would be very
beastly, for I should have balanced an evil greed against the
disgust and humiliation that would follow, and mired myself
knowing I did it ; but Charles, I think, went innocently in
quest of happiness and could not understand if he did not
find it. . . ."

Herluin looked up at the calm face of painted stone, and
was glad for Charles and for himself that the miraculous

Motherhood and the bright companies of Saints stood between earth and the fiery awfulness of God.

Then he went out into spring sunshine, and wandered back to the high town deep in thought.

" I shall be sorry to leave this sheltered life," he said. " But Marckmont I must have, for it belongs to me, and I to it. And now, whatever befall, my way to Marckmont lies through Ger. . . ."

Plegmund's eyes grew grave in his ruddy face when on that same evening Herluin spoke of Nino's and his own departure.

" Street of Anvils is become ill-famed, then ? " was the armourer's only comment.

Herluin laughed.

" You know it is not that. Not least of all my gratitude is that you never pressed me for my history. But Nino and I must seek our fortunes, sure of a welcome here when we pass this way again."

" That at least is well said," growled Plegmund.

" Are you going fighting, Herluin ? " demanded Berel, eagerly.

" Perhaps," replied Herluin. " But I hope not."

Nino Chiostra chuckled.

" Hope *not* ? " echoed the boy. " But, Herluin . . ."

" Master Herluin knows more of fighting than do you," came Marthe's crisp interjection.

" Although he was not out in the Jacquerie," murmured Nino.

" Poor Drogo ! " exclaimed Marthe unexpectedly. " Master Herluin, you leave a sorrowful house here opposite."

" And another at the corner," added Godelieve above her poised needle.

" Ay, and all because of a maid's disobedience," said Marthe. " Yon poor nobleman—I'll warrant the proud wench led him on."

" God rest their souls, all three of them, and comfort those they have left," muttered Plegmund.

" Ruan did right," blurted out Berthelin, flushing when he found they were all looking at him.

" None of them did right."

" Hamund is more to be pitied than any."

" Hamund ?   A fiendish wedded life *he* would have had ! "

" Mother, Alys was not wicked ; the young Viscount was to blame. . . ."

" What do *you* know of such matters, girl ? "

" I saw Ruan's father to-day ; he was bowed and wretched. . . ."

" Has not the Viscount a father ?   Ay, and a mother too. All their rank and titles cannot bring them an heir. . . ."

" Hamund will never have an heir now."

" But plague on it, husband, had that creature borne a son, he would never have known sure fatherhood . . ."

" Mother !   Alys was my friend."

" You are well rid of such a friendship ! "

Godelieve was crying now.   Herluin sat in silent discomfort.   In the corner Nino Chiostra discreetly hummed a tune.

The neighbours stared when, twelve hours later, Herluin and Nino rode in half-armour up Street of Anvils to dismount at Plegmund's door.   The humpbacked bellows-blower held their bridles whilst they bade farewell to the armourer's household and walked to Hamund's little shop at the corner.

" God speed you wherever you go," said the old craftsman, peering sadly across his littered bench.   "See, take these . . . I had intended them for . . . but never heed that now . . . take them with Hamund's prayer for your safety and achievement."

Whilst they were cramming the silver-mounted cups of horn into saddlebags already fully laden, Hubriton appeared.

" Almost I wish I were coming with you," he said, loudly enough for Godelieve to hear.

" Next time we are here perhaps you will be," murmured Herluin.   " And if not, we shall maybe have matter for the swelling of your chronicle. . . ."

Hubriton smiled ; but his smile vanished as he caught the tail-end of a gibe from Berthelin.

" . . . to see *him* on a horse would frighten even Joris of the Rock," the apprentice grunted.

Hubriton's gravity deepened into preternatural woe.

" Herluin, Nino, you are never going without holy water? "

" Eh ? " demanded Nino over his shoulder.   " Nay, now, we have offered candles and prayed . . . the rest is with the Saints."

" I was thinking of Franconians," continued Hubriton evenly.   " Best take a stoup of holy water to sprinkle on their tails."

Berthelin growled, but a diversion then occurred ; Drogo had come to his door, and, after a silent glare, had expectorated loudly and vanished.

" Now that," cried Nino clearly from his saddle, " that was how we spat in the Jacquerie ! "

Drogo's ferocious face reappeared ; Nino hitched at his new sword-belt and drew six inches of a shining blade.

" Your gift moves sweetly in the scabbard, Master Plegmund," he called aside.   " In Mantua, with just such a weapon, I was once too quick for the master of a bawdy-house."

There was an instant's silence in Street of Anvils ; the whites of Drogo's eyes were injected, for Alys lay dead upstairs, and none of the listeners had not thought of her.   Then Herluin swung himself on to his mare's back and headed her down the street.

" Farewell, all, and God be with you ! " he said to the group by Plegmund's door.

" Fiend split your puppy-guts, the pair of you ! " roared Drogo through the chorus of farewells.

" In Mantua, too," said Nino, " the pimp was loose of tongue . . . but even he had not yet bartered his own sister ! "

Crash !

A heavy door-bolt whizzed over the crupper of Nino's horse and struck the wall of Plegmund's dwelling.   The Tuscan grinned and tightened rein ; with a clatter of hoofs he wheeled his mount upon Drogo, bowling him backwards over his own threshold. . . .

" Farewell, sweet bully of the armourers ! " jeered Nino, reining back.   " God spare you from His blasting till we meet again ! "

Then Nino's steel cap was off, and Nino was bowing left
and right as he joined the waiting Herluin a score of yards
along the cobbled way.

" I wish I had done that," thought Herluin.   " Yet I am
glad I did not."

He waved his hand to Plegmund, and saw the trampled
Drogo lurch to his feet and shake his fist at Nino's back.   Then
their horses were trotting abreast past awed or scowling or
applauding faces ; but presently they reached the turn of the
street, beyond which none had seen the leave-taking.   Thereafter few looked up at their passing ; warm air engulfed them
at the smithy doors, and sweating men moved darkly against
showering sparks, whilst Street of Anvils poured its music
out into the calm spring day.

*Tink-a-tink-a-tink-a-tink!   Tink-tink!   Ding, ding, dong,
dock!*

So Herluin journeyed with Nino Chiostra up the western
side of that tract of country beforementioned, whose shape
was like the profile of a nibbled pear, having at its stem
Belsaunt, at its core Alanol, and at its apex Ger.   From
the north-western gate of Belsaunt their way lay along the
northern bank of Varne, which there ran brown amid the
springtime forest greens ; and they first drew rein beside the
broad moat of Olencourt, where Herluin heaved so noisy a
sigh that Nino smiled at him.

" Is she there, then ? " demanded Nino.   " Does your
lover's instinct tell you ? "

" Not it.   The Castellan is not here, for his banner does
not show ; but *she* may be.   In any case, the place holds a
sufficiency of magic, since she has looked on it so many times."

Nino shrugged his shoulders.

" Beware how you enjoy this misery," he counselled.

Herluin looked at the sage boyish face, at the green-brown
moat where water-lilies floated and swans ruffled the ponderous
reflected shape of Yseult's home, and lastly at the forest
ranges leaning far and far against the cloudy May-time
sky.

Enjoy his misery ?   Well, it amounted to that ; but why
not, since little else admitted of enjoyment ?   Nino did not

understand. Nino sniffed the scents of spring with no
Yseult to close the end of every brave or gentle thought.

Some day that lifted drawbridge might have come down
before Herluin — no, before *Raoul* . . . he saw himself
riding, gorgeously apparelled, pale and grave and glad, up
to the door of the great hall where once Yseult and he had
met, where now she waited for him with steadfast eyes
like stars. . . .

Presently he sighed again, and gathered up his horse's
bridle.

Towards sunset the travellers came out into open country
between a marshy bend of the river and a low tree-crested
spur of forest. Far ahead of them the returning curve of
Varne gleamed amid orchards and tilled fields, and midway
in the segment of rich land the fortified Inn of Harmony
crouched by the crossing of roads that ran to Angmer and
Pont-de-Foy. A windmill and a tower on the near bank
marked the bridge at Angmer, but Pont-de-Foy lay hidden
by willow-holts ; and in the courtyard of the inn green
surcoats bore the fleurs-de-lys of the vigilant Castellan.

" I think we will move on," said Herluin, softly. " Angmer
is too far aside, and we cannot make Ververon before dark.
One cup of wine here, and then straight ahead."

" This land I know," remarked Nino when they were on
their way again. " Just there, beside those grassy barrows,
John Doust and I came up with three Belsaunt merchants
fighting for their lives and goods against a troop of forest
thieves. What ? Yes, Plegmund was one of them ; he was
on his way to Château Saulte with armour for some lord or
other. And in the next bend of the river is a hidden ford,
right among the thickest of the woods . . . a wood-cutter
to whom John had done a kindness showed it to us, saying
it was a ford in his grandfather's time, before the Saultes
built Pont-de-Foy. You trample through bracken to the
water's edge ; the forest has hidden what road there may have
been. With a staff you may venture it in a dry October ; I
was up to the chin in one place, it is true. No one uses the
ford now."

Herluin listened ; the thought of the forgotten ford brought

a queer thrill to him—a joy in the twilit fringes of the forest,
in the cloud-darkened sweep of fields and woods bisected by
the rose-flushed steel of Varne, in the secret sound of wind
that drove into the afterglow—a joy mysteriously magnified,
as if he tasted all delight that men had had of earth and sky
and river in that place since the beginning of the years. . . .

For a moment Nino and he and all the world seemed
tranced, as though the shifting patterns of eternity were
frozen for his contemplation; some darkling splendour
offered, and he could not envisage it. A voice from God
seemed stirring in his mind, saying that all such splendour
came from God-ward; a voice from Beauty's self stirred
after, claiming that uttermost joy could ever have reached
him only through the clear brave eyes and strong sweet body
of Yseult. Yet beside and beyond these voices was a silence,
and in the silence a beating of wings . . . it seemed a black
gerfalcon drove lonely up a slant of golden air, and left and
right were roofs and towers and tree-tops, a far gleam as of
marshes, a jagged furious surf as of the sea.

There came an aching sense of quest in desolate and
forgotten places . . . the falcon lighted upon ruined battlements; he clung to high cathedral towers that trembled to
the clamour of their bells; he swept wide-winged across the
waste between the Singing Stones and Dondunor. . . .

" Poor tired futility," cried Raoul within his mind. " What
seek you? Yourself? Your happiness? The Sangreal?
How can *I* help you, who are myself? I think you will spend
your life in search of something lying behind the sunset,
something never to be found—or, if found, spoiled by finding—
and yet mysteriously to be sought for ever. Yseult might
have helped you to it, if she would, but none other of all God's
creatures . . . say, who will fly with a lonely falcon? "

Then Herluin jumped in his saddle, and his mare reared,
and Nino Chiostra swore and afterwards laughed; for out of
a clump of birches beside the way a great owl hooted, mocking
the unspoken question with a piercing " *Who-oo-oo !* "

" Were you dozing? " asked Nino.

" Day-dreaming. What are you up to? "

For Nino had halted and was standing in his stirrups
beneath a rowan that overhung the way.

" The damned souls of departed warlocks make such sounds," said he gravely, breaking off two sprays and handing one to his companion. " I am not too fond of such a place and hour."

" What ? " exclaimed Herluin, once more wide awake, " this from you, the devil most applauded at the Christmas Mystery ? "

" Ay, and even in the company of one who bears a pass-word of the brood of midnight. Of all your tales, my Herluin, I like least that one of the piping fiend with the stag's head. In any case, this empty road is not the stage by the south transept of Saint Austreberte, nor that grim poplar one of the bishop's pikemen."

Herluin looked round him at the darkening landscape, and drew a deep breath.

" It is not," he agreed ; and then : " The Saints be praised, it is *not*."

That night they slept in the mean inn at Pont-de-Foy ; and next day saw them riding in upland pasture country, where fortified farms of Honoy limestone guarded the sheep on the heights and the orchards in the hollows. Their second night was spent at Hastain, and on the third day they saw Ger. A league along the sounding coast they drew rein and stared into a smother of landward-driving cloud ; and there, now hidden and now clear, the promontory held its crown of towers aloof above the fighting waves. The salt was on their lips, and in their cloaks the wind ; and again Nino Chiostra doffed his cap and bowed from his saddle.

" Now must I school myself to call you——"

" Raoul. Call me aught else and you are a villain."

" *My lord Viscount* ; this once at least. What, can you first come in sight of so lordly a heritage and not demand your lawful title ? "

" That title I could do without," said Herluin-Raoul, shortly. " Baron of Marckmont is good enough for me."

Not for the first time he wondered if the Count Warden would expect his Viscount to live at Ger. A mean existence that would be . . . no, with the aid of the Duke of Saulte he would possess his barony and live unto himself. In any case there would be an end to these long wanderings and

sojournings amid strangers.   Herluin must vanish again, this
time for ever ; Raoul must live by the store of courage and
experience which Herluin might bequeath to him.

Gramberge came in sight at the moor's foot, and the
towers of Ger were sunk behind the seaward ridge.   Noon
was past, and speed became imperative. A single yellow-
surcoated man-at-arms looked curiously at the pair as the
geese of Gramberge fled before their trotting horse-hoofs ;
and at the far end of the village street Raoul realised that it
had taken him a year to make full circle around Moors of
Nordanay and Uplands of Honoy.

" What shall I find at Guarenal ? " he wondered. " Reine
mourning for dead Charles ?   No, not unless she came to care
for him since last I saw her.   The Baron will have to look
around again ; he will find noble popinjays enough in Basse
Honoy.   The Saints forbid . . . but what affair is it of mine ?
I suppose betrothal is become an ominous thing since I was
at Montenair."

Thereafter mooning visions of Yseult lasted him until
a bend of the road brought Nino and himself face to face with
the van of a steel-girt cavalcade.   Sweat started on Raoul's
forehead ; then he lifted his chin and squared his shoulders,
for behind the foremost riders swayed banners of familiar
device.

" These are the friends I sought," said Raoul to Nino.
" *Checquy argent and azure* is Le Véranger, and the red owl
is Guarenal."

" Glory to God and the Virgin," returned Nino with a
grin.   " I feared we were about to undertake this doughty
company."

And side by side they rode down towards the white goat's
beard of the old Vice-Warden and the sleek jowl of portly
Enguerrand.

" Give you good-day, my lords ! " cried Raoul.

" Death and wounds ! " exclaimed the peering Baron.
" It is the boy Raoul of Marckmont ! "

" No, by my hilt, you are wrong, my lord," amended the
Sieur du Véranger with twinkling eyes.   " It is Raoul of *Ger*.
Well met, my will-o'-the-wisp ! "

Their hands came out, their quizzical regard and questioning broke over him like waves ; behind them pages and men-at-arms stood in their stirrups or leaned sideways to discover why the troop had halted. Nino was made known with a wave of the hand ; and Raoul learned that on the following day the funeral train of Charles was expected to arrive at Ger.

" My lord, I grieve for your shattered project of alliance between our houses," he hastened to say.

" I must see the poor lad buried," growled De Guarenal, " and Enguerrand pauses with me on his way back to my lord Duke.   Now, will you turn about and ride with us, or shall a couple of my men escort you on to Guarenal ? "

Raoul hesitated for a moment.

Then : " We will come with you," he said.

On the low hill-crest above Gramberge, Nino Chiostra gave to the two-score men-at-arms behind him a short considering stare.   Then he edged his mount forward and spoke in Raoul's ear.

" A boon, Raoul—the first of your Viscounty."

" Granted, my Nino.   But what is it ? "

" That I may ride forward and announce your home-coming."

" Very well.   But, Nino . . . say I come with these my lords."

Nino nodded gravely, lifted his gloved finger-tips to the rim of his steel cap, and spurred out between Raoul and Enguerrand.   For a moment the three nobles watched his slim diminishing figure ; then the old Baron turned stiffly on the young one, and again Raoul found himself embarked upon a welter of explanation.

" Wardship is not dissolved with a sneeze," observed the Vice Warden drily at one point.   " I think you were wise to come in search of the Sieur here."

" And fortunate to find not only him, but you, my lord," put in Raoul.

" You seem determined to involve me in dispute with my lord Count Warden," growled the old man.   " But with my connivance you began to spin this coil, so I suppose that in so far as I may I must see you righted."

" God requite you, my lord," said Raoul soberly.

Then he inquired after Reine.

" She follows with dead Charles . . . oh, she is well
enough, I thank you," the Vice-Warden said. " She beat
me at chess a week ago, and now her falcons are better trained
than mine. Also she looses a very deadly arrow. But she
is not a boy. .·. ."

" Some day, my lord," commented Enguerrand, " a man
will thank God on his knees for that."

" *How now, De Guarenal, what ill-timed folly is this?
Do you connive at mockery in such an hour?* "

" No mockery or folly, Armand. Nor is the hour ill-timed.
We bring you your brother's son again ; in this day of sorrow
at least it is given to you to know the falcon brood unspent."

" *My brother's son! Let me see him!* "

Question, answer, and rejoinder rang like iron in the
thronged and silent hall of Ger. The Count-Warden was on
his feet, his pale eye glazed and vicious ; blunt visage and
bull-neck were encrimsoned above his fur-trimmed mantle.
At his elbow the thin face of his Countess, already grey with
grief, went green with incredulous rage ; and behind the two
great chairs clustered the staring chiefs of the household.
Men-at-arms and grooms and scullions gaped along the walls ;
by the door the surcoats and plate-armour of the visitors
splashed and barred the gloom, and midway between Count
Armand's scowl and the tilted beard of De Guarenal lounged
Nino Chiostra, smiling into the pink bewildered countenance
of John Doust. . . .

Raoul stood forward from between his friends, and met
his uncle's gaze as he had never before met it. His mouth was
dry and his knees trembled, but somewhere in him stirred
triumph and amusement.

" So ! " said the Count, harshly. " And why do *you* now
dare to show your face at Ger ? "

Then Raoul answered, so sharply that he scarcely knew
his own voice.

" Partly, my lord, to do a last poor honour to my cousin
Charles, God rest his soul . . . almost alone in this place he
showed me courtesy . . . and most unwillingly shall I stand

in his shoes. And partly I come to claim from you my barony, being now of age according to law."

" So ? " said the Count again, with a strange thickening of speech and a rising inflection. " This matter . . . you shall await my pleasure in this matter."

" So be it, my lord. At Guarenal, as guest of my lord Baron, I will tarry ; for none can believe you glad to see me, or me to see you. But here and now I ask you to pledge word that as soon as my brave cousin is laid to rest you will make full rendering of Marckmont."

" Sirrah ! " bellowed the Count, rising heavily from his place. " You add to the flat disobedience of a year the knavish impudence of this demand ? Before I move a hand to give you Marckmont you will lodge a month at Ger ; and in the meantime this little yapping cur that came to herald you shall stay as hostage for your good behaviour. . . ."

" No, by the harrowing of hell ! " droned a deep voice ; and swiftly John Doust bowled the slight figure of Nino Chiostra sideways towards the door, so that the latter's steel cap came with a metallic bump against the plated shoulder of stout Enguerrand. Enguerrand's mailed arm gripped the Tuscan's body and whisked it into the group of his own checquered surcoats ; a warlike growl arose on this side and on that, and fifty hands were laid on sword-hilts up and down the hall. John Doust backed slowly till he was level with Raoul ; and behind them the old Baron clashed a gauntleted fist on his shining tasse and raised a thunderous shout.

" Armand, in the name of God I conjure you set bridle to your wrath ! In rank and office you are my superior, but I taught you sword-play thirty years ago, and I will not see your father's last remaining grandson slighted and brow-beaten when he stands within his rights. He is tenant-in-chief, as are you, as am I ; give him the pledge he seeks, and let all men witness why he should not entrust himself to your fond guardianship before he enter upon his own inherit-ance ! "

" My lord, you go too far ! " boomed Armand of Ger. " Not you, but I, am Count and Warden in this place. For my sins this pup is now my Viscount . . . in the name of our lord the king I will make good my claim to his carcase. . . ."

" In my own good name I challenge that claim," returned the old Baron promptly.

" And in the name of Godfrey, Duke of Saulte, do I support that challenge," droned Enguerrand du Véranger.

Then Raoul, flushed and tense and fierce, took another stride towards the dais.

" My lord ! " he cried. " My lord ! I will not strain your famous courtesy by resting for a night beneath your roof ; but in the hearing of all present I would thank you that you steadfastly refused to deem me dead, preferring rather to collect mesne tithes from my poor barony of sand and water, than lawfully to hand it back to our lord the king ! "

At that shrill taunt the face of the Count Warden grew dusky-purple ; his towering figure swayed, and his mouth opened for a roar of rage. One arm went up as though to loose the swords of Ger ; then his pale eyes turned suddenly inward on injected eyeballs, his hand fell, and he crashed heavily backwards into his chair. It was as though he stretched himself and yawned ; but the yawn was hideously prolonged . . . it became a whine, a high desolating whine, and a white froth broke out along the strong bared teeth and straining lips. . . .

Tumult awoke in the hall ; Raoul stood staring blankly at his work, and behind him the old Baron's voice gave sense to the swift re-grouping on the dais.

" An apoplexy . . . God have mercy on him ! "

" It is the hand of God," said Enguerrand, soberly.

Nino Chiostra laughed a solitary laugh.

Motherhood and wifehood . . . sacred things. A livid mask of fury and hatred confronted Raoul ; the lean Countess spat at him and raised wild arms towards the roof.

" God's curse and mine on you for ever ! " she screeched. " Mary Mother grind her heel in your face ere Satan fork you into hell ! My son is dead, and you have slain my husband . . . every night will I pray for your blasting, for leprosy in your flesh, and black damnation of your soul ! "

" Nay, nay," growled John Doust, as the women pulled

their lady away, " meat and wine and temper went to his undoing. . . . Sieur du Véranger, I pray you stand fast on Herluin's other side."

Enguerrand looked round amid the subsiding din.

" Herluin's other side ? " he repeated. " Who the devil is Herluin ? "

A deathly silence fell in the hall when the Viscount's white face was first turned in front of his uncle's empty chair.

" The Count lives," said Raoul, shakily. Then, steadying his voice, he looked about him and went on.

" God is my witness that I sought no harm to him ; but what is come is come, and all here must abide by it. My lord Vice-Warden remains to administer the business of the Coast March ; and I remain as Viscount of Ger. If any feel disposed to quarrel with my authority, let him speak now ; for later will be too late."

A muttering rose among the men-at-arms, but no clear voice emerged. The visitors stood silent in front of their men ; Raoul sank sweating into the chair of state, and behind him Nino and John Doust leaned watchfully on their drawn swords.

Then gaunt De Castlon spoke from among the higher sort at the side of the dais.

" Ger is Ger," he said roundly. " I am for our new Viscount. Who is with me ? "

" I," said the steward, hurriedly. " And I," said the comptroller. " And I," growled a hulking squire. " And I," squeaked an excited page.

" And I, my lord Viscount. . . . I am your man, if . . . if . . ."

It was Griffon the executioner, kneeling before the dais, with hairy hands outspread and dull eye glazed with apprehension.

Raoul looked down at him and smiled.

" Up, Griffon," he said clearly. " Serve me as well as you served my lord Count, and all men will continue to . . . er . . . respect you."

Then Milo, the old captain of the men-at-arms, laughed aloud and drew his sword.

"Count or Viscount," he grunted, saluting, "I serve the
Ger who is on his feet to lead me."

Then many blades were out, and the hall rang for the
newcomer.

But Raoul had sinking feelings at his middle. It would
be harder to sit in his uncle's chair than in the armoury of
Campscapel, or in the loft at Belsaunt, or yet in a hollow oak
in the Forest of Honoy.

"Some would now name me fortunate," he reflected that
night. "Yet Marckmont is no nearer to my hand; Ger
which obeys me must constrain me also—and there will be
strange meetings on the morrow when they bring Charles
home. This was *his* home; I who receive his body am a
stranger. Yet when my uncle dies I, even I, am Ger. Where,
then, are pride and vengeance, that I find no joy in this strange
turn of the wheel? Some in my place would at least have
stricken off the right hand of Griffon, that poor obedient
churl. . . .

"I was cut out for a little lord at Marckmont, not for a
great lord here. When shall I know peace again?"

To this despairing question came no answer save the deep
snoring of John Doust in the antechamber, and the long
harmonies of sea and night-wind round and under the crags
of Ger.

On the brow of the rise beside Count Armand's gallows-
tree slim Robin Barberghe raised a mailed hand and halted
the last progress of his cousin Charles. In the moment's
silence, when only banners flapped and gulls and curlews
cried, the eyes of Raoul met the eyes of Reine de Guarenal
across the dark trappings of the funeral horse-litter. That
afternoon the brown girl rode side-saddle, and her cloak was
of sable velvet; between the puzzled scowl of Robin and the
whimsical stare of tall Alain her regard was sombre, for
although she had made no pretence of caring for the man to
whom she was promised, Reine paid a proper respect to his
memory.

Raoul inclined his head in greeting; the old Vice-Warden
told the newcomers of the Count's seizure and of the coma
that had followed it, and Raoul watched their realisation of

his status flicker on the faces of Robin and Alain.   But when
his turn came for speech he glanced first towards the girl.

" Friends, you are welcome, though most unwelcome is
the woe that brings you.   Beside the body of Charles, whose
soul God have in keeping, all harshness or dispute is stilled
and overpast.   I pray you, follow me in peace to Ger."

Then the Prior of Saint-Guthmund-over-Ger advanced to
cense the bier, whilst the chanting voices of his monks went
bravely up against the seaward wind ; and Raoul wheeled his
mount and led the sad procession down through salt airs and
light stinging rain towards the black-draped gateway of the
barbican.

As he went he realised his fair words to be provisional ;
he yet might startle Alain or round on Robin if either of them
overstepped restraints imposed by the occasion.   And once
they were his guests he found little to say to them, or they to
him ; only Alain chuckled deep in his throat as he flung his
gauntlets to a waiting page.

" In sooth, Raoul, you tricked me fairly when we last rode
together.   But I think you go somehow guarded against
witchcraft, for the beldame whom you stunned called down
such curses on you as never I heard before.   Since you are
here, and master of Ger, I doubt the potency of her enchant-
ments ; but I confess I gave her a gold piece to stay her
clamour and avert her face from me and mine that day."

Raoul laughed abruptly.

" I knew your heart was not in that employment," he
replied, taking the other's proffered hand.

But inwardly he said : " Alain, you need not even hang
yourself for me.   How can I quarrel with you, generous,
gallant fool ?   I come no nearer to Yseult than this, to clasp
the hand that . . . and in my secret knowledge and despair
is even a kind of joy ; for I find I wish these lovers well."

With such unseasonable meditation in his mind he let his
uncle's chamberlain and steward and comptroller guide him
through his duties as host and acting head of a great household ; and not until late afternoon had he a chance to speak
aside with the Vice-Warden's granddaughter.

" Well, Lady Reine," he said with a forced cheerfulness,
" what make you of your handiwork at Ger ? "

" *My* handiwork ? " demanded Reine, glancing up something grimly from her breviary.

Raoul looked down at her—at her brown long-lashed eyes, at the nobility and piquancy of her strong, sunburned face, and at the book whose gold clasps winked against the purple of her silken lap ; and his heart sank lest his vivid memory of this girl betray him, as memories of Rogier had betrayed him, into assumption of a friendship felt by him alone.

" Why, yes," he explained wearily. " You sent me off to Belsaunt thirteen months ago. The rest has followed like— like the flowing of a river. Or so it seems as I look back upon it."

Reine's fingers twitched aside the full folds of her gown to make room for him on the settle beside her.

" And are you sorry that I did so ? " she inquired.

" No . . . all things considered, no."

Comfort and interest rang in her voice ; Raoul seated himself, and watched the red smear of a wet sunset die out above the sea.

" There are strange tales of you abroad since last we met," said Reine after a pause.

" None stranger than the truth," Raoul wagered hardily.

Then he chuckled, remembering Alain's gift to Gunnore on the road from Montenair.

" Alain regaled you with these tales on your way hither ? " he hazarded.

" No. But when he visited our hold last autumn he told us how you dodged him . . . and how you came to be in his company."

" And you thought it base of me to smite an old woman ? "

" I thought you must be changed . . . but before that came word of your flight from Ger ; and it was said your bones were found picked clean by a tarn in the wild hills south of Gramberge. . . ."

" So ? Some time I will tell you my adventures, but now the watch-horn blows ; I doubt not the Barberghes are before the gate. I am changed ; only believe I am not yet come to beating peasant women over the head. And although I was a fool at Montenair, I was not the sort of fool Alain imagined me. . . . I pray you excuse me ; I must not leave Robin to welcome his own father and mother."

" No, you must not," agreed Reine as he bowed to her.

Then she looked comically up at him, so that he paused to see what was coming next.

" You and Robin," she said, " remind me of . . ."

" Of what ? "

" Tom-cats enthroned at opposite ends of a garden-wall."

" The figure is cruel but apt. You know my score against him ? "

" Yes. And Robin hates you because he injured you. Grandfather was furious when he heard of it. I think this hold is often over-full of Barberghes."

" So do I."

" But, Raoul . . . ."

" Quickly, I beg."

" *Did* you kill Lorin de Campscapel ? "

" Yes. From behind. He drunk, and I inflamed with a strong potion. Also I killed . . . but no, not even to you. I took the Butcher's signet-ring from his dead hand, and my Lord Castellan stole it. I have lied most valiantly and been believed ; when I tell the truth I am laughed at. And that is an infuriating thing, as any liar would agree. Ask me no more, or I shall begin to lie to you also. The habit grows. Farewell."

And, somehow relieved by this outburst, the Viscount of Ger marched down to the steps of the great hall.

The Fox of Barberghe had maybe thought to lord it in his brother-in-law's castle ; but his eyes went shrewdly to and fro in his lean face when he rode in, marking the owl of Guarenal, the checquers of Le Véranger, amid his own device of chevrons and the crowding sable falcons of Ger. To Raoul his words were honeyed ; no shadow of demeanour recalled the last occasion when the two of them stood at one time in the inner bailey.

But when it came to supper-time the Countess of Ger refused to sit at meat with her husband's nephew and her son's supplanter. So the Barberghes ate with the lady and her women in her own chamber, whilst Alain de Montcarneau went with Raoul and the rest upon the dais in the great hall.

H

And there Raoul sat wondering what tale the Countess might be spinning to her kinsfolk ; for around him the talk lagged uneasily, so that time and again the clamour of the waves rose faintly through the gusty dark.

" What news has my lord Count from Montenair ? " asked the old Vice-Warden after a prolonged pause.

Greedily Raoul listened for the answer, marking Alain's heightened colour and unwonted hesitation.

" News better told at another time and place," said the paladin at length. " When I ride south again, my lord, it is to celebrate my betrothal with the Lady Yseult de Olencourt."

For a moment Raoul was deaf and blind ; then he found sense to marvel at the stab of affectionate hatred which assailed him. And then his own voice was added, something huskily, to the polite and interested chorus of congratulation. . . .

" Indeed, my lord," came Reine's clear voice, " she is very lovely."

" Attend, Count Alain," chuckled old Guarenal. " There flies no ordinary courtesy."

" But she *is*," insisted Reine. " Lovelier, I hold, than even Yolande de Volsberghe or Ermengarde de Saulte."

Alain inclined his head and reached for his wine-cup.

" Cry you gramercy, Lady Reine ; I pray you will drink with me."

Over the silver goblet-rim Reine's eyes went past the flushed face of Alain to the white face of Raoul. Conscious of her scrutiny, Raoul twitched his features into the semblance of a grin ; but Reine had seen them lighten at her praise of Yseult.

" Oh, God, to be at Marckmont and alone," said Raoul in his heart.

Then he, too, thrust his cup against Alain's and drank with him. . . .

On the morrow Charles was laid to rest in the crypt of Saint-Guthmund-over-Ger ; and at the going-in to the burial the Countess took the arm of her brother of Barberghe, giving him wrongful precedence over Raoul ; but Raoul said no word, standing and kneeling behind the pair of them throughout that solemn rite. And at its termination, when the mourners passed from the priory nave and down a lane of serfs and fisher-folk towards the castle, Raoul saw one sunburned girl look oddly at the Lady Reine de Guarenal beside him, and then at the baby in her own sturdy arm.

" Saints only know," he reflected, " how many of my serfs-to-be go fatherless since the Viscount Charles came home."

XII

RAOUL'S DAY

" My lord, I hoped the Count Warden was recovered from his sickness. We are desperate men in my town; the Constable is at Hautarroy, and the Sieur Gilles will not budge without his father's word; the Duke of Saulte is gone south also, and the Castellan is not to be moved. Surely, we said, one great lord will somehow succour us, even though the king cannot. And now . . ."

The man from Alanol stood first on one foot, then on the other, and stared dejectedly at the Vice-Warden.

" If I were twenty years younger than I am, and if the Easterlings had not wind of the Count's plight, you might have counted on me," said the old Baron, grimly. " But I am here to look to the Coast March. I can do nothing. Who without a siege train and three thousand men can sit down before the Rock of Campscapel ? "

Then Raoul spoke, with his heart hammering in his breast.

" It may be I can deal with Jehan," he said.

Baron and messenger stared at him.

" In two days' time I will tell you," Raoul went on; and as he spoke his plan ran fierily in his mind. " But first, can you engage to raise the town as one man for a night ? "

" That can I," said the burgher, simply.

Indeed, his tale was foul enough. Red Jehan, snorting at his brother's charter, had resumed full power over Alanol. His riders held the gates, his writ ran mercilessly in the streets; no man's life and no woman's honour was safe against him, although the coffers of the town were drained to satisfy his greed. One hour of armed resistance, and a ward was sacked and burned; since then the wretched townsfolk had crept fearfully about their business, barring their doors when night spewed lust and murder from the barbican.

" The country-folk are scared of entering the place," the burgher pointed out. " The market languishes, the foreign

merchants are once robbed and flee to come no more. The
priests are mocked. and stoned, the very nuns are afraid to
show their habit beyond their convent wall.   In sight of God
and for the sweet sake of the Virgin Mary, lords, help us now
or we perish."

" Your name ? " asked Raoul.

" Pendred."

" Is that your tanyard by the foot of Wine Street, round
the corner from the Sign of the Red Dolphin ?   Yes . . .
oh, I know my Alanol . . . no matter how.   Now, Master
Pendred, leave me alone with my lord Baron . . ."

" Death and wounds, boy, what have you hidden from me
now ? "

Raoul outlined his plan ; and two hours later he and Nino
Chiostra and John Doust were riding, plainly clad and
lightly armoured, beyond Gramberge along the eastward
road. . . .

Charles was three weeks in his grave, and still Count
Armand lay between life and death, whilst the new Viscount
sat uneasily in his uncle's place.   The doleful history of
Modred, Prince of Britain, had stuck fast in bogs of
passion and enchantment ; nor, since Reine de Guarenal
had read and criticized it, did Raoul find relief in its
consideration.

" In truth, Raoul," said the brown girl straightly, " this
Modred has too many people in it.   I am forever falling over
some new name or some name half-remembered, a disturbing
shadow in my mind that sends me scrabbling backward
through your pages—or, oftener, gives me to blink and lose
patience and pass on."

" The greater part of life," said Raoul, " is a tumult of
disturbing shadows, and no more.   Perish your story with
one maid and two men in it, and an old nurse to open the door.
Must Pelleas and Lamorak and Gaheris have no inwards of
their own—must they stand in the corridor speechless and
foodless and loveless, until Arthur or Guinevere or Lancelot
address a word to them ?   If one should tell *my* story in small
compass, what room would therein be for a certain fair name,
the name of the Lady Reine de Guarenal ?   Yet, as I have

said before, her word swayed her grandfather in this room
where we now sit, and—lo ! the adventures of Raoul, who
was sometimes Herluin and sometimes Raoul again."

" But what could be said of her, except that she had a snub
nose and—fie upon her—wore no headdress until she was
past seventeen ? "

" Oh, she heartened a fool when every one was against
him.

" Nevertheless you would do well to strike out many of
the sounding names. To you they are something—you have
read deeply in the old romances ; but try your *Modred* on
grandfather, or Robin, or Enguerrand, and I vow they will
say you confuse them instead of getting on with the fighting
and the naughtiness."

" But I did not write for my lord Baron, or for Enguerrand,
and certainly not for Robin. I wrote to . . . to ease myself
of a burden, the burden of the mournful confusion which is
our life."

" Not *my* life, Raoul. I am well content . : . whilst I
can hawk, and hunt the beasts of chase, and watch the little
animals when they cannot see me. Then I love embroidery,
especially of banners ; and now I am doing an altar-cloth,
very fine ; I have archery and lute-playing and reading of
the *gestes* and ballads. For my duties, I learn to be châtelaine
at Guarenal ; and with that, and with the Holy Offices—oh, I
am tired and happy at the day's end. No mournfulness, or
yet confusion, comes to me."

" Never ? Do you never sit and watch the sunset, and
dream things not to be shaped in words ? "

" Oh yes, sometimes. But when that began to hurt I
stopped it for a while. . . ."

" I can never stay myself from doing it. The most part
of my life is preparation for such idle moments ; and when
I make them I cannot savour them. Only as they rise un-
bidden do they now delight me ; so that I begin to welcome
the thought of war, like any boastful swordsman who has
no wit or grace for anything else. Indeed, I had rather kill
men than animals, for men have generally done ill, and animals
never."

" Poor Raoul . . . did you love her very much ? "

Reine's voice was gentler than he had yet heard it ; the question drove him from his chair to a seaward window.

" I love her very much," he corrected dourly.

" *How* much ? "

" Enough to . . . to remember that she mocked my barony, my little lordship . . . enough to flaunt my new heirdom with its promise of lands wider even than the lands of Montcarneau . . . enough to plunder and rob and slay if it would anyhow advantage me with her. And yet, God help me, enough to wish her happy with Alain . . . and yet again, not enough to give Alain a chance of winning signal thanks and glory. . . ."

" You speak a mighty riddle, Raoul. How could *you*——"

" Ay, you do well to emphasize the pronoun. Yet it is true I travail with a secret that may never benefit me . . . but if it benefit not me it shall never benefit another."

Reine looked at him, he thought, as though he were a hurt and sulky child. But on the very morrow came the man from Alanol to Ger. . . .

" So we are not yet quit of this track, John and I," said Nino, eyeing the dark southward slopes of moor. " I hoped we were, when last we came northward ; but now I am content."

" I too," said John Doust, heavily. " I will not go to England until I have more gold than previously I lost to that accursed ship-master ; but now I am in no hurry, since the gaining of it seems likely to be lively . . . thánks to you, my lord."

" In good faith, John, though I be a shrimp and you an elephant, I will batter your bascinet about your ears next time you ' my lord ' me when we are alone," cried Raoul. " I would there were no need for it at Ger, but there some of the men-at-arms already hold me in sufficient light esteem."

" I wondered if you noticed that," muttered Nino.

" I noticed it well enough. This business we are now upon may remedy it."

" How so ? "

" Get a score of such lusty rogues killed in a rousing fray, and the rest will love you for ever. I know not why, but so it is, and lords and captains profit greatly by it."

Nino laughed.

"*Per Bacco*, Raoul, you are right. I feel there is great glory to be won in the shadow of your gerfalcon, yet . . . *you* will think too much for the enjoyment of that glory. I declare you are happier here alone with us than you will be in any pomp of victory."

"Perhaps I am. Indeed, I am. Saturn stood too high at my birth. But I cannot understand why, now, when I look back on my first flight from Ger, the days I spent alone and fugitive seem happy; for they were not happy at the time."

"Because the fears you had no longer press upon your mind as they did then. That easement makes remembered sun more golden and remembered skies more blue . . . I know it."

"You talk like a pair of poets," growled the Englishman.

"We *are* a pair of poets," chirped Nino. "Raoul, cry again that rondel you made the other night, when we had ridden on the sands by Merlin's Cove."

So Raoul declaimed *Sea-Magic* against a hum of insects and a stir of wind amid the pines of Nordanay.

> *The glimmering waves, along the midnight shore,*
> *Lifted and curled and crashed in emerald flame.*
> *Between the ragged clouds dim starlight came,*
> *And sad sea-music, surging landward, bore*
> *Faint-echoed fragments of entombèd lore.*
> *Yea, shouting tales of thrice-forgotten fame*
> *The glimmering waves, along the midnight shore*
> *Lifted to curl and crash in emerald flame.*
> *You and I will remember evermore*
> *The mad white horses that no crag could tame,*
> *The rock-ring'd cove with the enchanted name,*
> *The furious booming wind that beat and tore,*
> *While glimmering waves, along the midnight shore*
> *Lifted, and curled, and crashed in emerald flame.*

"*Brava!*" cried Nino. "Almost it makes me love the sea, an element which has no kindness for my inwards."

"Yes, that is stormily fashioned," admitted John Doust.

" But you were at Ger before midnight, and the wind was not
a gale till dawn. . . ."

" Oh, painful preacher of the truth ! " trolled Raoul. " It
is even as you say. Nor can any tale be thrice-forgotten.
But when Nino and I had come away, when there was no one
in the cove at all, that was how it looked and sounded. . . ."

" If I had not seen you letting daylight into forest
thieves . . ."

John Doust twisted his mouth to an almost imperceptible
slit, and cut his words off with a grunt.

" Somewhere there I slept the first night. . . ."

Mile on mile of sweltering heather, with a brassy haze
to veil the nakedness of Dondunor. Bees booming past as
though hurled from a sling ; curlews sharply black and white,
cutting wild curves in the fierce blue of the zenith ; rocks that
danced in the distance, and a glaring sun that drew sweat from
the very eyelids. . . .

" Up there must be the tarn where I slew the apprentice
. . . now we should bear southward . . . God, but the moors
are good."

" And my damned bascinet is nigh red-hot."

" In truth, John, you are wilting visibly. I myself could
welcome some small array of Raoul's glimmering waves.
What, must we push past that black cliff ahead ? "

" Ay. Thank your own particular Saints it is not raining."

" *Per Bacco!* What is rain ? Ere sunset I shall be a
little fried eel. Shut the oven door, said the salamander ; I
cannot abide a draught. Mary Mother, what pains our
Viscount takes to get us all eviscerated by this scurvy Jehan
de Campscapel ! "

So they came over the lowest eastern shoulder of the
mountain ; and when they had eaten and drunk they bathed
in a pool and donned their cloaks and hoods, that no strange
wink of steel might startle a lolling sentinel on any of Red
Jehan's watch-towers above Capel Conan.

" Dead ground between that clump of pines and the rock
like a goblin chimney. Follow the stream till the little water-
fall, then aim for Dondonoy."

H*

Nino memorised the route by speaking it aloud. It was John Doust's notion to hang the skull of a mountain sheep on a hawthorn bush above the Conan Beck at their place of crossing. And now they were in peril, for the watch-towers were less than a league apart. Clouds gathered about the sunset, and fantastic fires seemed lit in heaven behind the mountain.

"Red Jehan's version of discipline may work in either of two ways," said Raoul. "The watch-tower garrisons may all be drunk each night, or ranging wide till after dark. Nino, I am glad you counselled our carrying bows. Now, by the Rood, what *is* it ? "

Only a herd of scampering deer; but even John Doust had drawn quick rein and plucked at the hilt of his great estoc.

"Now we must drive straight through the pinewoods till we strike the stream again."

And, no man seeing them, they came in the last light to the tiny home of the anchoress beneath the Rock of Campscapel. . . .

"Holy sister ! "

A faint stir beyond the square slit in the stone; then a reedy voice, gentle and unafraid.

"Who speaks so late ? "

"Do you remember a boy who passed out through your cell in the autumn that is gone ? "

"A boy ? There were two boys. One came with my good lady and the girl . . . yes, I remember the other. I thought he was Saint Michael, come in a dream."

"Sister, I am he. I would pass in again."

"None has ever passed in this way . . . I have no light . . . but enter if you will and can."

Standing on John Doust's shoulders, Raoul fumbled for the trap-door in the thatch. At length he found and raised it, and with one leg thrust through he turned and gulped a mouthful of fresh air. Below him the Conan Beck ran noisily, a faintly-gleaming serpent barred by black tree-boles; far up the dark hillside a solitary light gleamed from some outwork of Red Jehan's hold. John Doust's face was a blur; the unhooded cap of Nino Chiostra glistened faintly in the starlight. . . .

Thud ! He had fallen on his feet, and was fumbling in
his wallet. Flint and steel gave light at length ; the taper
shook in one hand, and in the other rattled the keys he had
taken from hunchback Dirck that night eight months
before. . . .

" Sister, has no one ever come this way, save those three,
since I was here ? "

The bright eyes of the anchoress seemed dazed by the tiny
flame ; but the whitening head was shaken sturdily.

" Not one. I fear my lady has forgotten me."

" Was the girl slender ? And the boy small as I am ? "

" Yes. And the girl carried a great black cat."

" Did they ask concerning me ? "

" No. The boy was wounded, and they seemed in haste."

" Ah . . . well, sister, pardon my disturbance of your
rest. God willing, I shall soon be back, and then you will
sleep in peace."

Queer soul, on whose simplicity so much depended ! The
thought struck Raoul even as the key grated in the hidden
lock. . . .

This time the air of the passage was oppressively close ;
the flame burned ill, and the shadow of Raoul's sword-point
leaped along the dripping stone. Rats squeaked, their first
shrill outburst lancing the oncomer's vitals ; at the foot of
the stair a red-eyed couple turned as though at bay, and then
fled scuttering. . . .

Up and up and up went Raoul, shearing the matted cobwebs from before his eyes ; and though he halted at each
score of steps his head was whirling and his breath spent
when he came softly to the top step and the iron-studded door.

Then he leaned against the wall and choked back a laugh ;
for a great wooden bolt, unnoticed by him when he fled that
way, had been shot on the outer side of the door by the last
user of the secret stair.

" So, Jehan," whispered Raoul, " you do *not* know. In
two days more you shall have company."

Then he turned and stole down again, and in five minutes'
time was taking leave of old Clotilde. Once more she held
the light for him ; and John Doust gave him a bear's hug
when he dropped on the mossy bank above the stream.

" All is well . . . come . . . God be with you, Sister."

" God guard you, friend . . . good-night."

The taper was quenched, and with a faint jingling of bits, a faint trampling of riding-boots and horsehoofs, the wanderers faded into the forest, and only the Conan Beck swirled down the glen beneath the calm night sky.

For years to come, throughout Honoy and Nordanay, the octave of Corpus Christi was fated to be known as Raoul's Day. On the previous morning, after the burgher Pendred had left Ger, Raoul took a piece of charcoal into the winter parlour; and there, with his tongue-tip curling out of his mouth, he drew on the boards of a new-scoured table a much-smudged but reasonably accurate plan of the hold above Alanol. Then, for an hour or more, he hung above it with John Doust and Nino Chiostra, whilst the old Baron of Guarenal sat by them in his chair, silent save when they sought his counsel.

At length Raoul stood straight, grimacing at the stiffness in his back; and at his bidding a saluting squire ran off to gather the chief men-at-arms of Ger.

" My lord," said Raoul to the Vice-Warden, " will you lead the way to the hall ? "

" No, this time I follow our new Alexander."

Raoul smiled, but stepped out manfully towards the door.

" One moment, Alexander," came the voice of Reine, who had appeared during the discussion. " You have a very grievous smut of charcoal on the end of your nose."

In the hall, when the silent group of war-scarred retainers was collected by the dais, Raoul spoke clearly.

" Now let the castle gates be shut," he said. " And let none leave or enter by the low postern until I know his business."

" The herrings are coming in, my lord," objected the steward, whilst warrior looked on warrior at this unusual command, and another squire went out to see it done.

" God be good to all herrings, Master Steward, but this time they wait," replied Raoul. " Herrings were the death of one Campscapel; I would not have them prolong the life of another. Gentlemen and soldiers, which of you will follow

me to smite Red Jehan into hell? I can take no more than
a third of your number, for we may all be slain; but as I see
it our chance is good, and if you follow not I take my two
friends here, and five-score men-at-arms, and go without you.
Mine is no crack-brained scheme; my lord Vice-Warden has
approved it. Milo, you asked that Ger should lead you;
what say you?"

"I say you are very young, lord Viscount. Also you
speak in riddles. May we not learn more?"

"Only those who swear to follow me may hearken further.
You are my uncle's men, not mine; but those who come,
and live through one night's work, will not have reason to
be shamed."

Old Milo shook his head; but a round dozen of the
squires and sergeants swore, and forthwith trooped up to the
winter parlour to be shown the charcoal diagram and to learn
their parts.

Then Raoul took a crucifix, and each man kissed it,
swearing secrecy till his return; and in an hour the sweating
armourers of Ger were cursing the day of their new Viscount's
birth as they dealt with the needs of a swarm of clamorous
swordsmen. . . .

In the midst of the hum of preparation that same afternoon came two loud blasts on the watchmen's horn from the
gateway turrets; horsemen in checquered surcoats neared
the barbican, and Raoul—glittering for the first time in full
armour—had the drawbridge lowered, and gripped the hand
of Enguerrand du Véranger.

"What, here again so soon, my heart? In faith I am
glad to see you, but how comes it?"

"My lord Duke sends his condolences to my lady your
aunt, and would have further news of the Warden. What is
toward here?"

Raoul told him.

Soon after dawn on Raoul's Day the watchman's horn
was wound again. This time a single horseman broke across
the bridge; he came from Ostercamp, the last dark fortress
of the Coast March, with news that at the hour of matins
seven Easterling galleys had been sighted, standing in

to shore towards the undefended fishing villages between Ostercamp and Ger.

Old Guarenal banged his fist on the board in front of him, and looked at Raoul.

" My lord, I am pledged to the men of Alanol."

" I know you are, boy. I must see to this myself. Enguerrand, are you for coastwise blood-letting, or for more glorious hazard over Alanol ? "

" My lord, you honour me, but *I* am pledged to Raoul."

" I thought as much. Leaving me to explain to your Duke how you came to be hung at the Rock of Campscapel. Well, go your way. Ho, page, my armour, quickly ! De Castlon must take charge at Ger. . . ."

So, in the first warmth of the cloudy day, the great hold was four-fifths emptied of its garrison. Every war-horse was out of the stables, and half-a-dozen of Raoul's archers had to be dismounted and left behind ; not until the Vice-Warden's force had passed the barbican did Raoul wave his hand in the inner bailey. Then his own cavalcade swept two-and-two across the sounding bridge, whilst Reine stood by De Castlon on the steps and ground her teeth because she was a girl.

" Why, grandpa is more blithe than you," she said to Raoul when he kissed her hand. " Oh, I know you are not afraid, but . . ."

" I shall be afraid soon enough," promised Raoul. " Meanwhile, be good to my lady of Ger, poor soul . . . hey, what has Nino on his shield ? "

" A ram *passant* . . . why ? Oh, you mean he is not noble . . . as Jehan de Campscapel and you are noble."

" Your point is barbed as ever. Nino's father was noble, in any case. But I was thinking of a prophecy . . . oh, I will tell you later—if I can. Now it is time to go . . . and I thank you, cousin Reine, for warning me of smuts upon the nose."

" And *I* thank *you*, cousin Raoul, for your civility to one who is not someone else ! "

" Farewell ! "

" Farewell . . . and God be with you and your men ! "

So, jestingly till their last words, they parted ; and Raoul looked down at the waves of Ger and wondered if he should

see them again. At Mass that morning he had twice lost
the thread of the service by thinking of Yseult ; and now he
saw himself as being at ease with any maiden but the one
who really mattered to him.

"Dear Reine," he thought. "Yseult would have liked
her . . . at least, I hope so."

So, musing most unsuitably for one who led a raid, he
passed beneath the gateway of the barbican and tightened
his steel-girt knees against the stiff embroidery of his saddle.

"I must put all my wits to this one venture," he told
himself. "Why do I burn in scheming heat all morning
till the thing is well in train, and then grow cold and listless,
pondering it as though I had not planned it ? When fear
strikes through to my heart I suppose I shall fully apply
myself to war ; but until then I crave my own permission to
remain a poet and a lover and a fool."

Five minutes' poetry and love and folly were then left
to him ; for at the end of them a second solitary horseman
changed the tenor of Raoul's Day. This one seemed bent
on charging the column ; he waved his cap and yelled,
spurring madly along a track too rough to be called a road—
a track worn by the fisher-folk who came from the westward
hamlets to see what ornaments the Count Warden found to
deck his gallows-tree.

"My lord, you are of Ger—I pray you turn rein. Four
ships of the Easterlings are upon Karmeriet, and the herring
fleet is out ! "

"Karmeriet ? " exclaimed Raoul. "The Vice-Warden
is gone towards Ostercamp with two hundred men . . . but
no galley passed near Ger this morning."

"They came straight in from sea, my lord. Six more
were seen in the first light, making as though for Hardonek
or beyond. God blast them with His lightning, they are all
along the coast. . . ."

Raoul sat perched on Safadin, his great grey destrier,
and stared down at the woeful and beseeching face.

"I am bound on other business," he said shortly.

"Then at Ger—— "

"There are no horsemen left ; and no man leaves the
hold unless the town itself is threatened. Neither galley in

the harbour is sea-worthy ; help may come from Hardonek, friend, but I fear there is none for you at Ger."

Thump off his horse came the rider, tottering forward to fall on his knees in the heather at Raoul's stirrup.

" My lord, my good merciful lord ! " he bleated, with tears rolling down his cheeks.   " We are your people—you are the new Viscount—do not desert us in this dreadful peril ! My lord, they maim and rape and loot and burn if once they gain fair landing.   There are only a score of men in the village able to bear arms.   In the name of God and of Saint Guthmund, come and save us ! "

" Why the devil can they not flee inland and leave their houses empty ? " growled John Doust.

The man looked up at him.

" Our homes are all we have ! " he wailed.   " And there are some bedridden—*my* wife is heavy with child—we have a little tower that may be held for an hour or two, but my lord, they can pile wood about it and b-b-burn our people up ! "

Raoul looked out across the heathery waste, cursing the burden of this decision, whilst men-at-arms whispered and horses stamped, and in the nostrils of man and beast the warm scents of gorse and ling met the cool salt odour of the sea. Twelve miles along the winding cliff-top paths lay Karmeriet . . . and to reach the rock of Alanol Raoul had given his cavalcade no more than two hours over his own journey-time with John and Nino. . . .

The silence of his pondering was momentary, but to himself it seemed an age before he spoke.

" How was the tide by Capdelest ? "

" Half-full, my lord."

" Then we will come along the shore."

" God and Our Lady requite you, my lord, and have you in keeping for ever ! "

And with a wheeling and a stamping they were heading westward, where the messenger's path rose up and vanished above the first of the deep shoreward gullies between Capdelest and Ger.

Down the ravine turned Raoul, leaning back in his saddle as the charger slipped and slid ; and with shouts and oaths and vague metallic clamour man after man went rocking after him.

"In faith," said John Doust, reining in lest his mount trod on the crupper of Enguerrand's below him, "I shall never forgive this Raoul of ours if I am left with a broken neck in this damned gully, or an Easterling arrow in the guts down yonder."

"Pray rather that you may be spared for a stoup of boiling oil in the snout at Alanol," advised Nino. "For myself, I do not know this coast, but it seems to me you are most likely to be drowned."

Presently Safadin's shoes struck fire amid the scattering shingle at the foot of the ravine ; and the long line of yellow surcoats dipped and wound and clanged into column of fours upon the beach.

"Nino," said Raoul as he waited, "what badge is that upon your shield ? "

Nino looked down at the ram *passant*, gold on green, which he himself had painted.

"This is the ram of Chiostra," he said. "My father's arms I would not bear if I might ; but I will do what honour I may to the badge of my mother's commune. Runs your blood cold at this assumption ? "

"Not it. I only know that Jehan de Campscapel believes that death will come upon him behind a ram."

"*Ecco !* That is fair hearing. *Sono da Chiostra, son' montone.*"

With Nino's newly-fashioned motto in his ears Raoul touched spur to Safadin's flank ; and behind him rose the heavy drumming of horsehoofs upon firm sand. Then, for the first time, as the sea-wind beat on his face to the effortless stride of the great grey stallion, Raoul tasted a joy in leadership ; it was good to have launched a bolt of steel, with himself at the head of it, to the aid of the sturdy fisher-folk along the coast.

But on his right the grey-white tide, already breasting the Hardonek sand-banks, crept swiftly over the flat rock-strewn shore towards the base of the black cliffs of Capdelest. Raoul had not ridden a mile along the beach before he regretted this rash venture ; but now there was no turning aside, for the gullies grew steeper and less frequent, and to mount again to the cliff-top would have thrown away what time was gained and lost much more beside. And so he pressed on, his eyes set on the diminishing reach of sand between black rock and hurrying sea. Not Capdelest itself, but the lesser headland beyond it, was the danger-point; yet already at Capdelest the foremost breakers were slapping at the cliff's very foot, and the column trampled through shallow whirling water to regain sand on the further side. . . .

" God, we shall never make it ! " Raoul told himself, when the first spray shot high amid the distant rocks which littered the sand by the far horn of Merlin's Cove. Then his oath became a prayer : " God, let us make it ! Keep our horses' feet ! "

At length he turned in his saddle, and yelled across the wind.

" Form double file ! Let no man ride on the rocks—hold to the sand for your horses' legs ; bear knee to knee, and let the outer man grip fast on his neighbour's pommel ! "

And as he turned again he cried out to Enguerrand beside him. " Lead on ; I follow last of all."

Then Enguerrand drove his spurs deep and hurled his charger at the cliff's end ; and the backwash of a broken wave met the oncoming curl of a breaking wave and took him to the knees in foam. Raoul reined aside, and Safadin stamped once with a mighty splashing, thereafter standing like a stone ; and past him crashed and clanged and hurtled the shouting riders of Ger. Green water, ridged and ramparted with silver, roared under and about them ; bent figures disappeared in shooting spray, and strong hands clutched at arms or saddle-horns of men ahead of them, at bridles of destriers behind them, hauling a chain of flesh and blood and steel through a creamy welter fifty yards in length.

" On with you ! On with you ! Strike spur and trample the damned sea ! " shrieked Raoul, scarce conscious of his words ; and at the last he churned grey Safadin about and, with his sollerets and leg-armour full of water, drove furiously to the flank of the last rider of his troop. . . .

The man-at-arms grabbed at him and missed ; their mounts were separated, and Raoul made that perilous passage

alone with Safadin. Twice, in battle with surge and backwash, he thought the stallion's foothold gone, and once he
was nearly out of his saddle on the seaward side ; water smote
him as though it were solid, and he dared not sit upright lest
a breaker beat him against the glistening rock-face ten feet
away. . . .

A group of exultant men was straining to receive him ;
John Doust stood on a boulder, waist-high in water, with a
dozen dismounted riders linking him to safety round a jagged
corner, and as Raoul gasped and reeled and clung in his place
the Englishman's great hand fell clutching on his vambrace,
whilst the sea sank savagely away with a last tug at Safadin's
straining knees. . . .

So the tide which bore the Easterlings upon Karmeriet
failed to stay the rescuers by Merlin's Cove ; and with grey
Safadin thundering ahead the falcon surcoats swept along the
narrowing sands. And so at last Raoul and Enguerrand broke
round a shelf of rock and saw the dark hulls of the beached
galleys and the smother of smoke amid the little huts of
Karmeriet. On a low ledge behind the village rose the squat
shape of a tower ; the sea-wind drove the smoke towards it,
and under cover of that smoke the tiny scuttling figures of the
pirates bore—even as the messenger had prophesied—bundles
of straw and faggots, benches and stools and the poor household gear of the fisher-folk, to pile them at the base of the
tower. Arrows and bolts and pebbles big as a man's fist
rained upon the raiders ; as Raoul drew near he noticed mail
and even plate amid the latter, and when the screech of
discovery ran among them a tall man with a single silver wing
on his helmet could be seen directing the beginnings of
withdrawal to the ships. . . .

But warning came too late ; when Raoul snapped his
visor down and felt for his sword-hilt John Doust and a score
of men-at-arms were already separated out and bearing slant-
wise on the galleys. And with a mighty shout of " *Ger !* "
the horsemen were all among the cottages, hacking at fleeing
Easterlings, piercing them in the back with arrow and lance,
stamping them hideously into the sand and mud and ashes.

One red-faced rogue with a horned steel cap and a cuirass
of grotesque leathern leaves stood sturdily in Raoul's path

and let fly a shaft at Safadin's chest, but the point glanced off Raoul's knee-plate ; Safadin reared and struck out with his fore-hoofs, and something seemed to snap between Raoul's eyes. The man disappeared ; a stone, flung from nowhere, crashed on Raoul's shoulder-plate, so that he reeled along the stallion's crupper. Then he was upright again, knowing the snap between his eyes for the communicated shock of Safadin's iron shoes as they broke the Easterling's body. . . .

Reining in, he peered towards the ships ; one was already half-full of yelling pirates, and on the prow—like the Sieur Ajax when the Grecian fleet was assailed by the lords of Troy—stood the tall warrior with the winged helm, wielding a broad axe whilst his men strove to push off from shore. . . .

Round each galley a fight was raging ; half-way down the beach was Nino Chiostra, dismounted and running like a madman, waving a flaming brand snatched from some burning cottage, hooting with triumph as he neared a vessel and plunged into the water towards her waist. A moment more, and the half-furled sail was alight ; the shallows grew full of men who grappled and fell in blood-streaked foam, and at the seaward limit of the village a score of cornered pirates were dying man by man beneath the lances of encircling men-at-arms. . . .

Up by the tower was Enguerrand, directing the hurling aside and trampling out of already-burning faggots. Here and there lay yellow surcoats ; Easterlings were Easterlings, in spite of surprise and panic.

" My men begin to earn my fame for me," said Raoul between his teeth.

And he wheeled Safadin and fell to killing with the best of them. Days afterwards he recalled things felt, things seen beyond his sword-point or over the rim of his shield—black teeth in a yelling mouth, gashed arms flung wide to clutch at Safadin's bridle, jar upon jar of his own descending sword, and the distorted face of an Easterling boy whose blue eyes in one hour looked first on piracy and last on life—but at the time the furious images succeeded each other as in a dream, each wiping out its predecessor with a new hazard and a new atrocity. . . .

The leader with the winged helmet held his place until

a "man-at-arms impaled him from below ; two of his crew
leaped over the stern and swam far out until they drowned,
but the rest fought grimly to their end.   The villagers were
out of their tower, and with axes and shovels and scythe-
blades tied to poles they spread a lively carnage up and down
the shore. . . .

Not a man of the raiders escaped ; and when the four hulks
blazed in a row along the sand, Raoul turned up the shingly
slope and found his charger's way barred by a little mob of
fisher-folk.   Shouting, laughing, weeping, they closed about
him ; old men piped blessings, women kissed grey Safadin's
mane and bridle, or caught at Raoul's plated knees and feet,
at his scabbard and stirrups and embroidered saddle-cloth.
Children were held up to see the face of the sweet Viscount,
who would not give his people over to the terror from the sea.

" There, there, good souls," laughed Raoul, hoping the
tears on his cheeks would be taken for sweat.   " Make way
. . . make way . . . you shall have timber for your huts
again . . . I and those with me need your prayers this
night . . . no, we cannot come to kneel with you, for we
have other work to do."

And amid the clangour of bells from the tiny church went
up the shouts of Enguerrand and of John Doust, mustering
the scattered men-at-arms along the beach. . . .

Eight of the troop were dead, and more than a score
wounded ; of the latter, a dozen were left behind, the rest
electing to share the night's adventure.   So that it was with
less than a hundred mounted men that Raoul rode up the
ravine behind Karmeriet and gained the cliff track running
between Gramberge and Hardonek.   In Gramberge men
stood staring when the cavalcade bore up the crazy street and
galloped off towards Guarenal ; had not one injured man
fallen out of his saddle and been handed over to the care of
the village priest, none would have known whence this living
thunderbolt was launched, and even the dazed man-at-arms
could not enlighten those who tended him as to whither it
now sped.

" Well begun," growled John Doust, as he eyed the
shadows of afternoon along the ranges, " is nothing like
half-done."

"We must go by the way we planned," said Raoul, "or I would strike straight up into the hills at the first opening. What I most fear is premature defiance or attack by the townspeople. An armed man, with armed comrades by him, will not find it easy to hold a roof-tile whilst the wolves of Campscapel go lewdly in the streets beneath him."

"I should have thought them too well terrified to stir until your signal," came Enguerrand's mild voice.

"Sieur Enguerrand," chirped Nino Chiostra, "you have never lived among brawling townsmen. Not valour, but persistent unity, is their chief lack. I noticed our Viscount did not tell yon Pendred *how* we mean to enter the hold of Campscapel; and that was wise. *Per Bacco*, but a known road seems shorter . . . I think sea-bathing suits these northern horses . . . ai, ai, *sono da Chiostra, son' montone*. . . ."

"Pray that by midnight *montone* be not mutton," counselled Enguerrand with a smile.

Hard riding brought them at length to the point where they must leave the road; and there they halted, each man eating and drinking and sparingly watering his horse. Presently they were trailing in single file up bracken-covered sheep-tracks, men leading horses, horses crowding each other; and the first westering of the sun saw Safadin foremost in a helter-skelter advance along a heathery hog's-back that slanted down to the eastern spurs of Dondunor.

"This ride is like any other ride," thought Raoul suddenly. "I want to do things as other men do them, and yet to think of them whilst I do them . . . to see myself doing them as though I stood by. And when I pass into myself and fall to *doing*, as on the shore this morning—then I lose that faculty of watching which above all things pleases me. So that to do a thing whole-heartedly is not wholly to know that I am doing it . . . ay, life is subtle if one lacks the thews and sinews of John Doust, or Charles, God rest his soul . . . or, perhaps, of that Easterling whose face I split in the shallow water. . . .

"Some day—if any other day be left to me—I think those two sharp flames of thought and action might unite in me, and then I should engage in life indeed and miss no edge or

savour of it. That unity I dreamed Yseult might work in
me ; but she would not, therefore she could not. And now,
in the shadow of death . . ."

The morning's race and tide-passage and butchery, the
might of sweating Safadin between his plated thighs, the
surge of his own headlong war across the sun-scorched
heather, the promise of great and furious reckonings between
the now and the midnight—all these flared dimly for a space
in Raoul's mind. For with an inward quailing and alarm
he found the flame of this day's action to have burned his
cherished love to ashes ; heart-scarred, yet consciously heart-
whole again, he smiled to find himself shocked by his own
breaking out of slavery.

" And now in the shadow of death I am emptied of that
madness, and something sad because of it . . . for my folly
in loving her was greater than she knew. Be damned to her
and to all sweet shapes that promise a glory beyond fulfilment
of flesh and blood . . . if this be my last sun, at least it shall
not sink upon the shame of mine idolatry. Farewell, Yseult ;
and never wonder what a grief we might have wrought
together."

And since his thought of Yseult had largely been oblique
consideration of himself, it was with a mysterious sense of
selflessness that Raoul awoke from dreams and looked about
him at the stern helmed faces of his company.

" Dear Saints," he mused, " there is much to live for here
below. I do not want to die until I know more of it . . .
then why in the name of Michael Archangel am I plunging
through this red bell-heather to put myself in jeopardy of
Jehan de Campscapel ? What are *they* dreaming of—Nino
and John and Enguerrand, that grim man-at-arms, that
hulking archer ? Helms and bascinets are much alike, but
what a medley of imagining must fume thereunder !

" And now, you feckless chieftain, attend to your great
secret raid ! "

The sea-wind had died at noon, and not until sunset
dusted with gold the first tree-masses of the Forest of Honoy
did a stiff south-westerly breeze beat into the faces of Raoul
and his men and bring slate-coloured piles of cloud to the
shoulders of Dondonoy. There on the windy heights, just

out of range of Jehan's watch-towers, with twilight coming on and ten miles still to go, Raoul held rapid conclave with his three friends. . . .

"I spy our goblin chimney," said the Tuscan. "Now give me a squire and let me ride ahead as we agreed."

"Yes, Nino, go you on ; we follow fast."

With no uplifting of voice or horn from that point onward, they bore with speed towards the deepening shadows of the woods. In front went Nino, and behind him rode a squire with a white scarf dangling from his helmet. As the dusk deepened only that greying blur gave Raoul his direction ; once or twice John Doust growled out that Nino was wrong, but in the end he was able to draw rein beside the sheep's head on the hawthorn bush, whilst Nino's horse pulled up the far bank of the brawling beck.

A clattering and splashing rose, and again Raoul had a moment's pause whilst the tail of the column crossed the water. And now the thought of waiting eyes and swords in Alanol sent a shiver of excitement through him, and he commended himself to God and the Virgin and to his own particular group of Saints, lest later he forgot to do so.

Then Safadin was trotting through the evening odours of the pine-forest, and Raoul saw a great star peep blue-white through ragged clouds above the sombre western ridge, where still a rosy smear persisted behind the feathery tops of swaying pines.

Beyond that ridge lay Alanol ; behind him, with a medley of soft sounds blurred by the rushing clamour of wind in the woods, came the armed riders of Ger.

The vast bulk of the Rock of Campscapel stood up against the lingering green gashes of summer afterglow. The dull steel of the Conan Beck gave ghostly definition to the swaying branches of gnarled beeches, which seemed to wave defiance at the more orderly ranks of pines above them. The rueful squire whose duty it was to stay with half-a-dozen men beside the tethered horses stood with the low-voiced chieftains and received his orders with the best grace he could muster. . . .

Clotilde sat wide-eyed in a corner of her home ; beside her another squire stood on guard with a candle to light the men into the passage, and to see that none trod where he should not in the narrow cell. First Raoul, then Enguerrand, then Nino, then John Doust, was swallowed up in the arched way ; Raoul held a taper in his shield-hand, and Enguerrand had three unlit torches tucked beneath one arm. . . .

Again the rats and spiders scuttled ; echoes died as the passage filled with the clank and rattle of plate-armour, and presently Raoul set foot on the first stair. . . .

Up and up and up, until the dusty steps were packed with men, until Enguerrand must hand his torches to Nino Chiostra, in order to hold Raoul's taper for the opening of the door. . . .

To Raoul it seemed that his own loins were jelly, and that above them a spring was coiled at his midriff. The keys clinked in his mailed hand ; beside his upper arm flashed Enguerrand's stained sword-point, poised for a thrust if a thrust were needed. . . .

The lock grated, and a screeched whisper from John Doust sent silence spinning down the stair. Then Raoul drew the wooden bolt, and pulled open the door, filling the widening gap with his shield and clutching his sword as he had once before clutched sword two paces from that spot. Then he stepped forward, foining at the arras ; and no glow streaked the floor at his feet save that which came from behind him. . . .

With a gasp he parted the faded hangings ; all was dark in the armoury until Enguerrand followed him, and neither light nor sound came from the hole where Dirck had slept or from the chamber where Butcher Lorin died.

"No one cares for the harness as Dirck did," thought Raoul as he moved to the outer door and saw about him rusted corselets and littered helms. "And now for the turret stair and the signal to the townsmen."

He waited until the room bristled with balanced weapons, and then unlocked the second door. In the corridor, again, was darkness ; there the wind whistled eerily, and a faint sound of singing drifted from the direction of the Lady's Tower. . . .

"*Per Bacco !*" came Nino's muffled whisper, "I am now like to be delivered of a woundy sneeze. . . .

" Hold your nose, you gomeril," breathed John Doust.

" Sst ! Hark ! "

" Nothing ; only the wind. Now, John, you to the right ; Nino, be ready on the descending stair. The first two squires behind there, forward . . . that is the passage to the dungeon tower, and you must watch it . . . now, Enguerrand, with me. . . ."

And up the turret stair they blundered, until they came to a little leaded door and paused to light the torches.

" Now wait," said Raoul, " whilst I get my bearings in the dark."

And when he had circled the windy turret-top, marking the cressets over the main gateway and on Jehan's Tower, and the lit windows of the great hall which barred with gold the gravel of the inner bailey, he hung for a moment between two merlons, watching a sentinel move along the western ramparts beneath him.

" Poor devil, you are like to be the first," he thought.

Then he turned away and glanced at the black roofs of Alanol, whence many eyes must now be strained towards the keep ; and suddenly he was mad for the great reckoning to begin.

" Enguerrand ! "

Like a rising sun the portly vavasour projected himself and his blazing burden from below. Raoul grabbed the first torch, waved it wildly, and flung it—a whirling spinning gout of fire—out across the northern battlements and down into the black ravine between the castle and the town. The second and the third went after it ; and along the wind came a faint alarm of voices and the sudden fury of bells. Lights sprang to life in Alanol ; nearer at hand, in the castle itself, a man yelled out some unintelligible warning or command. An arrow whistled up past Raoul's helm ; more yells and a vague tumult woke in the hold of Campscapel, and Raoul and Enguerrand plunged down the pitch-black stair to where the torches of their men cast a red glow on bared teeth and strained, exultant faces.

Then Raoul beat the flat of his shield upon the stone beside him, and shouted at the top of his voice :

" No quarter for men, no harm to women ! Follow your

leaders, and lay on as you did this morning ! God and Saint
Guthmund for Ger ! "

And with a terrifying roar the yellow surcoats broke loose
in the hold of Campscapel.

In Alanol Red Jehan's night patrol had visited the gates,
and was scouring the taverns and brothels for comrades who
should have been in quarters, when the three thrown torches
flared aloft in the windy darkness and woke the town about
its ears. Amid arrows that flew from doors suddenly ajar,
amid tiles and pots and cobblestones that rained from roofs
and windows, the hardy wolves broke back towards the
barbican ; there the gate opened to receive them, and was
not shut again, for from neighbouring alleys poured a picked
band of townsmen. Patrol and burghers entered together
in a raging, snarling press, and the main gate beyond stood
barred, the drawbridge grinding aloft in the faces of those
who would have fled over it ; so that presently the outnumbered defenders of the barbican were trampled to death
or hurled into the stream two hundred feet below, ignorant
of panic in the hold behind them, knowing only that the gate
watch had delivered them over to their enemies. . . .

Meanwhile the drunken sport of the Red Count's Riders in
the castle hall had ended in a bellowing of commands, in a
snatching up of war-gear and a frenzied falling-on in ward and
bailey that rang to the war-cries of Ger and of Le Véranger.
At the first onset all was wild confusion for the garrison ;
men stumbled up from their mattresses, got steel in face or
throat or body, and fell to die where they had slept, or crawled
away to faint and stiffen in corners where death-laden torch-
light did not come. Fierce eddies of combat woke and were
stilled in gallery and guard-room and along the walls ; and
presently Red Jehan, with a dozen chevaliers armed cap-à-pie,
issued from his own tower above the inner bailey and
marshalled a half-hundred of bewildered men about the great
hall steps. There a fray locked fast that might have lasted
till no man of either side stood upright had not Raoul's
archers, from the ramparts, volleyed at short range arrows
which laid low old Bruin and a score of others, and sent a
rush of half-armed Riders, in search of cover, backwards on

to the blades of Enguerrand and his party as the latter stormed in at the far end of the hall. . . .

Never before had Raoul fought on foot in full armour; practice was one thing, and this mad mellay in flickering torchlight altogether another. He was no longer poet or dreamer; he was an armoured animal that fought and shouted and exulted, sliding forward a foot, sloping a dexterous shield, hewing and thrusting at every shape that bore no yellow or checquered surcoat, battered at in turn by axe and sword, guisarme and mace and morning-star. Nimble enough and strong in the arm, he dealt few blows which seemed to him to miscarry, and was not at first recognised as a leader of the attackers; unknown to himself, John Doust had bidden two doughty men-at-arms follow their Viscount closely wherever he might go, and with these two striking where he struck Raoul bore steadfastly towards the unyielding figure of Red Jehan. . . .

Jehan fought two-handed, with an axe; Ord shielded his master's left side, and the Count's own plate of proof withstood for long the blows that showered upon it. Man after man went down beneath his whirling weapon, and not until Nino Chiostra and he came together in front of it did Raoul hear Red Jehan's voice amid the howling din.

" *Face Campscapel, face Death !* "

" *Ger ! Ger ! Saint Guthmund for Ger !* "

" *Ai, ai ! Son' da Chiostra, son' montone !* "

And over against the raging Count was tilted the golden ram of the Tuscan commune.

At sight of it Jehan gave ground, then raised his battle-axe and struck a mighty blow which split the shield and broke the arm beneath and beat the little southerner senseless to the gravel; and as it fell Raoul hewed half the Campscapel's near thigh-piece from him. Then Ord lashed out with his mace, buffeting Raoul on shoulder-plate and gorget; and Raoul reeled away, to be propped by the men-at-arms behind him, and given a moment's purchase for his next forward tiger-spring that carried the full force of body and of spirit. . . .

" Face Campscapel, face Death ! " thundered Jehan, stepping forward and whirling a second blow at supine Nino;

but a voice as loud as his own replied, whilst a squire's shield
took the murderous axe-head sideways, so that it crashed wide
and bit into the body-armour of a man already prone and
dead.

" Saint George ! " roared John Doust, as his estoc flashed ;
and beneath its edge the Count's bright casque split open,
and the Count staggered and gave back again, blind with
blood and bellowing with rage. . . .

Now the black surcoats were thinning in the inner bailey ;
the yellow pressed them steadily into an angle of the walls, and
still the archers of Ger held keep and ramparts above them.
The squire sent to secure the southern gate was wounded and
his men beaten off, so that that way was opened half an hour
after the fight began ; and across the lowered bridge fled
many servants and not a few of the fighting-men of Campscapel.   Otherwise none would have lived to tell the tale, for
when Enguerrand had swept through the great hall he broke
out to the main gate, and put to the sword the hapless wretches
who held it.   Then that bridge, too, went down, and across
it poured the roaring burghers of Alanol. . . .

So it was that Enguerrand reached the inner bailey again
in time to see Raoul's sword up to the hilt through Ord's lean
body, and Raoul's shield riven, as Nino's had been, by one
of the last blows of Red Jehan's axe.

Raoul, very happy at last in killing, shrieked " *That for
Gervase !* " as his thrust went home.   Then he was thunder-
smitten and beaten flat ; some one trod on his helm, some one
else on his empty sword-hand, and one of his faithful men-
at-arms pitched dead across his legs . . . but he reared
himself on the elbow which still moved, and saw Red Jehan
—bare-headed, foaming at the mouth, his beast-face masked
with blood, one hand already smitten off, a tall squire's sword
and three pike-points in his vitals—borne down upon his
knees amid a heap of slain. . . .

" That is how heroes die," thought Raoul mistily.

Then men drew back ; John Doust's wet estoc swept a
wide circle in the torch-bright air, and Jehan de Campscapel's
red head leaped from its shoulders and bounded to Raoul's
side.

Raoul struck feebly at the ghastly thing, and fainted away.

At dawn, when all was done, they brought a score of whimpering women before him ; and, one, with a baby at her breast, he knew for Red Anne's old companion Agnes.

" Set that one aside," he commanded, pointing to her. " Give the rest food and let them sleep in safety ; any man touching one of them evilly hangs like a dog."

So Agnes was led alone in front of Raoul, who sat with Enguerrand amid the overturned trestles in the little hall of the keep ; and as the dawnlight grew she stared at her captor with a growing wonderment, for first he motioned the men-at-arms to seat and leave her, and then he pushed up the bandage which half-hid one eye, and gave her a weary grin:

" Well, Agnes ? Yes, I am Herluin . . . at least, I *was* Herluin. Tell me, now . . . but first, you are quite safe, you and your baby . . . tell me, what happened after I fled ? "

The dark eyes of Agnes widened, and defiantly she stared across the bundle of clothing in her arms.

" It is enchantment," she muttered sullenly. " Do not look on my baby, lord Herluin. He is Ivo's son—at least, I think so. But Ivo ran away with my lady and Lys, in November, soon after you had gone . . . and I was glad, because my lady was turned into a devil when the Butcher died, and Ivo loved her and forgot me . . . and she mocked him, because he was young and could not satisfy her witch's body . . . and on the night that Jehan slew the comptroller and Mathilde, a troop-captain tried to ravish Lys, and Ivo killed him, and they all vanished, Ivo being wounded."

" A merry hell, in sooth. It was time that some one ended it. But tell me, Agnes—what happened on the very night I fled ? "

" On that night . . . the Butcher was slain, and Dirck, and the Count of Saint-Aunay whom they had tormented. . . ."

" Ay. And the little captive Countess ? "

" She slew herself when Jehan came to see what had befallen his brother. Some said Satan had come in person and claimed the Butcher's soul because of the things done in the hall that night . . . and Red Anne swore Red Jehan had slain his brother, and Jehan swore it was Red Anne, and all the hold was in a tumult. Gervase was killed . . . Ord said

he saw you two fighting in the inner bailey . . . and we
thought you had run away because of that. . . ."

" I see. But Ord slew Gervase ; and this midnight, by
the grace of God, I slew Ord. And had you no word of Red
Anne or the others since they fled ? "

" No word at all. And it has been very grim in this hold
ever since. I would have fled too, but this little knave was
coming, and I had nowhere to go."

At that point the little knave set up a howl, so that Agnes
loosened her clothes and stuffed the point of a brown breast
into his mouth ; and Enguerrand looked from Raoul to
the whispering men-at-arms lower down the hall, and his
eyes twinkled for the first time in twelve hours, or maybe
fifteen.

" And now," concluded Agnes dully, " now my brother
would have killed me, only your men—if they are your men—
would not let him come near."

" Your brother ?   Out of Alanol ? "

" Yes."

" Would you take your baby to a convent ?   You, I doubt
not, could find work there ; and the child will thrive.   No
need to take the vows . . . besides, I doubt if they would
suit your humour."

" You mock me, Herluin.   What convent would do more
than give me a night's shelter ? "

" Come in my care to Our Lady of Montenair, and see."

" Hey, Raoul," interrupted Enguerrand, " you go from
here to Montenair, not Ger ? "

" Friend, I beg of you, lead back the remnants of my men
and give my greetings to the Guarenals . . . no use to send
them to my lady aunt, I fear . . . in that, being so far south
again, I must visit my barony whilst the chance offers.   John
and Nino, and a dozen men-at-arms, come with me—Nino
in a litter if he cannot ride—but the rest, when we have slept
a little and broken fast with the burghers, I give into your
hands . . . together with a not unwarlike tale to tell to my
lord Duke at Saulte."

" A warlike tale indeed.   Now, by the Holy Rood, I am
stiffening up . . . and the baby has had his fill . . . and
here comes John Doust—perish the man, is he beaten out of

iron ?—with something in a sack. Yes, Raoul, I will take your men to Ger, and do my best to look as if *I* had led them to victory. . . ."

" You remind me, John," said Raoul, drawing his hand away from the fingers and lips of the kneeling Agnes, " I have other luggage to take from here beside that little present for the Castellan."

And the strangest moment of all that grim return took Raoul by the throat when he pulled out of a palliasse the blazoned title-page of his ballad-book, and found behind the arras a dusty sword. The ballad-book itself was gone ; and Raoul paused by his old window and watched the summer sunrise gild the shoulder of Dondonoy.

" Well, Herluin ! " he whispered stupidly.

But the name meant nothing. Surely Herluin was another person, who had told Raoul of this sweep of forest and moor, of the black beard of the Butcher and the slim nakedness of Lys. . . .

The Viscount of Ger yawned loudly and tottered away down the winding stair of the Pages' Tower.

" I suppose it was I," he said aloud. " But I am Raoul, a creature emptied of love and youth and hatred and remorse ; and thirty of my men are dead or like to die, and Nino is sorely hurt, and oh, God, I am tired, tired, *tired !* "

XIII

THE MARSHES OF MARCKMONT

" My lord, they say the Castellan is gone to Olencourt, and will not return until Saint Jehan Baptist. And the Sieur Rogier is at Hautarroy."

Raoul peered up at the scarp of Montenair, whilst idlers in the village street gaped at his battered little troop and at Nino Chiostra's horse-litter ; the man-at-arms looked at the sack he carried, and John Doust chuckled and spoke.

" In a fortnight this other and most unsaintly Jehan will be higher than aught else under Heaven."

" Unfortunately true, my John," said Raoul, " but whatever betide I must rid me of this courteous obligation."

Then he bade the man-at-arms choose two companions and take the sack to Olencourt, where it must only be opened at the feet of the Castellan.

" But first," he added, " repeat the message that you bear."

" My lord : *My lord Viscount of Ger greets my lord Castellan ; since my lord Castellan has the signet of Campscapel he sends the sword-hand of the Count Jehan to wear it. Also he sends the head of the Count Jehan, lest there be any doubt as to whom the hand belongs.*"

" You have it. That and no more. But tell the Castellan anything he may ask you of the fray over Alanol. Tell him also that I have gone to Marckmont, and give him certain knowledge of the illness of my lord Count at Ger."

In this way the head and hand of Jehan de Campscapel went quietly in a sack through Belsaunt city. In this way Raoul's name flared through the northern provinces and was borne southward with an ever-growing increment of rumour ; in Belsaunt something near the truth was known, but in Camors and Elquitaine he had slain Red Jehan in single combat after sinking fifteen Easterling galleys on the high

seas and covering sixty miles of moor and forest : the whole
in something under eight hours.

And in this way—avoiding Belsaunt by a mile or less, to
the disgust of his followers, who would have liked a little wine
and boasting in the taverns—Raoul came at length to the place
that he called home.

A chill wind blew across the twilit marshes; from the
village of Olvay the last league of the road ran northward
between swaying poplars.   The trees and shoals of the east-
ward horizon were misted with rain ; in the west a jagged
streak of orange faded out beyond sharp-cut shapes of little
lonely farms.   Here and there a fainter gleam was reflected
from water ; the wild geese woke strange clamour, homing
in wedges between broken masses of swift slate-coloured cloud.

To Raoul nothing mattered but that he was bound for
Marckmont ; once there, in his own place, he would find ease.
His late achievement promised surcease of indignity ; he
smiled to think of Robin Barberghe's face when he should
hear of it.   But chiefly he valued that feat of arms for the
peace that should ensue in Nordanay.

" Still, there is always Joris of the Rock," mused Raoul,
" though he has held to south of Varne, they say, for a full
twelvemonth.   But one cannot blast the whole of evil and
disorder off the earth in one red afternoon."

" Now that," said John Doust at a turn of the way, " will
be your castle."

And out of the waste of brown-rippled water and bending
whistling reeds stood up the low smooth mound and the
four dark towers of Marckmont.   To southward of the hold
were the roofs of the village, the round church belfry, and
the moving arms of the windmill; northward only the low
causeway ran from the foot of the mound into the evening
distances.

" Yes, John, that is Marckmont.   Nino, we are all but
arrived."

" Praise to the Saints for that," groaned the Tuscan from
behind the curtains of his litter.

To John and Nino, Raoul reflected, Marckmont was a
place like any other place ; but to himself the very roadside

trees were friendly, the haystacks standing where stacks always stood seemed to bear welcoming faces, and even the little scurrying waterfowl were of good intent. Remembered cottages, a sable blur in the blue-grey murk ; tousled heads thrust over half-doors in the gloom ; a barking of dogs from gated farmyards of freemen ; a mighty clattering on the cobbled reach of street, and the belated blast of the watchman's horn from a tower-top—these led to the short gravelled rise between the tufted grasses, and at length to the edge of the moat.

The moat itself, half-empty after drouth, assailed the nostrils of Raoul with faint remembered stink. Beyond the stony sheer of the south-western tower a will-o'-the-wisp danced lonely in half-darkness over the nearer marsh ; and a bat fell from some machicolation and twirled above the head of the home-come baron. Steel-capped heads showed between the merlons over the gate, and beside the raised bridge a face hung grey in the blackness of a window-slit.

" Who are you ? " demanded the face, in a sonorous wail devoid of all expression.

Raoul gestured silently towards the falcon on the torn breast of his surcoat ; and the inquiry was repeated as though by some mechanical device.

" Who are you ? "

At Raoul's elbow the big Englishman exploded a roar of wrath across the stagnant water.

" Who are we, cheese-face ? Only the Pope, the Emperor, and bully Prester John ! Who, think you, wears this blazon ? Is this your greeting to your lord, Viscount of Ger and Baron of Marckmont ? "

" If you be Mogue, my uncle's steward," called Raoul, " down bridge and up portcullis."

" My lord, if you be my lord, show me a face I know. Doubtless you have heard how once a Duke of Volsberghe took Camors."

That was by dressing himself and his men up in Camors surcoats ; and Raoul beckoned forward two of his older men-at-arms.

" Here, look your fill," he shouted, smiling behind his beaver at the manner of this longed-for entry.

"Ay . . . ay, yours are Ger men, my lord. I had my lord Count's word to admit no armed party numbering more than six ; but since my lord is laid aside his word must lie aside as well. Your servant, good my lord."

Down thumped the bridge with a rattle of chains ; up grated the portcullis, and quietly the gates swung inward on oiled hinges. High across the black well of the courtyard a lit window marked the room where once the Countess Adela told stories to a brown-haired boy. . . .

"Saints," thought Raoul as he rode in, "how everything is *small* 1 "

The steward himself took Saracen's bridle, and Raoul sat for a moment staring down into Mogue's plump wrinkled face.

"Now do you know me ? " he asked.

"Yes, worshipful my lord. But I entreat you to remember that I may not lawfully assist you to administer your fief until you are confirmed in its possession . . . and until my lord Count recover I see not how. . . ."

"Save your speech, Mogue. I will stay as a guest under my own roof. But now let us have hot water by the gallon, a bed straightway for Master Nino Chiostra, some change of clothing for Master John Doust and myself, and then the devil of a supper . . . beef and venison, coneys if you have them, or a capon ; any pottage easily made—but above all, eels, chopped eels of Marckmont. For wine, the Estragon which the Cardinal Bevilacqua gave in memory of his visit to the Countess Adela . . . and hasten, for any love you bear to your own big belly."

"What is this folly of non-possession ? " growled John Doust, when Raoul and he sat in their steaming bath-tubs amid floating aromatic herbs.

"Oh, there is homage to swear and relief to pay, and my uncle to be quitted of his guardianship . . . no matter, we are here. John, you shall have hunting, fishing, and the best hawking in the north of this wide realm. Nino must make haste and mend his arm again . . . hey, Mogue ! "

"My lord ? " inquired the steward, poking his head and a bundle of clothing round the arras by the door.

"Regard the pink arms there of my friend John Doust.

In the small hours of this day they took from its shoulders
the head of Jehan de Campscapel."

Round as an O bulged the brown eyes of Mogue.

" Jehan de . . . oh, my lord ! Indeed your troop bears
signs of a great fight, but I knew not . . . ah, my lord, my
best felicitations to the Sieur de Jondoust ! "

Even Nino, in bed in the next room, forgot his battered
bones and the unhandiness of his attendant man-at-arms,
and began to laugh.

" *Vive le Sieur de Jondoust !* " he trolled.   " Ten
thousand little fleeting devils !   *Evviva il Signor di Nino-
chiostra !* "

Mysteriously happy were the fifteen days that followed.
Like a truant schoolboy Raoul galloped across and across the
dry third of his barony, visiting his villages of Olvay and
Cremalvay, hunting and killing two stags in the wild foot-
hills at the causeway's northern end, leisurely hawking along
the heat-hazed margins of the marsh.   Sometimes he poled
a flat-bottomed boat amid reed-locked fastnesses, fishing with
line and landing-net or torch and trident spear ;   or he idled
in willow-shaded waters, watching the battles of the young
swans, listening to the far boom of the bitterns, making verses
which he touched to life on the new strings of his lordly lute.
Also he practised sword-play with John Doust, and pondered
fierce chess with convalescent Nino ;   and in the cool gloom
of the little chapel he gave thanks for his double victory and
prayed for the souls of those of his men who fell in the winning
of it.

Often, and with perplexity, he thought of Yseult, and of
the fires of his late adoration, that died as suddenly and
soundlessly as once they rose in him.   Less often, with a
wonder kindlier and more shamed, he thought of Lys ;   and
in contemplation of those two sweet wraiths he arraigned the
planet Venus as a curse upon mankind.   The planetary body,
indeed, made a convenient scapegrace, for the love of Yseult
for Alain and the love of Lys for Raoul bore now too great
a likeness for one to be of heaven and the other of hell.

But on the sixteenth day of his sojourn at Marckmont the
world reached out to reclaim him ;   green surcoats sown with

silver fleurs-de-lys came swinging up the Olvay road, and
Raoul found himself looking something grimly into the grave
considering eyes of Rogier—Rogier, last of the three Olencourts to fail him at Montenair. . . .

" Here is your ring ; Fulk bade me render it to you," said
Rogier after their first constrained greeting.

Raoul smiled, and set the cumbersome signet on his
thumb.

" I suppose my lord Castellan sees no further use in it,"
he murmured.

" In faith, you may take it as you please," returned
Rogier, " yet no man for years has had aught from Fulk
which so smacks of apology.   Indeed, you have startled him
. . . and many another, not least among them my sister
Yseult."

Raoul looked calmly up, and Rogier curiously down.

" What said she ? " Raoul inquired, not without sadness
that now the answer mattered nothing to him

" That she had not thought you were one so savagely to
cut off heads or to send them abroad in such a heathen wise."

" Aught else ? "

" Well, yes."

" So.   That poor conquest bears admission at the last.
Jehan de Campscapel has lost his head ; therefore poor
Raoul had not quite lost *his* when he presumed . . ."

" Raoul, I was nowise pleased to hear you were so
crossed. . . ."

" Oh, it is all no matter now.   I entreat you grieve no
more, if you have grieved at all.   I am very content, with a
contentment too complete to please my lady your sister if
she knew of it."

Rogier laughed.

" I will pass that dire tidings of disenchantment back by
the way I heard the news," he said.   " To wit, my lady
Ermengarde de Saulte, who by God's grace will be my wife
before the year is out."

" What ?   You betrothed ?   My hand on it."

Some minutes later, as his page stripped the dust-whitened
armour from him, tall Rogier interrupted his discourse of
Ermengarde with a sudden exclamation.

" By the Rood, I have not told you.   On the octave of
Saint Barnabas Apostle our lord the King married the
Countess of Burias, Conrad standing with them under the
pall."

Raoul whistled.

" Conrad, hey ?   Legitimised at a blow ! "

" Ay, and created Duke of Burias that same afternoon."

" But there can arise no question . . ."

" Of Conrad's coming nigh the throne ?   No, there was
woundy talk of that in the marriage proclamation.   But
Volsberghe grinned in his beard as he bore one corner of the
pall, and Saulte stood mighty thoughtful at another."

" What said the Prince Thorismund ? "

" Oh, he took a maudlin pleasure in the aggrandisement
of Conrad.   The pair of them are thick as thieves.   They
lead a troop of noble brawlers . . . ducking the watch in
the river, dousing passers-by with wine from tavern windows,
waylaying market-women and tying their skirts above their
heads.   In short, they fill the court with sottish pranks and
beastliness."

Raoul grunted and was silent for some minutes.

" *But now you will be king,*" he quoted softly at length.

" Eh ? " queried Rogier as he approached his bath.

" Nothing.   A memory of Sanctalbastre.   Conrad's words
when the Cardinal Count took Thorismund away . . . but
tell me, Rogier, what said Alain de Montcarneau when he
heard of the end of Red Jehan ? "

" He was angered.   He named your exploit witchcraft,
and was sulky all the day when any spoke of it."

" Ay.   Had I loved your sister without capturing the
hold of Campscapel, Alain would have laughed.   Had I
captured the hold without loving your sister, Alain would
have applauded.   But in my doing both he finds a dark
presumption.   Dame Venus is a mischief and a scourge . . .
saving your presence, Rogier."

" Bah," growled his guest through a mask of soap.
" Some day you will think otherwise."

" Maybe," responded Raoul absently ; but in himself
his one-time query hardened to a curt rejoinder : *No one flies
with a lonely falcon.*   And aloud he said : " Well, if our lord

King René be hale enough to marry, he is hale enough to
confirm me in my barony.   Stay with me three days, Rogier ;
then we will ride together to Belsaunt.   From thence I go
to Hautarröy."

" You will have to cut your way through the Belsaunt
streets.   They hum with your fame and your adventure."

" Ay, if I were fool enough to go with yellow surcoats.
But I warrant the Marckmont blue and gold goes doucely
enough beside your lilies to the door of the Four Swords."

Evening at Belsaunt, and a little wind that crept with
dolorous music in the streets of the high town.   Raoul,
pausing in his cloaked and lonely stroll, saw the first star
caught in a stirring poplar-top beyond the garden-wall of the
Friars Minor that ran for a third of the length of Street of
Bells.   He would have liked to call at Plegmund's house, but
that he shrank from making himself known in his true person,
and shrank no less from any more deception of the armourer's
household that had given him so much kindness.   Thus he
contented himself with cocking a whimsical eye at the
window of his late bedchamber, and with one glance at the
gutter where the Viscount Charles had died ; then he passed
softly on his way amid the smell of cooking suppers and the
hundred noises of the twilit city. . . .

" *Herluin !* "

He spun on his heel to confront the speaker of his one-time
name.   Hubriton stood sombrely regarding him—Hubriton,
lank-haired and something haggard, with a book beneath
one arm and a basket of eggs on the other.

" Why, Hubriton, I was musing and walked clean past
you.   Give you good greeting ;   how are all our friends in
Street of Anvils ? "

" You have not been there, then ? "

" No . . . no . . . there are reasons.   I stay at an inn
for this one night "

" I have not been to Plegmund's house for nigh a month,"
said Hubriton grimly, " but when I was last there they were
all merry enough."

" How so ? "

" On the Friday after Holy Trinity, at the Assembly of the

Armourers, Berthelin was admitted a journeyman of the craft ; and four days later he and Godelieve were betrothed."

" Ah, I am sorry . . . for your sake."

Raoul let his voice die away, and stared discreetly down the street into the emptying market-place.

" Better Berthelin than Drogo," said the clerk, harshly ; and in a lower key he added : " But I had shot my bolt and failed ; Godelieve would have none of me. Yet it goes hard to dwell so near, knowing no respite save in labour over squabbles of evil-tempered craftsmen."

Hubriton glanced down at his eggs and essayed a smile.

" Folly to put them all in the one basket," he said. Then, more blithely : " But now, what inn is yours ? I will take home my hopes and fears and, if it please you, join you for a stoup."

" My inn is the Four Swords," said Raoul reflectively, " but . . ."

" You do not want me," muttered the clerk, quickly. " So be it. The Four Swords is over grand for . . . indeed, I perceive you are different, Herluin."

Raoul frowned.

" Not so fast, Hubriton. I am the same, although I am also different. I want you well enough . . . ay, to ride to Hautarroy and further. But we will find some quiet tavern for what comes next. Go, leave your eggs and join me here. I will wait."

So, after dark, in a little ale-house at the corner of Street of Spurs, Hubriton took employment as secretary to the Viscount of Ger, and learned some of the facts which later he embodied in that chronicle whereon this tale is founded.

" Now perish me," he said when warmed with wine, " if I do not remember your query concerning such an offer of service. . . . I took it for a jest, and here am I accepting it as gladly as a drowning man accepts the end of a flung rope. But I think I shall have little cause for shame in your service, Herluin . . . your pardon, Sieur Raoul."

" Civilly said, my Hubriton ; but I pity the robber baron whose conscience lay in your keeping."

" I doubt not he would soon find a keeper more to his liking. And you . . . may send me packing if I dare to

J*

disagree with you, but I do not think you will hang me in a drunken jest."

Raoul sat silent for a while ; then he asked a question.

" Hubriton—what, to your way of thinking, chiefly marks a man's nobility ?   Nobility of heart, I mean, not blazoned quarterings."

" That he have power over others," came the prompt reply, " and strength to refrain from any wanton use of it."

" But if he have no power over others ? "

" That he will never let himself be bullied into evil-doing."

" H'm.   Yes.   But these things are covered by the laws of chivalry and by obedience to Holy Church."

" These things and many others, Sieur Raoul.   Much folly and much wickedness among them."

" What folly ? "

" Say, the pride of Paladin Roland, who flung away the rearguard because he would not blow his horn.   Is that not celebrated as a famous deed of valour ? "

" Yes.   But the wickedness ? "

" Holy Church is holy, wherefore men bow to take the blessing of the Abbot of Saint-Maur-by-Dunsberghe, keeping their pretty daughters out of his sight the while.   And what a misery was loosed in that crusade against the men of Albi, when the crusaders won salvation for their souls with all black beastliness. . . ."

" But the men of Albi were heretics, convicted of most evil . . ."

" Ay ; but they did nothing worse than what was done against them with the blessing of the bishops.   It was the blessing, not the deeds, which made the difference betwixt black and white."

Raoul thought suddenly of Lys, of Sabelle of the Coven of the Singing Stones, and of grotesque and valorous Gunnore of the Coven of Culdesang.   As tenant-in-chief and soon to wield high justice, middle, and low, he might himself ere long be setting engines to wrench the joints of just such curious lively creatures as these which had befriended him.

" But, Hubriton, is it wrong to take the Abbot's blessing because the Abbot is a wencher ? "

" Wrong for me, because I feel it so."

" You set up *your* authority against . . ."

" No ; I bow with the rest. I am no martyr to my own poor opinions. Yet I feel it to be wrong."

" But why, if the Church . . ."

" My lord, I do not know. It is something that happens in a man's soul. At least, it has happened in mine ; and by your face, by my knowledge that you are not one to hand me over to the Bishop, it has in some sort happened in yours."

" But . . . where is truth, if not in keeping of the Church ?"

" The truth, or part of it, is in each man who lies alone on hill-tops and in forests thinking of it. Or so it seems to me. Even the Sieur Jesus went into the wilderness."

Raoul crossed himself, and Hubriton went on.

" There was no Church to tell the truth to *Him*."

" But, Hubriton, the Sieur Jesus had the truth from the Beginning. . . . I know that that is a mystery, and that we cannot understand it ; but surely the truth is there, given by Him to the Church."

" It has something altered . . . my lord, if the Sieur Jesus came again his Church would do him to death as an heretic, a blasphemer, a leader astray of poor folk."

Uncomfortable honesty stirred Raoul to a measure of agreement. Something in him fastened hard upon this heresy, shifting and lightening his burden of confused belief. . . .

" To have the power, and to refrain," he mused upon his bed, when moonlight silvered the Belsaunt roofs and Saint Austreberte's chime came shivering down the midnight air. " There is much valour in my Hubriton. His are brave thoughts that win him little ease. But for myself, I think the Sieur God has been very merciful to me, showing me things vile and best avoided."

He thought of the Counts of Saint-Aunay, Alanol, and Ger ; of Alys the sister of Drogo, and the Viscount Charles ; of the mother of Charles when she cursed her son's supplanter.

" Yet it seems to me," said Raoul soberly to a shaft of moonlight, " that to be merciful to me the Sieur God has been very hard upon some other people. For I must pass as one of the happier sort ; I have power and a taste of fame, and never a man went better friended. Yet something blurs

my life with deep confusion ; the lonely falcon wanders in a
fog of melancholy.   Mercury drives me forth to seek, and
Saturn mocks me when I find.   With my heart at Marckmont
I must set my mind on Ger.   Strange that a falcon, not a
swan, was shown to me in that weird vision by the Inn of
Harmony, when Nino told me of the hidden ford of Varne. . . .

" There may be much to divert me at the Court in Hautarroy ; but I wager a day will come when Saturn claws my
inwards with lust of loneliness and silence. . . .

" Until that day I must move as the world moves, flame
of action ousting flame of thought.   For what is leisure to
Thorismund and Conrad, to Rogier and Alain, is to me a
labour of wits and body.   Because the great stone devil
overlooked me at my birth . . .

" Until that day . . ."

Raoul slept.

Midnight at Hautarroy, and twelve weeks later.   In the
great parlour of the Hôtel de Saulte a prince, three dukes, and
a gay company of lords and ladies ; among them Raoul,
Baron of Marckmont, Viscount of Ger, blood-cousin to
René of Neustria, and something of a problem to the Lady
Ermengarde de Saulte who sat beside him. . . .

Since coming to the Court, Raoul had knelt before his
king, holding his strong brown hands between the palsied
hands of René, whilst the clerks wrote and the heralds slanted
their trumpets, and Hubriton demurely counted out the
feudal dues in bright new coin.   Nino Chiostra, too, had stood
behind Raoul at that ceremony — Nino, newly come from
Marckmont, and amused to find himself comptroller to a
baron ; and with John Doust as captain of his men-at-arms,
and Piers du Véranger, a twelve-year-old kinsman of Enguerrand, for his page, Raoul had entered on a courtier's life.

For a month he had hawked and hunted, diced and danced,
watched cock-fighting and the baiting of the bears, followed
the king to Mass, and talked and yawned in resplendent
antechambers — himself no less resplendent in velvet cloaks
and satin pourpoints, with parti-coloured hose, with jewelled
hilts and girdle, with shoes having pointed toes six inches
longer than his foot, or with thigh-boots eclipsing those which

Robin Barberghe wore that far-off day at Ger. And Raoul's achievement over Alanol had stood him in good stead amid his younger peers, few of whom had borne arms beyond the lists ; for without it his aloofness from their grosser pleasures might have occasioned comment of a kind to be checked by violence only. But his discreet demeanour pleased the king and the Cardinal Count of Estragon, who now was Chancellor; and Raoul was chosen to accompany old René on a short summer progress through the central provinces of the realm. At its conclusion he was made chevalier ; and, moving as his world moved, he found amid its pageantry small time to mope with *Modred, Prince of Britain.* Nevertheless the making of his songs throve sturdily ; so sturdily, indeed, that the grave Duke of Saulte had his eye on the corner of his parlour whence Raoul watched the company across the comely shoulder of the Lady Ermengarde. . . .

"But, Raoul," Ermengarde was saying, "you will abide at Hautarroy for the Michaelmas jousting ? "

"Not I," responded Raoul. "Already I strain the patience of my good friend the Vice-Warden ; he cannot warm my uncle's chair for me for ever. And there is Marckmont to be visited. . . ."

"And Yseult to be avoided," he read in the kind blue eyes of Ermengarde ; whereupon he approached his lips to the gold cloisons of the nearer horn of her great head-dress, that none might overhear his slow protesting murmur.

" There is a worse thing for a dog than to be given a foul name and hanged."

Ermengarde's shapely head came round ; her eyes, and the pink oval of her perfect face, were almost piteous with bewilderment.

" What thing is that ? " she demanded.

" That he be called a duck," said Raoul solemnly, " and drowned."

Ermengarde smiled, but it was plain she did not understand. Raoul had captured her attention by talking of her lover Rogier; with Ermengarde, moreover, he felt safe amid the sickly airs of passion and intrigue that crept about the court. Yet safety at her side involved him in amused exasperation ;

for he had discovered that Ermengarde believed him still
to harbour desperate passion for her friend and future sister-
in-law Yseult. And neither his jesting, nor an habitual
serenity, nor even flat avowal of whole-heartedness, drove
the awareness from her glance or muted the compassion in
her voice.

"Preserve me from constancy in love," thought Raoul,
"if it breed such weary disregard of time and circumstance.
The way of a man with a maid is naught to the way of two
maids' tongues with a man . . . and all because I took the
hold of Campscapel."

Then he smiled, for his vexation could not stand against
the gleam of the white Saulte shoulder and the warmth
of the red Saulte wine. Across the one, with vision en-
hanced by the other, he gazed contentedly along the lordly
room. . . .

Bronze candelabra hung by chains from the blue-coffered
ceiling ; dull crimson arras shimmered with cloth of gold,
Damascus carpets broke the blue and yellow pattern of the
floor-tiles, and the honey-colour of oak panelling was varied
and enriched with flower-shapes of gold and black and red.
High up in the wall six windows set with rich stained glass
made blue and silver of the intermittent moonlight. When
talk and laughter waned the wind crooned organ-deep in the
enormous chimney, or the hand of the Duke's chamberlain
on a tasselled signal-cord woke harmony of harps and flutes
and horns behind the emblazoned screen of the minstrels'
gallery. Pages flitted serenely to and fro, with the Saulte
bars red and gold on the dove-grey of their tunics, and in
their hands tall silver cups that winked in the light of a
hundred candles. Conrad, Duke of Burias, magnificent in
crimson, and the daft Count of Lestembourg, bizarre in lizard-
green, made a brave double foil for the central figure of all—
Thorismund of Hastain, slim in white satin from throat to
toe, with his hair a flame above the beauty of his chalk-white
face. . . .

"The little sot drinks twice to Conrad's once," mused
Raoul, watching his princely cousin. "Preserve me also
from inconstancy in love, if it must paint such shadows
underneath my eyes. But what a fool he is . . . ah, now

he smiles . . . it needs a dancing manikin to make him smile."

For the acrobatic dwarf of the Duke of Burias, borrowed for the occasion, came stumping all in scarlet from behind a curtain, bowing this way and that before he struck up a little shuffling dance to the twang of a zither in his keeper's hands. The goblin gestures of long arms and tiny legs, the somersaults and hand-walking, and most of all the periodic bump as the creature sat heavily backwards, bouncing on his behind to stand straight up again without a bending of the knees—these set the glittering company in a roar. But Raoul watched the manikin's unsmiling face, a face as dreadful as that of a dissolute child, with blear-eyes, saddle-nose, and twisted lips ; and in one momentary hush he heard young Guy de Saulte speak aside to the Duke of Burias.

" Shall I give him wine ? "

Conrad's dark face twitched ; he showed white teeth in a frank transforming smile, and Raoul strained his ears to catch the quiet reply.

" Not in the presence of these noble ladies.   But after, if you will.   We might have in a woman of the town ; I warrant you will find it comical."

" I warrant I should find it foul," reflected Raoul, tossing a florin high in air, " but none here can compel me to look on it."

The dwarf saw the coin coming, dodged to meet it, and caught it in his wide gap-toothed mouth ; then he stood on his head and twiddled his red boot-soles in gratitude.   Silver, and even gold, began to tinkle and roll around him ; and only a muffled yelp when he had disappeared gave knowledge of his claim to keep them.

Then Lestembourg was calling for the harp ; and very merrily he sang *Now Raveth Alured*, and—when pressed for more—a song about a maiden's knee.   And at length Raoul himself was strumming the company to silence, with his eyes on Saints Barnabas and Paul, who preached to the men of Ephesus along the dusky arras by the door. . . .

" A love-lilt for sweet Ermengarde," he thought with malice, and sang his song *Excalibur*.

When Merlin brought him to the lake
  To take the brand Excalibur,
Pendragon seemed but half awake
When Merlin brought him to the lake
The brand Excalibur to take ;
  But lo ! The shining steel astir,
When Merlin brought him to the lake
  To take the brand Excalibur !

But little thought had Arthur then
  Of Guendolen or Guinevere.
He heard the thunder of his men,
And little thought had Arthur then
Of Guinevere or Guendolen.
  The witch-prow cleft the haunted mere ;
But little thought had Arthur then
  Of Guendolen or Guinevere !

Amid languid applause the Duchess of Saulte pulled a wry face.

"My lord," she protested, "you make an unseemly jostling of loves in good King Arthur's heart. Surely sad Guendolen was well forgotten before the true love came along."

"Your poet knows it is not always so happily contrived," said Conrad of Burias, courteously.

"Hey, cousin," called the young prince mirthlessly. "They tell me you are a very devout lover. Show us the metal of your love-music."

"What, my lord Prince ?" responded Raoul. "In presence of so many masters of love-craft—ay, and so many skilful mistresses ? "

Caressing the strings of the great harp, he counted among the crowd eight past or present loves of Thorismund ; two among them already hated Raoul for his mild inattention to their veiled advances, and most of the others seemed mindful of his *double-entendre*.

And in a deeper than the usual hush he began his *Song Against Coquetry*.

Her will I not admire,
  Nor her defence assume,
Who bids desire mount up as fire
  To fly away in fume.

Count not the raptor's blame
  Ere all excuse be shown ;
Who jests with flame deserves the same
  For torment of her own.

Her only will I sing,
  Who, challeng'd by the Boy,
Or bids him wing or crowns him king
  In courtesy and joy.

This time the soberer part of his audience cried praise of words and singing alike, but Thorismund of Hastain screwed up a pettish mouth, and the half-drunken Lestembourg broke out in mournful laughter.

" Why, what a vexed morality is this !   Marckmont, would you deny their sport to hunter and quarry alike ?   In faith, cold fish come out of the sea at Ger ! "

Raoul smiled and shrugged his shoulders.

" But, in truth," he replied roundly, " they are as happy there as any lizard preying on jewelled flies along parched walls of Hautarroy ! "

Thorismund chuckled at the riposte, and raised his voice again.

" Nay, cousin, these are doleful airs.   If you have proper passion in you, let us hear it ! "

" Something, my lord, more heartening for disconsolate ladies," cried the pretty Duchess of Camors, who had ruled the Prince for a month and could afford to mock her rivals.

" Something less subtle, of your mercy," laughed the Duke of Burias.

" In effect," groaned Lestembourg, " something contrived by another poet, if any such be now admitted to exist."

" By the Mass," said the big Duke of Saulte, looking round on his guests, " your task is set, my lord.   I confess my curiosity to hear how you accomplish it."

Raoul bowed from his stool towards the latest speaker.

" I have here a ballade, my lord Duke, which has in it passion known to all ; also it heartens a sad lady, showing her that a man who heeds her not need not of necessity be thinking of some other lady.   Also, I trust, it is not too subtle even for a lizard's understanding—ay, lizards might sing it, for they have long tongues. Your servant, my lords and ladies ; I sing to my lord Prince this my *Ballade of Ger*."

Then, striking a swift chord, he straightened himself up and sang again ; and as he sang he saw that he had them— soldiers and great dames, popinjays and trollops too.

> *The sunlit streets of Hautarroy*
> *Are filled with ladies, fair and free ;*
> *By garth and pleasance of Honoy*
> *The roses riot on tower and tree.*
> *The wine's deep red in Beltany,*
> *And many a lance is splintered there ;*
> *But give to me the northern sea*
> *And the iron crags of windy Ger !*
>
> *In high Baraine are skilful spears*
> *For boar and bear that fume at bay,*
> *And javelin-swift the falcon clears*
> *The frowning oaks of Queranay ;*
> *The cities of Camors are gay*
> *With carven gems and costly ware :*
> *But my heart's away to Nordanay*
> *And the iron crags of windy Ger !*
>
> *Merry and long are tale and song*
> *By tavern fires of Elquitaine,*
> *Where undismayed the hamlets throng*
> *Round the proud abbeys in the plain ;*
> *Yet who would turn me strives in vain,*
> *By threat or argument or prayer,*
> *When I lift rein for the fells again*
> *And the iron crags of windy Ger !*

At the end of his third verse Raoul turned, singing the *Envoi* full at the flushed and quickened face of Thorismund of Hastain.

> *Prince, in the van of your command*
> *Look for me, when the trumpets blare,*
> *Sword in hand for the sounding strand*
> *And the iron crags of windy Ger !*

Prince and dukes, ladies and lords and chevaliers and all, united in a shout of applause that filled the lofty chamber and brought Raoul half-pleased and half-disdainful to his feet.

" Now, fiend fly off with me if ever I heard a braver song ! "

cried Thorismund. " My lord Duke, I ask your leave that
we pledge my good cousin in a goblet of your wine . . . and
Raoul, I pray you, I command you, send me a copy of your
great ballade before the night comes round again ! "

" My lord, my naughty lord," trolled the Duchess of
Camors, " if the crags be of iron, need the Viscount be also
of iron ?   One line of twenty-eight with ladies in it ! "

Raoul bowed, with a glance aside at Lestembourg, who
now was hiccoughing praises with a hand on his gemmed
sword-hilt.

" Nay, gentle Duchess, ask my lord there ; if the sea be
cold, the fishes are cold therein."

" Ask rather the townsmen of Alanol," said Conrad of
Burias, lifting his wine-cup with grave eyes fixed appraisingly
on Raoul's face.

" My lord Prince, my lords and ladies, you do me too much
honour," protested Raoul as they drank to him ; and amid a
swirl of music from the minstrels' gallery he regained his chair
beside the chair of Ermengarde de Saulte.

" Raoul, I love your brave ballade," said Ermengarde.
" When did you contrive it ? "

" During the late progress of our lord the king."

" How long were you in shaping it ? " demanded the Duke
of Saulte.

" Between a sundown and a sunrise," answered Raoul.

" Name of a name," exclaimed the Duke. " When I
was your age I expended near three weeks on the making
of a very scurvy little vilanelle. How do you go to the
work ? "

" I know not, my lord Duke. The memories and dreams
are there, but of the weaving wind that frets them into rhyme
I am not master."

" The p-poet's images," droned Lestembourg with a
portentous gravity, " are in his mind, but dead, like new-born
lion-cubs, which only after three days are enlivened by the
r-roaring of their sire or the fierce ex-exhalation of their
dam."

" My lord, you have but set my query at a remove,"
objected Saulte. " What sound or breathing moved my lord
here to our enchantment ? "

" The sound of beauty," said Conrad of Burias half to himself. " Ay, and the breathing of pain."

" Maybe you are right, my lord Duke," was Raoul's smiling admission ; but Ermengarde glanced sideways at him, and her transparent thought set the smile awry on his lips.

Beauty and pain.   Conrad, too, had a life of his own behind the glare of the court—even, perhaps, behind the muttering of those about him who already moved to raise him one day in the stead of Thorismund.   And at the dark duke's words that thing befell Raoul which he had foretold to himself at Belsaunt in the Inn of the Four Swords.   Saturnine lust of loneliness and silence clawed at him ; instead of candle-light and silk and gems, instead of bright eyes, painted lips, and the white slope of dainty shoulders, he saw . . . a mound with four towers and a causeway, with poplars swaying in the twilight and water lapping brown amid brown reeds and dull green bulrushes. . . .

" Why, Raoul," Ermengarde was saying, " if you hold your Ger in such esteem, I must not marvel that you will not delay for the Michaelmas jousting."

" Michael Archangel rot the Michaelmas jousting," thought Raoul ; and aloud he murmured : " Ger ? It is not yet mine, and when I am there I hate it.   My home is Marckmont in the marshes. . . ."

" But . . ."

" But there are no rhymes to *Marckmont*, and many rhymes to *Ger*.   *Videlicet*, dare, glare, stare, that I have not used."

" But, Raoul . . ."

" Ay, I fear I am no true poet.   Your true poet shreds his very heartstrings down the midnight wind.   I must confess to deeps beyond the sounding of my verses.   For even had I rhymes, not for a king's ransom could I fashion a *Ballade of Marckmont*.   Where there is peace of heart there is no versifying ; or so it is with me.   A thing must fret before I round on it with a goose-quill.   And iron crags, to speak sooth, are something sharp to sit upon."

Ermengarde stared dubiously at him, striving to force this flippant Raoul within the bounds of her obsession.

" Alas, yes," he added softly.   " I once made verses to
Yseult also.   But it is six months since I inked paper in her
honour.   And to-morrow I start for Ger.   A most unpleasant
place, I swear.   Great swingeing draughts on the back of my
neck.   My uncle scarce distinguishable from a corpse, my
aunt's each glance at me a dagger.   Endless disputes between
farmer and forester and fisherman.   A salt cake over everything.   Gulls wailing like unshriven souls.   Sea-fogs . . ."

" You travel by Montenair ? " interrupted Ermengarde.

" No.   I shall go by Hastain for the better road.   Yet if
you have letters for Rogier, my war-captain John Doust shall
carry them himself."

" Gramercy, Raoul.   You will not leave before mid-day ? "

" No.   Does that give you time enough to write ? "

" Yes . . . yes."

" One *yes* for Rogier, one *yes* for Yseult," thought Raoul.

" It is not yet October," murmured Ermengarde.   " The
roads will not be very bad to north of Belsaunt."

Raoul sighed.; and on the following afternoon a packet
sealed with the Saulte device went with his gear from the
north-western gate of Hautarroy.

Ger, and the bedside of the moribund Count Warden ;
weary hours in the great hall, with eyes of plaintiff and accused
fixed on Raoul's face, and only the twitch of old Guarenal's
nose-end to remind him that there still was humour in the
world—for Reine was visiting her kinsfolk in the south, and
Nino was left behind in Hautarroy to gather certain payments
due to the Baron of Marckmont from sub-tenants of his small
lands in Baraine. . . .

Then a two-days' journey, with Gunnore clasping a purse
in her great red hands and roaring praises down the road
behind his laughing troop . . . with Denise de Saint-Aunay
white and red and white again as she stood before him in a
guest-room of Our Lady's Abbey at Montenair . . . and at
last a quiet afternoon at Marckmont, with little Piers du
Véranger to hand him dry clothing, and the voice of Nino
Chiostra delicately raised in the adjoining room. . . .

" Hubriton, give me a rhyme for Mogue.   In sooth it is
not far to seek.   Fiend fly off with this thing—I have split

my quill again.   Hubriton, cut me another quill, for the love
of the golden swan.   Now here is . . . no, that is eels.   I
never thought when first I put on hose that I should rise to be
comptroller to a lord to whom are due ten thousand eels a
year.   Ten thousand fleeting little devils, rather ; it gives
you a griping of the guts to think of them.   Ah, here is what
I sought.   Item, eleven dibbles ; item, six flails for the
threshing, one having a broken swiple ; item, eight sickles ;
item, five scythes ; item, fifteen harvest-bottles of wood,
having stoppers, and carrying-cords of horsehair.   Three of
the stoppers are lost.   But a murrain on it, do the five
scythe-men each bear three bottles of ale to the fields ?   And
if so, how comes it that we have twelve stoppers left ? "

"It may be, Master Nino," came Hubriton's grave reply,
"that each of the Twelve Apostles took a stopper under his
particular protection."

"Ay, ay.   But is it a wonder the Marckmont serfs are
fatter than any I have seen since I came out of Tuscany ?
Now here is Captain John, a tidy scarlet from his bath.
Hubriton, you have slaved all day.   Lay down your pen.
To-morrow we will begin by reading this list you wrote in
the sheds, and checking the items off here.   Now we will cast
work to Lucifer who fathered it, and go play ninepins in the
hall till supper-time."

"Ha, Nino," said Raoul, entering from his bedroom,
"do you not know it unlucky to burn three candles in any
but a consecrated chamber ? "

Nino looked up, with a smudge of ink on his round brown
cheek.

"Sieur Raoul, I would have you know this chamber is
consecrated by the suffering of Hubriton and myself, plough-
ing for hours through the mess bequeathed us by that
runaway rascal Mogue.   Were it not for Hubriton I had long
ago cast myself in the mere.   Hearken : whilst you and John
flew hawks towards Cremalvay, we have laid bare a dozen
—ah—mogueries . . . he sold five hundred of your eels and
pocketed the price . . . he lent your bull three times, for
a consideration not inapposite, but lacking in profit to you
for years to come . . . and when he fled he carried off a
serf and a pack-horse laden with arms. .   ."

" Queer soul," said Raoul reflectively. " I suppose we shall never know what ailed him. He might so easily have stolen more."

" You take it coolly," Nino admitted, with a shadow in his honey-coloured eyes.

" Why, must I stamp and roar and startle the little water-fowl ? " demanded Raoul with a smile.

" I wish you would," grieved Nino, frankly.

" Ay," chimed in John Doust. " Rot the man who chatters all day at the mystery of rivers ; but, Nino, I swear to you by Saint Wilfrid that not thirty words have escaped this lord's lips all the day. ' There goes a fox,' he said ; and once, ' Do courtesy to the tiercel ; he has not tasted the quarry.' And as we rode homeward, it was ' Piers, these two hares to the priest's house, with my greeting.' And that was all."

" My lord," began Hubriton suddenly, and as suddenly stopped short, fiddling with his long goose-quill and finally thrusting it into the wooden ink-pot before him.

" Well ? " asked Raoul, wearily.

" There is a maid below . . . she stood at the gate this morning, but she says you saw her not ; and to-night she was in the kitchens when you rode home. After Mass she was wedded to Kymlog the swineherd. She is bond ; the man has nothing for the marriage-due. She awaits your pleasure."

Raoul hooked his thumbs in his belt, and stared for a moment at the steady flame of a candle, so that when he looked up at his three companions the green image in his retina blurred their watching faces. Then Turpin, a favourite boar-hound, pressed a heavy head against his master's thigh ; and by the door slim Piers halted, sneezing quietly aside from the steaming cups of spiced and heated wine which he had carried up the winding stair. . . .

Kymlog was the first of Raoul's serfs to marry since his lord's entry into Marckmont ; and John and Nino, Hubriton and Piers, waited silently to see what use their moody Baron might make of his *jus primae noctis* with penniless Kymlog's wife.

" John, how do you advise me ? " Raoul asked at length.

The Englishman rubbed his pink jaw with powerful fingers, and his little blue eyes twinkled.

" Take the maid," he growled. " She will do you a mort of good. I know your scruples in these matters ; but by the harrowing of hell I would give you every plump wench in your barony if thereby you shook off these desolate humours."

" And you, Nino ? "

" Beshrew me if I know what to say. I am half of a mind with John. Knowing your trick of argument, I feel you think of Kymlog ; but Kymlog seems to me one with his pigs, that is to say, *your* pigs. Your delicacy will be wasted on him."

" What says Hubriton ? "

A kindly malice sparkled in the black eyes of the secretary.

" My lord, have you seen the maid ? But yes, you saw her when you gave permission for the marriage. She is comely enough, with dimples and to spare, and the miller's wife has given her a trim gown. The gleam in her eye may be for Kymlog . . . but I would swear that by the set of your chin she is now like to be grievously disappointed."

Raoul laughed aloud, and pointed to a little pile of gold nobles by the open strong-box on the table.

" *Retro me, Sathanas !* " he said. " In faith, am I become so glum that even Hubriton would sacrifice me to myself ? Nay, give her one of those and bid her be off to the swineherd's hut ; the due is remitted. Piers, serve that wine to Captain John Doust and to me. A health to you all, you villains, and prosperity to Kymlog's nuptials."

Over the goblet-rim John Doust's regard was comical ; Nino made an entry on a roll and pushed a coin across to Hubriton.

" What have you written there ? " demanded Raoul.

" *Saints Simon and Jude Apostles* : This day my lord Baron cast an unthreaded pearl before his swineherd, and after the pearl gold, value . . . *half a mark.*"

" Out upon you, Nino ; are my rolls a vehicle for your scurvy wit ? "

" Eh, but your children's grandchildren will look at them, saying : *Here Mogue the steward fled, and a low fellow named Chiostra took hold of the accounts. He was later drowned, when the Baron Raoul bade him rake the moon out of the marsh.* And so I win my niche in story."

"Rather be off and see what ails your blue gerfalcon. She was sickly enough when Piers took our birds to the perches half an hour ago. Hubriton, set aside these cursed rolls; then bring me my tablets, and light another candle. And then go throw at ninepins; for I will not have you wear yourself to a ghost in my affairs."

"At it again?" groaned John Doust, levering himself up from the window-seat. "Then I will depart; for if I stay here I shall snore, and you will set brute Turpin on to me, and my end will be brief as Nino's and less tidy."

But when he was alone Raoul did not at once sit down to the table. Instead he stood by a glazed and leaded window, looking out into the marshland dusk.

Only the sails of the windmill and the tops of the ranked poplars moved in that wide sweep of dark earth and grey or steel-bright water. Blurred in the coarse glass, the last red bars of sunset faded out; the rising wind kept up a low continuous humming about the creviced stone, booming softly at intervals in the great chimney. The fire crackled companionably, and from time to time the great hound Turpin sighed in his sleep and stirred his black nose on his brindled leg. Once a wedge of wild geese slid grotesquely beyond the distorting panes; here and there a light awoke in cottages along the margin of the fen.

"Saints Simon and Jude Apostles," mused Raoul. "This night a year ago I must have slept in Plegmund's attic over Street of Anvils. *Tink-a-tink-a-tink-tink.* And all my thoughts were of Yseult and Marckmont. And now Yseult is nothing, and Marckmont is my own, and even Marckmont fails me at the last.

"Something I need that has escaped me. It has been near, and I have missed it; for my thought of it is a kind of baffled memory. Here all things minister to my delight, and only the delight is lacking. Was Nino right—do I want to wring the colour from the sunset, to rake the moon out of the mere? Or were all of them right, Nino and John and Hubriton—is *that* the simple explanation of my woe? Death and damnation, it is not; that, too, is only a symbol in the end. A symbol of some harmony known to the Sieur God, who swung the planets on their chains and bade them now oppress and now sustain us. . . .

" Some day I shall marry, I suppose. Soberly and by agreement, as befits the ruler of Ger and Marckmont. And to whom? Some well-dowered doll out of Basse Honoy or the South. There are two—or is it three?—Saulte sisters younger than Ermengarde. God send they are less stupid. Or some young heiress like Denise . . . poor little Denise, the Constable is fallen out with the Castellan because each claims her as his ward. These maids are played too much as pawns between the castles and the chevaliers. . . .

" And some day later I shall have an imp to go abroad upon my saddle-bow . . . out there, across the marshes on grey afternoons. . . .

" *See, imp, brown-yellow agrimony. Rub the flowers between your hands; they smell like burnt cedar-wood. But if you dry and burn them they drive away the flies. And it is good for the cows when they cough in the marsh-fogs. And the purplish flower is potentil; its name means ' powerful.' If you cut yourself it stops the bleeding. Look, the queer bird, the bittern; he sees us and stands quite still, staring up at the sky. But if you go near he will fluff up his feathers and thrust his long beak at your eyes. . . .*"

Raoul came to himself and smiled. Many times would the willows shed their leaves before he showed the flowers and birds to a small boy, or taught him how to walk on stilts through the shallow water. Many times would the November mists sheet all the marshes, and the sun peer redly through the shortened days, and John Doust's bellow, as he drilled the men-at-arms, ring for miles in the windless air. . . .

" Come," said Raoul, turning from his window. " It is time to make an end of *Modred, Prince of Britain.*"

And presently his melancholy flowed from him into the minds of his creation. Nimüe wove her snares with the green eyes of Yolande de Volsberghe, daughter of the Constable; Pelleas passed from mortal sight on the shore of a lake like that which broadened from the marsh beyond Cremalvay;

and beneath a doom-red sunset Camelot took on the spires of Hautarroy.

Christmas he spent at Marckmont, where the marshes were frozen for weeks at a time, and where above the snow the leafless woods receded under a leaden sky. Wolves howled among the Olvay oaks ; beneath a waning moon Raoul saw them trotting boldly on the ice beside the sable shadow of the causeway. He himself loosed the death-arrow at the wild boar whose head adorned the Christmas supper-table ; and he himself bound up the gash which one great tusk had opened in Turpin's flank. Not only his own men-at-arms and servants, but also the whole village, feasted and drank at his charges, and men shouted to each other that the good days of the Countess Adela were come again ; for Mogue the steward had displayed a merciless rapacity towards the peasantry. And if Raoul—standing in his vaulted kitchen beside the slowly-revolving carcase of a roasting ox—was suddenly aware that only the parsimony of Mogue had made possible his, Raoul's, generosity, no such consideration clouded the animal satisfaction of Kymlog the swineherd, whose face shone drunkenly in the light of the roaring fire as he watched the fat drip into its wooden gutter.

Raoul, too, drank heavily that night, but was still able to command two of the soberer men-at-arms to carry Nino Chiostra to bed. Even Hubriton was merry ; John Doust disappeared from the public festivities at an early hour, and Kymlog never missed his comely wife. True, a child was nearly drowned in the great horse-trough, and suspension of curfew meant that one thatched hut was burnt to the ground, whilst there was colic and kindred distress in the courtyard ; but the village silence of Saint Stephen's Day bore testimony to the quality of Raoul's meat and wine. . . .

And in the twilight of the last day of December Raoul found himself looking down at the weather-beaten face of the old war-captain Milo, who knelt stiffly before him and brushed his hand with a frost-rimed moustache and icy lips.

" My good lord Count, your uncle, the Count Armand, died two days ago, when the tide turned at dawn."

" God rest his soul," said Raoul, crossing himself. " And

does my lady the . . . the dowager hold to it that I murdered
him ? "

" I fear she does, my lord. But the Baron of Guarenal
begs you will come to Ger as speedily as roads permit."

" H'm. That will I. Up, Milo ; yours are a new horse
and sword for bringing me these tidings. Piers, go see to
Captain Milo's comfort."

And presently Milo was answering his lord's questions
between gulps of steaming wine.

" The lonely falcon goes to eyrie, then," thought Raoul.
" There will be little time henceforth to wander aimless up
a slant of golden air."

At supper that night he smiled to hear John Doust,
Captain of the Men-at-arms of Marckmont, overtopping
with tales of transmontane war the stories told for his admiration by Milo, Captain of the Men-at-arms of Ger.

" They are both lying," he told himself. " Neither will
admit himself a less experienced soldier than the other.
And Milo will never forgive John because he, Milo, did not
come with us to the ending of Jehan de Campscapel. The
men who take kindly to war are children at heart ; witness
the blades I led on that foray, who ran at my stirrup and
cheered when last I rode to Ger. But I . . . by God and
by Saint Guthmund, I will have peace along my marches
and my coasts."

And on the following day the new Count led his troop—
Nino beside him, John Doust and Milo abreast behind—
northward across the causeway and into the Forest of
Nordanay.

XIV

THE CRAGS OF GER

" For God's sake, Reine, stand backward from the verge."

Raoul's fingers crisped on the rampart wall behind him ;
fear tightened about his heart at sight of the girl's slim figure
a pace from the cliff-top.

Pale January sunshine lit the impish face she turned on
him ; fierce January wind beat back her crimson cloak and
flattened the short crimson riding-frock against her knees.
Behind her a cloud-shadow lay violet on blue-grey sea ; two
hundred feet below her the waves curled inward with curt
rushes, slapping viciously along the rocks, whilst across the
harbour the glistening base of the headland was alive with
stalking ghosts of spray.

" Why, Raoul," Reine exclaimed, " you are going green.
Is this the hero of Karmeriet and Alanol ? "

" It is the owner of the fish-basket in which they will
gather you up if . . . *ah, Reine !* "

His voice broke out of control. Empty space tugged at
his loins as he started forward to catch the girl's arm and
wrench her bodily away ; for one spurred boot had slid
wickedly to the very edge.

" Ouch ! " cried Reine. " Death and wounds, my lord,
let go ! "

The mock oath and the mocking title, the sun-dazzled
blink of long dark lashes, the warmth of a firm round arm
beneath the velvet sleeve, set Raoul's blood free-coursing
once again ; but not until the pair of them were sheltered by
an angle of the wall did he loose his companion and scowl
into the brown derision of her eyes.

" Do that again," he threatened, " and I—I will have you

chained to the wall of the keep garden. Are you altogether
made of iron ? "

" Not altogether. Not my arm, I swear ; that is bruised
for a week. Why, stupid, are you angry ? What a fuss for
nothing ! I have robbed gulls' nests enough before to-day."

" So have not I," growled the man. " I would not stand
where you stood for another barony."

" Then what were you doing out here ? I saw you steal
away, but I thought you could not mean to flee the hold
again—especially in this direction."

" No, I am no gull. At least, no sea-gull. I came out
here to be alone."

Reine looked at him, and smiled, and turned away.

" No gull indeed," she said over her shoulder. " Let the
lone falcon brood in peace upon his crag."

She moved towards the postern in the high grey wall, and
Raoul stared after her in a kind of dour perplexity. Reine
had no coquetry or malice, and her choice of words rang very
oddly in his ears. In six strides he had overtaken her.

" Wait for me, Reine. Being with you is the same as
being alone. This castled state demands a castled temper
foreign to me. There is á curst dispute along the coast, and
it is hard to be both disputant and judge."

" I know," returned the girl. " Foreshore rights and
rights of wreck. I heard the steward bleating after you.
And since you saved the fisher-folk, no doubt they feel it
right they should defraud you of just dues."

" That is it. But Charles, God rest his soul—sometimes
I wish that Charles had lived to quarrel with them in my
stead."

Reine wrinkled up her little brown nose and stared across
the harbour ; and Raoul glanced at her and laughed.

" Hey, I forgot," he confessed. " *You* would have shared
this squabble with him ; *you* would have carried these keys
and walked of right in the keep garden."

" Talking of gulls," said Reine serenely, " they are flying
in from sea. I trust we may reach home before more storms
break on us."

The postern clanged behind them, and Raoul shot the
bolts and turned a key in the great lock.

" I wish you a fair journey," he muttered, " and more joy of your company than would fall to me."

For Armand of Ger was two days buried, and already his widow was leaving the hold, braving all discomforts of winter travel rather than stay in shelter of Raoul's towers. Raoul had set apart a minor estate in Elquitaine for her sole use and occupation, and thither her nephew Robin Barberghe was now to escort her. To Guarenal the old Vice-Warden and his granddaughter would accompany them, there to entertain them on the first night of their journey. Officers of the Coast March, too, with clerks and rolls and strong-boxes, would ride to the Vice-Warden's castle, now become their centre of administration ; and with them Enguerrand du Véranger, a new-made March Lieutenant. Already the Fox of Barberghe—loud in his praises of Raoul for the latter's generosity towards his widowed sister—had left with his own lady for their hold in Basse Honoy. Gilles de Volsberghe and Rogier de Olencourt had gone, with the banners of Constable and Castellan that graced the funeral rites of the dead Count Warden ; the dozen lesser lords and chevaliers had followed, so that by noon Raoul would be alone with his own men and his own windy coasts. . . .

" Do you still cherish your old enmity with Robin ? " Reine asked, as Raoul dropped the shining keys into a pocket at his belt. " I deemed it ended when Charles died."

" Think you Robin deemed it ended ? "

" Yes. Or so I hoped. I never liked him, but at least he has shown grace these latter days."

" Strange if he had not," said Raoul, grimly.

" You mean, it is well to be civil to you in your own hold ? "

" Just that."

Reine was silent until they had entered the little garden of the keep, where fruit-trees cowered in a row beneath the northern wall, whilst draggled barberry and rowan disputed the dank corners. Then, pausing on the gravel path, she laid a gloved hand on the bough of an apple-tree, and shook a shower of glistening drops to the dark earth.

" That, too, is strange," she said, looking thoughtfully up at her companion.

" What else is strange ? " asked Raoul absently, his mind on the turmoil of preparation in the inner bailey ; for they had passed along a rampart - walk and seen the horses being harnessed once again to the great horse-litters that would carry southward the Dowager Countess and her women.

" Grandfather said of you, when we heard how you had taken the hold of Campscapel : *That Raoul will be implacable in strife ; beware the man reluctant to slay beasts when he takes to the slaying of men.* I found it hard to believe ; for since I saw you first, not yet two years ago—a boy half-scared of his own daring—to me you have barely changed. So that I chide you, as now on the cliff-top. But I am a maid, a nobody ; and you are a famous captain. Yet I have spoken with you as though you were another maid, because you talk so little of achievement and legality and the idleness of the serfs, and so much of songs and legends, of places you have seen and queer folk you have met. But now I begin to believe it indeed . . . is that where you will chain me if I offend again ? "

She motioned towards a rusty stanchion that served in summer-time to bear an awning in the north-east corner of the garth ; and Raoul hooked his thumb in his belt and frowned at the unoffending iron.

" But," he objected, " *I* have spoken with *you* as though you were another man. Nevertheless in the past week no woman in this hold—no, not the Countess of Barberghe's haughty self—has moved with more sedateness than have you. And yet you wonder that I, too, am grown up ! "

Reine's mouth twitched ; and after a moment Raoul gave a chuckle that was half a groan.

" In truth," he said, " I never thought to find you in the same galley with Ermengarde de Saulte."

" How ? "

" Why, Ermengarde would have me always a youth, laden with love half-monstrous, half-absurd—a two-headed calf of a love that bleated and was blind. Indeed, she was offended to be told that I could not sustain, and that Yseult could not inspire, a hopeless deathless passion of the kind esteemed in old romances."

Reine looked at him and laughed the deep abrupt laugh of a boy.

" Yseult I believe is generous," she said.   " She could laugh without malice to hear you.   But Ermengarde would mightily enjoy your dying of love.   She is all woman."

" From your tone she is to blame for it."

" Oh, she is as God made her.   But a woman withouι manly generosity is a horse-leech, and a man without womanly perception is a clod."

" Stern Reine !   That damns a moiety of humankind."

" A moiety at least."

" Among them Charles, God assoil him."

" Why do you talk so much of Charles ?   But you are right . . . Charles had the clod's two eyes for a woman."

" Which are ? "

" The eye of contempt and the eye of desire.   No wonder women look for gold and gear beside.   Charles, it is true, was kindly in his scorn ; and we had been betrothed five years."

" You mean, you were used to the thought of marriage with him ? "

" Yes.   And now it is all to do again."

" What ? "

" Our lord the king, to still this strife betwixt the Constable and the Castellan, has given grandfather the wardship of your little heiress of Saint-Aunay."

" Denise ? "

" Yes, Dionysia, as we call her who have not saved her from dire peril in the forest.   Some time next summer she will be with us.   And grandfather, poor soul, must hasten my betrothal before I am put in the shade ; for they say the little Lady Dionysia is very fair."

" Ay, she is fair enough, but . . ."

" Fie, what a moody acquiescence !   Robin and Gilles pricked up their ears at knowledge of her coming."

" They would.   I saw her in October, on my way north from Hautarroy.   She was shy, and called me ' Herluin,' and then was shyer than before."

" Poor she !   But in faith, Raoul, has Yseult drawn off all fiery humours from your heart for ever ? "

" No ; but she has made me mightily wary of them.   Good

K *

soul, she was once ashamed of my devotion ; yet nowise so
ashamed as I have been."

" Now that is false, or cruel, or both together."

" Neither.   My earliest adventure seemed to need a fair
face at the core of it.   Yseult's came neatly to my eye.   All
that I sought, when I fled hence from the whipping-post, I
bound together and named *Yseult*.   In brief, she was a . . . a
symbol, and it is hard on oneself to make a symbol of another
mortal creature."

" Harder on her, if you should marry her."

" True.   But of that there was never any danger.   And
when, between Karmeriet and Alanol, I found the shadow of
the whipping-post gone from my heart, gone also was my
so-great love."

" But why were you ashamed ? "

" For my idolatry.   That I allowed her slightingly to
speak of Marckmont.   That I came to smile at what was
sacred to me.   That I spent the words of love in a madness,
whereby they are dimmed if . . ."

" If ever you need them again ? "

" Yes."

Reine snorted.

" Saints witness you are not so old," she gibed.   " I who
had qualms before a warrior Count am now a very hag
for counsel.   Dear foolish Raoul, I have small faith in your
discrimination as a lover ; but should you fall again into
this weakness, take heart against your shame.   If the match
be a fair one, and the maid less stupid than Meldreth in the
song, do you not see she would rather you had kept a boy's
clean silly dream till manhood—harming neither Yseult nor
yourself—than have gone the way of half your peers in other
men's beds and houses of ill-fame ? "

Raoul stared down at the sunlit earth and up at the windy
sky.

" As man to man," he said, " that is fair hearing.   But
as maid to maid, where got you all your wisdom ? "

" The serpent whispered it to Mother Eve.   Doubt not
the little Saint - Aunay has it also.   You did her great
service, and she is young enough to find no irk in gratitude ;
she yet may carry those keys of yours in the wards of Ger."

" Denise will never do that."

Reine stared.

" Why, here is the strict warrior-Count again ! " she exclaimed. " Are you so very sure ? "

" I am. Twelve hours before I found Denise in the forest I . . . I . . . it was my sword quenched her father's torment in the keep of Campscapel."

" Oh ! " whispered Reine.

She looked away, and with a curious thrill Raoul observed his jeering counsellor become again a contrite little maid.

" Your pardon," she said, oddly. " You have so many secrets, Raoul. But there is now one less for me to trample on in jest."

" It is nothing. Come, there is this fearsome leave-taking toward."

Reine moved ahead along the path, but at the keep door she wheeled and again confronted him.

" One moment," she commanded. " I have remembered why I sought you on the cliff. It was your rondel that you showed us yesternight, the *Rondel of Hill Country* that I so loved."

" I will make you a copy of it," Raoul promised.

" No, there is no need. Hear me, have I it rightly ? "

She clasped her hands behind her and looked him squarely in the face. Colour crept beneath her sunburn, and her voice was hushed and a little shy ; but to the end she held his grave considering gaze, and gave him his swinging rhymes without mistake or hesitation.

> *Mine be the grey and the golden weather*
> *Far in the heart of the windswept hills !*
> *War is the woe that a madman wills,*
> *Wine is a fool's or a coward's tether,*
> *Love hath redden'd his white wing-feather :*
> *Love is a cheat who laughs and kills :*
> *Mine be the grey and the golden weather,*
> *Far in the heart of the windswept hills.*
> *Perish the sword and the vine together,*
> *Shatter the harp that torment thrills ;*
> *Mine be the flume that a freshet fills,*
> *The drone of bees in the purpling heather,*
> *The blue and the grey and the golden weather,*
> *Far in the heart of the windswept hills !*

" *There !* " she finished, with eyes grown merry again.

" You have it, Reine ; and never did I like the sound of
it so well."

" Last night it kept me awake until I had remembered it
entire ; but I was not sure of it. I must wait to hear it sung
until you come to Guarenal ; do not forget you are pledged
to us for the Easter solemnities."

" I will not forget."

In half-an-hour the leavetaking was over. The implacable
dowager had given Raoul her last stare of hatred, whilst even
Robin Barberghe bit his lip in some embarrassment. The
drawbridge rang to the outgoing horse-hoofs ; Raoul cloaked
himself and mounted to a turret-top, watching—as he had
watched two years before—the sparkle of steel fade on the
crest above the hamlet of Gramberge. Then he turned, and
for a desolate while stared down along the gull-loud crannies
of the cliffs.

" This foreshore mischief ended," he told himself, " I
will unearth poor *Modred, Prince of Britain*, and whelm him
utterly at last in the sea-fog at Camlan. . . .

" There will be snow to-night. Then, if the wind drop,
we shall have frost and the chance of a wolf-hunt. . . .

" I wonder whom they will find to marry little Denise ?
I wonder, too . . .

" I . . . but what ails me, now ? "

For his right arm grew stealthily flexed at his side, as
though of its own volition. His right hand opened, and the
fingers curved as though to enclose with gentleness some fair
and friendly thing—the bough of an apple-tree, the muzzle
of a worshipping hound, or even the round arm of a brave
and lovely girl.

Raoul thrust the hand from beneath the furred edge of
his cloak, and stared at it. Then his face flamed, although
there was none but a wheeling gull to see him.

" Sieur God," he said, " I think I have another secret
from her now."

And all around him the north wind shrilled and hummed
in the worn stone, whilst gathering cloud and rising sea
spread gloom and fury on the crags of Ger. . . .

On the Wednesday before Easter, with only Piers du Véranger and half-a-dozen men-at-arms behind him, Raoul rode to Guarenal according to his promise. · That night he heard from the old Vice-Warden what news from southward had broken the winter silence of Nordanay ; for a season of deep snow and shattering storms was lately overpast, and no lord in those fastnesses knew much of the recent doings of his neighbours. That night, also, Raoul gave *Modred* finished into Reine's hands ; and he played chess with Enguerrand and dared not look at her whilst she began to read it. Enguerrand beat him twice ; and finally he laughed and went to the harp, singing song after song for the diversion of the household, tiring himself in order that he might not lie awake too long before the morrow.

It seemed the old Baron planned to build, on the high ground six leagues to northward of his hold, a new march-tower to overlook long reaches of the roads to Ostercamp and Ger, and a wide sweep of the indented coast between them ; and as serfs were already digging space for the foundations, Raoul accepted invitation to ride to the site with Enguerrand if the morning of Holy Thursday were fair.

" I too," said Reine, looking up from the thick manuscript upon her knees. " I must gain strength to follow all these chevaliers to their untimely graves."

" The grey and the golden weather, hey ? " smiled Enguerrand. " The golden is well enough, but Raoul may keep the grey to himself for all I care."

" Name of a name," protested Raoul, " my verse is not my creed. I sing the moors, but for the most part leave them gladly to the witches and to Joris of the Rock. . . .

" Joris will spare you a curse, my lord, when he hears of your new tower," he added, turning to the old Vice-Warden.

But the Baron of Guarenal nodded in his chair, and it was Reine who motioned to the pages for candles to light them all to bed.

" Joris is south of Varne," said Enguerrand as he rose. " Since autumn he has not been heard of in the Uplands of Honoy. Poor pickings for his kind in our late weather. One day, God aiding us, we will yet ring him round and finish him."

"Amen to that," said Raoul absently; for he was watching Reine, whilst in him rose a dreadful hope that trampled all the past to unconsidered dust.

"Ha, but the pines smell sweetly!" exulted Reine, tightening bridle and twitching the quiver at her hip, so that the free tip of her four-foot hunting bow danced wildly behind her head. "Golden weather for spadework, Enguerrand. It is not graves they were digging, Raoul; why do you look so glum?"

"Do I look glum? I slept very ill; and when I slept I had an evil dream."

"It came a night too early, then. Is it not on Good Friday Eve the nightmare rides across all Christendom? Tell us your dream."

"No."

For in that dream Raoul and Reine had stood together on the crags of Ger; and from the postern Charles came creeping on them, sword in hand. Raoul had fought a ghastly dream-fight with numbed sinews and a bending blade; and Charles in the end smote heavily downward and vanished. But Raoul, groping at his love to save her, grasped only a warm severed arm, whilst far below a plume of spray sprang lightly from the crest of a green incoming wave . . . and Raoul, starting awake with a groan of horror and despair, had stared into the face of little Piers du Véranger, who shivered with cold and fright in the first grey of the dawn, clutching a candlestick that dripped hot wax upon his lord's disordered bed. . . .

But now it was near mid-day; Raoul and Reine and Enguerrand, with two squires following after, were riding down steep sledge-tracks from the heathery crest where serfs dug through the peat to naked rock for the founding of Guarenal's tower.

"Never before have I heard a dreamer refuse to tell a dream," cried Reine. "Many a time have I broken fast with grief, after asking a guest in courtesy if by chance she dreamed in the night. Oh, they have always dreamed . . . and neither commendable sense nor mirthful furious folly, but dreary mysteries of pilgrimage and apparition which only the

dreamer can expound.   Sometimes they make it up as they
go along . . . but their voices change between the dream
and the falsehood."

" Saints witness I am glad of my refusal," Raoul said.
" Come, let us ride a mile along the Gramberge way."

" We must be home by the hour of nones for the alms-
giving," Reine reminded him.

" Time enough yet.   Somewhere on the right hand,
beyond the first rise of the road, six silver birches grow
before three great pines.   Among them I hid my sword and
mail when I came from the Belsaunt tourney.   I would greet
those birches again ; they were good friends to me. . . .

" And yet," he added, " no better friends than my uncle's
whipping-post, which is now mine."

Enguerrand chuckled.

" Carve on your whipping-post," he suggested, " this
legend : *Under God ridded I this realm of Lorin and Jehan
de Campscapel.*"

" Nay, why pitch on the whipping-post ?   Saint-Aunay,
God ease his soul, had his own share in that deliverance.   So
had Robin Barberghe, and the Bishop who gave the tourney,
and Red Anne who took me for her page, and the witch-
women who befriended me . . . and both of *you.* . . ."

" Enough," groaned Enguerrand.   " I yield the point."

" It is shame to stop him," said Reine, laughing.   " Anon
we should have heard how many angels stand upon the point
of a needle."

And she began to whistle the air of *Now Raveth Alured*
in time to the beat of Jehanet's hoofs on the sandy road ; so
that presently Enguerrand looked at her and ventured a mild
rebuke.

" Do you not know it is said that the heart of the
Blessed Virgin bleeds each time she hears a woman
whistle ? "

" More likely it bleeds each time she hears a woman hush
a child with such a tale," said Reine ; and then : " See how
the thorns bud on their landward side.   The May-flower will
be heavy this new year."

" At sundown I should not linger hereabouts," Enguerrand
confessed, eyeing the twisted shapes amid the rocks.   " To-

night, they say, the hawthorns groan for shame of the Crown
that was woven in Pilate's hall."

The three of them crossed themselves and fell silent for a
space ; and suddenly Raoul drew rein and flung up a hand
to halt the rest.

" Your birches ? " asked Reine.

" No.   Listen ! "

The horsehoofs thudded to silence.

" What is it ? " muttered Enguerrand.

" *Bells !* "

Borne by the stiffening sea-breeze far along the steep edge
of the moors, the chime of bells strove faintly with the song of
thorn and pine.

" Gramberge," said Raoul.   " But it is no alarm of riot,
for they are ringing a triple peal.   Yet why to-day ? "

For from the *Gloria* in Holy Thursday's Mass until the
morning of Holy Saturday the bells were ritually dumb ; and
there amid pines and sand and flowering gorse the riders
stared at one another and down the rugged road towards the
coast.

" Come," said Raoul, touching spur to his horse's flank ;
and with its mirth abated the little cavalcade drove westerly
at a full gallop, whilst on the left the moors towered ever
closer, and each turn of the way brought sharpening clamour
of the bells ahead. . . .

And when the straggling hamlet burst on view a sinister
and darkening breath seemed blown athwart the brightness
of the day ; for the mean street was empty save for a mongrel
dog that fled at sound of their approach.   House and hovel
were still and shuttered ; no one stirred by well or smithy or
in the half-ploughed fields.   But still the squat grey belfry-
tower, that stood across the graveyard from the church,
hurled steady clangour into the windy air.

" What ails them ? " cried Raoul, standing in his stirrups.
" Is it the plague ? "

Enguerrand, watching the church as they approached it,
suddenly set his left hand on his sword-hilt.

" Someone is spying from the leper-squint," he said.
" And beneath the bushes by the chancel is a man with arrows
in him."

Then, as they checked their horses to a trot, the door of the priest's house burst open on their left, and the little priest himself came stumbling out. The riders stared, for his pale face and grizzled hair were half-concealed by a bandage, and as he signed the Cross at them he was fain to prop himself against his door-post.

" In God's name, Father Andreas, what is amiss ? " barked Raoul through the uproar of the belfry and the clatter of hoofs.

" Thank God you are come, Sieur Count," groaned the priest, his thin face drawn with pain and lit with, a curious exaltation. " But is this all your company ? Were you not set upon ? "

" This is all—but set upon by whom ? "

" Then for God's sake and the Lady Reine's, go—you are well horsed and armed. *They* feared to stop your coming and may not stay your going—ride hard, break through to Ger, and send us aid ! "

" Break through to . . . damnation, man, you are distraught ! What ails you—who has hurt you—who are *they* ? "

" Beast-headed things that came upon us in the dawn— ay, you may cross yourselves, lords and lady. They chased a queer thin wench out of the moors . . . I took her in and would not yield her up for all their yelling . . . and they came skipping in the street and struck me with a club, and slew the bailiff and two more who ran at them, for they were black and swift and hard to see in twilight . . . and ever since sunrise they have beleaguered us with arrows from the thickets and the moor behind . . . and they have sworn to bring down Joris of the Rock. . . ."

" Joris ? *Here ?* "

" Ay, Joris of the Rock. *Now* you will ride, Sieur Count, God helping you . . . I beseech you tarry no longer ! "

Count and March Lieutenant looked at the priest, at each other, at the dark slope of moor that sank into dense brushwood high above them ; and from the latter, as if to quicken their perceptions, came sailing a long shaft that sank up to its feathers in a thatch across the street.

Enguerrand swore and seized Reine's bridle, crowding white Jehanet beneath the priest's own overhanging eaves.

K

The squires drew in likewise, and Raoul leaned distractedly out of his saddle towards the priest.

" You believe Joris on his way ? " he demanded.

" I do not know . . . I have not heard speak of him for a year . . . but the serfs believe it."

" Where are they all, the peasantry ? "

" After the first onslaught they barred themselves in the church, old and young, bond and free, having carried in the babes and the bedridden. Three, stouter than the rest, I sent on foot for aid. My man Imbert rode on the bailiff's horse for Ger, but none of them has come again, or any help of their sending, unless indeed you . . ."

" We met no one. Go on."

" The voice said they were dead to a man, and the horse taken. . . ."

" The voice ? What voice ? "

" About the hour of terce a . . . a great sweet voice cried out of the orchard thickets, so that I might hear, and those in the church as well . . . saying that if I did not render up the wench before the sycamore-shadow touched my wall, we should have Joris of the Rock down by mid-day or a little after. . . ."

" It has a grisly ring of certitude. Go on again."

" And that those in the church were safe, but that all outside should perish and the hamlet be sacked and fired . . . so that the serfs burst out and battered at my door for me to cast the poor wretch forth . . . but I withstood them, and they dared not break in beneath my crucifix . . . instead, they scattered for their huts, weeping and cursing most vilely, to gather such gear as they could and drag it into the church . . . and one I heard who screeched that God was always harsher than the devil, and none rebuked him . . . so when they had gone I took hyssop and sprinkled holy water from my windows, and sent my maid-servant to ring the peal of exorcism, for there was no one else. . . ."

" How many are there of these archer-fiends ? "

" Three I saw, but by the arrows there are more."

" But they are scattered and few if they must send for Joris to do their work. You and your wench and this fugitive can each ride pillion ; we can break through to Ger and leave the serfs to their perplexed allegiance . . . ah, one of you behind there, to the belfry and in God's name stop the clamour of those bells ! "

" In God's name I commanded them to ring," came the priest's mild protest. " But the wench within is nigh senseless ; her ankle is broken and her arm torn with an arrow . . . she lost much blood, and more when I broke it out. Sieur Count, she will die on your saddle-bow . . . I beg you will take my servant and leave me with the other . . . and by the dear Sieur Jesu I conjure you, get you gone before it is too late ! "

The younger squire had thrust his horse to the belfry and disappeared within ; the triple pealing slurred, and sudden silence buffeted Raoul's ear. Then the squire came out, with a comely peasant-girl who rubbed red palms together and grinned to find so many fine folk round her master's door.

" I will see this wounded creature," Reine announced.

She slid from her saddle and crowded past the priest into his dark dwelling ; protesting further at this extension of delay, Father Andreas reeled after her.

" That belfry," began Enguerrand.

" Yes, it might serve for an hour," said Raoul. " Come and look at it."

The belfry was some fifteen feet square and thirty-five feet high, two-storied, with bell-ropes hanging through pierced roof and floor, and only splayed slits to give light if the narrow door were closed. There was no inner door to the winding stair, and nothing but ends of rope and part of an old broken harrow in the ground-floor space ; Raoul ran up to the room above, and found it empty save for dust and cobwebs.

" Now, leave me here with Father Andreas and this runaway," he said when he joined Enguerrand below. " My horse will carry the serf-girl if she rides half as grimly as she rings a bell. Reine and she at least should win to Ger."

" If these damned archers have any force it will be laid to ambush us on that same road by now," objected Enguerrand. " It is well past mid-day, and there is yet no Joris ; this place has stout walls, and you and I—and Reine with her bow—can hold it an hour. Let the squires go—they are stout men both, and one or two make a worse mark than five."

" So be it," said Raoul after a moment's fret. Then, with
one eye on the church door only thirty paces from them, he
added : " Go you and bring priest and all down here, and let
the squires stay with us until our garrison is set. There is no
knowing how frightened serfs may jump. Ay, take both
horses ; we must risk losing them. They can graze in the
priest's orchard."

Immediately he was alone Raoul was aware of a dull
terror ; but he thought of Reine in her crimson riding-cloak
—a fair mark for an archer on the crest towards Ger—and he
knew that with her at his back he would fight as he never
fought before.

" This might be a stranger leaguer than that of Capel
Conan," he reflected, scanning the dark skyline far above
the hamlet ; then voices burred in the church, dying down
as he glanced in that direction, whilst hairy faces moved
obscurely behind rents in the horn-filled windows.

" I warrant them doubly scared that we take no heed of
them," he thought. And a moment later : " Just Saints,
here is a queer procession."

Round the corner of the priest's house strode Reine, with
her bow unsheathed and strung and an arrow set. Behind
her came Enguerrand, nursing the limp and ragged shape
that was the fugitive ; and on either hand of him, so that
their horses shielded Reine as well, the squires rode at a foot
pace with bared blades. Last of all came the peasant-girl,
one arm around the tottering priest, the other swinging a
great bundle from which protruded the top of a silver
altar candlestick ; and at sight of this deliberate progress a dull ferocious tumult swelled in the church, whilst
arrows shot from far above began to fall and flicker in the
street.

" Close archery would drop the half of us," thought Raoul,
" but maybe Enguerrand was right, and they ambush the
seaward road."

He stepped forward, hoping to draw arrow-shot from the
rest ; but a bolt creaked on the door of the church, and he
spun round, plucking out his sword.

" Stay where you are, you swine ! " he shouted. " Or by
the Rood you will need scant carrying to your graves ! "

Then Reine was close upon him, and her voice rang coolly in the windy air.

"The priest was right," she said. "Our bag of bones went off into a swoon when Enguerrand lifted her. But she is gentle of speech, and muscled like a sturdy boy."

"Best get them all upstairs," counselled Raoul. "Enguerrand and I can hold this tower a week, so be it Joris has no mangonel."

Reine's smile blazed out upon him with a dark and terrible enchantment.

"It is plain we are not upon your crags of Ger," she said.

Then she was gone inside ; and as Enguerrand paused to manœuvre his burden through the narrow entry Raoul blinked at it, and stared, and brushed his empty hand across his eyes. . . .

Beneath a tangle of mouse-coloured hair the still face against Enguerrand's shoulder was grey behind weather-burn, grey and haggard and pitifully thin ; but there was a brave pinched daintiness about the nose and mouth.

"Holy Mary ! " said Raoul between his teeth ; and he rounded on the waiting squires, whilst Enguerrand gently handed up the stair to Reine the frail and fugitive anatomy of Lys. . . .

"Now ride for Ger ! " he snapped. "Seek out the Captain Milo and the Captain John Doust ; tell them to bring as many men as they can mount, half archers at the least . . . and let the small horse-litter follow them. Separate if you are waylaid . . . and God go with you. *Ride !* "

The squires had wheeled their horses, ready for his word ; the flash of a saluting sword from one, the grunt of a half-swallowed oath from the other, and they had crashed away behind the huts and stacks and across the open fields.

Raoul drew a deep breath and looked again from moor-skyline to church door ; and presently Enguerrand's voice fell sharply from the parapet beside the bells.

"They are half across the ploughland," he called. "They ride a score of yards apart. They are through the first thickets . . . by the Mass, they are under the pines and out the other side. They are up on the near brow . . . they are shot at . . . God speed them, they are gone ! "

"Every slit is shuttered," said Reine's voice from the
door-way. "Commend me to your ancestor who built this
belfry. Look here."

Raoul turned and entered, staring as she pointed. A
little trap-door lay open above their heads, so that an archer
kneeling in the upper room might ply a bow at murderous
range for any coming in below.

"My post," claimed Reine, as Enguerrand lumbered
down the stair. "And there is a slit in front of it as well."

"Saints send we do not need them, all the same," was
torn from Raoul in such a voice that Reine looked quickly
at him. But before she could reply there came a growl from
Enguerrand beside the door.

"Archery closing in," he said. "*And by God we were
only just in time.*"

Over his shoulder they peered at the high moor; and
Raoul felt a dryness in his mouth, for crag and hummock
of the topmost crest were alive with dozens of bounding,
slithering men.

Then they slammed and locked the door, shooting across
it two iron bolts and a great bar of wood. Enguerrand
kicked and wrested from the rotting harrow two wooden
lengths with which he plugged the narrow window-slits,
swinging the strong shutters to behind them. Then, in a
gloom lit only by the arched crack over the door and the dim
square of the trap, they pounced upon shreds of rope and
tugged the remains of the harrow across the earthen floor.

"That great nail over the door should bear this wrack,"
Raoul had said. "Let it hang loose. If they beat the door
down it should devilishly hamper them."

So the three comrades lifted the heavy criss-crossed wood
and secured it to dangle flatly against the narrow doorway;
and as Raoul fastened the last knot Reine left them, to peer
down a moment later from the trap-way above.

"The serving-maid is on the roof," she said. "Father
Andreas tends the poor wench; she is coming round. What?
Yes, we will keep our shutters barred or ajar; but I shall
shoot from this slit until you need help below."

"Now would I give a year's rents for a suit of plate
complete," grumbled Enguerrand. "But here we are,

without even a shield—nothing but swords and jerkins and thigh-boots."

" Here is a little hunting-targe," said Reine. " It came in the cloak with the priest's gear upon it."

" Yours, Enguerrand. There is more to hide of you than of me."

" So, but I will guard the right hand of the door. And Raoul, there is only one weak spot in our defence . . . for they will not use fire, I take it. I mean ladders."

Above them Reine spoke to the priest, and then leaned down again.

" Some took their ladders to the church," she said.

" Ay, well, at the worst Raoul can keep the roof, and I the stairway here. Yon parapet is three feet high in the crenels . . . good enough if you crouch and let men rise before you strike at them."

And when Enguerrand had set the hunting-targe upon his arm there came a little wind-stirred hush in the belfry of Gramberge.

" God and sweet Jesu and the Blessed Virgin, save ! " prayed Raoul simply in his heart. " Save our bodies if it may be so ; but do not suffer any of us to fall alive into the hands of Joris of the Rock ; and send swift aid from Ger ; and whether we now live or die, take *all* our souls in holy and eternal keeping. . . . Amen."

He opened his eyes and looked again at the trap-way. Reine had turned from the slit and was watching him.

" Reine," he said hoarsely, appalled yet glad that it was he who had to say this thing to her. " If . . . if the worst befall, and there is no hope left . . ."

Reine flipped her dagger-hilt and nodded, calmly holding down a hand with two slim fingers extended.

" Good," muttered Raoul ; then he crossed himself, and dared not look deliberately at her any more.

The quiet voice of the priest sounded from above ; then the muffled cry of the serving-girl rang down the winding stair.

" *Coming across the fields.*"

" Coming," said Reine ; and she raised her four-foot bow.

And, after a stranger moment than any, there swelled

around the tower a crackle of shouting and a padding of many feet.

"Hither axes!" boomed a jovial voice. "This meat is tenderer raw than roast! Rufin, a ram and ladders . . . Madoc, iron to break mortar out and pegs to mount upon . . . bowmen, rake the slits and let no head show on the roof! Axes amain!"

There followed a sudden yelp and a roar of brutal laughter.

"*One*," counted Reine; and the first thunder of the axe-heads fell upon the door. . . .

Spears thudded in the slits against the wooden plugs and shutters. Tiles, tossed by the serf-girl over the parapet, crashed among the cursing axe-men; presently picks began to chip and clink between the stones of the tower.

Said Raoul: "They may pick away till midnight, if devils keep faith, and if there be no ladders in the barns."

"If devils keep faith!" grunted Enguerrand; and once more Reine's voice came clearly down to them.

"Someone at least keeps faith," she called. "A woman in man's clothes sits a horse by the church door as if to guard it."

"So!" cried Raoul above the din. "And has she red hair?"

"I cannot see . . . ah, now they have a great log from the wood-pile."

"Ay, now the fun begins indeed," growled Enguerrand; and every other sound was blotted out by the first crash of the ram. . . .

Six and seven times the splintering impact sounded, and still the stout wood held in jagged inward-slanting shapes. Through the gap Raoul saw scattering bodies, striding legs encased in leather, swords and pikes and guisarmes with lowered points; Enguerrand and he stood back, one at each side of the doorway, and between them burst a sudden hail of arrows that streaked amid the bell-ropes and bit at bare stone beyond, rattling and rebounding harmlessly about their knees and feet.

Axes again. The burst bolts clanked, the wooden bar hung down and fell, the pointed fragments flaked and flew, the harrow-hatching swung and clashed to a rain of smiting

iron . . . steady pike points raised its lower edge, and a
first brave ruffian stooped and crowded buckler and steel
cap and blade into the gloom. . . .

Raoul struck at the pike-heads, cleaving the nearer one
from its shaft ; down slewed the hatching on the attacker's
inbowed shoulder. Enguerrand whirled in a blow that
split the cap and the skull under it ; the outlaw stumbled
on his face and sprawled half-through the opening amid the
wreckage of the door.

Began a thrusting, snarling madness round the entry,
with hands and weapons driving in the hatching, and the
defenders stabbing through and under it. Pikes bored cross-
wise at their knees, and they backed ; but as a second
bucklered figure stepped across the pike-heads they danced
at him together and spitted him twice over. He, too, pitched
forward, pressed by those behind, fouling the pike-heads as
he fell ; and over his bowed back Enguerrand sped a wicked
thrust into a tugging pikeman's throat. Raoul tore the
buckler from a limp arm and took it upon his own ; the
hatch fell thudding and hung as before, and the attacking
press thinned out and scattered a second time.

" 'Ware arrows," muttered Enguerrand, backing along
the wall.

" *Four !* " said Reine above them.

Raoul dropped on one knee and slanted his buckler above
the corpses to peer from beside it.

" They are sticking shields on pikes to make a kind of
siege-cat," he said, wincing as an arrow beat into the buckler-
face. " Ha, there is Joris . . . a great lank rogue with a
pointed golden beard . . . *Wow !* Reine has dropped the
man in front of him ! "

" *Five !* " chanted Reine in the half-hush.

" *A sagitta volante in die, a negotio perambulante in
tenebris, ab incursu et daemonio meridiano,*"droned the little
wounded priest behind her ; and through the Psalm cut a
husky voice unheard of Raoul since Herluin's last night on
the rock of Campscapel.

" Lady, whoever you be, who is it fights below ? "

But Reine cried only : " Ladders ! They have joined
three ladders that will top the tower ! "

" I go to the roof," called Raoul.

" Bring arrows when you pass, as many as you can find."

The two men groped and grabbed, and with a score of shafts in his buckler-hand Raoul dived up the narrow stair.

" *Six !* " snapped Reine as he strode into the upper chamber and spilled the arrows by her knee ; and out of the corner gloom beyond the praying priest came a quiet cry :

" *Herluin !* "

Raoul straightened up and peered at the ragged shape half-risen from the floor.

" Yes, Lys, it is I," he said. " Lie still for your wound's sake ; all here are your friends."

Then he turned and bolted up to the roof, wondering even at that pass if men were often so glad as he to escape into a battle. . . .

Up there the arrows searched the crenels and rasped the tiles of the stair-head ; now and again one smote a bell and bounded off with a *ping*. The serving-maid lay between stair-head and parapet, her chin propped on her hands, her bright eyes fixed on the seaward ridge where the road from Ger ran down.

" Keep low, Sieur Count," she said. " I have thrown all the tiles I could make to loosen."

Raoul dragged himself out beside her, and with his sword began to poke about to loosen more. Then a tumult of renewed attack burst round the base of the tower, whilst from all sides the arrows whistled upward.

" They may get through the doorway with their cat," thought Raoul, " but it is useless for the stair. Enguerrand is strong as an ox, and there it is one against one. And Reine sows death as they crowd in."

" The ladder is against the western wall ! " piped Father Andreas from below.

Then Raoul gave the serf-girl his cap and bade her set it on an arrow to draw fire at a northern crenel, whilst he crouched midway behind the threatened parapet.

Scrape and slither of wood against stone, feet stamping on the rungs, slapping of arrows into the wooden beam above the bells, and the exultant grunts of mounting men. . . .

" First after you with the women, Joris ! " yelled a great voice beyond the crenel on Raoul's right.

" No," snarled Raoul, rising with buckler poised to guard his head. " First off your ladder into hell ! "

And he smote furiously between the merlons at the ascending bascinet, ducking down as it disappeared, marking a grisly falling clatter amid the roar of assault. . . .

The second man he beat down with a great gash in the face. The corselet of the third withstood his stroke, and the rogue got an elbow on the parapet ; but Raoul charged with the flat of his buckler and hurled him off the wall. The fourth attacker swung a morning-star so that the spiked ball bounded on its chain in the flat of the crenel ; and Raoul slid his bucklered left hand up and gripped the chain, lunging his point into a brawny throat. The downward tug on the chain relaxed, and Raoul laughed—stemming his laugh with an oath as an arrow swept through his tumbled hair, its feathers brushing harshly across his temple.

Shrinking back, he dragged at the morning-star, but its haft was powerfully clutched from below ; for a second Raoul hung on, and then let go. The iron ball flew off the surface of the stone, and a shield-rim wavered above the crenel's edge. Raoul split it, and pulled his sword away ; and a jumble of prayers and curses began to stutter from his lips. . . .

How long that nightmare lasted he could never tell ; but his arm began to ache with the burden of flail-like blows such as he had not known were in him. Dimly he felt a scratch in his left shoulder, and saw an arrow drooping from his jerkin ; dimly he heard the serf-girl scream, and knew that a second ladder was coming beside the first. . . .

The blade of an upthrust guisarme screeched on the merlon side at his shoulder ; once more he grabbed and tugged and slashed, and the guisarme came away in his left hand, whilst in front of him a hairy face grew white and sank its jaw on the crenel, so that a black beard splayed grotesquely out along the reddened stone. Raoul struck out again, but in the mid-stroke pain ran hotly through his forearm ; his hand flew open, his sword whirled out and flashed and was utterly gone. . . .

Remained the guisarme. Clumsily Raoul swung it about,

as the top rung of the second ladder came into the crenel on his left. His right arm, transfixed and numbed and bleeding, yet permitted him to set the hook of the bright blade against the wood ; and with all his remaining force he thrust the ladder away from the wall. Its angle was steep, for the climbers feared to break it with their weight ; and Raoul had one glimpse of clutching hands and a desperate helmed face between the upper rungs . . . then the weight went from his weapon, and a mingled crash bespoke the ruin below.

" Next time it rises I am done," he thought ; and as he turned to the other ladder he heard the serf-girl scream again . . . again and again and again.

" She is hit," swirled in Raoul's mind. " This is the end."

Behind him a bell boomed sharply, as though its rope were clutched by a falling man in the struggle at the stair-foot ; in front of him the ghastly bearded face had vanished, giving place to a lean bareheaded youth with red-rimmed eyes, with a great knife caught between long yellow teeth, and with one knee already planted on the wall. . . .

" One more," gasped Raoul, and lunged beneath a rising sword.

Not the blade of the guisarme, but the spike behind it, went somehow home ; the outlaw missed his sword-stroke and toppled forward, clutching Raoul by the belt. There behind the parapet they grappled, Raoul hammering his buckler in his enemy's face, whilst above his head the fist that had held a sword now held the knife . . . the knife poised high to end all love and lordship and bright earth for ever. . . .

Then Raoul was gripped from behind ; over the buckler-edge one red-rimmed eye gave him a hideous wink. The yellow-toothed mouth blew a sudden incredible howl in his face. The hand on his belt flew off and away, to be dashed across lean brows ; between its horny fingers protruded the slim shaft of an arrow driven deeply in by the sturdy serving-maid. Hand and face and arrow and lithe body reeled away and toppled back across the wall to disappear.

" Praise God, my lord ! " sobbed the girl in his ear as she hugged him round the waist. " Look up—we are saved— they flee in terror—here are all your men from Ger ! "

But Raoul leaned on her and on the merlon beside them,

staring down at Red Anne by the church below. The Mistress
of the Coven of the Singing Stones was cloaked and hooded
and armed with sword and bow ; her hood had fallen back,
and between a dark close-fitting cap and a fierce sun-browned
face her braided hair made a sharp blot of colour against the
grey church wall. Between her knees the bailiff's horse
plunged amid shouting, scattering outlaws ; but she checked
him roughly, and the great sweet voice that Father Andreas
knew rang out across the din of rout and onset.

" Joris, this way—there is yet time ! "
The fair head of the outlaw chief flashed at her thigh ; the
grey horse bounded forward between the bushes, Joris loping
alongside with one hand on the stirrup-leather and the other
swinging his sword. Rider and runner vanished into the
moorward thickets; that now were full of leaping, scurrying
fugitives ; and from the shallow opposing slope came a
drumming rush of horsehoofs and a deepening roar of ' Ger ! '

Clutching his wounded arm above the transfixing arrow,
Raoul turned, and saw his yellow surcoats break fanwise down
over orchard, tilth, and pasture ; and first of all — half-
armoured and unhelmeted, with dark curls blowing stiffly
back, with face death-white and furious and sword-point
swinging low—slim Nino Chiostra charged astride great
Safadin. A score of yards behind came John Doust,
swearing thunderously by Saint George and by the harrowing
of hell ; and behind again were Milo, and the grey chamberlain De Castlon, and Hubriton clinging grimly to his saddle,
and squires and sergeants, men-at-arms and archers—one
blur of fierce, bronzed faces, foaming destriers, falcon coats,
and steel. . . .

" So," said Raoul, and sat down lumpishly on the tiles of
the stair-head ; and then, to the laughing, weeping girl beside
him : " Can you bandage an arm ? "

" Yes, Sieur Count," and there came the rip of a smock
above a bared brown knee.

" Tighter . . . no, leave the arrow alone . . . one thing
at a time. Your name ? "

" Juliana."

" Bond or free ? "

" A bondwoman, Sieur Count."

"You are a brave wench, Juliana. You shall be freed to-morrow. Take my cap as a token."

And with the arrow through his arm and Juliana's tearful praises in his ear Raoul lurched down the belfry stair.

In the first floor room Reine sat grimly on the trap, which would not altogether shut ; for a great pike-head, thrust up from below, had been caught and held when she slammed it down. Lys watched calmly from her corner, and lower down the stair the priest was bent above the swearing Enguerrand.

"Sieur Count, this lord is wounded, and I cannot move him," cried the priest.

"Nothing to heed ! " laughed Enguerrand below. "Nothing to . . ."

"Nevertheless he has fainted," groaned Father Andreas. "Is . . . is Juliana still alive ? "

"Here, Father."

"Come you and help me ; he is bleeding."

"Damnation!" muttered Raoul, leaning sickly against the wall. "Reine, open the trap ! "

Reine tugged at the door and tore it open, so that the pike swung down and thudded below. Then, setting her hands on the edge, she looked at Raoul with a little contraction of her war-sullen face.

"I will see to him," she said ; and she and her slim gripping fingers went after the pike.

"She might have seen to *you* first," Lys whispered.

"She might not," said Raoul.

"Above there ! " came the great voice of John Doust from the belfry door.

Raoul lurched forward and knelt at the edge of the trap.

"By the scabbard of Michael Archangel, Count Raoul, I am glad to see you ! " boomed the Englishman.

Two faces stared aloft—John's red and sweating and quizzical, Nino's pale and grim and running with tears of relief.

"Captain John," called Reine from the stair-foot, "will you climb the ladder and come down the stair to lift the Sieur Enguerrand ? I have stopped his bleeding, but we cannot shift him."

" That will I, Lady Reine . . . and God be praised
we . . . you . . . they . . . ah, now the ladder, by the
harrowing of hell ! "

" Your John will be a courtier yet," said Reine to Nino
Chiostra ; and then, looking round at the darkling shambles
in which she stood, she added wearily : " This was *our*
harrowing of hell ! "

Nino gulped and motioned her out into the sunlight.

" I would tell you, Lady Reine," he began hoarsely, " your
squires are safe, though the younger was twice wounded ·. . .
I would you had seen our muster when they broke in . . . *per
Bacco !* That *he*, and *you*, and the Sieur Enguerrand who
came with us to the ending of Red Jehan, should go in hideous
peril, well-nigh a bowshot from the barbican of Ger ! Ten
thousand little fleeting——— "

" Men-at-arms ! " cried Reine, with a catch in her laugh.
" I pray you send a few to clear this floor and help us carry the
Sieur Enguerrand and the poor wench above."

The two dark heads passed out of Raoul's range of vision ;
Raoul glanced over his shoulder, and saw the witch-girl's pale
eyes widen in her brooding face.

" There is a litter coming for you, Lys," he said.

" To carry me whither ? " she demanded, strangely.

" Ger."

" Indeed, my great lord Count, you had better have given
me up."

" Why ? "

" Who is the round-chinned archer who fought so
well ? "

" The Lady Reine de Guarenal."

" She is one reason *why* ; but there are many others.
Yet I would I had found strength to slide my knife into her
back."

" God help you, you are sick to madness," muttered Raoul,
helplessly.

Lys blinked malevolently at him and reached out feebly
for the crucifix which Father Andreas had laid upon the
floor.

" God does not help me," she whispered, " but the devil
will." Then, with a sudden hoarse upraising of her voice :

" *Come here, you little droning priest, and watch me spit upon this fond . . .*"

But Raoul had shuffled to her on his knees, clapping one hand ungently over the dry, blaspheming lips, and groping with the other for the crucifix ; and although his pierced arm throbbed in torment, his fingers were still stronger than her own, so that he tore away the little laden cross.

" Be still ! " he hissed ; and for reply Lys set her teeth in the edge of his hand and slipped back, fainting, on the cloak where they had laid her. . . .

John Doust came trampling down the stair ; Raoul, still stupidly clutching the crucifix, found Father Andreas beside him, and felt a stir of desolate mirth. For in the battered but exultant face of the heroic little priest was admiration for this edifying spectacle.

" My good lord, may God Almighty and Merciful uphold you for . . . ah, is the poor wretch dead ? "

" No. Swooned away again."

And presently, when the shuffling and tramping had begun downstairs, Reine and a proud excited squire of Ger came up the steps together ; and the squire saluted and gabbled a message from old Milo to the Count.

" Eleven outlaws we have slain, my lord, and fourteen more are taken. Joris won clear—your horse and the rest are stolen. Shall Captain Milo pursue across open moor ? "

" No. Clear the woods as best you may, but leave the moor. I want no men lost in the bogs and gullies."

" And the prisoners, my lord ? "

Raoul pondered for a second only, glancing down at the still brow of Lys and up at the wide eyes of the perspiring squire.

" Behead them instantly," he said.

By sunset Nino Chiostra and fifty men-at-arms had escorted Reine to her home ; by sunset, too, the serfs of Gramberge—pardoned, but mightily afraid—crept in their street again beneath the eyes of John Doust and a score of archers posted in the belfry tower. Four more of the outlaws' heads adorned a yew-tree by the church before old Milo called off his bows and lances from the margin of the moor; and little Father Andreas knelt with his servant Juliana before the altar and opened a grateful heart to the Sieur God.

But in his hold of Ger the Count Raoul passed from the bedside of the smiling Enguerrand and sought the bedside of grave Lys, whom the chamberlain's wife had bathed and clothed and tended, so that she lay softly amid pillows and stared through window - glass across the sunset - reddened sea.

"Well, Lys," said Raoul, heavily, "this was a strange rencounter."

"No stranger than aught else," she murmured, without turning to look at him.

"True. But tell me, if you are not too weary . . . how did it befall ? What were you doing by Gramberge ? "

"Fleeing from Red Anne. Ay, times have changed. You made a very hell-cat of her, Herluin . . . Sieur Count . . . that night you slew the Butcher and won down our secret stair."

"*You* knew, then."

"Yes, for I gave you that draught which was to bring you to my bed. And by the bones of Huon the Foolhardy it *has* brought you in the end . . . but not as I intended. Indeed the bed is yours . . . and this silken night-shift much more comforting than heather on the open moor."

"But did you not tell——"

"I told nothing to any one. Red Anne I had already once deceived for you ; to betray you after you fled would only have made known my earlier treachery. And Ivo, besotted by love of Anne, would have ripped me up if I had looked askance at her. . ."

"Why did you quarrel in the end ? "

"I stole the last of the jewels of Campscapel that Red Anne carried with her. See, they are there on the hutch, in the little leathern purse. I fled last sundown from the Singing Stones . . . and Anne and Ivo and the coven hunted me till dawn. It was Ivo planted the arrow in me, I believe ; but they did not know I was hit. Ivo was madder than ever to show his devotion, for Anne has given herself to Joris of the Rock a time or two, and Ivo weeps and rages but cannot

break away. Last summer we peddled packs to Hautarroy,
and Joris met us in the forest as we came again. He and
Anne knew each other of old ; and even he cannot hold her
against her will . . . you know how she ruled the Riders
of Campscapel."

" Ay."

" There are some of them, now with Joris, who escaped
your slaughter above Alanol. Anne could have turned them
on him with a word."

" But what is Joris doing so far north ? "

" After you took that hold there were many of Jehan's
cattle straying wild in the hills. Joris came north before the
winter closed and slew a mort of them, storing their hides and
horns in caves on Dondonoy. A week ago he forded Varne
and trailed through the forest, bringing five-score men and
many ponies to collect his store. He and some of his cronies
were to join us on the morrow by the Singing Stones. Among
them was one Rufin, who men say is a bastard of Jehan
de Campscapel ; and by his face and bearing I can well
believe it."

" You fled from Rufin too ? "

" Ay."

" What did you mean to do ? "

" I hoped to win into Basse Honoy, but they headed me
back across heather. I would have aimed for Dunsberghe,
where I have friends of a sort. I could have opened a house
there . . . yes, virtuous Herluin, Count, great warrior,
paladin . . . a brothel for ease of silly sailormen. But
now . . ."

" But now ? "

" I do not know. You wake old mischief in me. Your
voice began it, yonder in the belfry. Life at your hands is
an evil gift."

" Ah, you are hurt and weary now. Here you are safe ;
you can recover health and strength and . . . and go your
way in peace."

" Ay, I was always one for going in peace, was I not ?
I tell you your mercy is more devilish than anything I feared
from Rufin or Red Anne. One time I swore I would have
joy of you ; and when my trick miscarried I swore that if I

met you again you should love me or kill me. And now
I have seen your dainty archer . . . so what choice is left?
This is your witchcraft, Herluin . . . yes, I will call you
Herluin. Since you kissed me in Red Anne's antechamber
I have been almost chaste in body, and in spirit altogether
chaste . . . so that my old companions have mocked me
beside the Singing Stones, and one, less wary than the
others, mocked my knife into her. But it was not the name
of your Holy Trinity that beat me off you; it was the touch
of your boy's clean mouth on . . . no, it is all no matter
. . . do not go for a moment."

"Promise me one thing, Lys."

"What is that? Do you want me to enter a convent?"

"Promise me that you will speak no word of your . . .
your witchhood here in Ger."

"Ha! It would be fair revenge, would it not, to let
myself be branded as a witch in your own hold . . . tried
by the Prior of Guthmund's-over-Ger, and handed over to
the secular arm . . . valiant secular arm that goes in a
sling because it defended me!"

"Be silent. Well you know I . . . I would slay you
myself rather than see you burn."

"Hey, I should lift my throat for that dear blow. But
have no dread; what if you were called away, and it fell to
another, less squeamish, to have the burning of me? I
would not appear in my smock yet awhile—I am not so fair
as I was. You have my word."

"Then I will leave you now."

"*My lord!*"

Wretchedly Raoul turned.

"Will you kiss me once on the mouth, as if I were a little
maid? I cannot stab you; see, my dagger is on the hutch
beside the purse. And I will not ask you again."

Raoul strode back to the bedside, stooped, and kissed her.
Then he stumbled away; and as he passed the hutch the
gleam of the dagger-hilt caught his eye, so that he paused
and pouched the weapon before laying hand upon the door.

"My lord!" came another and clearer call; and once
more he wheeled, and his eyes blurred at the sweetness of
the witch-girl's face.

" You will think me foolish, but . . . can any come
climbing in at that window there ? "

" What ? No, unless he had wings. There is a straight
drop of two hundred feet and more into the sea. The cliff
overhangs. But the wench who tends you will bar the
shutter. Are you afraid of . . ."

" Not now. But the sea sounds angry. Is it high tide ? "

" Not until midnight. After an hour or two you will be
used to the sound of the waves."

" Ay, doubt it not. Give you good-night, my . . .
Herluin."

" Give you good-night, Lys."

But at Ger upon Good Friday morning they came crying
to Raoul of an empty room and an unbarred casement ; and
grimly he strode along his corridors to stare through the
open window at grey cliff and heaving grey-green sea.
Nothing of Lys remained but the light imprint of her
body in the bed, the little leathern purse of jewels on the
hutch, and between two stones of the deep window-splay a
shred of soft white silk that fluttered to iron derision of
the wind.

And at Guarenal upon Good Friday evening Raoul sat
alone with Reine by the fire in the Vice-Warden's little
council-chamber ; and there he told her the story of Lys as
he had known and moved in it.

" Almost I wish . . ." said Reine when he had finished.

" Wish what ? "

" That you had made her happy . . . once. For you
could not have kept her happy. None can do that for
another, for happiness comes from the Sieur God."

" Lys would have said, from the devil. She had wildness
in her blood . . . she loved that roving and tumultuous life.
There may be others by the Singing Stones in this night's
wind and rain, but not brave Lys."

" And nevermore brave Lys," said Reine ; and her own
dark compelling loveliness seemed stern or tender as the
firelight glowed or waned upon it.

" Which are you, Reine ? " asked Raoul, watching her ;

and only her grave considering eyes told him that he had said the words aloud.

" Your pardon," he muttered, and rose unsteadily to his feet ; for he had not meant to approach his latest secret by way of the desolate tale of Lys.   And as she said nothing, he went on : " Let us join the others in the winter parlour."

He moved to the door and unlatched it, looking back ; Reine stood up, but still she gazed into the fire.

" I do not know what you meant," she said coldly, " but it may be I am both."

Raoul stared at the latch, clicked it, and opened the door an inch.   Outside in the corridor was darkness and a whistling wind ; and suddenly he was overborne by panic and starvation.

Softly he latched the door again ; and as he turned the girl turned also.   For a moment they stared the length of the shadowy room ;   then, silently, they began to walk towards each other.   As they moved their faces altered ; when they stood a pace apart there seemed no need for words.   Yet quietly and wonderingly they spoke each other's name.

*   *   *

" *Look, Reine . . . our dawn across the sea.*"

" *Dawn !   O but I have slept !   Now hold me up . . . up, up.   Yes . . . it is like the coming of the Chalice of the Sangreal.   And after the Marckmont silences it is wild and strange to hear again the surges and that little faëry song of wind.*"

" *It hardly ever fails in this high place.*"

" *Harsh warrior, you bruise my side . . . dear lord and love, are you even at home at last in your hold of Ger ?* "

" *Where you are is my home, brown sorceress.*"

" *Flatterer with the face of a stone devil . . . O greedy one, be still !* "

" *I will not be still . . . the east is full of red-gold plumes . . . the waves are shaping and hurling up to us feathers and sword-blades of sound.   They sing the song of Raoul and of Reine."*

" Raoul . . ."
" Reine."

*   *   *

So the new life began.   For Reine and for their children, in the troublous years that followed, Raoul bore the peace of Marckmont in his heart; but to all Easterlings, and forest thieves, and evildoers whatsoever, he was the black gerfalcon in eyrie on the crags of windy Ger.

THE END